To Lisa

Hope you like your Uncle's book. He's a pretty good writer.

Love,

Aunt Tessie

FAREWELL TO THE MOCKINGBIRDS

a novel

by

JAMES McEACHIN

the rharl publishing group
16161 ventura boulevard #550, Encino, CA 91436

the rharl publishing group

rharl and colophon
are registered trademarks of
the rharl publishing group

isbn 0-9656661-9-0

printed and bound in the united states of america

lyrics to lift every voice and sing are by james weldon johnson

this book is a work of fiction

"— The time has come for us to carry out the sentences of the court. This morning we must die. At the clearing in the woods our government has prepared for us, we will go to our deaths representing the greatness of our race, the dignity we hold as men, the distinction of our soldiering, and knowing well our only aim was to serve the country honorably."

— Obie O. McClellan,
First Sergeant, King Company,
24th United States Infantry (Colored.)

December 21, 1917

based upon an actual event

Preamble

She suffered a penalty of progress and welcomed the year 1917 with the promise of war. She carried out that promise on April 6th, when her national leaders laid aside 1914's Proclamation of Neutrality and countered Germany's outrageous aggression with a formal Declaration of War. And so, in less than three years, a conflict which had gained momentum with the assassination of an archduke and his lady in the far-off capital of Bosnia, had engulfed all of Europe, Asia, and Asia Minor, now reached out to the last major power, and became a World War. The United States of America, for the first time in its comparatively young history, mobilized its untested greatness for global conflict.

Our involvement, said the leaders, was to make this the war to end all wars; the war to end injustice and tyranny, to rid the world of the likes of Imperial Germany and its sabre-rattling, land-grabbing leaders. This was to be a fight for freedom, for decency, for the oppressed; a fight for all mankind, for all the things America stood for. The beneficiaries of the greatest society in the world could not stand idle.

A new energy swept the country. Old aversions and lethargies gave way to such high-sounding phrases as *Over There, To The Trenches, The Stars and Stripes, Yankee Doodle, The Great American Eagle,* and *On To The Glory Of War.*

No place was more active than the office of the Secretary of War — and understandably so. In his office rested the might of the United States. In his hands rested the awesome responsibility of executing the orders of a president whose re-election slogan the year before had been *he kept us out of war* — a president who now had to decide exactly what the nation was going to do in a far-flung war that had already destroyed more property than any war in the history of mankind.

Also facing the Twenty-eighth president was the troubling little issue of the Negro in uniform; his loyalties, his worth, his courage.

The war had suddenly elevated the usually drab military stock to noble and prestigious heights. Every man, every unit, would be touched by war. But it introduced a question that had buried itself in tradition and had lain low in America: On the stage of the great world drama, what was to be done with the man with the lowered standards? Should he — *could he* — represent the great nation abroad? And when the war was won should the man with the lowered standards be heralded and welcomed back to the docks in re-nown? What, the questions continued, was to be done with the colored man?

The advisors met. A decision was made.

With 10,000 Negroes already in the nation's military, it was ruled that the exigency of war did not permit the obliteration of the long-established views of the country. Thus, from Richmond, Virginia, on April 24, 1917 the following Associated Press message was telegraphed to recruiting stations:

NEGRO RECRUITING HALTED
NO MORE NEGROES WILL BE ACCEPTED FOR
ENLISTMENT IN THE UNITED STATES ARMY.
ALL COLORED UNITS FILLED.

The wire did not please everyone. "The secretary of war is in grave and unpardonable error," argued the Chief of the General Staff. "How can we, in light of demanding more manpower, and doing all that we can possibly do to get Congress to urgently pass this new Selective Draft Law, go before the mothers of this great country and say 'give us your sons' and, in the same breath, turn to the colored people and say 'no sacrifice needed'?

"The great General John J. Pershing and his American Expeditionary Forces cannot fight this war alone. It must be remembered that nothing consumes men like the treachery of war. And especially a war of this magnitude. We are no longer chasing Indians, Spaniards, or Mexicans. Those days are far behind us; the world has changed. We are now facing a cunning, diabolical enemy who has already lost more men than we have in our entire Regular Army. And this same enemy has vowed to sacrifice even more in his quest for world domination. Now I ask you: if you commit your best red blood to this, what will you have left for the future of America?"

"The future of America will remain secure," said a senator in defense of the secretary, "and so, I might add, will its traditions."

"I am, as are you, Senator, concerned and aware of the country's traditions," the general argued, "and that is why I hope it is known by everyone in the nation that if it were the prestige of the United States Army that was at stake, and that alone, my long career in the military would compel me to agree with you. But since it isn't, and since the very life of this democracy is at peril, I must argue for what is best for the country. Notwithstanding your views, Sir, the present Table of Strength of ten thousand coloreds in the military is simply not enough."

"It is enough to afford their race adequate representation," said the senator.

"But not enough," countered the general, "to supply the demands of war."

The press agreed with the general.

"There are times," concluded a Washington editorial, "when it is altogether tolerable to restrict the number of coloreds serving in the military. But to do so at this preposterously low figure of ten thousand, with perhaps another ten thousand in the National Guard, is wrong. And then to restrict those numbers at the expense of others in this hour of peril, when the most conservative estimates indicate that under the proposed Selective Service Law more than three million of our other boys may be called to arms, is totally reprehensible and carries with it the tinge of treason."

The government's position changed. The Negro would serve in force.

When the great machinery of World War I shifted into high gear, from the four corners of the country the blacks came. They poured into the nation's draft boards and registration centers in such unprecedented numbers that by the end of October 1917 there were 737,626 black registrants, of whom 75,697 fresh-faced blacks already were swelling the ranks of the nation's military. Even more would come. In the end, 2,259,527 blacks had registered at the nation's draft boards. Nearly a half million would actually serve the great cause.

Not all of them would serve with acceptable distinction.

in memory of the troops

Chapter 1

Miles away from Washington and the dark clouds that gave way to rains of global war; miles away from the draft and registration boards that would eventually give hope, shelter, and faded honor to thousands upon thousands of blacks in 1917, there stood Gift Chapel. It was squat and white. It was on the grounds of Fort Sam Houston in San Antonio, Texas. It stood alone.

The night before, by order of the adjutant general, the post commander had assigned a detail of soldiers to strip the memorial building of all signs of the Deity and ready it for the largest trial ever to be held in the military — indeed, the largest to be held in the history of the nation. The trial was to hold two other distinctions. It would be the first general court-martial of the Great War; it would be the first en masse trial involving soldiers of the Regular Army of the United States. Court observers agreed there should have been one back in 1906. If there had been, went the consensus, there would be no necessity for this one.

By 0600 on a morning that welcomed an unseasonably cold November 1, the San Antonio soldiers had completed the task of converting the remote post's only chapel into a court. The huge white cross that had topped the steeple had been temporarily replaced by the Stars and Stripes. Now the building appeared aloof and dwarfed.

Inside, there had been changes as well. Notable was the absence of religious artifacts, Bibles, and hymnals. There was no altar. The dark brown pews were still there, but to the left of them and dominating the wall was a roped-off area that sent bone-hard benches splintering up three levels. The 63 prisoners were seated on the benches. They were all black, and, except for one, boyish Jody Cunningham, they were Regular Army. They were not draftees. They were volunteers from all parts of the country.

Overall attempts at theological annulment proved futile, and the isolated structure stood strong in the image, saying that it was still God's house. But not to the military. God, His disciples, and all that was His was out, and despite the stand-strong image, the chapel was now an Army of the United States Military Court.

It was a strange setting, but to make sure there was no confusion as to purpose and scope, another U.S. flag, topped by a brass bald eagle, was placed corner-right. It was joined by the tasseled and pale-blue colors of the 24th United States Infantry Regiment (Colored.) Both the flag and the colors were flanked by two rigid-standing, military bearers just a few feet to the rear of three connecting and slightly elevated, arched tables. They had replaced the 4'2" pulpit and were without cloth cover or adornments. The prisoners' fate would rest at the tables.

Occupying the tables and attesting to the Army's determination for speed and efficiency for trial, there would be 13 high-ranking trial officers. They would consist of two brigadier generals, eight colonels, and three lieutenant colonels, all from the high command.

It was 0656 hours. Court would be convened in a matter of minutes. To ensure absolute order in the court, the prisoners' guards had been doubled. As an added measure, tight, uniformed guards stood throughout the room, their bayoneted Springfield rifles held at port arms. All white, mostly military, and dressed in the Army's 1917 Class "A" uniform, a sea of spectators with hardened faces packed the pews. Some stared at the black faces in the roped area. Most did not.

The seconds ticked away. Soon through the thin walls Sgt. Yeager, the big Irish NCO — the noncommissioned officer in charge of the guards — heard the marching footsteps approaching. He quickly abandoned the parade-rest stance, clicked his heels in attention, and barked, "Except for the prisoners, *ATENNNHUTTT!!*"

The assemblage complied with snap.

After a momentary silence the double doors of the chapel swung open and allowed another burst of chilled air to enter. No one thought about the cold.

Sgt. Yeager barked again. "*Court's* in sessssionnn! Preee-zziiiding Off-fiss-ser, Brigadier General Curtis V. Hawley!!"

Through the doors came another flag bearer. He was followed by the 13 trial officers. Grim-faced and determined, they moved in step, snappy and in single file. In the lead was the no-doubt-about-it, legendary court disciplinarian, Brig. Gen. Curtis V. Hawley. A stocky, gruff Kentuckian, he had close-cropped hair and the face of a bulldog. A lone star glistened on each epaulet of his tight-fitting tunic. Without wasted motion, he led the detail past the pews of spectators, who included Capt. Lloyd Whitney, the commander of I Company, and Captain Harland J. Farrell. A scholarly, patient, undecided 41-year-old man with light hair capping a once athletic frame, he was the commander of Company K.

Forward of Capt. Farrell, in the first row, was Lt. Col. Briggs, the Third Battalion commander. Directly before him were two long tables, one for the trial judge advocate, and the other for the defense. Off to the left were the unspoken objects of the ceremony, the 63 prisoners. Most of them were in their mid-20's, and they were the only blacks in the court. All soldiers, all members of the notoriously proud 24th U.S. Infantry (Colored), they now were disheveled, stripped of insignia, and sitting quietly and only partially attentive in the roped-off area cornered by guards and, from a certain deceptive angle, appeared to be centered by an unlit, pot-bellied stove. Hued light from the stained-glass windows cast an abstruse touch to the setting.

En route to the elevated table, none of the trial officers looked in the direction of the blacks, nor did they look in the direction of Capt. Farrell, the white commander of the disgraced Company K. Their eyes remained straight ahead.

When the trial officers reached the elevated tables, Hawley, as President of the Court, stood behind his chair for a split second, then sat. The other trial officers did likewise. With the spectators still standing, the brigadier got right down to business.

Because of the length and gravity of the charges, and because the Army had taken the extraordinary step of appointing a veteran general to preside over the court, it was expected that he would take a moment or two to read the accompanying Statement Of Agreed Facts submitted to the court by both prosecution and defense. There would be no such reading.

Everyone knew why they were there, that less than four months ago these *soldiers* went on a murderous rampage and violated law after law after law.

For those in attendance, what made matters worse was that these *soldiers* were not recent volunteers. They couldn't claim the ignorance of the draftee. These were regular Army. *Colored* regular Army. These people had been beneficiaries of a government that had fed, sheltered, and paid them when nothing else in life had been available to them. These people were veterans, and except for one, they were hardened to the ways of the military. They had been trained for war, but there they sat — as beasts, useless and disgraced. Their presence in a military court brought into sharp focus the entire question of coloreds in the Army of the United States. The nation had made a mistake.

The one-star general was automatic. The one-star general was firm.

"The discipline and reputation of the Army of the United States are deeply involved in the manner in which military courts are conducted and justice administered; the duties, therefore, which devolve upon officers appointed to sit as members of the court are of the most important character. That these duties may be discharged with justice and propriety, it is incumbent upon all who are witnessing these proceedings to do so with decorum, and in a manner which precludes distraction. The court will not tolerate anything to the contrary. So saying, we shall proceed pursuant to existing regulations."

"*SEATS!*" commanded Yeager, the big NCO in charge of the guards.

The court sat quickly, and quietly. The guards assumed the parade-rest stance. They would maintain the position throughout trial.

The brigadier general cast a stern eye over the room. "The court calls for challenges."

The prosecutor, a man slightly over the age of 50, stood. His mustache was thick; his face, immovable. He was sturdy, elegant, and deceptively tough. "Colonel Paul A. Boatner, the trial judge advocate. No challenges to the court, Sir."

"Noted," responded the brigadier. He looked at the table for the defense.

The assistant, wanting to rise to her feet, held off in deference to her superior, Maj. P. D. DeBerg.

DeBerg, a brilliant man during his youth, had been through many court battles. But this was his last. He was tired, old, and sick — and he was afraid. He was not afraid of dying. He was afraid to meet his Maker knowing that he was participating in what he thought was a blasphemous and irreligious use of His lower house. He used the term *lower* house because the chapel was not a temple.

Temples were for God's chosen.

No one really knew what the major thought about blacks. No one really knew what he thought about blacks in the military. No one knew what he thought about the case. He never commented. In September, when he was given the assignment of defending, the only thing he had made clear was that his second assistant had to be "someone different." Lt. Wilmona Jennings was assigned the case, thus becoming the first female officer ever to participate in a military tribunal. When she first reported to the old defender's office in October, a month before trial, she hadn't so much as raised an eyebrow. But not so now with the court. With his first assistant, a Captain Donald Thoren gone, from the moment the lieutenant walked into the court, she commanded all eyes. She also elicited all manner of under-breath comments. Most didn't know there were females in the Army of the United States. Most didn't know a female could even attend a court-martial, let alone participate in one. For the defense, she was not expected to be a plus.

"From the defense," the brigadier said, louder, "the court calls for challenges."

The seasoned woman of 47 stood. She was tall, and her hair was tied in a tight bun. It was auburn and streaked with gray. It went well with an angular face. Her accent was pronounced — clipped and precise. Records indicated she had been born and raised in England. Manchester. The daughter of missionaries, the Rogans, she had graduated from the University of Manchester, having majored in law. She had been in the United States three years; two in Washington, she had spent her off-duty days and nights learning court-martial procedure.

If the lieutenant was nervous on her first case, she didn't let it show. She put her eyeglasses on and said with seasoned poise, "First Lieutenant Wilmona Jennings, assisting Major P. D. DeBerg, counsel for the defense. No challenges to the court, Sir."

The Brigadier General/President of the Court stared at her for a moment, then looked in the direction of the prosecution and proceeded according to the manual. "Any objections to the court as now constituted?"

Col. Boatner stood again. "None from the prosecution, Sir."

"From the defense?"

Again Lt. Jennings stood. "No objections from the defense, Sir. But the defense would like —"

"Charges," Brig. Gen. Hawley said, abruptly cutting her off. The woman sat.

The general again called for the charges to be read.

For the reading, the young officer sitting next to the prosecutor abruptly stood. He adjusted his glasses and said, "Captain Theodore Algonquins, assistant to the trial judge advocate, Sir."

"Noted," said the brigadier. "Charge."

The captain tersely read from an opened manila folder, copies of which were already in the hands of the trial board. "In time of war, violation of the 64th Article of War."

"Specification," the brigadier said, calling for the additional reading. He was routine and harsh.

Someone in the court coughed. "Excuse yourself," ordered the general. It was probably said for effect. It didn't matter. A young second lieutenant rose and quickly left the court. The brigadier said again, "Specification."

"Specification," responded the prosecution. "In that the accused personnel of Company K, 24th United States Infantry, Colored, having received a lawful order from Captain Harland J. Farrell, United States Infantry, commanding, to lay down their arms and return to their tents, the said Captain Farrell being in the execution of his office, said troops did, on 25 August 1917, at about 2020 hours at Camp Logan, Houston, Texas, fail to obey same."

"Charge," said the brigadier general.

"In time of war, violation of the 66th Article of War."

In the manual of court-martial the term *specification* was designed to be a question. From Hawley it was a command.

"Specification," he said again.

"Specification. In that the accused personnel of Company K, 24th United States Infantry, Colored, did on 25 August, 1917 at about 2020 hours create, incite, cause, and join in the seditious and mutinous act of breaking and entering the Supply Tent and unlawfully removing arms and ammunition therefrom, and subsequently firing at, and holding an officer of the Army of the United States at bay, Camp Logan, Houston, Texas."

"Charge," called Brig. Gen. Hawley.

"In time of war," said the prosecution.

"Specification," the brigadier again called.

"Specification. In that the accused personnel of Company K, 24th United States Infantry, Colored, did, on 25 August 1917, at about...."

The indictments hammered on. Virtually every charge read carried with it the penalty of death or life imprisonment, yet there wasn't the expected somberness in the roped-off area. It isn't that the blacks weren't interested, or that they weren't harboring stress and fear. A lot of them simply chose to ignore the weight of the charges, or sought to deflect them by doing something other than concentrate on the proceedings. Some sat with a stoic indifference, some sat with wandering eyes, some wondered why the prosecution would use the term "K" Company as opposed to what they preferred, King Company. King Company was the full military designation they had always used. King was designated by the Army Field Manual. Thought the prisoners: the contracted "K" Company was insipid and carried no weight; it was disrespectful and sounded white.

Not including regimental, battalion, or company headquarters, The 24th U.S. Infantry Regiment (Colored) was composed of three battalions. Understrength though they were, each battalion consisted of three line companies.

Aside from Headquarters Company, Companies I, K, and L — Item, King, and Love — made up the Third Battalion of the 24th.

From inception, from the earliest days of the military, Item and Love didn't rank with King. They were feeble and unmanly names. The U.S. Army Field Manual, responsible for the designations, had no such concerns. The Army said the names were clear-cut, eliminated confusion, and would therefore stand unchanged. The Item and Love designations survived the years, but they were not used with the frequency of King.

In the 24th U.S. Infantry Regiment (*Colored*, always parenthesized), the K Company troops lived up to the name. They were kings of the regiment, best of the battalion, in their view. But now there they sat along with a few members from I and L Companies, surrounded by a detail of white guards and listening to a series of deadening charges in a roped-off area in a church on a post they were not familiar with.

As the charges continued, and unseen by the guards, a few of the King men broke boredom by mischievously spitballing each other. Others sat on the hard pine benches, deflecting the force of the charges by doing nothing but playfully rolling their eyes at each other. One or two felt the call of sleep.

On the first row, attitudes were different. Peter P. Curry, the one-time company clown who now suffered with swollen hands and head wounds, was mindless and deflated. As always, his pal, young Jody Cunningham, was by his side. The unit's only draftee, Jody had a face that was fresh and childlike.

Centered on the bench was the defiant Cpl. Thelonious Poole. The high-cheeked, lanky, 38-year-old corporal sat with his arms folded as if daring the world to say anything to, for, or against him. Because of his surly appearance, the kinky-haired and medium-complexioned man from Mississippi commanded the guards' attention more than any of the others.

But it was "K" Company's first sergeant, Master Sgt. Obie O. McClellan, who commanded the court's attention, and that of many of the spectators as well. He was an enigma. He was not much to look at, he was of average height and weight, and there was nothing intimidating about his appearance. But all knew he was the unquestioned leader of the group and, as some said, the reason they were there. And, as the charges would maintain, he was the mastermind of one of the darkest chapters in the annals of military history. Never before had one man led such a vicious and unremitting assault on the populace at large.

The dark, aging, bespectacled soldiering mystery sat alone with his thoughts. The other members of the company on the bench were clearly respectful of him. They allowed him as much room as possible, and so for the most part, it could be said, the first sergeant was alone. The seating arrangement and the court-martial itself hadn't changed anything. First Sgt. Obie O. McClellan had always been alone.

The reiteration of the prosecutor's statement "*In time of war*" created a paradox in the first sergeant's mind. Several times he thought about the premonition — or, more accurately, the nightmare — that had plagued him over the years. Whatever it was called, it was there, at the forefront of his mind, and it never left any doubt as to the trial's outcome. But as inevitable, riveting, and indescribably final as the real end was sure to be, it was the words "*in time of war*" that mesmerized him. It was peculiar. The first sergeant was peculiar.

The First thought about the term *in time of war* over and over again. The words had seized his mind before, but not in the same troublesome way.

McClellan had always felt there was equality in war. In war, he believed, there was progress; blacks would be appreciated and would contribute on an equal footing. As an example, he recalled, once the seeds of war spread to all the white military encampments and finally sprouted on the three black regiments, the colored soldier, for the first time, became important. It had been a simple thing then, but he, and indeed all the blacks in the military, felt enormous pride when, up north, the First Separate Battalion, answering the call to colors, was assigned the duty of watching over the water-supply system in Washington, guarding the six huge reservoirs, the Potomac River projects, and all the power plants in the District of Columbia. It was an honor, some said, that was comparable to England's Guard Regiment, where only men of undoubted loyalty and character were selected to protect the crown. McClellan felt, as had all career blacks, that The First Separate Battalion's assignments — *in time of war* — were sure signs that the Army's insecurity about black competence and loyalty was over. He sat there remembering that in June, back in Columbus where he and the Company had been stationed, he had other thoughts along those lines. Being accepted as loyal, *in time of war*, as wonderful as it was, did little to dispel the Army's long-held belief that the blacks didn't have the courage to fight. It did nothing to eradicate the long-held beliefs that the blacks were slack, indifferent, and lazy. Nor did it eliminate the long-held beliefs that the blacks were close to being freaks of nature, and, as such, had no will or reason to fight. He, like all the others, had heard over and over again that war is noble and heroic, traits that surely could not be attributed to a race that had no pride in country or self. There was only one thing that could create a wholesale change in America — *war*. *In time of war*, thought the First.

The assistant trial judge advocate was now reading another charge. There were more to come, but the quixotic first sergeant's mind was already back in Columbus, New Mexico.

King Company might have mutinied in Houston, but it was the anticipation of war that gave it impetus.

Chapter 2

For years Columbus, New Mexico, had been the home of the 24th Infantry U.S. Regiment (Colored). Even before the threat of war, King Company, under the authoritarian direction of the first sergeant, led the 24th's Third Battalion in soldiering excellence. The achievement didn't come without cost. Although they wouldn't say it was because of McClellan, two company commanders had come and gone. There was something fearful about the man. He was unlike any Negro they had ever seen. Like granite, he was unreadable. And since most whites had never dealt with a black in a leadership position, they gave him room. Thus the First was allowed to adopt his own policies.

As the war closed in, First Sgt. McClellan wanted everyone and everything to be in place. Since they were Infantry and it was going to be a foot soldier's war, there was no doubt they would be first to respond to the nation's emergency. Consequently, under the First's leadership, weekend passes were restricted, and furloughs were held to a minimum. The Company was not fully equipped — indeed, no black companies were. Whether by design, or other reasons supported by the government's outright fear of putting too many weapons into black hands, the troops didn't have sufficient arms of any kind. But while the Army's slight might have slowed the other blacks, it didn't stop McClellan. Even before the outbreak of war, the troops of King Company spent their weekends turning sticks and broom handles into rifles and manufacturing makeshift targets, tanks, and grenades so that during the week they could train morning, noon, and night.

The First had always been unremitting in his training efforts. He was so unremitting, in fact, that when Capt. Farrell, the new company commander, arrived, he had to order the First to ease up on the schedule. McClellan complied, although only partially.

Meanwhile, the overseas war effort was gaining momentum as German submarines continued to menace the sea. They had destroyed dozens of ships since the great Cunard liner Lusitania sank two years earlier off the coast of Ireland with the loss of 1,198 lives. In rapid succession, the British passenger steamer Arabia was sunk; the hospital ship Britannic went down in the Aegean sea; and the transport Iverria was lost. A month later, the liner Lanonia was torpedoed, and the American steamers Healdton and Aztec were blasted from the Atlantic. War was indeed coming closer to the United States. The U-boats continued to prowl.

Deciding on a course of action, the President wanted to arm all merchant ships. Eleven U.S. senators filibustered against him. Countering them, he said that they had "rendered the great government of the United States helpless and contemptible."

England, to outsmart the Germans, tried *"dazzle-painting"* her ships. The U-boats were not confused by the painting mishmash and could soon boast they had sent 11 million tons of war-needed goods to the ocean's bottom.

With senate approval, the United States finally enacted an embargo against the Germans, and U.S. destroyers were sent to convoy the merchant ships to Britain. The allies launched a series of offensives, and on June 13, Gen. John J. "Black Jack" Pershing, nemesis of the marauding Mexican bandit Pancho Villa, and his staff arrived in Paris without incident. Thirteen days later, under command of Gen. Siebert, the first contingent of American troops arrived in France ready to do battle. No Negroes were among them.

Back home, blacks the Army over were waiting.

King Company was still training.

In Washington, with President Wilson now able to promise the allies unlimited support, and the new Selective Service Act in full swing conscripting an Army of 500,000, everything about the war effort was still good news to the blacks. The 9th and 10th Cavalry and the 24th and 25th Infantry — the Regular Army's four black units — were waiting in the wings in unparalleled anticipation. Getting ready were the nearly 10,000 blacks in the National Guard of several States.

The cadre of the Army's 24th were more expectant than anyone else. The 9th and 10th might have been more famous, having ridden with Roosevelt's Rough Riders at San Juan Hill during the Spanish-American war back in 1898, but the 24th — the *Deuce-Four*, as some called it — was the regiment of choice.

It was generally believed that Gen. Pershing favored having blacks in the military, and it was a general belief, too — unsupported by fact — that if and when the blacks were called to join the American Expeditionary Forces in Europe, the Infantry would be called first. The 24th was infantry.

The battalion was ostensibly stationed in Columbus to guard the borders against further Mexican intrusion. There was concern, too, that the Germans would forge a German-Mexican alliance against the United States. But all that was laid aside. Rumors were rampant, and the latest spread like wildfire throughout the 24th's Third Battalion. Word had it that the Third Battalion — companies "I," "K," "L," and Headquarters — would be moving out in a matter of days.

McClellan of King Company, though pleased at the prospect,

took a wait-and-see attitude. He continued to put his troops through the paces.

Chapter 3

It was late in the day of June 14th on the training fields of Columbus, New Mexico. Lunch, the daily staple of hardtack and pork n' beans, had been particularly unappetizing. In the King Company Mess Tent the evening before, flies, roaches, maggots, worms, and other undesirable little specks had attacked the rancid lard and carried the feast over to the syrup, flour, and sugar. They spent the night assaulting the pork. By midmorning on the field, diarrhea struck again. The company had already gone through the hustle and bustle of mock skirmishes, and the men were hoping to end the day with something a little less engaging than hand-to-hand combat training. First Sgt. McClellan thought otherwise and ordered more rounds of trench assaults. For the abdominally gassed and pained, he ordered target practice from the prone position. No one was pleased — particularly those positioned next to the bloated. Capt. Farrell, there along with the men, said nothing. And so, once again, King Company was still in training when the two other line companies – I and L — had long since called it a day.

Time on the field was rough on everyone. The sick were getting sicker; the unsick were getting grumpier. Training supplies were low. And the equipment, already showing it couldn't stand up to the oppressive New Mexico heat and the sunup-to-sundown rigors demanded by the first sergeant, was giving out. True, some of the men did not have real weapons. Some were using muskets. But most of the rifles and sidearms had been fired into uselessness long ago. Worst was the machine-gun section. All but two had to "make do" by simulating fire and voicing *rat-a-tat-tat's* at the German cutouts.

On the last series of rounds, McClellan, walking up and down the firing line, noticed one of his soldiers was not firing. Nigeral O. Carter was his name. He spoke the language with a trace of an accent.

"What's wrong, Trooper?"

"No firin' pin, Sir," responded the young African-born soldier.

"An' the sight-piece is missin'."

At the same time, a machine gunner at the end of the line held up his trigger-housing unit to show the sergeant his weapon also was shot. McClellan hollered back to his corporal who was standing with Field Sgt. Dukes about 20 yards behind the line. "Poole! I thought I told you to check *all* the weapons before coming out this morning!"

"I did check 'em, Sarge. I started at 0530 hunnert hours."

Capt. Farrell, the C.O., moved forward to give the housing unit a quick look and called back to Poole. "Is this the best you can do, Corporal?"

Poole answered with far more vehemence than he would have done with the first sergeant. "With what I got to work with, YES! That is the best I can do." He jammed his fists to his sides defiantly. "Ain't nothin' no different than the uniforms an' all the rest of the equipment we ain't got. I bet'cha if we was white instead of a bunch'a goddam niggers, the Army — "

"*POOLE!*" McClellan shouted.

The firing stopped. The first sergeant's voice had that kind of command over the company. Everyone looked on. "Number One," he blistered, "you do *not* challenge an officer in the Army of the United States! Number *Two*, profanity is out! I've told you before, and I will tell you again: in the presence of the troops you will, at all times, employ your best language, never your worst! *Three*, there is the distinct possibility your God is black. He or His name is never to be demeaned! And finally, the term *'nigger'* is an age-old vulgarism inappropriately donated to the black race by a tongue-troubled white race. It has, in fact, nothing to do with your heritage, and is therefore not yours to claim. Do you read me?"

Poole said nothing. It was not that he was avoiding the question. He was thinking.

"Do you read me, I said?!"

"Yessir."

"If you've got it, now let's explore it. For the benefit of the troops, if you're called a nigger, and you are not a nigger, who then, *would be* the nigger?!"

"I dunno," the corporal said.

"That instrument resting on your shoulders is supposed to house a brain. Use it! Now, I say again: the word *'nigger'* is an English vulgarism ascribed to your forefathers before they got off the boat. If your forefathers were ignorant of it, and you do nothing to embrace it, *who*, then, *would be* the nigger?!"

Poole scratched and tugged at his upper ear lobe in serious thought. He finally ventured, "The ones who did the donatin'?"

"See to it that it remains that way."

The uncomfortable white company commander broke his silence. "It's about that time, Sergeant."

Cpl. Poole overheard it and mumbled to Sgt. Dukes, the ancient field sergeant with the sagging belly. "He was s'pose to say that a whole two hours ago."

Sgt. Dukes didn't appreciate the comment. "Poole, why don't you just get on out of the Army?"

"If other doors was open, I wouldn't be here in the first place."

Sgt. Dukes gave him a look and moved over to where McClellan was standing. "We gonna wrap it up now?" the older sergeant asked tactfully.

"Call it, Dukes," McClellan said, his irritation evident.

Sgt. Dukes moved away, unhooked his whistle, and gave it three blasts. All training activity came to an immediate halt. The men gathered their gear and, without any verbal orders, raced to form the company formation.

Pvts. Yancy and the African-born Carter, two who also doubled as company drummers, automatically snapped on their snare drums and stood at the end of the first and second squads of the Third Platoon, tapping out the off-patterned "preparation" theme. Pfc. Simms stood in front, poised with the company guidon. The dust still hung in the air. In less than a minute and a half, King Company was formed and standing tall — waiting for McClellan to give the marching orders.

Facing the formation, and with the captain in his normal position of five paces to his left rear, the first sergeant called the company to attention, did an about-face to the company commander, saluted him, and accepted the order to march the company back to camp.

McClellan did an about-face and studied his rigid troops. At this point not a muscle dared to move. The staredown was prolonged until the First bellowed, *"KING COMPANY!"*

"King Company!" Dukes repeated.

"Right — "

"Right!"

"Face!"

The company did as ordered, simultaneously shouting *"One! Two!"* as they were required to do whenever a one- or two-step maneuver was required. Only the young Japanese, Toho Fujiyama, was a hair off in making the snappy turn.

The first sergeant thundered again, "Right shoulder — "

"Right shoulder!"

"Harmz!"

The rifles, like the machine guns and tripods, crackled to their shoulders.

"Stand tall!" McClellan barked.

"Guidon!" Dukes called.

Simms, the guidon bearer, scurried to the front of the First Platoon to head the formation.

McClellan then yelled, "Drummers!"

"Carter, Yancy! Set!" Dukes called.

"Forrr-warrrd," McClellan yelled after the two drummers were in place.

"Fooorrr-warrrrd!" Dukes repeated.

"Haugh!!"

On the First's command, Carter connected with Yancy in pounding out a strong cadence. Seconds later they changed patterns. The snapping drums crackled with a new rhythm, and 154 strong, with Poole, Sgt. Dukes, and Capt. Farrell joining the first sergeant alongside, the company moved out smartly. They were smart, that is, except for the captain, Toho Fujiyama, and one or two others who marched midranks and couldn't be easily seen by an outsider.

Capt. Farrell, in the flanking position, had a problem. He was unsoldierly, and terrible at marching. He had no sense of cadence and no rhythm, but he attempted to satisfy the situation by giving it a valiant try.

Two miles later the captain was still simply walking at a fast pace.

The battalion area was at the end of an extremely long dirt road. The first thing that came into view was a 7 x 12 A-framed guard's booth that sat about 300 yards forward of a host of company-size, olive-drab tents. It was paralleled by rusted barbed wire. A long pole, representing a gate, stretched across the roadway. Serving as an archway was an 18-foot sign that was boldly lettered: "BLACK LIGHTNING." It was framed by two enameled bolts of black lightning outlined in crimson. Centered was the wording "HOME OF THE TWENTY-FOURTH UNITED STATES INFANTRY (COLORED). The word *Colored* was in parentheses. The wording *Columbus, New Mexico,* rounded off the bottom. Proudly presented, too, on both sides of the sign were the insignia and campaign awards denoting outstanding service in the Spanish-American War.

Beyond the gate the surroundings were precise, with huge olive-drab (O.D.) tents flanking the main road and forming their own lines of dull symmetry. On most evenings one could still hear the dying sounds of an Army post that had just called it a day. The sounds would last until dark, until shattered by the arrival of King Company returning from the fields.

Not that I and L's return had been quiet, but King's return always created a stir that couldn't be ignored.

McClellan would wait until about 200 yards away from the archway and then call for the guidon. Simms, already setting the smart pace in front, would jam the dark blue KING-emblazoned banner razor-straight up into the air. He would keep it there until the next command. Dukes would call for the first and second drummers, and Carter and Yancy, responding as one, would stop tapping and get set for a change of rhythm.

With the guidon still skyward, and when exactly 100 yards from the archway, McClellan would scorch the earth. "King Company! — What are we gonna do?!"

In tight, penetrating unison, the company would respond: "Soldier!"

McClellan would holler again. "What'd you say?!"

"Soldier!"

"I can't hear you!"

"*Soldier!!*"

"How're we gonna soldier?!"

"Together!"

"I can't hear you!"

"Together!"

"Guidon!"

Simms would then arm the banner smartly out front. He was ready for the *sound-off.*

"Alright! Let's stir it up! Delayed cadence," called the First. *"Count!"*

"One! Two! Three! Four!" The first count was paced, and then they would shout, *"One-Two-Three-Four! OneTwoThreeFour. OneTwoThreeFour. OneTwoThreeFour."*

"Break it down, Black Lightning!" McClellan hollered.

Simms would snap the guidon to the upright position. Instantly, almost as if automated, the company would make a move and then slow to a powerfully measured pace. At the same time, they were readying themselves to sing a stanza of their adopted anthem the First had discovered the only time he and Dukes had been on furlough. They went to Tennessee's Fisk University to hear the famed Fisk Jubilee singers.

King was less than a hundred yards away now.

"Nigeral O. Carter! Yancy!" Sgt. Dukes called, sending the drummers' hands into a flurry of motion.

"Stomach in, chest out! Heads held high!" First Sgt. McClellan would command. *"Lemme hear you, King Company! Sing a song!"*

The chorus of James Weldon Johnson's yet-to-be-published *Lift Every Voice And Sing* would herald the approach.

"SING A SONG, FULL OF THE FAITH
THAT THE DARK PAST HAS TAUGHT US.
SING A SONG FULL OF THE HOPE
THAT THE PRESENT HAS BROUGHT US.
FACING THE RISING SUN

OF OUR NEW DAY BEGUN,
LET US MARCH ON 'TIL VICTORY IS WON."

It shouldn't have worked but it did. It was pageantry. Stunning. The chorus of the song, already written for a low register, was voiced a full octave lower. The melody was rich, and was stretched in such a fashion as to make it almost haunting. Along with the precision of the delayed footwork that matched the delayed cadence came an exhibition in soldiering. Though it was dark and the presentation was done every time the company returned to post, the comments from the bystanding troops who had raced from their company areas just to see them were of the highest praise. Except for the NCO's — the noncommissioned officers Sgts. Odums and Williams, first sergeants of the neighboring companies I and L — there would be no jealousy, a trait well-known in the military. Here, except for those two Firsts, who often would make it their business not to be around when King returned on post, there was only envy for a unit that could march as no other unit could.

Farther down, the company would reach the battalion area, where they would give another demonstration, then *half-step* all the way to the cluster of tents that partially boxed the end of the main roadway. The air-tight formation would swing to the left. A few yards more and King Company was home.

Except for neatness and absolute order, where even the dirt fell into conformity, the pride of the Third Battalion's home base looked no different from any other. Platoon-size tents lined both sides of the field. The Orderly Room headed up one end of the company, the Mess Tent and Supply Tent footed the other. Two ceremonial cannons stood by the Orderly Room's entrance near a spot where the guidon was kept.

When McClellan marched the troops past the cannons into the area, they knew from the way he was calling cadence that, as good as they had been, they were in trouble. They were right. He halted the company at midfield, gave the appropriate commands, and didn't mince words.

"You were piss-poor out there today, and your marching back to quarters failed to impress."

The First was standing erect in front of the formation, and his voice was demanding more. "You were not at your soldiering best. The whole notion of soldiering is not new to you. You are volunteers. The Army didn't find you. You found the Army. And when you found the Army, you found a home. And now that there's a national emergency and for the first time in your history you will be called upon to represent *all* the people of the United States overseas in battle, you *will* do better. The nation deserves — and I will accept — nothing less than your soldiering best. Tomorrow you will bring me your soldiering best. And to make sure that you get a proper start on the way to your soldiering best, reveille will be at 0400 hours!"

Every man in the formation felt like bursting into tears.

"*Fo'* o'clock in the moanin'??"

"Lawd, Lawd, Lawd."

"Have some mercy, Sarge."

"Please show some mercy."

"As you were!" the first sergeant said, canceling his own order. "Your reading, writing, and hygiene classes will be at 0400! Your morning exercise, to be followed by your morning chow, will be at 0300! Reveille will be at 0200! And if I hear another peep out of you, you won't sleep at all! And you will not eat at all!" He waited to see if there would be any further comments. Despite the long faces of disappointment, there was absolute silence in the ranks.

"Dismiss 'em, Dukes," said the First.

As McClellan headed for his tent, which was next to the Orderly Room's big tent, Dukes gave the command to disperse, and the company broke ranks.

The captain, a quiet, scholarly man, had been standing silently alongside McClellan. He couldn't have disagreed more with his First, but he certainly wouldn't say it, though he did saunter off in the direction of the Orderly Room, mildly reprimanding himself for not at least saying something to the sergeant.

Farrell's reticence was partially understandable. He was new to the Army; he was new to the regiment, the battalion, and the company. He was an engineer, knew little or nothing about the Infantry, and had never commanded before. Worst of all, coming from northern New England, he had never been around blacks before. But he had heard about the problems experienced by the company commanders who had preceded him. McClellan, no doubt, had a lot to do with the departures.

For more reasons than one, the sandy-haired captain didn't want to be swallowed by that same stigmatic weakness that apparently befell the other C.O.'s. He, of all people, couldn't afford that. As he had been advised before getting to the regiment and the battalion, and as he had said to himself before getting to the company, he had to be careful. He was quiet by nature, but too much quietness could be interpreted as unmanliness, and that could be dangerous. Around the blacks, he was told, *always* speak up. Find a target, find a big target and assert yourself. Do it as soon as possible.

Maybe it was because of McClellan, but the captain hadn't asserted himself. Several times on the field he had tried to achieve something close to it with Poole. He hadn't really succeeded, and he knew it. Since being there, however, and having observed the insolent corporal, Farrell knew the opportunity would present itself again. It did. Sooner than he thought.

The captain stopped, turned towards the cluster of men heading into the First Platoon tent, and called to Boland.

The heavy-walking young man knew what the captain wanted. He automatically stopped talking and double-timed towards the Supply Tent at the far end of the company. Poole, the Corporal of Supply, saw him, muttered something under his breath, and deliberately walked the other way.

"I'm going up to the Officers' Club at Battalion Headquarters, Corporal."

"What's that got to do with me?" Poole asked, his question ringing with insubordination.

"You have the keys to Supply," the Captain said. "Open it so

Boland can get the pillion wheeler."

"In the Army it's called a moto'cycle. *Sir*," Poole said sarcastically.

"I don't give a damn what it's called, Corporal. Open the goddamn Supply Tent." Capt. Farrell surprised himself. As a Quaker, he was surprised even more for having used God's name in vain. "And I'm giving you fair warning, Corporal. From this point on, do *not* correct or question me!" He waited on the *yes, sir.* It didn't come. "Have I made myself clear?"

Poole still said nothing.

Have I made myself clear, Corporal?!

Poole finally mumbled, "Yes, Sir," and moped off.

The captain wasn't satisfied. "Double-time!"

Poole continued sauntering.

"I want you to *double-time* to that Supply Tent, Corporal!"

Without energy the corporal picked up speed.

The company commander was more than pleased with himself. Farrell didn't see him, but looking on from the front of his tent was the first sergeant. He did something unusual. He almost smiled.

Carter, removing his snare drum on the way to the First Platoon tent, bumped into Simms heading to the Orderly Room to perform his other duty as part-time clerk and called him. "Hey, Simmsy, lemme know if I got any mail up in the Orderly Room."

Carter's timing was off. Roosevelt, Menyard and Andrews, always seen together and comprising a slaphappy, toe-tapping, clowning trio who took nothing serious, draped arms around each other and broke out in rhyme:

"Mail? Mail? Mail!???
You can't read, an'yo' momma can't write;
If it wont for the Army —
You pickin' cotton all nite!"

Organizing and dispatching the long arm of the draft across the great nation was a Herculean task. It was made all the more difficult by the failure of many eligible young men to register as required by law, and by hurried and error-prone draft boards that tried to do their best in the face of an unprecedented emergency. In the dark nooks and crannies of the country, the problems were particularly acute, because the government had no way of knowing exactly how many men were qualified for service. Records weren't kept, and in some places officials simply didn't know that such a thing as a birth certificate existed. The government hoped to correct the omission by relying on rural officials to conduct searches and, at the same time, to spread the word that a war was going on and certain young men were invited to attend. On the surface, at least, this appeared to be a fairly workable move. But Washington soon learned that employing rurals to serve as draft officials was fraught with danger. Ineptness had women, children, and the dead called for duty.

Though it had lost intensity, a hoopla continued to be raised in the North that Negroes would demean the prestige of the military. Yet, save for the fear of arming blacks and treading on the memory of the Confederate Army, many southerners were anything but concerned. They were comforted by the mistaken idea that the government wouldn't dare arm and train blacks in the deep South. Indeed, some southerners thought the "Northern" Army — as the United States Army was called by some — would be the ideal place to unload some of the more "slack, ungrateful, and uncooperative young coloreds who offered no promise and showed no respect for the good and solid traditions of the South." After all, the coloreds of today were not like their forefathers. They were becoming unmanageable. They were slack and unproductive, they were not working the soil, they congregated in unacceptable places, and they were slow in moving out of the white man's path. They were also showing interest in white women. And in the 50 or so years since slavery, many had begun to look the white man directly in the eye.

Drafting young coloreds was acceptable to the South.

The advent of drafting blacks, however, wasn't restricted to North and South. The draft extended East and West as well, and every State contributed to the great cause. The quiet Rocky Mountain State of Wyoming, with its 97,914 square miles, was very enthusiastic. She gave the nation all the blacks she could. Ninety-five.

One of them was Jody Cunningham.

He was getting close to being 12 years of age.

· · ·

First Sgt. Obie O. McClellan's was a four-man tent, but he occupied it alone. Two things stood out — the neatness of his clothes, and the many books that topped the makeshift shelves.

As usual the sergeant showed no signs of fatigue after the long day on the field. Normally after cleaning up a bit he would tend to a few company matters and spend the major portion of the evening reading. When he entered the tent this time, he lit the lantern and was taken aback by the curled figure asleep on his cot. It was pitifully ragged, exhausted-looking, and definitely in the wrong place. The papers sticking out of the back pocket of his thin corduroys were draft orders. With a look that suggested he was feeling sorry for the intruder, the sergeant studied him for a moment, removed the orders, and spent a moment or two looking them over. Then, as though reaching down to gently lift the visitor, the First put a hand under the cot and flipped it over. The weak body went sprawling into the corner. McClellan stepped to the door. "Field Sergeant Abraham Dukes!"

Dukes, on his way to the Orderly Room, changed directions and responded, "Comin', Sergeant."

"On the double!"

When Dukes entered the tent, the first sergeant was back to scanning the orders. Dukes was surprised to see the boy, still reeling in the corner. "In *your* tent? Who is he? Better yet, *what* is he?"

"His orders to report says his name is Jody Cunningham."

"*Orders to report?*" digested Dukes. "You mean *that's* a draftee? You ain't *tellin'* me, this is the kinda stuff we gonna be receivin'? I mean, this boy don't belong in the Army. Partik'lar in the Deuce-Four. He belongs in a crib or somethin'. We gonna send him back?"

"How?"

"I'll go next door to the Orderly Room and have Simms to buy him a ticket."

"With what?"

Dukes was stopped. He looked at the scared youngster. "You got any money to get back home with, Son?"

The boy shook his head in the negative.

"S'what I figgered," Dukes said. He helped the boy to his feet. "Sure is young. An' sure don't look like them new draft boards is gonna be doin' things right. S'pecially in the South."

"The State of Wyoming is not in the South, Sergeant," McClellan said.

"Wherever he's from, it's almost criminal. How old is you, Boy?"

"Age is not going to have very much to do with it, Dukes. The whites are in charge of the Boards. There's a war going on. If there's a prospect of getting killed in the war, the registrars in that part of the country only want to know two things. Is he black and is he breathing."

"On them two he 'pears to qualify."

"The battalion is understrength, so we'd better start getting used to it."

"I ain't gon' never get used to nothin' like this. How we gonna make a man out'a somethin' like him? He won't even make a good scout."

"Two?"

"Get him out of here, and assign him a bunk. Have Poole uniform him, and bring me two."

"One apiece. That scoundrel Pete Curry was on guard at the rear gate, and nobody but Pete Curry would send him in here."

"But, Sergeant, this boy shouldn't have to be diggin' a hole because of Curry's foolishness. Curry, yes. He should dig 'til the cows come home. But not this boy. An' I still say he's just too young to stay. An', Mac, I hate to say it —"

"Then, don't."

There was nothing else to be said.

When Sgt. Dukes led the boy out of the tent, they went next door to the Orderly Room tent for the keys to Supply.

Something entered the old sergeant's mind as they marched across the field. It had little or nothing to do with Pete and the boy's disciplinary action — having to dig two six-by-six-by-six holes in the ground with the small entrenching shovel. It was more than that. For years, in one way or another, and in this outfit and another, he had been at the first sergeant's side, and never once had they had a dispute. Nor did he ever question a decision or counter-mand an order. Now, because of this nice little fellow tagging along behind him, he had to. Though scared to death, as anyone would be when encountering First Sgt. McClellan, the boy looked like the happy hayseed. Dukes assessed that he came from a sheltered life and that he would be missed by a loving family — but even if not, as far as he was concerned, the boy presented a major problem. Beyond the hayseed look, the naiveté, the loving family and all, the boy was simply too young. He was too young in years, too young in mind, and too young in appearance to be in the Army. No ques-tion, the boy *had* to go. It was as simple as that. They hadn't been paid in a while, and there was no money in the till but somewhere, thought Dukes, he'd find some. This evening he would carry out the first sergeant's orders. By tomorrow night, though, this little country bumpkin would be gone.

The old belly-hanging field sergeant didn't know it, but what he was thinking would have broken the boy's heart. Jody was all for being in the Army now that he knew what — and where — the Army was. When he arrived in Columbus earlier in the day after the long, sore-footed journey, he had been directed to the front of the Post, but he wouldn't go near it. With the boldly painted black lightning, the campaign awards, the gate, the fencing, and the out-and-out austerity of the place daring him on, he didn't know what he had stumbled into. He was too scared to go forward, and too tired, hot, and hungry to turn around. Besides, he didn't know what to turn around to. Helped by accommodating strangers, he had taken days to get this far. Now not knowing what to do, he found him a spot and sat on the side of the road.

An hour later, and still not secure, the boy decided he would approach the daunting place from the rear.

It was late in the day when he neared the rear gate, and it was only after he saw the outline of the tents some ways down the road that the idea began to sink in that he had found what he thought he was looking for. He became breathless with awe. He had never seen anything as big and spacious as an Army post. Coming from a hidden town in Wyoming, he had never seen anything *period*.

Jody's arrival at the guard's booth was a boredom-breaker, and it didn't take Pete Curry long to realize that here was somebody ripe for plucking. For Pete, the timing couldn't have been better. Guard duty was the most boring of all chores, and being on guard at the rear gate, especially for anyone as active as Pete, was the absolute pits. The booth was hot and tiny, and activity was nil. The long, monotonous, pebble-thick dirt road to camp was a natural sleep-inducer, offering wide-awake contentment only to the lizards, ants, and carefree butterflies. Pete hated the rear gate assignment. First Sgt. McClellan knew he hated it, and he was most magnanimous in repeatedly giving it to his trouble-prone young soldier. The First knew that one day he would catch Pete sleeping on post. Pete was determined never to let it happen. Sleeping on post was a severe court-martial offense, and for someone like Pete, it was a guaranteed six months in the stockade — at hard labor. Pete didn't necessarily mind the six months, but the hard labor was another story.

On the afternoon of Jody's arrival, Pete was on the stool in the booth. Fearful of being caught napping, he had already danced in place, sung, screamed, yodeled, done push-ups, plucked his eyebrows, and was working on the eyelashes when his head went down again. It snapped up when he dreamt he was hearing the first sergeant's footsteps. The sequence repeated itself several times. Determined not to get caught, he resorted to parting his eyelids with little twigs from a bramble bush, a ploy that allowed him to see the ragamuffin bouncing up to the gate with a sack tied to the end of a long stick carried on small shoulders. Foggily through the twigs, Pete confirmed what he thought he saw and waited for the figure to get to the booth. When he did, Pete stepped gingerly from the guard's booth. At first he thought Jody was a delivery boy, but when he saw the official-looking papers sticking out of the youngster's hip pocket, he knelt in the boy's presence. His head bowed in mock servility, he introduced himself as Peter P. Curry, guard-private to arriving royalty, and with a welcome that would have charmed the Hun, he stood and again bowed to the visitor, whose thin eyebrows were still arched high when he saw the bent twigs in the shifty eyes. Telling the youngster that he had lived a lifetime waiting for this moment, Pete removed the stool from the booth and set the openmouthed visitor down. Continuing the act, he brushed a tear from his cheek, put the visitor's sack in the corner of the shack, and brought out the scissors. To the boy's relief, Pete finally removed the twigs. After batting his eyes several times, he reverently put the scissors to work, cutting two stars on the boy's already tattered shirt. Pete loved that part. He loved watching his barbershop-inspired fingers at work.

All done, he stepped back and saluted. "This is the first time I done ever been in the presence of greatness," he said. "Yo' Honor, I am touched."

The boy didn't know what the greeting or the stars meant, but he was ever so thankful, ever so humbled. Apparently so was Pete. He bowed again, gushed more fake tears, and asked the young visitor where he was from. Jody, overwhelmed, breathlessly explained that he was from Wyoming and that he had been told there was an Army somewhere around and he was supposed to be part of it. He wondered if he was in the right place.

"Suh," Pete said, choking back another crocodile tear, "not only is you done landed in the right place, but for somebody of you statute — you is in the *only* place. These very grounds ain't been the same since we heard you was comin'. And *you* is the only reason I've been standing ou'cheer waiting. An' I'm soooo glad you're here, Suh. I am soooo glad to see you."

"Is that why you had them things in your eyes?"

"Amen. They was to guide you home. An' you done made a body happy. But forget lil' ol' humble me. I'm just a lowly lil' Deuce-Four sentry. I just been stannin' ou'cheer sacrificin' my all, waitin' for greatness to show up. An' here you is. Our Holiness. I would rest myself at your feet, but I must stand so's I can direct you to your private livin' quarters. S'cuse me, your private *temporary* livin' quarters. I say 'temporary' because your permanent quarters up at Regimental Headquarters is bein' occupied by some scamp who ain't got no business bein' there. But don't you worry, Yo' Majesty. I got me some lowly understrappers workin' on gettin' him outta there at this very minute. An' I'm personally gonna take some actions against the cuss who let 'im get in there. But in the mean, I'm s'pose to direct Yo' Holiness to King Company. Get that? 'King Company.' Kings of the Regiment? Aces of the *Deuce-Four?*"

Pete wanted a reaction. He didn't get one. "Watch my mouth. See the lips movin'? *Kinnnngggg Kumpeenee. Now* you say it."

"Kang Kunney."

"No, no, M'lord," Pete said. He sent his fingers slicing through the air like a concert master and spent the next several minutes teaching the boy how to pronounce the name. Then when he thought he heard the sound he wanted to hear, he curtsied.

"*M'lord*," said Pete, "you say it so good, the crown we done picked ain't worthy of yo' head. An', Suh, that head of yours is gonna make the jewels look like rust in the sunlight. If we didn't already have a king, you'd be it."

"But I thought you just said I was."

"No, Yo' Highness. You will be in the *company* of kings. What you actually is, is ruler. Potentate. Crowned head of state. Lowly lil' King Company was just constructed in your honor."

"King Company was?"

"But say it right, Suh. *Kinnnngggg Kumpeennnee!*"

"*Kahinnnggg Khumpennee!*"

"Ooooh, how you do do justice to the sound. You make it sound like angels is tiptoe'n through the shadows of violets and tulips. Please say it one mo' time."

"*Kinnnngggg Kumpeennnee!*"

"What melody. I now know why you is the noble man that you is. I can now see why this whole thing was constructed, erected, and resurrected in your honor. We ought'a change the name of the whole regiment an' put it in your name." Pete hopped into the booth and grabbed a piece of paper and a pencil he had no use for. "In fact, let me make a note of this. 'Pete, start on that in the mornin'. Get the boys t'gether. Do do somethin' for this nice lil' visitah. Put this b'fore the board.' Yo' name agin?"

Jody told him. Pete wanted to know if the name was spelled with one "x" or two — and if the "x" or the "x's" were in caps.

Jody didn't know. Pete couldn't have written it if he had.

The boy told the funny man that he was "funnin'" him.

Pete responded with a solemnity a priest would envy. "M'boy, the one thing I never do is fun 'fore the sun goes down. This whole camp thing was constructed, manufactured, assembled, fabricated, an' re-actualized in your honor. It's all for you." Pete popped back out from the booth. "Now, Yo' Majesty, let me show you how to get to *Kinnnggg Kumpeenee*. And when you get to *Kinnnggg Kumpeenee*, the first thing you gotta do is go in this tent — *yo'* tent. It's right next to this big one called the Orderly Room, the one with cannons in front of it. Now, if a man comes in there wearin' some stripes on his sleeves, don't you pay him no attention. He's your personal servant. Might even be good to tell him to wait outside. Anyhow, get yourself plenty'a rest 'cause you — as thee honor-ee — is got some mighty big people to meet in the mornin'. People like General Pershing, an' Custer. An' wear that same shirt. Them stars I just cut puts you right up there with 'em. An' they looks good on you."

Pete returned the stick and sack, stepped back, and saluted the boy again.

Jody waved goodbye. With the sack swinging lively on his tired shoulder, he bounced happily down the camp road.

• • •

Jody wondered if he would ever see the prankish fellow in the little booth again. He hoped so. He liked him. But there was a more immediate concern. "What's a six-by, Mister?" he asked. Glad to be out of the tent, he was still trailing the swiftly moving Sgt. Dukes across the grounds to the First Platoon tent.

"I ask'd you in the tent, how old is you, Son?"

"I dunno."

"You don't know your age?"

"No, Suh."

"You ever heard of a birth certificate?"

"Nosuh."

"You ever been to school?"

"School? Nosuh."

"Where'd McClellan say you from?"

"Wyomin'."

"That's where it gets real cold in the winter, ain't it?"

"Yassuh."

"Never heard of no colored folks bein' in that part of the country. They must be tryin' to get rid of 'em, sendin' somebody to the Army as young as you is. What part of Wyomin'?"

"Chugwater."

"Chugwater? What kinda name is that?"

"S'where I live."

"You got family?"

"My momma."

"What she do for a livin'?"

"She used to work for Mr. Buttercup."

"Doin' what?"

"Ranchin'."

"A woman doin' ranchin'?"

"I used to help out. But she ain't doin' it no more. She been too sick. An' I'm gonna be a little worr'd about her this winter with me not bein' around to chop wood an' everythin'."

"Don't worry, you'll be there."

Jody didn't quite understand how. They walked on for a bit,

then he asked, "Do they pay you in the Army, Mister?"

"There's been a slight problem of late, but it's twenny-one dollars. Once a month."

The boy stopped. "Oh, my Lord! Twenny-one dollars!"

"And no cents."

"Wow!" Jody said breathlessly.

"Wow' what?"

"This'll be the first time I ever made any money."

"Maybe you was too young to get the money."

"But my momma wont."

"You tryin' to tell me your mammy was working for nothin'?"

"For food an' a place to stay. 'Most everybody there do that."

Sgt. Dukes stopped and looked at him. "If you was to be gettin' money, what would you be doin' with it?"

"Send it home."

"Wouldn't keep it for yourself?"

"Nope."

Dukes looked at him carefully. Only somebody with a good heart would be thinking like that. "You look like you starvin'. When's the last time you had somethin' to eat?"

The youngster gave it a thought. "I can't r'member."

Dukes hadn't planned it, but he ended up in the Mess Tent and made the youngster a sandwich from some of Mess Sgt. Willie Powell's leftovers.

Under the row of lights in the Mess Tent, which was much brighter than McClellan's, Dukes could see the boy much better. It reaffirmed earlier thoughts.

Field Sgt. Dukes sat and watched the hungrily munching boy like a hawk. There was no doubt about it, he was simply too young and innocent to stay. Dukes didn't like going against McClellan's orders, but this was a face that couldn't grow serious peach fuzz. To throw him into a company of loose-talking, profane-thinking mid-20-year-olds and rob him of his innocence before he had a chance to sample life was wrong.

As Dukes intently watched the youngster, he began thinking about himself. The old sergeant's mind went all the way back to what it was like when he first arrived at an Army post. What a day that was. He was, as the saying goes, full of piss n' vinegar — young, expectant, and ready to take on a man's world. Strangely, he remembered, he had no fear and wasn't afraid to mix with a barrackful of strangers from all parts of the country. He welcomed being away from home, away from the small confines that limited a young man with a purpose. Young Dukes was all for the Army. Thirty or 35 years later, he was still all for the Army — and even to this day, not having a uniform to wake up to would kill him. It almost happened once.

It almost happened to both him and McClellan.

Watching Jody caused the field sergeant to think of something else. What would life have been like if he had had a son? The thought pushed him back even further. What if 35 years ago he hadn't run away from the oldest city in the State of Georgia and, to use the term McClellan often used, "found a home"? That would have been somewhere around 1886 — '87, maybe? But what if he hadn't found the Army? Would he have married? Had family? Certainly there wouldn't have been a life in the Army. Like most of the coloreds, if he had remained home, he never would have even heard of an Army. He would have been home, tied to a woman — untraveled, ignorant, and dull. What would the woman have been like? What was marriage like? What's it feel like sleeping with a woman on a regular basis? What's it feel like to roll over and find somebody's in the same bed with you — night after night? What a sad thought, he chuckled to himself.

Although Abraham Dukes wasn't his name back then, he was the same person. That aside, when he was young, many times he had awakened with a woman, but then – daylight — and he was back home, back on post, back to the safe confines of the military. That's the way it was. In the Army, you hit and run. No strings; no commitment. Didn't need any. The Army was there. For the dedicated — the good soldier — that's all anyone needed: Army. In the Army there was — and is — no room for *anybody* but Army. In the Army there is no room for *anybody* but Army. The Army has always been its own fraternal order; its own matrimonial structure; its own world. The Army is all things to a man — parent, wife, mistress and offspring.

But what if by mistake he hadn't found Army? What if he had gotten stuck 'way back there in Savannah? What if by some quirk of fate, marriage and family had happened? Maybe he would have had a boy like this one sitting across from him. What if the years had passed and the boy had had a son? Ol' Sgt. Dukes would'a been Grandpa Dukes. Suppose the grandson — he'd now be a little older than this boy — but what if the grandson came to him and said, "Grampa; I've been hearin' about this thing called the Army. Sounds excitin'. Think I'm gonna join it." Would Grandpa have approved? Well — yes; and no. *Yes*, Grandpa would have approved if the grandson had had to endure the hardships of 1882's Georgia that he had faced. *Yes*, if he had had to face a life of knowing nothing, being nothing, and living in a mud-caked shanty with planks so spaced you almost didn't need doors to go in and out. And a big fat *yes*, if he had had no choice but to grow up in the same Georgia with the hate, the lynchings, the fear of the whites, the no-work and no-hope-for-work except for that of a field hand, which — looking back — is something *Sergeant* Dukes never had to do. *Grandpa* Dukes would have done it, but not *Sergeant* Dukes.

And the 'no'? Well, it'd have to be a *no* to the grandson if he was talking about 1917's Army. No, definitely not. He would not have approved. No, because the Army of today — the 1917 Army — was not the Army of old. It was too new. Too modern. It had too many machines, too many cars and motorcycles and other contraptions that would eventually bring the foot soldier to ruin. This had proven itself before, and it would do it again. Even as late as the month of May, he remembered. Last May, the battalion had to go on a 30-day assignment to Arizona — and they had the audacity to *ride* to the train station in trucks. The Columbus depot was less than 15 miles away, and they rode! Infantrymen *riding*? Ridiculous! In the old days they would have marched. Not to the depot. *To Arizona*. There was no doubt about it, the foot soldier was changing. And another thing, thought the old sergeant, along with all the coddling and babying that was going on now in the military, the new Army was too sanitized. They were talking about bacteria instead of backpacks, raingear, rubber to protect the boots, and all sorts of sissy and nonsensical things. Even soap and water were getting to be an issue. Scuttlebutt had it that the troops were going to have to bathe once a week. Even the horsehair toothbrush had undergone a change. Worse, they were going to be *"required"* to use them. *Daily!* Required to brush the teeth – *daily?* Who's teeth *are* they? McClellan — and he should know because he reads a lot — but he said that a lot of changes like that were coming and that one day they were going to do something called "vaccinatin'"people. Syphilis and gonorrhea were going to be treated by needles instead of ramming an instrument up the penis opening and letting the pus and blood flow; consumption and whooping cough were going to be fought with pills. *Pills?* To add insult to injury, they were going to bring the outhouses indoors and call 'em latrines. *Latrines?* Taking a dump in a *luh'trine?* Whoever heard of relaxing butt muscles in something like that? An' imagine how *that's* going to smell. An' there's something else. Nowadays they don't sleep outside. They bivouac. *Biv'wak?* What's *that?* And what's that got to do with anything? No, there was no stopping this new Army. They had already changed the color of the uniforms. What was wrong with the ol' two-tone blues and that yellow bandanna? Nuttin'. And there was another bothersome thing about this new Army. It was too much without personal contact. Nowadays you would hardly ever get to see the enemy. Even at that the modern Army killed with too much ease. Not satisfied with these new things called tanks they copied from the Brits, they have artillery shells that can shoot forever. They've got liquid fire, and another new thing that the coloreds don't have. It's still called a machine gun, but it fires with so much heat, it's gotta be cooled by water. The modern Army's got new mortars, and this thing called a grenade. You carry it by hand, pull a pin, throw it, and if it hits right, you can kill four or five men at one time. It's worse than that shrapnel that other Englishman invented. And now they've developed gasses that can blister the skin, choke the throat, and kill a man in a matter of seconds. They have helmets instead of hats, cartridge belts, maps that make no sense, and commanders who sit behind desks and talk about fighting wars in foreign countries with names so strange they don't even belong on earth.

Without doubt, the new Army was leading itself to ruin.

Leaving the mess hall and continuing across the field to the First Platoon tent, the old sergeant, his mind heavy with resistance to modernity, asked the boy how long it took to get from Wyoming to Columbus.

Jody was still cramming his mouth with bread he had pocketed. "Most a week, 'cause I got lost. The white folks wouldn' let me ride no train. What's a six-by, Mister?"

"You'll see," said Dukes. "The main thing is, you found us. An' I'm gonna tell you somethin', Son. If you want your *temporary* stay here to be slightly more than pleasant, you better learn there ain't no 'misters' in this here man's Army."

They reached the First Platoon tent and Dukes led the boy inside. "An' don't feel bad when I do you a favor t'morra," he said.

Jody didn't know what the sergeant was referring to and walked on happily, still pinching on the bread. It had gotten gritty and sandy in his pockets, yet he was too hungry to let it remain untouched.

Inside the tent, the field sergeant walked purposefully down the aisle. He pointed to an empty cot and kept on moving. Jody continued to follow him. "You're gonna sleep in that empty cot back there for the night. B'longs to Rochester. He's on guard. He won't need it 'til morning. But don't you go gettin' too cum'ftable."

The youngster stopped, took a look at the cot, and held his breath. Finally he asked, "I'm gonna have a real sleepin' bed?"

"What'chu been doing? Stannin' up every night?"

"Nosuh. But I never had a real sleepin' bed. My momma ain't, either. An' one'a these days I'm gonna buy her one'a these."

Sgt. Dukes didn't hear it. He was already down the line, moving in on the foot of Pvt. Peter P. Curry's cot. Having worked guard duty earlier, Pete was sleeping peacefully. As McClellan had done earlier with Jody, Dukes grabbed the side of the cot and sent the scrawny 20-year-old miscreant reeling, then turned and marched back up the aisle. Heading out, he collected Jody and called back to Pete, "You got exactly sixty seconds to be out front."

Pete sputtered. "What'd I do?"

"Sixty seconds. Clothed," Sgt. Dukes said. Once out front, he stood and closely eyed the thin second-hand of his most prized possession, an action made all the more interesting because the hand didn't move and the field sergeant couldn't tell time.

Pete wasn't fully clothed and didn't quite make it in the allotted 60 seconds, but he managed to burst outside in fairly good time.

Inside, Jody had been too enamored of the cot to see Pete. Now he swallowed. "Hey, it's you!"

"Why looky there," Pete said in return. He chuckled. "Did His Majesty, the gen'ral, have hisself a nice lil' snooze?"

Sgt. Dukes, responding for Jody, told Pete that one day somebody was going to hand him his head. Saying nothing more, he escorted them down the field and into the Supply Room, where he wasted no time in conducting his search.

The Supply Room, another company-size tent, differed from the Orderly Room and Mess Tent only because it was far too crowded. It was musty but neat. Old blue shirts, trousers, leggings, helmets, .03 and .30 Krag-Jorgensen rifles — mostly broken — lined both sides of the room amid some training equipment. To the rear, near a broken Harley-Davidson sidecar motorcycle, he found a wooden box containing entrenching tools. In short order, Sgt. Dukes put his hands on the two shovels he had been searching for. He handed one to the bewildered Jody and shoved the other into Pete's hands.

"But, Sarge," Pete protested. "I didn't do nothin'."

"You sent this boy to the first sergeant's tent. You're lucky you're gettin' off by diggin' a hole in the ground."

"But, Sarge —!"

"Shut. Up." Dukes had separated the words as he went over to a clothing stack that was behind a long counter. Without questioning Jody as to size, he found a hat, a pair of o.d. trousers, a shirt, and socks, and tossed them, along with some safety pins and a pair of boots and leggings, to Jody. "These'll do 'til you see Corporal Poole in the mornin'." The field sergeant then asked himself why he would have Poole uniform the boy in the morning if he was going to arrange a ticket for him to go back home sometime later in the day. But thinking on a different level, if the boy and his mother were too poor to even have a bed to sleep on, what was he going home to? It was hot now, but sleeping on the floor in a Wyoming winter? The boy had already said that the woman was sick. If she was as fragile and as small-boned as he was, somebody wasn't long for this earth.

Dukes didn't like what he was thinking. Putting the thought on hold, he led the pair back outside and around behind the tent, then over to the rear of a row of out-houses. While Sgt. Dukes was thinking of one thing, Jody was thinking of another. As Jody had started to change clothes, displaying nothing underneath his soiled shirt and tattered pants, he whispered to Pete, "Do I gotta pay for these here clothes an' stuff?"

Pete lifted his eyes as if to say, "Is you crazy?" Suddenly he changed his mind as opportunity knocked. He whispered in return, "I'm puttin' up the money, but you gotta see me on payday. I'm gittin' everythin' for half price. Includin' the shovel. See? By stickin' with me, you're already ahead of the game."

Outside the tent, 30 yards away and still saying nothing, Sgt. Dukes methodically paced off two areas and said, "You will dig a hole six feet long, six feet wide, and six feet deep. You will report to the front gate guard when you have dug the hole measuring six by six by six. The front gate guard will come and check the hole that measures six by six by six. An' you will be done diggin' the hole measurin' six by six by six by the time reveille is sounded."

Again Pete started to protest, but he was silenced by the field sergeant's look. Jody, still not fully understanding, started to put the little shovel into motion. He waited, however, until Sgt. Dukes had cleared the area before tactfully questioning the logic of digging a hole and covering it back up. Pete replied that they were talking in code.

Careful not to injure his fingers, he laid his shovel down and cleared a spot to lie down.

"M'boy, let me quote: Special Order #222-5555. It says, and I quote, 'Pete and the sarge will talk in code whenever Pete and the sarge is got somethin' important to say.' Since we is friends, let me un-code what he was sayin'."

"He was sayin' we gotta dig two holes with these tiny shovels, an' we gotta cover 'em back up."

"The good sarge was sayin' that *you* had to dig two holes. I have to lay down here an' oversee 'em, so's I can be close to 'em. S'the best way to do the measurin'."

"An' he said that in code?"

"Certainly."

"Didn't sound like it."

"I'm givin' you the *meanin'*."

"The meanin' of the code?"

"The meanin' of the *meanin'* of the code. An' I ain't s'pose to do that."

"Why not?"

"We at war. An' you is in King Company. We is kings o'the hill.

An' the rules o'the war says that when peoples o'the hill in high positions, such as me an' the sarge, is got somethin' to say to each other, they say one thing while the people listenin' is thinkin' you're sayin' another. That way, they'll be thinkin' they hearin' one thing while they is really hearin' another."

"An' you in a high p'sition?"

"So high I been treated for nosebleed."

"So you way up there?"

"From where I sit, birds look like they flyin' underground."

"So you real high."

"I get tired lookin' down on the moon."

"Well, if nobody down here can hear you, why do y'all have to go through all'a that codin' stuff?"

"To confuse the foe."

"Foe?"

"Foe. Like 'fo they get to us, we gotta get to them. Foe means the enemy. Spies an' all."

"Lotta them 'round here?"

"A slip of the lip will sink a ship. Y'ever heard that before?"

"Nope."

"You will. An' after your basic trainin', you'll be havin' a code all your own. An' learn it good. New Mexico is the birthplace of enemies. They got more enemies here than cactus"

"Really?"

"S'why we're here. You don't think the Army would put a whole — and, see — there's that word *hole* again. Like the sarge, I almost used it in code. But you don't think the Army would station a whole regiment like the Deuce-Four in a place like this if we wont here for somethin' important, do you?"

"Don't s'pect they would."

"Well, they didn't. R'member I was stannin' at the gate when you got here?"

"How could I forget that? I told'ja you was funnin' me."

"I was testin' you. Now, y'got any idea why I was really out there?"

"You said it was to meet me."

"Noooo." Pete said, getting more comfortable. "I was out there because I had just come back from shippin' a boatload of spies to Washington."

"You funnin' me again."

"Nevah. Where you from, lil' mascot?"

"Wyomin'. Ever heard of it?"

"Course," Pete said confidently. "And how are things at the White House?"

The Officers' Club, slightly less than two miles from King Company and less still for companies I and L, was a small wooden building located at the western edge of the post's main headquarters building. After duty the executive officers and company commanders from the battalion would gather there and, more often than not, be joined by a few officers from the regiment.

The tables in the club were small and square. They had a look of bamboo that matched the bar but clashed with the olive-drab paint.

There were about two dozen officers in the club when Farrell arrived, and, as always, most of the attention centered around Lt. Col. Briggs, the battalion commander. He couldn't be heard at Farrell's table, but the tall, thin man with the grayed horseshoe hairline was expounding his opinions on the war from the largest table at the rear of the room.

Capt. Farrell, new to the regiment, didn't know what the colonel's views were, but if the battalion commander were like most senior career officers — particularly Infantry officers — he couldn't wait for the taste of blood. The captain was of a different stripe, and in that sense he should have been grateful to his first sergeant for being the last to bring his troops in from the fields. Being last meant that the K Company commander would be the last officer to arrive at the club. Since seats were at a premium, the captain had a good excuse for maintaining his distance. Farrell's lateness and seating placement, and sometimes failure to show up at all, were not lost on the battalion commander, however. From the outset, Briggs had reservations about the captain. He thought his new company commander dainty and unmanly. Farrell thought the battalion commander was a buffoon, talky and vainglorious.

In the strict sense of the word, Capt. Farrell was not a soldier. Unlike the other officers in the regiment, battalion, or club, he would never be a soldier.

Harland Farrell was a quiet man, a transplanted Easterner. Born in Lancaster, Pennsylvania, he was studious but was known to criticize himself for remaining with his old-line *Inner-Light* Quaker association too long. He married while studying engineering at Boston's School of Engineering. Upon graduating, he moved to Maine and joined his wife's family. There he joined the Reserves, thinking it would be politically advantageous. To keep ties with the military after ROTC, and with sole thoughts of future security, he joined the ranks of the inactive reserves and benefited greatly from the association. Recommending, gaining inside information, and working on the Army's many engineering projects through and with his wife's father, he was living a secure life. But — and not solely because of the coming war — Farrell was not a happy man. He had never been a happy man. He wasn't satisfied with the way he had done things. He wasn't the builder he wanted to be. He engineered nothing of significance, and to his way of thinking did nothing to benefit mankind. Worse, even at this late date he was still in anguish because of an overly stringent, pacifist upbringing. He was not proud of his ties to the military. At one point, as his wife was later to say, during his second year of marriage he was despondent. So troubled was he that, unknown to his wife, and well before there was talk of war, he went back to Boston and tried to resign his commission. Drunk, he failed in the attempt. Had he not been fearful of hometown chastisement and serious conflict with his father-in-law, he could have returned to New England, claimed pacifist or Conscientious Objector status, and quite possibly been freed of military obligation. Confused, he elected to wait. While he waited, the globe shrank.

Internationally, the feeling was that the United States, seen as isolationists, could not possibly remain aloof. Europe — indeed the world — was a wreck. Nothing could be discounted; anything was possible. The Serbs were being blamed for the death of the heir to the Austro-Hungarian throne; Poland was without a government; and Belgium was just a "scrap of paper." France was in trouble. The Czecho-Slovaks were controlled by the Austrians, as were the Armenians and Lithuanians. Italy was angry. Compounding defeat and revolution, typhus was sweeping Russia. The Turks were set to do battle with the Central Empires. Vienna sent an ultimatum to Belgrade. Rumania was gearing up for war. And Japan, her treaty with Great Britain be damned, continued her aggression in Kiao-Chau, China. Set to conquer all were the Germans. Defensively the United States activated her Reserves.

• • •

"Brandy," Farrell said to the black uniformed waiter on TDY — tour of duty — with Headquarters Company. He tightened the club's only empty chair closer to the table where Capts. Lloyd Whitney and Kurt Reed, the company commanders for the neighboring companies of I and L, were seated. The lesser-ranked Warrant Officer Bill Froelich, of Headquarters Company, was seated there, too. Farrell was friendly to all three of them. "Whew, sure was rough out there today. And this New Mexico sun can really be scorching."

"What the hell are you trying to do, Farrell, trying to make the rest of us look bad?" Capt. Whitney asked lightly. "Do you realize the hour?"

"It's almost bedtime," Reed took a drink and chided.

"Just scoring points, huh, Captain," Warrant Officer Froelich commented.

"No. Just doing what has to be done, I guess."

"You been scoring any points lately, Warrant Officer Froelich?" Whitney directed the question at the short officer seated diagonally across from him.

"I don't have to," Froelich answered, matching impoliteness with aggressiveness.

Farrell broke in. "It's never me wanting to stay out in the field. It's the first sergeant."

"Hey, remember my first words to you when you got here? 'Never allow a First too much room,'" said the chatty warrant officer. Again he irked the I Company commander. Whitney simply did not like the man.

To get away from Froelich, Whitney said to Reed, "First sergeants can really be pains, can't they?"

"First sergeants are more than pains," Reed answered conversationally. "But how would you like to run a company without one?"

"Can't," Warrant Officer Froelich answered.

"How the hell would you know?" Whitney snapped at the pudgy man again. "Have you ever been out in the field?"

"Give him a break, Lloyd," Reed said. "Just because he's up at Headquarters *playing* soldier, doesn't mean he isn't trying."

"I'll give him a break, all right."

"Do that. But you still didn't answer the question."

"What?"

"How would you, Captain Lloyd Whitney, commander of Company I for Item, like to run a company without a strong First? Better yet, let me change it," Reed said. "*Could* you, Captain Lloyd

Whitney, company commander of Item Company, run a company without a First?"

"Hell, yes."

"You lie, Lloyd. You couldn't run that company without Odums," said Reed. "Just as I couldn't run mine without Sergeant Williams."

"It's no lie," Whitney retorted. He didn't bother to lower his voice when the black soldier/waiter returned with Farrell's drink. "If it were a white company, I couldn't — or wouldn't — want to run a company without a First. But commanding coloreds? I'd be better off. A helluva lot better off."

"Why?" Froelich asked.

"If you must know, and I don't see why you should," Whitney answered, "but if you must know, first sergeants are intermediaries. A First is a go-between for the company commander and the troops. The company commander has to be the supreme authority. The danger in having a colored First, particularly one who thinks he's God's gift to the Army, is that he forgets the role of intermediary and thinks he's the superior. Like yours, Farrell."

"Yeah," said Reed. "But how many McClellans are there around?"

"None," answered Froelich.

"I sure as hell hope not," Whitney said. "Coloreds are dangerous to begin with. Make the mistake of teaching them how to string two adjectives together and they go crazy. You ever hear McClellan when he's talking to those ignoramuses of his?"

"Yeah, I have. He knows his stuff," Reed said. "But what you were saying before, Lloyd, doesn't always happen. And the benefits are: a strong colored First knows his men a hell of a lot better than we do."

"He should," Lloyd Whitney countered. "He's a nigger and so are they."

The statement pushed them into silence. Farrell, already quiet, took a drink and ordered another. Froelich, for no apparent reason, started chuckling to himself. Reed and Whitney looked at him. To dismiss what he was thinking, Reed emptied his glass and spoke to Farrell. "As the new kid on the block, I'll bet my bottom dollar you're sorry as all hell you ever ran into that bunch of yours, Farrell."

"Wasn't my idea."

"Being here wasn't mine, either," Reed said.

"Nor mine," volunteered Whitney, the C.O. of Company I.

"Nor mine," added Froelich. The short, weighty, dark-haired officer who worked at Headquarters Company went on. "I love the Army. But this is ridiculous."

Lloyd Whitney was on him again. "What the hell do you have to complain about? You're always saying something like that. You're not a field officer. You're up at Headquarters, doing nothing but sitting on your stumpy fat ass all day."

"Lloyd, I keep telling you — you shouldn't talk to an executive officer like that." Reed teased.

"He's not an executive officer. He's a warrant officer. It's a stupid rank that means nothing. It's a hybrid. Besides a bunch of Africans, there are two things that don't belong in the Army, hybrids and Hebrews."

"Not nice, Captain. Not nice," Reed said to Whitney. He knew the ruddy, pleasant-faced captain from New York was about to launch into another series of racial declamations.

It was a nightly occurrence. With Froelich sitting there absorbing it without uttering a single defensive word, the Company I commander would start with the Jews and then unload the thick of his venom on the blacks.

It was rare, however, that a captain would speak so openly about the dilemma of commanding a company of troops he so despised, as Whitney did — and he had been with the battalion for well over a year. The quietly offended Farrell thought that the Army was wrong — dead wrong — in not transferring Whitney and all the Whitneys in the regiment to some other units. But then, he reasoned, if the Army reassigned all the officers who didn't like blacks, the blacks would end up commanding themselves. That brought up another interesting point that needed confirmation. It was a bit naive, but the question had to be asked. Farrell was about to break his silence and form the question differently when something else came from Warrant Officer Froelich. He took a sip and spoke from out of the blue.

"I'm not a field officer, thank God, but I'm reading a — "

"You bet you're not a field officer," Whitney interrupted.

"Right," Froelich said importantly. "I'm an administrator — "

"You're a waste of time. You shouldn't be sitting at this table. You're an overgrown clerk. You ought to be wearing one of those dresses your family sells back there in the garment district."

"Let him finish what he started to say, Lloyd," Reed said.

"Thank you," said Froelich. "I'm reading this book that says, 'the best way to handle coloreds with guns is not to say too much to them. Keep the fear hidden.' What would you say, Farrell?"

"I don't know," the commander of King Company said. He rubbed a finger thoughtfully around the top of his glass. "I'm a living example of the loneliness of command, looking for understanding."

"Doesn't tell us much, does it?"

"He never tells us much," Froelich said, switching back to the issue. "Okay, see if you agree with this: In the same book, Teddy Roosevelt said, 'Speak soft but carry a big stick.' Any comment from you company commanders?"

"Yeah," Whitney said, again being rude. "That would be something a Jew would remember."

"Back off, Lloyd!" Reed said. "Why are you always on him?"

"He deserves anything he gets."

Farrell already knew the answer, but still seeking confirmation and hoping to tone matters down a bit, he wondered aloud if anyone had ever seen or heard of a colored officer in the division. Whitney volunteered that there were none. He threw in an invective and again said that there were none, that there should be none, and that the Army had already gone overboard in having colored noncoms.

Froelich, recovering from the insult, again supported his nemesis. He said that there were fewer than a dozen colored officers in the Army, over half of them were chaplains, and they were needed for the labor battalions. "But no matter what," he said, "the Army is not about to put a colored in charge of a company of colored infantry." He added that it had been tried in the Union Army but it never worked out. One black had even attained the rank of major.

"That's quite high," Reed responded.

"You think that's something?" Froelich continued knowledgeably. "There was one colored from Virginia who was elected a U. S. senator."

"Really?" asked Farrell.

"Yeah," Froelich said smugly. "But he went to Washington and the senate refused to seat him."

The conversation stalled for a moment. Froelich, trying to ingratiate himself even more, went on. "Speaking of President Teddy Roosevelt and his big stick, anybody remember hearing about the White House dinner he had for the colored leader, whasitsname?"

Whitney said dryly, "So what?"

"Well, a southern senator got wind of it and got so mad he called him a dog."

Whitney, as if having expected more, swallowed his drink. "Calling a nigger a dog? Is there a difference?"

"Probably not," responded Froelich. "But the senator was calling the president a dog. And then apologized to the dog. Ha, ha, ha."

Kurt Reed filled the embarrassing void. "Where you from, Harland?"

"Maine," Farrell replied.

"What part?"

"St. Agatha."

"Small town?"

"Umhuh."

"Like it?"

"Yeah."

"Born there?"

"Pennsylvania."

"Where 'bouts?"

"Lancaster."

"Nice place?"

"Yeah."

"Children?"

"Two."

"Boy and girl?"

"Two girls."

"I've got two and two," Reed said.

"I'd like more," Farrell said. "Two boys, maybe."

"The wife for it?"

"She wouldn't mind. Probably would've started already if I hadn't been snatched up for this."

"Mine's had enough," Farrell said. "But I still might try for another when I get back."

"Maybe a half n' half?" Froelich asked, trying to be funny. He was overlooked. Reed continued to Farrell.

"Where'd they muster you from, ROTC?"

"Umhuh. Inactive Reserves."

"What kind of work did you do?"

"Engineering. Worked for my father-in-law. You?"

"Construction. Small firm. They grabbed me out of Artillery. National Guard," Reed said. "And I'm still wondering what I ever did to the U.S. Government to get activated, and then draw an assignment like this."

"If you're like most of us," Whitney cut in, "somebody thought there was a little German blood in your history. Or maybe in your wife's. It's either that, or they don't hold out much hope for you as an officer."

"Speak for yourself, Lloyd," Reed said.

Farrell looked over at the senior officer's table and saw that the officers were about to stand for the lieutenant colonel's departure. One of the officers at the table said something. Briggs laughed, reclaimed his seat, and ordered another drink.

Withdrawing his look, Farrell asked, "How did the battalion commander draw this assignment?"

"Don't know," Kurt Reed said. "Senior officers don't discuss such things with peons."

"You're not a peon," Whitney said to Reed. "You're from New Jersey. You're a peed-on."

"Better to be peed on in Jersey than crapped on in New York," Reed responded.

"Touchy, isn't he?"

"No," said Reed, the commander of L Company. "Just allergic to half-asses with big mouths."

"Hey, a Jerseyite and a New Yorker. You two are neighbors," Froelich said. "You're supposed to love each other."

"What the hell would you know about love?" Whitney asked.

"A hell of a lot more than you."

"The hell you do."

Reed spoke up. "Hey, c'mon, Lloyd, enough is enough."

"Where's Colonel Briggs from?" Farrell asked. He was trying to steer the conversation in another direction, not realizing that Whitney and Reed were not seriously at each other's throat.

"The colonel came from the Point," Froelich said.

Farrell was surprised. "Lieutenant Colonel Briggs came from West Point?"

"Yep. The United States Military Academy at West Point," Froelich confirmed. "Taught there."

"Now I'm surprised. And disappointed," said Reed, who had been with the battalion only a month or two longer than Farrell. "I've always thought to be able to teach at West Point you had to have a brain."

"Don't underestimate him, Kurt," Froelich cautioned. "He's smart. Very smart. And he knows his history."

"And doesn't like coloreds," added Whitney. "That's what makes him my kind of commander."

"Lloyd, how come you don't put in for transfer?" Farrell asked.

"You don't know how many times he's tried." Reed said, laughing. "And still trying."

"And still stuck," Whitney said drearily. "Why'd you ask, Farrell? Thinking about a transfer already?"

"No. Just wondering. Curious."

"Meaning problems."

"No, I'm fine," responded Farrell.

"I can tell you're a bit shaky," said the I Company commander. "And I'll bet it's because you don't know how to handle coloreds."

"I don't have a problem," Farrell insisted.

"You gotta have."

"Well, I don't."

"Sure you do. Admit it," said Whitney. "No use trying to hide it. We've all gone through it. Trouble and worry go with the territory."

"C'mon, Lloyd, you're trying to scare the guy. What worry?" Kurt Reed asked. "You may not like them, but your men have never given you any trouble."

"The hell they haven't."

"What kind of problems do you have?" Farrell inquired.

"Name 'em."

"No. You name 'em," Reed said.

"Yeah, go ahead, Lloyd," encouraged Froelich. "I want to hear this."

"Who'n the hell's talking to you?"

"Lay off a him, Lloyd, and answer the question."

"Alright," said Lloyd Whitney. "How about discipline, for starters? Coloreds can't be disciplined."

Reed laughed. "Is that all?"

"I don't have that problem," Farrell said.

"Nor do I," said Reed.

"Both of you are lying sonsabitches," the I Company commander responded. "Maybe you haven't been here long enough, Farrell. But there's not a company commander in the regiment who doesn't have — or hasn't had — a problem with disciplining a bunch of blacks. And that's just for starters."

"And —?" Kurt Reed prodded. "C'mon, Lloyd, don't hold back. What else?"

"Well, if you really want to get serious, there're the problems with hygiene, lateness for reveille, shiftlessness, insolence, insubordination, belligerence, drinking and gambling. And practically everything else under the sun you can name. And you almost have to be a tribal chief to talk to 'em. It gets my goat, trying to communicate with these asses. Most of 'em have never heard of a thing called grammar —"

"Hey, hey, hey," Reed cut in. "A minute ago you were just complaining because McClellan knew so much."

"If he knew that much, he wouldn't be here."

"Christ, the guy can't win. If he talks properly he's wrong; if he doesn't, he's wrong. What do you want from him?"

"Screw McClellan and you, too, Kurt," Whitney said, dismissing Reed. "What I was getting to is that the coloreds speak English like goddamn foreigners. And they can't learn a damned thing. I still have some in my company who — after all this time — and hearing the command every day, can't tell *left face* from *right face*. And get this: It took three weeks — *three solid weeks* — for Odums, my first sergeant, to learn how to find north on the map. And he used to be a prizefighter, or so he says. He was supposed to've traveled. I mentioned east and you know what he did? He went looking for his mess kit. And a compass? Forget it. Shooting a back-azimuth? Don't even mention it. Setting up a skirmish? Out. The nomenclature of a machine gun? Not on your life. Diagramming a skirmish? You've got to be kidding. Transmitting messages by wire? Not on your life. And don't let any of 'em get excited. Then you can't even hope to understand a word they're saying. They sound like a bunch of damned monkeys scratching and fighting in a barrel. Put two coloreds in a room and get 'em steamed up, and I defy you to tell me what they're saying. Now, let's say —"

"Hold it a sec, Lloyd," Reed interrupted.

"Let 'im finish, Kurt," Warrant Officer Froelich said. "I'm enjoying this."

"I wasn't speaking for your benefit," Whitney said, and directed his attention back to Farrell and Reed. "Now, let's say the Army goes haywire and compounds its mistake by sending these ill-speaking, ninny-brained, ignorant asses overseas. Somehow, through another mistake, these imbeciles end up on the front lines — say, forward of the Brienne Le Chateau. Napoleon went to school there. The French have it, the Germans want it. Getting it will be a moral victory. Better yet, let's move to the trenches — say, the trenches of the reconquered part of Alsace. It's wet, and muddy. It's been raining on and off for days. The whole place is stinking with dead bodies; you can't tell one from the next; you don't know if you're stepping over or on friend or foe. It's like the battle of Passchendaele. We're being bombarded by German artillery; Boche shells are blowing up position after position. The rifles, grenades, and machine guns are doing — whatever. Fog is misting on the ground. It's so thick you can cut it with a knife. Now, they throw pyrocellulose at us; mustard gas, the works. We know an all-out attack is imminent. We can tell what's coming by the concentrated shelling. They're bombarding the living hell out of us. Some of the troops they're gonna hurl at us fought the Russians. They were in on the defeat of the First Battalion of The Chasseurs d'Afrique. They're not afraid of anything. Now they're ready for the big time. Us. They're going to charge with everything they've got. They want to make mincemeat out of us. We're the big, bad Americans. Invincible. We've fought our way from Conde-en-Barrois to the subsector of the Verdun. We've exhausted everything. We're down but not out. We still have our bolo knives to fight with. And we're still breathing. Our sector is cut off from you, Harland. K Company is totally surrounded. So I gotta get in touch with you, Kurt. I need fire power from L Company. And I need it in a hurry. The wireless is out of order. I go to my company runner. Now get this: in clear, concise English I give him your location. I tell him what to tell you. I repeat it — word for word. I don't miss a syllable — not a noun, verb, adjective, or conjunction. He's excited, scared; shaking like a leaf. I calm him. I ask him to repeat what I told him to tell you. He starts. He gets the first word so screwed up, I think he's working for the goddamn Germans. I ask him to start again — slowly. Take your time, I plead. He starts again. Now he's so confused he can't even understand what *he's* saying, let alone what I told him. I'm lost. Totally goddamned lost! I try again, asking the S.O.B. for the *third* time. He starts gibbering again. By the time this bastard gets to the second sentence, I'm ready to wave the white flag. I'm surrendering. I don't mind being killed by a German, but to be killed by a nigger fighting the English language is just a little too much to take. And, Kurt, if you or God and company can understand *one* word of what the black sonovabitch will be saying to you, I'll kiss your ass and the colonel's nuts on the doorstep of the Kaiser's retreat."

"Hear, hear," said Warrant Officer Froelich, applauding. He motioned the waiter for another round of drinks.

"Sounds like you're being just a little unfair, Lloyd," Farrell said, breaking the silence that followed Froelich's display.

"No, he's not," said Froelich.

"Yes, he is."

"The hell I am. And I don't need you to defend me, Bill," Whitney said to the Jewish warrant officer.

"I'm like Harland. I think you're 'way off the mark," Reed said. "And not only that, it seems to me you've forgotten something."

"Oh?" Whitney asked. "What? I should end up carrying the message myself?"

"No," said Reed. "With everything you've said, you didn't mention the colored man's will to fight."

"His will to *what?*"

"You heard me."

Whitney was aghast. He bolted up in his chair and sputtered. "No, I *think* I heard you, Captain. You couldn't have said what I think you said. Particularly if you're talking about fighting in a declared war."

"Then let me say it slowly," Kurt Reed emphasized. "I said you forgot the colored man's will to fight — and I'm talking about in a declared war."

"What a bunch of crap," Whitney fumed. "And even if the bastards did have the will — which they *don't* — and never will have, they still couldn't do it. Fighting a war requires intelligence."

"And courage," Farrell said quietly, supporting Reed.

"*You,* coming from all-white Maine?" Whitney pushed. "*You,* an Inactive Reserve — an ROTC officer who's probably never seen one goddamned colored in your life until you got in the Army — you're telling me the colored man has *courage?* This unfit, lazy sonovabitchin' slacker whom I've grown up around in New York, and have commanded for two years — you're telling me *he* has courage?"

"He has a hell of a lot more of it than I have."

Capt. Harland Farrell, the commander of K Company, had dropped a bomb.

"Would you repeat that?" Lloyd Whitney asked. The words were measured, his look was strong.

"When it comes to war," Farrell said in a matter-of-fact quietness, "the colored man has more courage than I have."

Even Reed sat upright. He tossed a look at Whitney, then at Froelich. Finally he addressed the K Company commander. "What the hell are you saying, Farrell?"

Froelich joined him. "Do you know what you're saying?"

"Yes, I do."

"Buddy," Whitney said challengingly, "I think you'd better explain yourself."

"We were talking about courage," Farrell responded thoughtfully. "I don't have it, and I don't want it. And as far as this war is concerned, I'm not certain I should participate in it."

It was another bomb. It was larger than the first, and the fallout was all-encompassing.

The table fell into a deep silence. They were close to getting up and leaving. Everyone looked at each other — all, that is, except Farrell. His glass was tilted and he was staring at the bottom of it.

"Hey, c'mon, Fellas," Reed finally said, lightly, hoping to ease the tension. "Can't you see the guy's joking?"

Kurt Reed wasn't successful. Harland Farrell did nothing to help. The table lapsed into a deeper quiet. It was a most dangerous area, and everyone knew it. Now the K Company commander knew he shouldn't have come close to even *thinking* about making the remarks. They were about as treasonous as one could get. Farrell knew, too, that if he tried to clean up, or worse, if he continued on to express his true feelings — the deep, but still unsealed Quaker feelings he harbored about the war and the military — there would be hell to pay. Not that he wasn't already in trouble.

The waiter returned with the drinks Froelich had ordered. Farrell didn't see him. He was absent. His mind had shot back to a plan he wished he had executed when he was a civilian. It would have kept him out of the military altogether. He hadn't done it, and he was in the Army. Stuck. Soon though, very soon, he would go to his fall-back plan. But the residual effect, then as now, was going to be costly. It was going to be costly to him and his family. After all, resorting to a fall-back plan that called for being drummed out of the military in time of war was akin to being court-martialed as an outright traitor. Worse, his wife, the daughter of a retired colonel and the man for whom he had worked, and who was responsible for aiding him with those government contracts even in those early years, would be humiliated beyond repair. Again the captain felt nervous over the untimeliness and possible implication of his remarks.

No one gave it thought, but if one found himself defending Farrell's side — that is, defending the seeming hard part of the statement — the part involving his participation in war, it had been tempered by the use of the words *should* and *not certain.* As for the other part, all he said was that, in speaking of courage, the coloreds had more than he did — when it came to war.

Though doubtful it was on anyone's mind, what the K Company commander said had unassailable validity, applying the adage *He who has least, has most to gain; he who has nothing, has nothing to lose, and could therefore attack with recklessness and abandon* — an act that was often interpreted and heralded as courage. Of course the argument on the other side could have been used as well: *He who has most to protect, protects most fiercely.* That, too, was often construed as heroism.

But none of the aphorisms entered into the captain's thinking. Nor did the added statement *I'm not certain I should participate.* This notion, according to the military, by any yardstick — by any measure — was an out-and-out court-martial offense. Somehow or other Farrell overlooked that part and concentrated on the more ambiguous first part, dealing with the coloreds. Still, even if it did not carry the obvious weight, there was the irrefutable fact that this was the military, and the nation was at war. He was an officer in the Army of the United States, and he was doubting his courage. And even if, for some strange reason, only the first part of the statement were reported to Lt. Col. Briggs or any other superior, he would be in more trouble than he could ever have dreamed. And being shot was not entirely out of the question.

Interestingly, Farrell was not so much worried about Lloyd Whitney. Despite his bigoted and militaristic contentiousness, Whitney was too upfront to create a lasting problem. He said what he meant and what he would do on the spot. He wouldn't hold back. The relationship would, of course, be strained — not that they were that close in the first place. But the narrow-minded C.O. of I Company wouldn't go behind his back with the knife. Reed was okay. But the stubby little fat man was another story.

Farrell sat there regretting and worrying about Froelich. Even with an apology, he knew this pusillanimous little kiss-ass warrant officer would not dismiss what he had said. No, he would give it the right read, and he wouldn't let it remain at the table. At the proper time, he would undoubtedly add something to it. But just in case, Farrell bit the bullet, apologized, and was set to steer the conversation away from himself. Reed did it for him.

"So, Bill, you said Colonel Briggs taught at the Point?"

"Until he had a small run-in with the higher-ups," Froelich answered. His mind was still on Farrell. "The brass got even by sending him here. Not a bad move on the Army's part, though. He knows coloreds."

"He does?"

"Like a book," Froelich said. "This isn't the only colored outfit he's served with."

"And Froelich would know," Whitney said, his mind still dampened by Farrell's remarks. "Pushing papers up at Headquarters, he's in everybody's business."

"I've told you before, I don't 'push papers.' I'm an aide, *Herr* Whitney," Froelich said, childishly stressing the Germanic *Herr*.

Whitney, as if making an attempt to get over the earlier concern, leaned over to the dampened Farrell. "Since you're new to the Regular Army and Infantry, let me explain, Harland. Colonels have aides. But not our colonel. As you can see, he has a pudgy little noncombat Jew who thinks he's an aide."

"At least he isn't contaminated with German blood," Bill Froelich responded.

Whitney turned crimson. "You sonofabitch. You or your kind aren't good enough to have German blood in you."

If the departing battalion commander hadn't made a timely stop at the table, matters would have gotten out of hand. The assault would have come from Reed, the Protestant captain from L Company. It is doubtful Warrant Officer Froelich would have gone further. Offensively, he had gone as far as he would go with the man he believed hadn't drawn a better assignment because he was part German. In that regard, Froelich was right. There were many officers assigned to the regiment whom the Army considered questionable.

"Gentlemen," said Briggs, dissipating the heat. He motioned with his hands for the men to remain seated and not stand at attention. "I think my line officers will be interested in learning we will be receiving traveling orders in the morning."

"*The* orders, Colonel?"

"The orders, Captain Whitney. Traveling orders."

"This is amazing."

"I'd say it's more like a goddamn crime. But you boys can write your wives and sweethearts and tell 'em that we're off." The colonel looked to his newest company commander. "Farrell, the news should make that trigger-happy bunch of yours feel pretty damn good."

"Better than that, Colonel." Farrell said, hoping to diffuse even more of the heat he had created earlier. "And I can tell you one thing, Sir, they are ready. If not with equipment, certainly in spirit."

"Don't eliminate us," Whitney said, contradicting what he really felt, "we have a pretty anxious group, too."

"But not as much as L Company," said Reed.

"Yeah, but 'L' stands for lazy," Whitney said, trying for humor.

"And 'I' for ignorant," Reed countered.

There was more good-natured ribbing and laughter. "Coloreds in combat," Froelich mused. "We never thought that would happen, eh, Colonel?"

Briggs rested a foot on the rung of Froelich's chair as he spoke. "Like I said, I think it's a damned crime. It goes to show you, you take what used to be a pretty damned good modern Army and let the slackers and know-it-alls back there in Washington get their hands on it, and anything's liable to happen. Things are changing, Boys, and not always for the better. It sure as hell is not like the old days. It's not the Army I remember."

"It's not the one I remember, either," Froelich said gratuitously.

"Didn't know you'd been around that long, Bill," Whitney said.

"He hasn't," Col. Briggs said. "What's it been, Bill, three years?"

"Four, Sir," Froelich said. "Two with you."

"Well, you've been a good boy."

"Thank you, Sir," Froelich said.

Whitney gave a small, derisive chortle.

"Think the Germans know we're coming, Colonel?"

"Like anyone of reasonable intelligence, Reed, they can smell coons on the move."

There was a smattering of laughter, with Froelich taking the lead. Capt. Farrell, taken aback by the remark, said nothing. Briggs noticed that he hadn't laughed with the others. "It's just a figure of speech, Engineer, don't let it throw you."

"Some figure, Colonel," Farrell said.

It was a nervy rejoinder from his newest officer. After a long, heavy moment, the lieutenant colonel started to depart. He took a step or two toward the door, then came back. "How would you have phrased it, Farrell?"

"Phrased what, Colonel?"

"What I just said."

"You mean about the men arriving in Europe?"

"To fight."

"I wouldn't have said anything, Colonel. I would've kept my mouth shut and let their soldiering do the talking."

An uneasy silence spread over the table. The other officers weren't about to break it. Briggs stared at Farrell for a taut, evaluating moment, then said to Warrant Officer Froelich, "See to it that I am awakened at 0600." To the others he said, "Delay your company reveilles until 0800."

New Mexico promised Columbus another pure but searing day. It was 0745, and the temperature was rising steadily. First Sgt. McClellan, having been notified of the battalion's reassignment by Farrell late the previous evening, already had King Company on the field. They were all there, that is, except for Pete and Jody. They were supposed to be at the rear of the Supply Tent, still digging.

The formation was made up of 165 men. This time it included orderlies, KP's, and cooks, all standing at attention. They had been standing at attention for 15 minutes. Three minutes later, Capt. Farrell came out and joined them.

Unlike King Co., Companies I and L felt no need to be early and, in fact, were happy with the late reveille. They were in the process of falling in at 0755. Back at the entrance to the battalion grounds, and over the fading sounds of bugles, four motorcycles generated trails of dust as the riders aimed them into the individual company areas.

When the rider skidded into the King Co. area, he stopped, removed his goggles, dug into the saddlebag, dismounted, and started to go into the Orderly Room.

"Over here!" called the expectant captain.

The driver remounted and quickly zoomed to the formation. He saluted, handed the captain the envelope, and sped off.

Capt. Farrell gave the envelope's contents a quick read and said, "At ease!"

The company was more than willing to assume the more relaxed position. Anything was better than standing at "attention."

The captain looked again at the paper that had been contained in the envelope and then at his First. He cleared his voice, took a step forward, and announced, "Since this war began some months ago, I know you have been hearing about the exploits of some of your contemporaries, and I know just how anxious you've been to join them on the field of battle. I know, too, just how diligently you've applied yourselves in training since I've been here, and you've done it under the most difficult of circumstances. It is not easy to train for war if you have little or nothing to train with. It is not easy to train for war if you are not certain you are going to war, particularly because of who and what you are. But you have managed to overcome, to which I can only say that I am proud. I am also proud to announce that your patience in these regards has not gone unrecognized. Having talked with Colonel Briggs last night, I would like to share the communiqué just received by him this morning and forwarded to us. It reads, under today's date:

'TO LIEUTENANT COLONEL HEINRICH KLAUS BRIGGS, COMMANDING OFFICER, THIRD BATTALION, 24th U.S. INFANTRY (COLORED). SUBJECT: TDY PRESENT ASSIGNMENT AT THIS STATION TERMINATED. COMPANY COMMANDERS OF THE THIRD BATTALION WILL, EFFECTIVE IMMEDIATELY, PREPARE THEIR UNITS FOR MOVEMENT.'

SIGNED, COLONEL RUSSELL J. SARNO,
COMMANDING, 24ᵗʰ U.S. INFANTRY (COLORED).'

The captain paused dramatically and continued. "Gentlemen," he said, scanning the rows of joyful faces, "with the American Expeditionary Forces under command of General Pershing in need over there, I don't think I have to tell you, you're —"

The captain's last words were never heard. The troops fired off a roar that sounded as if it had been powered by Zeus. Hats tossed in the air soared to a height that almost blocked out the sun. The troops whooped, yelled, hollered, sang, and, as if music swirled the area, they grabbed each other and danced. Outbursts and commotion rose from the other company areas as well, but they couldn't override or even match King Company's.

The rhyming trio of Roosevelt, Menyard, and Andrews draped arms around each other and came up with an instant rhyme to fit the occasion. Amid the hollering, they stumbled around, mugging and buddy-buddying it at the end of the 2ⁿᵈ Platoon's formation:

"Where? Where?? Where???
Over yonder, said the man;
we long gone.
An' if it wont for the Army —
we be's sittin' at home!"

Pete and Jody, fired up by the noise, left the disciplinary area. Because of Pete's inactivity, the digging had lasted all night. The two peeped from the other side of the Supply Tent, watched for a moment, and were overtaken by the jubilation. As Pete boldly led Jody towards the assembly, they were cheering along the way. When they reached the 1ˢᵗ Platoon, Pete spotted a reserved Sgt. McClellan standing in front, next to the captain. Abreast of them was Sgt. Dukes. Unlike Farrell and McClellan, the old soldier was practically dancing a jig. Pete caught his eye and sent him a nice "How-do-you-do" wave, then nudged Puerto Rico Hicks, the joyous young man standing next to him, and asked what was going on. Puerto Rico responded that they had just received the news they had been waiting on. The battalion was going overseas. Pete almost fainted. Visions of all sorts of leggy, gartered foreign women danced from the streets of Paris and directly into his head. Together they headed for his bed. "Overseas!" he sputtered to Jody. "Did'ja hear that, lil' mascot?! We goin' overseas!"

"Wow," said Jody, still bewildered.

Pete saw how confused his new friend was. "It's over that way. Past the Mississippi and about a mile past China."

With the celebration still going on, Dukes said to the First, "Well, Mac, looks like we finally gonna make it, huh?"

"Seems that way," McClellan said laconically. His intuition was working, and he was strangely unenthusiastic.

"After all we done went through," Sgt. Dukes said, his mind on the past.

On the surface, what Dukes had said seemed innocuous. However, it carried more weight than one would have thought. It certainly had greater implications than McClellan wanted to go into, particularly while the captain was standing there. Sgt. Dukes, not knowing what the first sergeant was thinking, started to go into it further. McClellan quickly halted him by ordering a dispersal of ranks. He then moved off, catching up with the captain who was strolling across the field, his head low and his hands clasped in back. He was on his way back to the Orderly Room.

The two walked in silence for a few steps. In the background they could still hear Dukes hollering. "An' git that packin' done. An' done in a hurry! Bag and baggage in front of the Orderly Room A.S.A.P! An' I want you men from the Second, Third, and Fourth Platoons to strike the first sergeant's, the Supply, and the Mess Hall tents. First Platoon, assist in packing, and then strike the Orderly Room! On the double! I want everybody workin'!!"

McClellan saw that the captain seemed pleased for the men.

Something told him the captain was not pleased for himself. The First finally broke the silence. "Captain, when you were addressing the men, I noticed you said '*you're* on your way,' instead of '*we* are on *our* way.'"

"Yes, I did, didn't I?"

"Any reason for that, Captain?"

"None that I'd care to go into."

• • •

In the First Platoon tent, some of the troops had dashed in and were busy striking cots, packing bags, and the like, while the trio was still rhyming and clowning at the opposite end. Pete stood on his cot and dropped his vision of things to come.

"Me an' General Pershin'. A team made in heaven. An' after we wins the war, when I come back home to Philadelphia wit' all'a them medals poppin' off my sweet li'l ol' chest, the girls is gonna be huggin' me, kissin' me an' everything. I can hear 'em now. 'Oh, Peet-tee, Sweet-tee, my hero. Come here, my lil' ever-lovin', sweet-tastin' Prince Charmin'. Let's let our love do the celebratin'.' Ha, ha. ha. But, in the meantime — in the in-between time, while I'm over there, all I'm gonna be doin' is Parla-Voo-Fran-Sayin'. Ha, ha, ha."

Jody was laughing with the rest of the men, but he didn't really know why. He tugged at Pete's sleeve. "What's that Parla-Voo mean, Pete?"

"That, my friend, is Jerusalem talk for 'welcome home, Pete, you been gone too long.'"

Further down the line, Puerto Rico called over to Chin, one of two Chinese that had been assigned to the company. "Hey, Hong Kong, after war, you go back home, huh?"

"I go Tokyo," John Chin said. "Start own war."

"Make sure you winnit, else you're going to be back with us."

"I don't mind," Chin said, laughing. "I almost colored."

John Chin spoke in jest, and part of what he said was unnervingly prophetic, but he was glad to be there. Since he wasn't born in this country and there were laws denying Chinese American citizenship, he felt that being in service would help turn the tide.

John Hong Kong Chin, Carlos Rodriquez, Pepe de Anda, Dow Lee, Toho Fujiyama, and others of non-European ancestry represented an American dilemma. They were not black, but they weren't white. Except for young soldiers like Chin, most of them, while not claiming to be white, thought the idea of assigning them to black units offended sensibilities and insulted their race. And while, they said, they had nothing against coloreds, per se, it simply was not right for the Army to treat them as coloreds and assign them to colored units. Concern over the matter was muted, and despite a number of protests, desertions, AWOL's, and outright failure to consider the military as a career, for the most part the Army's position remained largely unchanged. The men were not white, so they would not be assigned to white units. The Puerto Ricans presented no problem. With the United States claiming Puerto Rico as a territory and eventually conscripting thousands of its young men into the Army in the process, both the volunteers and draftees were automatically listed as citizens and *coloreds*.

The Army's failure to readily change classification devastated Toho Fujiyama. Suicide was never far from his mind. Before leaving his homeland, he had never heard of — nor seen — a Negro. There had been none on the boat, the docks, or the train — on either side of the Pacific. But once here, and once he became aware of the blacks' standing in their own country, he immediately fell in line and learned to detest them and everything they stood for.

A gifted young man tapped for homeland leadership, Fujiyama was from Gifu, a small farm-belt city in southern Japan. Along with others, he was sent to this country specifically to learn the military. For Fujiyama, disappointment was swift. He and his back-home backers were outraged that the U.S. Army would assign him to a unit as base as the *kokujins*. They were beneath even the contemptible Koreans, people whom they still did not like, and a people they had invaded and subjugated more than 325 years ago.

To be with the coloreds, in the Japanese view, was *kokujoku* — a loss of face. It was perfidious and underhanded, and came close to violating international law. The reaction was nothing more than an overreaction on the part of the class-conscious Asians, and contrary to what they thought, the assignment was not a violation of international law, because no international law ever dealt with the subject. Even if there had been, few Americans would have been concerned about what some nonwhite people on a far-away archipelago thought. Except for their interest in China, they were too insignificant to matter. On the world stage they would never matter.

The Japanese militarist thought differently.

It had been almost 50 years since the feudal period when the shoguns and local warriors ruled the land of the Rising Sun. In 1868, the emperor had been restored to his rightful place, and the country's sealed doors opened to western trade and industrial technology. A peek out of that door led to the effulgent sunshine of expansionist policies. To conquer, Japan would need a powerful military with bright, well-rounded young men.

With an eye to the future in the Imperial Army of Japan, young men like Fujiyama were expected to learn everything they could about the *Beikoku*: its history, its people — and in the unlikely event of war somewhere down the road, its military.

King Company and the rest of the Third Battalion had hardly gotten the first tent down before a cyclist sped into the company area with another envelope, this one addressed to the commanding officer of Company K. Simms took the envelope and immediately delivered it to Capt. Farrell. When the captain opened the envelope, he stood motionless. He was stunned. Getting over it, he uttered a profanity and quickly told Simms to have Boland stand by with the motorcycle. Simms did as ordered.

When Boland arrived with the cycle, the captain grabbed his attaché case, headed for McClellan's tent, then changed his mind and left with Boland. Twenty minutes later he was at Battalion Headquarters, moving swiftly and grimacing as he headed into Battalion Cmdr. Briggs's office.

When the captain entered, the lieutenant colonel, not pleased by the torn look or the gruff entrance, finger-snapped the men who had been striking and packing from the office out into the hallway.

"I didn't notice your salute, Captain. But I'm glad you're here.

I was just about to send someone to your company to get you," the colonel said. He looked down as if to review a memo that had been placed on his desk before he arrived. "There is an extremely pressing matter I have to discuss with you."

"I hope it is about rescinding these orders, Sir."

"I don't rescind Sarno's orders, Captain," Briggs said. "Furthermore, this is about a matter I consider far more serious. I want to hear from you, what are your feelings about not going overseas?"

The question didn't catch the captain off guard, but it forced him to lie. "I have no feelings, Sir."

"So, then, you would have no objections to going overseas — to fight?"

Farrell wouldn't comment. He was on dangerous grounds. He knew Froelich had written the report that was on the desk.

"By your silence I take it you would have an objection?"

Still no comment from the captain.

"This is a serious matter, Captain."

"I fully realize that, Sir," Farrell said at last.

"And your answer?"

"Sir, we're going to Houston, and the troops —"

"Forget the goddamned troops! I'm talking about you, Captain!" snapped Briggs. "Will you — or will you *not* — go overseas to fight?"

The captain stood there wondering what he would have said had the orders been for overseas and not Houston. Finally he surrendered. "I go where I'm assigned, Colonel."

Briggs didn't believe him for a second. He was right in not believing him. Yet, the lieutenant colonel wasn't nearly as harsh and as indicting as he could have been. Momentarily letting him off the hook, the battalion commander looked at the orders the captain had dug out of his briefcase and said, "Knowing your company and your first sergeant, I gather you're here to argue on their behalf?"

"Yes, I am, Sir," Farrell said, relieved. "And it's in conjunction with last evening's conversation about going overseas."

"Before you go any further, let me clarify. Yesterday evening I did not say this battalion was going overseas."

"Yes you did, Colonel."

"Don't contradict me, Captain. Now, what I said was, the battalion will be receiving *traveling* orders. One of the papers you're holding in your hand there just happens to be *traveling* orders."

"For Houston, Texas."

"To get to Houston, Texas, requires traveling."

"I know that, Sir. But we were led to believe the traveling would be to Europe."

"Farrell, if you've jumped the gun and told your troops something you shouldn't have, that's something you're going to have to deal with. To repeat — no matter what your understanding was, I did not give a destination last evening. The tenor of my conversation dealt with the fact that we're moving out. And that's *exactly* what we're doing. Moving out. That other piece of paper you're holding states, better yet, I'll quote it verbatim. 'Subject: TDY. Tour of Duty: Present assignment at this station terminated. Company commanders of the Third Battalion will, effective immediately, prepare their units for movement.' That is a *direct* quote, Captain. And the direct quote does not say one word about going overseas."

"Alright then, Sir — and not to be argumentative — but last night you *implied* the battalion was going overseas. If you remember, you even made a crack about the Germans smelling coons on the move."

"That, I was wrong in saying."

"I'm glad to hear you say that, Sir, because I thought the remark was — "

The colonel interrupted. "I was wrong because Germans aren't the only ones who can smell the sonsabitches on the move."

Farrell was stung into silence. The colonel noticed the look that went with the silence. "Do you have a problem with that, Captain?"

"None that I'd care to go into at this time, Sir."

"Then all of your problems are allayed?"

"No, Colonel," Farrell replied, holding his ground. "I have a problem when promises are violated."

"I've told you before, and I will tell you again: You were not promised a destination."

"All right, then, Sir, you implied we were going overseas."

"Implied? What the hell does that mean? The Army operates on orders. This is not the ROTC."

"I know it's not, Colonel. But it seems to me that after all of this training and preparation, the order to go to Houston doesn't make very much sense. If the division commander knew —"

"Hold it, right there, Engineer. You don't even know if we are attached to a division. But even if you did know, I'd still say you're going too far. I don't mind you blowing off a little stream, but you don't *think* for the Army. You don't *think* for the higher-ups, and I wouldn't let my two months in the *real* Army or my wide-eyed idealism get me into trouble if I were you. Or I should say, get me into *more* trouble."

"I'm sorry, Sir. But I was merely thinking that maybe the decision could be appealed at a higher level."

"How imbecilic can you get?"

"Begging the colonel's pardon, but it's not imbecilic to question logic."

"Who in the hell are you to be questioning the Army's logic?" Briggs flared. "Now, let me tell you this, young man: the Army is not stupid. The War Department is not stupid. Division is not stupid. *I* am not stupid. Headquarters is absolutely right in making the decision not to send these people to the front. I can attest to that. I know the colored man; I know his history. I've commanded them — *twice*. And I'd a damned sight rather be in Houston with them than on the front lines. Now if the French, stupid enough to listen to the British, want coloreds over there to fight, let 'em keep on wanting. They're Europeans. They don't know any better. We do. The United States has a tradition to uphold — and it doesn't include the coloreds. Our flag — Old Glory — should never be wrongly represented or degraded. Personally, I'd rather die a thousand times than to see that happen. I say to you again, the coloreds simply are not good enough to —"

"Again, begging the colonel's pardon —"

"Don't interrupt me! Your trouble is, Captain, you've lived a life of isolation. You haven't been with — or around — coloreds long enough to know which end of their asses are up. You don't know a damned thing about them. You haven't commanded them, you haven't studied them, and you don't know them or their history — if they *have* a history. But until you learn something about them, it's best you keep your mouth shut. Now, I'm reminding you, this country is at war — fighting a first-class enemy. The General Staff made a decision; Colonel Sarno has made a decision. And I wholeheartedly agree with them. The colored man is palpably unfit to fight.

"Understand this: Our country has had an Army since June 14, 1775, created when the Continental Congress authorized a Continental Army, the fruit of whose victories, incidentally, you now enjoy. Nowhere — and I repeat, *nowhere* — does that mandate or those victories say anything about coloreds. Now, the United States' position, the Army's position — and *my* position — are no less than that of the Father of this Country — who happened to have been the leader of that first Army. I say that because Washington himself didn't want coloreds in combat and took them — belatedly — only after they started to fight for the goddamn British. Lincoln didn't want them in the Civil War, and took them — again belatedly — only because he was forced to. Jefferson, while he might have wished the coloreds were something else and was base enough to've hankered after one of their unwashed women, described them as improvident and weak in facility. Fifty years ago even the Irish in New York — when they should have been worried about the potato famine in their homeland — rioted, killing and wounding hundreds in the process — because they didn't like them. And let's not even mention Webster's dictionary. It describes black as evil, sinister, ugly, objectionable, and unclean. And I *don't* disagree.

"Now, as to Army, there have been armies on this earth for nearly as long as there have been people. In prehistoric times, when men fought against each other in groups with spears and stone axes, they organized and fought in formation. It was an army. Four thousand years ago, when men started using horses and crossbows to fend and attack, *that* was an army. In Biblical times, with Pharaoh and that bunch, there was an army. Assyria and Persia had an army. Today, with our modern mechanization and with our organizational skills and abilities on the field of battle, *we* are called Army. Infantry, Cavalry, and Artillery. *That* is an army. We have been called Army for a long time, and I'll be damned if we — or anyone else you've ever heard of in all of human history — ever suffered a defeat because a colored wasn't in it. And I say that, knowing that this Army has been involved in no less than a thousand engagements since its creation. I suggest you read your history and get your priorities straight, Engineer."

"I don't know anything about that, Sir. But I do know something about — "

Briggs cut him off again. "If you don't know anything about it, then I suggest you keep your mouth shut and start learning. And start learning in a hurry. The United States Army is not composed of fools." The colonel picked up the memo. "Nor is it composed of officers who come into my office saying one thing — and could be shot for sitting in an Officers' Club making treasonable statements."

It was an odd and offhand way to bring up the subject, but the colonel had a definite threat in his voice. Despite the threat, his look suggested that the subject didn't have to go any further.

Farrell didn't know what to say. Briggs kept his eyes on him, and then, as if allowing the captain a way out, but still in a tone that sounded very much like a warning, asked, "Anything else,

Captain?"

"What will we be doing in Houston, Colonel?"

"We're going to Camp Logan. 'Camp Logan.' Does the name mean anything to you?"

"No, Sir."

"Don't you know anything about the Army at all? If you do, it certainly doesn't sound like it. Logan is a white post. Now, let me ask you, at an illiteracy rate exceeding seventy-some percent, what would you expect the coloreds to be doing?"

"I don't know, Colonel. Training draftees, recruits?"

"You're reinforcing imbecility, Captain."

"We won't be training draftees?"

"Hell and all its dominions will freeze over before a colored trains a white — *in anything.*"

"Why can't they train them, Sir?"

"Goddamn, Man! Has common sense completely abandoned you?"

"Then, Sir," Farrell said, depleted, "what will we be doing in Houston?"

"Logan is a construction post. These people will be servicing and guarding the construction work going on there. And I'm expecting them to do a damned good job at both."

"Colonel, I don't want to be argumentative, Sir — "

"And you'd better not be — considering," Lt. Col. Briggs said, referring to the memo.

Farrell understood the implication and began easily. "Low IQ's or not, Sir, the men are still soldiers. And if I can go back just a bit, Colonel — "

"If you do, you'd better do so carefully."

"I may not know their history, or as much as you do, Sir, but I do know the Negro soldier fought under Roosevelt when he was in the service, and he commended them."

"So what?! And who in hell gives a damn about what that overbloated bag of wind did? If Roosevelt had cared all that much for the coloreds, they wouldn't be here in New Mexico guarding the border against a bunch of goddamned Mexican bandits."

"Sir," Farrell said, trying to get a point across without sounding combative, "the battalion *fought* under him."

"Twenty years ago! And did you ever stop to think of *who* they were fighting under him?"

"The enemy of the United States."

"A bunch of goddamed outlaws!"

"But still the enemy, Colonel."

"Cubans, Farrell, Cubans! The goddamned Daughters of the American Revolution could've defeated 'em! Now get the hell out of here and get your company ready for movement before you wind up on charges."

Realizing the danger, Farrell turned to leave. He had to be wondering why the battalion commander had allowed him to go as far as he had.

"Captain," Briggs said, further surprising him by moving from behind the desk and escorting him to the door. "Let's not forget what I'm holding over your head. And let's not forget the seriousness of it. Now, I'm not the sort of man to hold things against my officers indefinitely. Thirty days after we are in Houston, I intend to destroy this memo. I use the word *intend* because my actions will depend on your actions — whether you become the officer I hope and trust you can be. You've made an interesting start by arguing for your boys — wrong as hell, but interesting. It shows me that you are stronger than I initially believed, and that you do have character. However, my great concern now has to do with what you would have done had the orders been for overseas."

What the colonel was asking, in other words, was, *would you have gone overseas?* Farrell knew it and stood at the door, his mind lost in thought. He was lost in more ways than one, but he wouldn't let it show.

"I think I know the answer," the battalion commander said. "And if you are wondering why I'm being tolerant of you, it's not because of your views or because you're new here. It's because I don't envy what you are going through."

"What am I going through, Sir?"

"I've been reviewing your 201 file. I find it interesting. I empathize with you."

"Empathy? Stemming from what, Sir?"

"You were a Quaker."

It hung for a moment. The captain couldn't respond. The battalion commander added, "Fifty years ago I was a practicing member of the Latter-day Saints of Christ. *Mormon* to you. And I was a damned good one. And then I grew up. I hope you do the same. Good-day, Captain."

Speechless, the captain saluted and walked away, wondering.

Briggs waited until the slowly departing captain was partway down the hall and called after him. "Farrell," he said, stopping him, "you were not entirely wrong. When Teddy Roosevelt was a colonel in the Army of the United States, he commanded the 9th and 10th Colored Cavalry units, along with his Rough Riders. The coloreds like to think that they saved the day at San Juan Hill because they charged the Spanish stronghold singing. I won't argue with that. Maybe they were colorful, and Roosevelt did commend them — though personally, I think he was — as usual — stretching it. But ten years ago, as President of these United States, he also threw a battalion of the sons-a-bitches out of the service for rioting and disgracing the uniform. That was in Texas. I say again, read your history, Engineer."

• • •

Twenty-seven minutes after the K Company commander had had the talk with the battalion commander, the members of his company were on the field. Although they were standing at attention under a flaming sun, the good news still weaved in and around the ranks, and out front, where the Orderly Room had stood, where the crates, steamer trunks, bags, and company gear were stacked, the captain stood alone. The trucks hadn't arrived yet, and the only one who showed concern was First Sgt. McClellan who also had to be wondering why the captain, returning from Battalion Headquarters, had ordered him to form the company when there was still so much work to be done.

Now he was wondering why the company commander had to go to Headquarters in the first place.

On the way to the formation, the first sergeant noticed that the C.O. walked slower than normal and wore a deep, thoughtful look on his face.

When the captain was in position, the first sergeant saluted him and received the order to *"parade rest"* the men. The First gave the order, turned to his commander, and said, "Captain, you may now address the troops." It was said cryptically.

"Address the troops?" the captain thought as the First stepped aside. *"How would he know that? I could have ordered the men into assembly simply to receive moving orders."*

The company commander dismissed the thought, glumly took two steps forward, and momentarily lowered his head as if reluctant to say what was on his mind. Raising it, he was brief. "Gentlemen, I was in error. Our orders are for Houston, Texas."

After a stunned silence it hit, starting from the formation's front. The stoic McClellan, never one to fully display emotion, put his hands on his hips, muttered something, and grimaced.

Sgt. Dukes, equally defeated, slammed his omnipresent clipboard to the ground, and cursed God.

Poole cursed God and the Army.

In the ranks, the men were crushed. They looked like whipped dogs on a short leash. Every head was heavy. Not a man in formation, including the apron-wearing cooks led by Mess Sgt. Willie Powell at the end, accepted the news without hurt comment. The bursts overrode the rhyming trio, and only Pete, shouting in Jody's ear, was heard to say, "Awww, shucks! There goes all'a my Parla-

Voo-Fran-Sayin'!"

His blessedly uninformed partner asked, "Can't you do it in Texas, Pete?"

McClellan had had enough. "At ease in ranks! You're soldiers, and, as such, you will do *what* you are told, *when* you are told! And you will do it *without* question or comment!"

The company fell quiet under the attack, but the faces remained long and dreary.

Farrell indicated he had nothing else to say. McClellan called the company to attention, did an *about face*, and saluted the departing captain. He watched as the C.O. sauntered back to where the Orderly Room had stood. What he would do when he got there, thought McClellan, remained to be seen. The tent was down, some of the bags were packed, and a number of crates were ready. But the trucks weren't there yet, and there was no place to go. Had the captain remained close to the formation, he would have learned more about his First.

"Parade rest!" the bespectacled sergeant ordered. The men snapped into the more relaxed yet more formal position than *at ease*. His voice was taut. "Bunker Hill, Lexington, Concord, we were there. The colored soldier was there. Having fought with — and for — the Father of this country, the Union Army, and nameless uprisings; after dying with Custer, chasing Billy the Kid, and capturing Geronimo, it is apparent the United States colored soldier is not fit to represent the United States overseas in battle. And so we must go to Texas. In so doing, I want each and every one of you to remember — in what has been called our black Dreyfus Affair — which in itself is ludicrous because the dishonored Frenchman never had to go through what the battalion went through, but in 1906, almost eleven short years ago, by order of President Roosevelt, the War Department — without benefit of trial – threw a whole battalion of our boys out of the Army because of trouble in a place called Brownsville, Texas. It happened in August. August thirteenth, to be exact. Up to that date, the coloreds had served with distinction and loyalty, but it did no good because they were not believed. There was talk of throwing every single black face in uniform out, and never letting us serve in the military again. It was the first — and *only* — time in the entire history of the Army that something like that had been done. But first time or not, it still happened, and those Brownsville memories are not dead. Neither they, nor the cause, will die. I want you to remember that the trouble started less than two weeks after the arrival of the colored troops. Plant it firmly in your minds — and any other place you are not currently using, to include your nightly fingered instruments — that the trouble started because a peg-legged white woman *said* that she had been attacked. Needless to say it was a bald-faced lie. No one — and I repeat, *no one* — touched that woman. But the whites would not listen — and then it was on. It hit the proverbial fan. There was more trouble than anyone expected; the shootings and killings were *not* started by the colored soldier. But the coloreds, soldiers and civilians, paid the price. Now understand this: there are some good and decent people in the state of Texas — and I am convinced the city of Houston has more that its fair share. But don't expect anybody there to love you simply because the country is at war and you are in uniform. You are not the conquering heroes; you will not go there thinking you are. The camp there is Camp Logan — white, and one of the Army's oldest. I don't know what our assignment will be. I have not conferred with the captain, but, knowing Army and what it thinks of us, I can imagine our duties will be limited to nothing higher than guarding the post. It is beneath what you've been trained for, and far less than we had hoped for. But we are still soldiers, and we will still be contributing. The old soldiers used to say, '*Ours is not to reason why; ours is but to do or die.*' King Company will arrive in Houston *doing*. We will detrain soldiering. We will march to — and through — Camp Logan *soldiering*. We will soldier as we have never soldiered before. Still, as coloreds, we will arouse fear and suspicion. At no time during our stay will Houston be a bed of roses, so prepare. That does not mean I want any head-scratching, Uncle Tomming, or yielding to Jim Crow; nor does it mean I want you to be any less than you are. It does mean that the uniform is not to be desecrated, and I will brook no trouble. In the interest of harmony, albeit patently artificial — and not all that one-sided as far as lust is concerned — you will maintain a distance away from the white woman. You *will* — at all times — respect the black woman. Upon encountering the white man, you will not tip your hat or bow your head, nor will you step off the walkway or roadway in any act of subservience. You will, at all times, look the white man directly in the eye, thus telling him you are singularly proud of the independent validity of your manhood, hence your black-ness. In the face of the white man, no matter what you are doing, both your conduct and your posture will always command respect. If his ignorance prevails, and your race is demeaned, I want you to continue on your merry way, for it is a well-known fact that if you stop to throw rocks at every dog that barks, you will never reach your destination."

The First studied them for a moment. "Do you read me King Company?"

"Yes, Sergeant."

"I can't hear you!"

"Yes, Sergeant!"

"What'd you say?!"

"YES, SERGEANT!"

"*LEMME HEAR IT!*"

"*YES, SERGEANT!!*"

• • •

After the packing chores had been completed, the troops still had time on their hands. The trucks to take the equipment to the depot had not arrived. McClellan welcomed the delay. It allowed him time to rehearse the march from the city of Houston to the

Camp Logan post.

Capt. Farrell had purposely missed a part of the speech, but now he was back. He stood at the edge of the company area and watched most of the rehearsal. The troops were impressive. The *sound-off* was snappy and the singing great. McClellan had come up with some new formations for which Poole mysteriously managed to produce some new instruments.

In the end, though, the captain considered the whole exercise a waste and strolled off wondering if he should have stopped his First.

When Farrell returned two hours later, the company, still with backpacks and haversacks on under the blazing sun, was still practicing. On top of that, Poole came to him for permission to borrow more drums from Companies I and L. They would augment the ones he had already stolen.

• • •

He had never been good at marching. He had given King Company more than he thought he should give. His hurt was now insurmountable. There was something all too defeating in going to Texas where the white troops were stationed and in his being assigned to a company of blacks. The fact that they were notoriously proud meant nothing, and it had the young Japanese telling himself he couldn't take it anymore.

While the troops were rehearsing their entrance to Houston and the Logan post, Toho Fujiyama fell to the ground. He had been marching in the ranks of the Third Platoon, and Sgt. Dukes, bringing up the rear, saw him fall and ran to his side. The young soldier didn't look ill, but he convinced the field sergeant that he was, and said that if he could get some rest and be alone for a little while, he'd be okay. The trouble was that the tents were down and no trees grew on the blistering company grounds. A caring Sgt. Dukes came up with the idea of having two of the men, Boland and John Hong Kong Chin, assist the soldier to the nearest spot of shade.

They complied, taking the young man to the other side of the crates and baggage where the Orderly Room had stood. When that was done, the two men returned to the field.

Roughly 40 minutes later, John Chin got permission to go back and check on the homesick soldier, who really hadn't cared for him, probably because he was Chinese. But at least he was Oriental. In the year Chin had been there, Fujiyama had spoken to him only once, and that was merely to tell the Chinaman that if he had been a Korean, he wouldn't have spoken to him at all.

Toho Fujiyama was not where John Chin and Boland had left him.

After a short search they found him.

The body was behind the stacked Supply Room equipment at the other end of the field. The head was tilted against a crate. The eyes were open. The figure was curled as if it had been kneeling, and blood had gushed from the nose and mouth. The abdomen was soaked.

Toho Fujiyama died from a bayonet plunged into his stomach. He had done it with such force that a clear two inches of steel was sticking out of his back.

The young man from Gifu, Japan had no shoes or shirt on. He had left no note.

Chapter 8

Unlike Capt. Farrell, who was so repulsed at seeing the thoroughness of the suicide he couldn't stop throwing up and again left the area under the guise of notifying Headquarters, the first sergeant viewed Fujiyama's body without much of an outward reaction. Inside, he had mixed feelings. He knew that the young man had despised being with the blacks. Intuition and attitude alone had told him that. Not that the young Japanese had been surly or insubordinate or anything of the sort; rather he walked around in a lone and dismal fog, dejected and depressed.

For a foreigner, Fujiyama spoke the language well, but no one would have known. He was remote, uncommunicative, and close-mouthed to a fault. Even when he was marching and he was required to shout out the hard, responding cadence during *sound-off*, he did so only when the First was looking at him directly. Even then it was in a manner that indicated he'd fall back into a darkened silence as soon as the First's eyes were diverted.

As he stood by the body, longer than he thought he should have, and almost as if he were guarding it, McClellan knew that the Japanese considered hara-kiri an honorable way out. He knew, too, that Fujiyama's act was done purely out of indignation. What bothered the First now was that he hadn't realized the depth of the young man's resentment. More troubling: if he had known, what would he have done?

It was an interesting dilemma. Here was a young man who, for all intents and purposes, felt that in a country that was wasteful, without civility, and lacking in purpose, it was truly dishonorable to be with their worst. But McClellan wondered was the feeling of dishonor truly his fault? The young man was a zealot who came from a sternly isolated and nationalistic culture that held practically everyone else's in contempt. But for whatever reason, he didn't realize that his nationalism and culture were no more appreciated by the people whom he abhorred. It was ignorance, not so pure and simple, but it was ignorance all the same. In all honesty, questioned the First, could ignorance, then, have been the young man's fault?

McClellan was still pondering the issue as he sent a detail to Regimental Headquarters with the body.

When the body was returned for disposal, McClellan was still pondering.

• • •

They were hours late, but the trucks finally came, and the company, along with the rest of the battalion, followed the equipment to the station. When they arrived, there was another wait. Eventually the train arrived, the men boarded, and by 1600 hours on that excessively hot June 4th, the members of the Third Battalion of the 24th United States Infantry Regiment (Colored) were on their way to Houston, Texas.

The sections containing Companies I and L preceded King Company, and as the train pulled out, some of the faces of disappointment had already given way to animated conversations and mild horseplay. Ten minutes into the journey, the backpacks and haversacks were off and the card games started. Soon the cheerful sounds of harmonicas, comb-blowing, spoon-rattling, Jew's harps, and other pocket-size instruments swept along the aisle and, more often than not, clashed with two banjos, three cowbells, several kazoos, and a lone washboard. In another car, further back, the men broke out in song. Throughout the train, though, most of the men sat gazing out at the passing scenery. Some contented themselves by catching naps, two of the men played jacks. Others brought out the dice and clogged the narrow aisles with their favorite game of chance.

In King Company's section, Boland sat up front with Simms. Junius Rochester later swore they were holding hands and making eyes at each other. Though it's doubtful they would have been that open with each other, particularly with the first sergeant and other NCO's around, there could have been partial truth to the statement. A genuine affection did exist between the two young men.

Pfc. Adrian Simms, the guidon bearer and part-time company clerk, was a strikingly tall, light-skinned, passive fellow with features and tendencies that were not strictly masculine. At night, when he was off duty, there was a decided lilt to his hips. That was only at night. And only when he was off duty. When he was marching with the guidon, leading the company, Simms was like a gazelle gliding through the wilderness, agile and flowing, ramrod straight; elegant and polished. No one marched better; no one was more impressive. Sgt. McClellan said there was not a soldier in the regiment who could outsoldier his guidon bearer, nor could one cut a more striking figure when he marched.

He was right.

Pervis Boland, on the other hand, was a tragedy. Beefy, and sluggish as a snail, when he marched he looked like a tub of asphalt on the way to meet a cement mixer. He was one big lump.

John Hong Kong Chin said he didn't know which was worse, marching in front or marching in back of the bowlegged, mechanically-inclined young man. In front, he kept a constant bulge in his pants; in back, he waddled. Puerto Rico Hicks said it was like marching with a runaway tank; they could never be sure of his direction.

But Simms genuinely liked the company runner. And the company runner, part-time cyclist and mechanic genuinely liked the guidon bearer. They liked the way each other moved. Although Boland had a young miss back home and he often talked of marriage, Adrian Simms caught his eye. Their union was inevitable. Columbus, New Mexico offered nothing; the military post, even less. The nights were lonely, the two were nice to each other, and whenever they could, the guidon bearer with the effeminate lilt and the mechanic with the bulge in his pants would steal away. The night was theirs.

Yancy, seated about midway in K Company's third car and behind the rhyming trio of Roosevelt, Menyard, and Andrews turned from the window and sighed. "I sure ain't into goin' to no Texas."

He had hardly gotten the words out of his mouth before the fun-loving trio swung their heads around and sprang into action:

"— *Texas?* — *Texas?*? — *Texas*???*
Be thankful that'cha goin, boy —
Where's yo' brain?
If it wont for the Army —
Y'couldn't ride no train!"

Down the line, Pete Curry was holding court. Facing him was Jody's happy face. Centered in a gathering of regulars, his buddy was on a roll, his short arms and smoothly working fingers in constant motion. Boasting about what he would do when he eventually got overseas, he started off in France but the world was in trouble. Full of peppy animation, Pete crucified names and assassinated geography. Cities in the Orient found themselves bypass-ing normal borders and being plopped onto places no map on the planet would understand. Russia was in the heart of Turkey. The Lusitania was not a ship but a place. King Constantine of Greece was a cook. The European command post where he, with insignifi-cant help from Generals Belgium, Bulgaria, and Budapest, had slipped behind enemy lines, landed in Des Moines, Iowa, and com-manded the troops from the muddy trenches of Arizona. The Rhine was in Italy; the Danube, in Switzerland. Poland was in Luxem-bourg, and Denmark was the back door to Austria. From Sweden and Munich, the capitals of Great Britain, the livewire would fight his last campaign. Home would come the hero.

"An'," Pete said, "when they stops the music, an' I comes down the gangplank an' steps onto that red carpet and bow to my adorin' public, it's gonna be a time to make your mouth water." He sighed, his pinkie extended. "An' when my public releases they holds on me, the first thing I'm gonna do is go get me some lye and potatoes, so I can make me some *konk*. Then I'm gonna konk my hair. S'gonna be real nice n' purdy. Slick. An' I'm gonna put a part in it. Girls like that. Makes runnin' their fingers through the curly locks easier. Then I'm gonna get togged down. Slick. Dressed to kill. An' with all'a the money the Gov'ment's gonna give me, I'm gonna go out an' get me one'a them real luscious Texas redheads. Tall. Legs a lil' bowed. Then you wanna know what I'm gonna go an' do?"

"Yeah," said Puerto Rico. "Go out an' get lynched."

"The rope ain't been made that's good enough for this neck," said the runt of a soldier. "No. If me an' my honey falls truly in love, I'm gonna bring her back to camp an' ask the colonel to marry us."

•••

Sgts. Odoms and Williams, the NCO's from Companies I and L, had joined Sgt. Dukes and Cpl. Poole near the rear of the car, where they discussed the Texas assignment in detail. Led by both Odoms and Williams, they concluded that nothing could be done about it, so the best thing to do was to make the most of it. They then tried to cut the conversation off by suggesting that the assignment was temporary. Sgt. Dukes disagreed.

Poole, for a brief moment, became untypically positive. Maybe it was just to get a rise out of old Sgt. Dukes.

"Course, there is one good thing about all'a this," said the Supply corporal, "we ain't gotta worry 'bout no more supplies. Whatever them white boys got, we gonna get — to include some good food. An' more guns." He didn't get the expected reaction from Sgt. Dukes, so he looked across the aisle to the company mess sergeant and said, "We gonna steal everything they got, ain't we, Mess Sergeant Willie Powell?"

The dried-up cook with the stained teeth didn't want to get involved. Rolling a cigarette, he moaned, "I ain't gon' be botherin' them white folks."

"The first sergeant said he want no trouble, Poole," Dukes finally said.

"Stealin' from white folks ain't no trouble," Poole said. "It's an art. An' think'a all them years they been stealin' from us."

"Stealin' what from us?" Sgt. Williams of L Company asked.

"Everythin'."

"Name me one thing we got that the white man want?"

Poole said without hesitation, "Our manhood, for starters."

Sgt. Williams knotted his face. "Sheeeet."

Sgt. Dukes, singed again by Poole, rose and kneed his way to the aisle. "Lemme get away from this fool," he grumbled. Dukes was on his way to the rear of the car to join McClellan.

Poole hollered after him. "If you don't think we ain't got nothin', Sergeant, go on up to the front of the train an' dance for the officers. Sooner or later, they'll steal that, too — an' make you feel guilty for havin' rhythm in the first place."

"You better hush your mouth. McClellan's sittin' back there," said Odoms. "He hear you talkin' to Dukes like that, he'll lynch you."

"Sho' will," agreed Williams. "That's the one person you better not let him hear you talk to like that."

"I ain't worried," Poole said. "Don't nobody scare me."

They rode in silence for a bit, then Sgt. Williams said to Odums, "Mac sho' cares 'bout that old man, don't he?"

"They been together a long time," Odums responded.

"How long's it been?"

"Too long," answered Poole. "He's too old for the Army, anyhow. I don't see why he's still hangin' 'round. He should be back down in Georgia, pickin' peas and shuckin' corn, 'stead of havin' his jaws tight 'bout not fightin' in no white man's war."

"S'ain't no white man's war," Sgt. Williams responded.

"Then whose war is it?" Poole asked cynically.

"Everybody's."

"Then how come 'everybody' ain't in it? How come we on a train, headin' for Houston?"

"Poole, you askin' for it."

"Sho' is," concluded Sgt. Odums of I Company. "You just itchin' for trouble."

First Sgt. McClellan was seated in the rear, staring idly out the window. He was past his thoughts of the young Japanese, and was thumbing through a book when Sgt. Dukes slid in next to him. Beside him was another book the First had apparently been leafing through. Sgt. Dukes picked it up and squinted at the picture. On the cover was a picture of an unimposing white man.

"This the book Sergeant Newton gave you before we parted company?" Sgt. Dukes asked almost in a whisper. Newton, under a different name, was someone they both had known some years ago.

The first sergeant nodded affirmatively.

"Boy, I miss that ol' trooper," Sgt. Dukes said, letting his words trail off. He hoped that the mere mention of the name would start a conversation that would take them back to the early years. He was thinking specifically about 1906, the year the first sergeant had alluded to in his speech before leaving Columbus. Dukes waited, but he didn't get the response. Keeping his voice low, he asked, "Where you think he is now?"

"I don't know," McClellan answered.

"Think he ever got back in?" Dukes whispered.

"He's found a way."

"Like us, huh?"

McClellan didn't respond. Not that he didn't have anything to say, he simply looked out of the window in quiet. Dukes felt like talking. He picked up the book and looked at the cover again. "Of all people... why would Newt give you a book about a white man?"

"Because he was a good white man."

"Mighty unusual," said Dukes. "Who is he?"

"Senator Joseph B. Foraker of Ohio."

"What'd he do?"

McClellan turned from the window. "He was the only man with courage enough to challenge the President when he dishonorably discharged the battalion."

Sgt. Dukes leaned over, almost whispering again. "He challenged the *President* of the United States about *us?*"

"Yes, he did."

"For what we did?"

"For the wrong the Army did."

"Good Gawd, A'mighty," Sgt. Dukes said, catching himself as though he had spoken too loud. That would have been difficult to do, considering the noise of the train. Besides they were alone in the back seat. Still Dukes insisted on being conspiratorial. "Tell me about it, Mac."

McClellan didn't have Dukes's concern and spoke in his regular tone. "There isn't much more to tell."

"Well, what'd he do? How'd he go about doin' it? I mean, you said he challenged Roosevelt. I mean, them ain't no small potatoes."

"He conducted a campaign for a fair hearing for the battalion. He wanted President Roosevelt to reopen the case, so that the truth could come out. The president wanted no part of it. The senator kept pounding, and he said to the president, 'They ask no favors because they are Negroes, but only for justice because they are men.'"

"M-y-y-y Gawd," said Dukes. He held the book closer to his ancient eyes so he could study the white man's face. "To think that a white man — a senator — said that about the Twenty-fifth. It almost restores your faith in mankind."

McClellan didn't comment.

"So, what happened? Was we — " The old sergeant stopped, looked around suspiciously, and whispered, "Was *they* ever cleared?"

"The dishonorable discharges stood. And they're still standing."

Dukes sent his mind back. Again he wanted McClellan's mind to go back with him, but he could tell that the First was not inclined to do much more talking on the subject. He would give it one more try. "I hate to bring this up, Mac, but do you think the same thing could happen again?" Sgt. Dukes was extremely hesitant. McClellan wasn't.

"We're still colored. We're still Army." With a chilling calm he added, "We're not going to Brownsville, but we're still going to Texas. The people are still white. Attitudes haven't changed. And they still have guns."

"And so do we."

The old cigar-chomping sergeant with more than 35 years of service under a hanging belly hated saying it. But he had to. He said it again. "And so do we."

McClellan didn't think he should have said it.

What the two men were talking about — and what McClellan had referred to in his speech back in Columbus and was now skirting — was the incident that had taken place in Brownsville, Texas in 1906. When the incident was officially researched five years later, it was listed as the Report of the Proceedings of the Court of Inquiry to the Shooting Affray at Brownsville, Texas. It contained 12 volumes, published by the U. S. Government Printing Office. Overlooking the many inaccuracies, the report told about how, on a hot August night, three companies of Negro soldiers of the 1ˢᵗ Battalion of the 25ᵗʰ Infantry were stationed at Fort Brown, the old Mexican War encampment on the edge of Brownsville. On August 13, at about midnight, two weeks after the arrival of the black battalion, fueled by a report that there had been an attempted rape of a disabled white woman the previous night, and supported by strong antiblack sentiments from a sizable Mexican-American population, a fusillade of shots rang out in the pitch black corridor that separated the fort and town. Knowing nothing of the alleged rape attack, and assuming they were under attack by a local mob because they had constantly spoken out about the ill treatment they had received in the short period of time they had been there, the blacks fired back. When the blacks had finished, a young white man lay dead, and a police official had been wounded. The next morning Companies B, C, and D were ordered into assembly on the parade ground at Fort Brown. They were told that if the guilty did not step forward, all would be discharged. No one moved. It was a "conspiracy of silence," said the Army. It was an act that resulted in an executive order dismissing the blacks from the military without honor and without a hearing. They were to be "forever debarred from re-enlisting in the Army or Navy." The order was carried out by Secretary of War William Howard Taft, who was later to become the President's hand-picked successor.

Foraker, the courageous Senator from Ohio, put his career on the line by demanding justice for the blacks and by demanding a more thorough investigation of the incident. The investigation was never done, and he paid the price at the polls. The senator's political career was over. Still continuing to fight from his home, he was offered any post he desired by the president if he would cease his troublesome ways.

The former senator would not compromise and died fighting for the cause.

Among the men who had been dishonorably discharged from the 1st Battalion of the 25th U.S. Army (Colored) almost 11 years ago were two men who were not involved in the uprising. They loved the Army. One was Abraham Dukes. The other was Obie McClellan.

Like Newton, they had different names then.

The Third Battalion officers were seated comfortably up front on the train, where the seats were spaced and padded. The cars were a lot less crowded, and the air was not heavy with the odor of sweat. Drinks in hand, almost as it had been back at the club on post, the officers were gathered around Lt. Col. Briggs. He was explaining to the younger officers how it had been in the old days. There was much he could talk about.

The son of Austrians, Lt. Col. Heinrich Briggs was born in Coeur d'Alene, Idaho, on October 28, 1862. After much difficulty, he entered the United States Military Academy at West Point, New York, by appointment in 1882. Graduating in 1886, he served in the Indian wars, the Philippine Insurrection, and the Punitive Expedition in Mexico. He rose through the ranks with relative ease. After assignments at the Infantry and Cavalry School and Ft. Leavenworth Officers' School and War College, he returned to West Point, thought he knew more than anyone else, and was bounced to the 9th Cavalry (Colored) for a brief stint before moving on to the 24th's Third Battalion.

Briggs was born with an air of superiority, and most thought his being relegated to commanding a battalion of blacks, on two occasions, would have brought about his end. For a career officer, both were considered Siberian commands — commands that took him out of the limelight and secretly raised questions as to his competency. The commands would surely eliminate any and all thoughts of becoming a general. Some thought that with his ego fractured, he would retire or go so far as to resign his commission in protest. If he didn't do something along those lines, he would certainly change his ways. He didn't. Still puffed with arrogance, he walked around as though he were above it all. While the Cavalry's assignment was temporary, the 24th's was not. And as vainglorious as Briggs was, it was obvious he would not like being assigned to the 24th permanently. For some field commanders it very well could have been a career-ending assignment. What the colonel's detractors didn't know was that as long as he felt certain in his mind that the coloreds weren't going to war, he wouldn't complain too much. The next war, he believed, was going to be a serious war, a war of conscience — certainly not good for anyone who had dabbled in Mormonism in his earlier days. It was even worse for someone who had a deeply hidden, inborn fear of war. Besides, he had nothing against the Germans.

Most of the up-front trip with the lieutenant colonel was spent with his again talking about his days at West Point, a conversation that always fascinated his junior officers. Briggs also talked briefly about the Philippine Insurrection and the Mexican Expedition, then touched lightly on possible problems that could occur in Houston. According to him, black troops had participated only insignificantly in the two aforementioned conflicts, but were still "feeling their oats" after all this time. It was his view that in Houston, black importance to the military had to be minimized.

Capt. Reed brought up the subject of discipline and the issuance of passes once the men had settled in on the new post. The colonel expressed a great deal of concern about allowing the men to go into town at all. One of his fears was that there were a few white homes and one or two stores close to post, and to get to town the men on pass had to go through that area. Warrant Officer Froelich jokingly suggested outfitting the blacks with leash and collar. Even with Briggs the joke didn't sit well. After the quiet, Whitney suggested no passes at all.

Although the L Company commander couldn't have been — or, knowing Reed, shouldn't have been — serious, his comment did lead to the notion that perhaps no passes should be given until the troops had had an extended breaking-in period, or at least until the whites had gotten accustomed to the idea that blacks were in the area. Reed voiced his opposition to Whitney's idea by saying that such a restriction could lead to a ban on passes altogether. This wouldn't serve anyone's best interest, he said. A restriction of any sort would be tantamount to undeserved punishment. He added that no matter what measures were taken, it would be virtually impossible to keep the men on post without suffering a plethora of AWOL's.

Saying nothing, Farrell agreed with Reed. Farrell had other concerns, as well. He felt that because of the bitter disappointment of being in Texas, not only should there be passes, but the number of men allowed to go on pass should go beyond the norm — and the passes should be issued immediately. Saying almost what Farrell was thinking, Capt. Reed restated his beliefs, then continued. "The point I was trying to make, Colonel," he said deferentially, "in line with what you're probably thinking, is that we can't keep them cooped up on post all the time. I mean, it's hot; we're in Houston. Something is bound to give if we don't let them out to let off a little steam on a regular basis."

Briggs yielded. Even he knew that a temporary ban on passes could be problematic.

"Tell you what," he concluded, "let's let them get settled in for a couple of weeks. Then put them on a regular pass schedule."

"To go where, Sir?" asked Whitney, not at all familiar with the area.

"There's a pretty big colored district in town. They'll have to pass through that small outlying area of whites, but that's alright. If necessary, we can place MP's on the road to keep them moving until they get to where they're supposed to be."

"The San Felipe district, it's called," Froelich added. "And it's contained."

"What colored district isn't?" Whitney asked.

"I know the area," the colonel said. "We shouldn't be getting any complaints about Jim Crow among their own people. Might turn out all the better for 'em. There're plenty of 'crows' there," the colonel chuckled. "But few Jims."

Most of the officers didn't get the meaning. *Crows*, the colonel meant, were black women.

"Any other ideas how to keep 'em loose, Colonel?" Whitney asked.

"Yes. It's an idea that comes from the president of something called the Houston Tea and Sewing Club. According to Colonel Stout, the post commander at Logan, they want to give the boys some sort of welcome. I wired back, suggesting a watermelon party," Lt. Col. Briggs said.

"What is the Houston Tea and Sewing Club, Colonel?"

"I understand it's a social club. Probably a bunch of bleeding-heart old women who don't have a damned thing to do all day but sit around, drink tea, and dream up a bunch of crap. If they're like others I've seen, I can tell you this: all of them have got one foot in the grave and the other on a banana peel. They're old, scared as hell, and looking for something to hang onto. This time it'll be the coloreds and conscience. What a damned combination. Coloreds and conscience. That's a contradiction if there ever was one."

It was one of the few times Whitney and Froelich gave each other agreeable looks.

The colonel continued. "And to ease their conscience, these old biddies want to do something for the poor, mistreated colored soldier. I'm told this flat-assed head of that Houston Sewing and Tea garbage — whoever she is — wants to invite the sonsabitches into her home for tea."

"But there's nothing really wrong with that, is there, Colonel?"

a lieutenant from the battalion asked.

"Inviting coloreds into your home?" Briggs flared. "Hopkins, you're a bigger ass than I thought."

"But, Colonel —"

"Shut up, Lieutenant," Briggs said, cutting the young officer off. He swung his head around to his aide. "Froelich, assign some colored MP's to the district as soon as we get there, and put some guards on that road from Camp Logan."

"Yessir," Froelich said, pulling out his pad to make a note.

"Now — and this is something that has concerned me all along," the colonel said. "I think what will work to our best advantage is that these birds will now be servicing, and we can go a long way toward eliminating all that unnecessary combat training — which doesn't do a damn thing but fire them up. Oh, and that reminds me, Engineer." He turned to Farrell, whose mind appeared to be wandering. "Farrell —"

"Yes, Sir?"

"Your battalion commander is talking. Are you paying attention?"

"Yes, Sir."

"Because this concerns you."

"Yes, Sir."

"Now, Whitney, Reed and you, Farrell, you company commanders must take into account that some of these people have never seen colored doughboys in uniforms before, just as I'd bet a lot of the coloreds have probably never seen the American flag before, or, at least, coloreds marching under the flag. But, whatever, the troops must detrain silently. We will assemble on the street in front of the railroad station. I will call the battalion to attention, and I will give command back to you company officers. My staff and I will then depart with the Logan commander and his staff. You will march to Camp Logan in silence. And Farrell, make sure that first sergeant of yours doesn't start with all that rabble-rousing singing and clowning when they march. This is the Army, not a sideshow."

"But, Colonel — " Farrell began.

"And, come to think of it, where'n hell did they get all that non-sense from in the first place?"

"It's been said that the song is the Negro national anthem, Sir," Froelich answered.

"*The Negro national anthem?!*" The colonel bolted upright in his seat and hotly blustered, "The *Negro national anthem!*"

"That's what I'm told, Sir."

"What a bunch of crap!" Briggs raged. "And just who'n the hell are the niggers that they've got to have their own anthem?! Jesus Christ Almighty! This country is going to hell in a handbasket."

The L Company commander asked, "Would you rather they sing the Star-Spangled Banner, Sir?"

"Reed, you can be court-martialed for less than that," Briggs threatened.

The train rumbled on as the group fell silent. The battalion commander couldn't get over the anthem idea. He sat smoldering. "*The Negro national anthem.*"

Capt. Farrell felt that he had to get his point across. "Er, Colonel, Captain Reed was planning on having his company do the same as King Company — that is, to march with cadence-calling. But only when they go through the gate."

Reed swung around. "*What?*" He had said no such thing, didn't know where the idea came from, and didn't want to get involved.

Farrell returned his look, seeking vocal support. He would get none from the L Company commander.

Farrell concluded by saying, "I will see to it, though, Sir, that the singing and cadence-calling will be toned down in city limits."

"There will be no 'city limits,'" Briggs fired. "This battalion, Companies I, L, K, and Headquarters, will march *silently* through the *back road* of Houston to Camp Logan — if there is a back road. At Camp Logan they will march *silently* through the gate and *silently* to the rear to pitch tents and establish quarters. From this moment on, *silence* is the order. At no time will there be any drums, tom-toms, Congo drums, voices, jigging, or any other kind of African antics used to intimidate the good and decent citizenry of Houston or the good American soldiers stationed at Logan."

"But, Colonel —"

"Don't *but Colonel* me! You're in enough trouble as it is! My God, Man, show some common sense! Can you imagine what you'd feel like if you were one of the good soldiers at Logan, or if you happened to be one of the good citizens of Houston, and saw a bunch of black illiterates marching — *with guns?!*"

"Could be pretty intimidating," Froelich said.

"Certainly could," Whitney said, not so much to support Froelich as to score points with the lieutenant colonel. "I'd sure as hell be concerned."

The colonel snorted again. "The *Negro* national anthem. What a load of garbage."

Capt. Farrell said nothing further and returned to his seat, knowing all was lost. King Company would not be marching.

There were problems ahead. The King Company commander's first sergeant had rehearsed the troops for hours preparing for a bang-up entrance to the new post. And now nothing. Farrell also sat with the thought that in order to make the Logan arrival really special, he had given Poole permission to borrow some instruments, mostly drums, from the other companies. Although he hadn't seen all of the rehearsals, he had seen the end, and that was enough. The company was in fine form. The captain admitted to himself that he had initially been wrong in thinking that the rehearsals were a wasted exercise and that at some point he should have stopped his First. But when he went away for awhile, he gave McClellan the benefit of the doubt. The first sergeant had been right, and before boarding the train — not that he relished talking to him at the time — he made a point of going to McClellan. Farrell told him that it appeared that the company had managed to overcome the overseas disappointment, that he was proud, and that he had never seen the company quite so magnificent. McClellan replied, "We'll be better in Houston."

Those words wouldn't leave the captain's mind.

When the train finally hissed and belched into the Southern-Pacific station, it was late evening and there were many more people than anticipated. Especially interesting was that the black battalion had been scheduled to arrive a full 11 hours earlier. This lateness created a stir, particularly among those who were unalterably opposed to the move. The rumormongers went to work, creating hope in some groups by saying that the Army had finally gotten the word that the blacks weren't wanted and had changed its mind at the last minute. Hopes sagged when the train finally did pull into the station, but there was no trouble from the opposing group. In case of trouble a strong but unnoticeable contingent of police was on hand. The military had agreed that maintaining a low police profile was a wise decision on the part of the city fathers, as were their efforts to calm nerves and, for those who remembered, eliminate thoughts of Brownsville.

And so, in the main, with the arrival of the black battalion, the bystanding whites tried for containment. They weren't entirely successful because they were too curious. Questions had to be answered. They snooped, scrutinized and analyzed.

Yes, the coloreds were in the real Army. Yes, the coloreds did wear the uniforms of United States soldiers. Yes, they did have a real American flag. And no, they were not guarded by white troops. Other questions came and went. But, again, outright ill will was submerged. There were no "niggers, darkies, or coons" signs jamming the humid air as there had been in Brownsville years ago, nor were there any shouts or facial signs of hysteria. Nothing was said or done to counter good order. That said, still there was a whiff of trouble in the air. It was backed by one lone black effigy hanging in back of a storefront. It was uniformed. It was hanging quietly out of view of almost everyone.

First Sgt. McClellan saw the distasteful effigy, but said nothing. Like the rest of the battalion, he would have missed it had he not been called to the side of a warehouse building by Capt. Farrell on another matter.

From where they were positioned, the black civilians couldn't see the effigy. Neither could the troops. Even if it had been more prominently displayed, it is doubtful the troops would have been aroused. They were far too engaged in the reception they were going to receive from the surprisingly large number of black civilians who were smiling in anticipation of the arrival of "their kind in uniform." The blacks were not allowed free access to the railroad station or to the troops. They were restrained in a roped-off area, and, unable to see the troops at first, they were a bit concerned. The welcoming committee was all white, and those whom the welcoming committee had greeted were all white.

Lt. Col. Briggs, having benefited from a long line of handshakes, salutes and military protocol, was the first to emerge from the station. He was greeted by the commander of the post, Col. Bradford Stout, who led the way out to the Houston street and discreetly stepped back to allow the Third Battalion commander to wallow in the limelight alone.

Besieged by reporters and photographers, Briggs beamed a while longer, then was trailed across the street by his subordinates from Headquarters Company.

Reed's men evaporated the Houston blacks' dismay, and the blacks of Whitney's L Company put them completely at ease. Watching them, the black civilians started applauding and cheering. Unlike Reed, Capt. Whitney was unimpressed. He didn't like it, either, when the proud welcoming grew louder as Odums and Williams, the first sergeants of I and L, took their positions in front of their companies. Blacks in charge of blacks was something the black civilians had never dreamed of.

Indeed it was a proud moment.

King Company, slightly delayed because of the long walk from the last section of cars, automatically stirred something deep in the black civilians. While the company did nothing attracting except to exit with tight militarism, the crowd sensed something special. The welcoming became almost thunderous.

The last two to exit the station were Pete and Jody. Before disembarking, Sgt. McClellan had made it clear that the company, like the other companies, would form on the street in front of the station. He said that there would undoubtedly be civilians there, but under no circumstances were they to talk or make contact with any of them.

Apparently Pete forgot the rule. When he came out front, it was but an instant before his eyes wandered over to the roped area. He fell in love. Standing forward in the crowd was Nellie Moore. An ample woman with just a touch of hair under the fold of a doubled chin, she was grinning broadly and waving a laced lavender handkerchief that matched her purple outfit.

Miss Moore was not one of the world's all-time beauties. Light-skinned and loud, she was about twice the size of Pete, and on a good day she could crush the runt. It was to be a good match because Nell — as she preferred to be called — loved younger, under-sized men, and Pete loved older, oversized women.

With hormones jumping, he nudged Jody. "Why, lookee thar. Is I been bless'd, or is I done been *bless'd*."

"What?"

"Over-r-r-r *thar-r-rrr*," Pete said, pointing, waving, and grinning coyly. "Now *that* is class. An' no doubt *mynnne*."

Knowing Pete was up to something, Jody exercised good sense. "I'm goin' to where we s'posed to be," he said, meaning he was going to where the company was forming. "I think you better do the same, Pete."

"You do that. 'Cause this is a case for the lone wolf. An' the lone wolf is in *luuuuv*."

It took but a moment for Pete to close in on the segregated. He winked at Nell and asked importantly, "An' what's this lil' ol' congregation doin' behind a rope?"

"You stay 'round here long enough an' Mr. Quackenbush will have you behind one," somebody in the crowd said, laughing.

"An' just who is this Quacken-fella?"

"The headhunter."

"The who?"

"You'll find out. He'll get to you sooner or later."

"Th' only thing is gonna get to me," Pete said, leveling in on the heavy-hipped Nell, "is this lil' rosebud right here."

"Ooooh," she cooed, "you say the sweetest things."

"An' there's mo' where that comes from." Pete delicately worked his fingers and nipped at her breast. "If there's mo' where these comes from."

"There's a whole lot more," Nell said, trying to show more body fat through the crowd.

"When can I see for myself?"

"When you ready."

"I might be ready right now," Pete said. He seriously thought about dropping his rifle and backpack, ducking under the rope, and leaving the Army behind. "An' who might'cha be, Hun-Bun? Wha'cho name?"

"My friends call me Nell."

"A name straight out'a the folds of *heaven*!" Pete gushed, his hands slicing nicely at the air. "Pete the Sweet is mine."

"I like that."

"An' I like you. I like you so much, I might be tempted to go home with you right now."

"I'm ready."

Pete again thought about ducking under the rope. He looked back at the formation and saw Jody waving urgently. "Tell you what, why don'cha write down all yo' partic'lars – since I knows me an' you is gonna be doin' some serious reconnoiterin' later on. Maybe even *too-night*."

The fat lady went into her purse, extracted a piece of paper, and roughly mapped the way to her house. "In case you have trouble, just ask anybody where Nell's is. Everybody know me."

"They don't know you like I'm gonna know you."

"You can say that again," Nell said invitingly.

Someone in the back of the crowd called out, "Hope you don't mind if she's a 'lady of the evening.'"

Pete laughed. "Not as long as she don't mind if I'm a 'gennemen of the night.'"

Nell loved it. She bubbled and gave Pete the address. When she saw he had difficulty reading, she said, "I'm right across the street from the saloon called Verl's."

Pete grinned, pecked her on the cheek, and promised he'd be there sooner than expected. He backed away, blowing kisses and bowing to the crowd.

Watching him from the balcony of the building across from the train station was the policeman Elmore Quackenbush. With him was his assistant, Ananias Blanchard.

Pete's conversation at the segregated area was able to last as long as it did because he wasn't seen by any of the company's NCO's. They were on the side of the warehouse building with Capt. Farrell. The building was beside the railroad station and just across the intersecting street where McClellan had sighted the effigy. Though the effigy was still on the sergeant's mind, he said nothing to the others and concentrated on what the captain had to say.

Again the company commander had bad news. He told his cadre that they would not be allowed to march into Camp Logan as rehearsed, and he emphasized that there would be no sound-offs, no cadence-calling, singing, drums or anything. They were to march out of the city limits and arrive on post in silence. Silence, he repeated, was the order of the day. The captain was quick and to the point.

Poole, still burning from the morning news and because they were even in Houston, was really on fire. He circled around, saying, "Ain't this a bitch! Ain't this a bitch!"

"Easy," McClellan said to his corporal.

"So, what'n the hell is we supposed to do, Captain?"

"Just as I said, Corporal." Capt. Farrell again quoted Col. Briggs. "Silence is the order of the day.'"

"Meanin' as good as we is, an' after all'a that practicin', an' after what I done went through back there in Columbus, bustin' my butt to get some'a that stuff to make us look good, an' sound good —"

"That's enough, Poole," McClellan said. There wasn't an ounce of strength in his voice.

"No, Sarge. No, it ain't enough. I don't mean no disrespect, but I'm gettin' sick an' tired of this crap," Poole said, his temper rising even higher. Ordinarily he wouldn't have dared to speak to the First with such anger, or even a tenth as much. If he had, the first sergeant would have been on him like a disease. But McClellan didn't stop him. Neither did field sergeant Dukes, who stood quietly by.

Poole hotly continued. "First this mornin' — gettin' the orders to come here, an' now this. It ain't right, Sarge. You know it ain't right. An' they know it ain't right. Every time we turn aroun', they come up with somethin' new. They stickin' it to us, an' they want us to keep on bendin' over an' grinnin' while they doin' it. They tryin' to break us. They want us to come here shufflin' like we still on the plantation. That's what they want our people to see. They don't want us comin' here lookin' an' actin' like soldiers. They want us comin' here — in a place we ain't got no business bein' in the first place — appearin' before them white folks out there and them no-soldierin' white boys at camp, lookin' like we ain't even in the U.S. Army; like we don't deserve no respect, like we just a bunch'a rag-tag niggers lookin' for a home."

"Are you through, Corporal?" Capt. Farrell asked, and at the same time wondered why the First hadn't said anything further.

"I ain't gonna be through til' we get some respect. I ain't gonna —"

"Alright, Poole, you've said enough," McClellan said, this time with strength, having exercised more patience with his corporal than he'd ever shown before. "You've had your say, now get back out front with the company."

"And when I form it, what do you want me to do?"

"I want you to first tell Carter and everyone who has a drum or an instrument that they can carry them, but they are *not* to use them. Tell the men that we will be marching silently to — and through — Logan. There will be no cadence-calling."

"And after I tell 'em that, then what do we do?"

The first sergeant's mind went back to the effigy. "We rise above it."

Out of sarcasm, Poole asked, "How?"

"By doing what we do best," the First said it in a quiet voice. "We do it by proving we can take anything anyone has to offer. We do it by soldiering."

The answer was not at all to Poole's satisfaction. He walked away in a huff.

McClellan watched the corporal as he rounded the storefront. So did the captain. When the lanky corporal was fully out of view, McClellan and the captain exchanged looks. They walked away separately. Dukes followed his first sergeant. None of them said anything.

Fortunately Pete had made it to the formation before the NCO's and the captain. No one was happier than Jody. He didn't want his pal getting into more trouble and, since he had never done it except at the rehearsal before they left Columbus, he was insecure and needed someone to coach him on this marching thing.

Out front, with the reporters and photographers still swarming around, a preening Lt. Col. Briggs completed waving and smiling to the still-not-committed white populace, then positioned himself to actually take charge of the battalion. It had been a good arrival, he thought. There had been no trouble. He and his staff had been given a good welcome by the Houston establishment and

Camp Logan's command. He wasn't exactly overwhelmed by Col. Stout, the Camp Logan post commander, but he reasoned that Stout was not an Infantry officer and was someone who could be easily dismissed.

Over the noise of the trucks en route to camp with the crates and equipment, the colonel accepted the *"All present and accounted for, Sir"* reports from the company commanders standing in front of their formations. He surprised them and Col. Stout, the post commander, by standing midstreet and giving a brief speech. Clearly it was for the benefit of the crowd.

"As your battalion commander, let me remind you, you boys are here in Houston, Texas for the sole benefit of guarding construction work in progress at Camp Logan. The duration of this assignment is unknown. But while here, as your commander I expect you to be on your best behavior and not do anything to affront the good and decent citizens of this fair city. Remember you are guests here, just as you will be guests at Camp Logan. Do not abuse their hospitality in the city. Do not abuse the hospitality of the good American soldiers on the grounds of their post. Again I remind you, you are laborers. Guards. Do not let that uniform you are wearing tell you anything different. I hope I have made myself clear." Then, as he had not done in ages he loudly commanded, "BA-TAL-YUNNN! 'TEN-SHUTT!"

The company commanders echoed the command, and the cadre of officers and 645 black troops, already at attention, stood motionless.

"RIGHT!"

"Right!" repeated the C.O.'s.

"FAA-CE!"

The battalion made the turn to face the long road to camp.

"Company commanders take charge!" Lt. Col. Briggs directed as he moved off importantly.

The colonel loved the show of being in charge, of seeing an entire battalion respond to his commands, doing exactly what he told them to do. The only thing wrong was that this was a battalion of colereds. He couldn't get away from it. It was a loss of prestige and, speech or no speech, an old thought plagued him. An officer of the Point should not have been relegated to commanding coloreds. He wondered what the post commander thought. Whatever it was, Col. Briggs was not going to allow it to get to him. Col. Stout was only a post commander of a construction camp.

The battalion commander wasn't quite as firm in his resolve as he had thought. When he climbed into the first of the waiting staff cars containing the officers from Logan, he shifted a look at Stout. Briggs, for the first time in a long time, began to feel embarrassed. He had studied — even taught — at West Point, and he was a battalion commander. But he was a battalion commander of coloreds. That couldn't be ignored.

The company commanders saluted the five departing staff vehicles, stood alongside their companies, gave "sling arms," and followed up with the seldom-used *column* commands.

King Company was last in the order of march.

At about the time the battalion left the crowded streets of Houston and settled on the long dirt road that led to Camp Logan, several loaded trucks sped by. They were the first of 10 such trucks that had backed up to the station for what would be several trips. The fifth truck was driven by P.K., a short civilian whose voice came close to sounding like a hyena's.

P.K. saw the troops walking in columns on the road ahead. It was his moment. He cackled and double-clutched the truck. Instead of driving down the center of the road, he drove to the side and in the direction of the trailing column of troops. Since they were last in the line of march, they were the King Company men. Hearing the roar of the oncoming truck, they automatically ducked for cover.

Almost careening over, the truck got stuck in a ditch, but P.K. wasn't troubled. Grinning, he tried to push the gas pedal through the floor. The big wheels spun, making the holes deeper. Alternately shifting from first to reverse, he rocked the big vehicle until it was free. He then gunned it and zoomed down the road off-center, kicking up enough dust to almost choke the battalion. Safely away, he spun his head around, checked the damage, and in that irritatingly high-pitched voice laughed hysterically.

When P.K. drove up to the gate, he was still laughing. Pvt. Clay Tanner, clipboard in hand, was on the gate.

"Hey, Clay, I see you got company comin'."

Tanner lifted the gate and handed him the log for signature, which for P.K. meant drawing a short straight line. "Yeah," said the guard, "we been waitin' on 'em."

"Shore is a heap of 'em. I never know'd they had no niggers in the Army."

"Lot of us just found out."

"Seems downright un-Amerucum, don't it?"

"Almost."

"I just had a lil' fun with 'em," P.K. said, handing the log back, after having trouble drawing the short straight line.

"What'd you do?"

"Blew a lil' dust in their eyes. Hee, hee, hee."

"Hope you didn't blow too much." Clay said, laughing with him.

"One of 'em's gotta see how to drive your truck."

P.K. gunned the truck away.

When word spread through Camp Logan that the blacks were actually on their way, a horde of white soldiers gathered at the never-used rear gate. The entire rear section of the post had been cleared for the battalion's segregated use and so thorough were the demarcation lines, the section easily could have been another encampment. The whites never spent time at the rear of the post, although a few days earlier a group had researched the area with thoughts of forming some sort of welcoming for the blacks. Word went out that the idea was being discarded. No one was able to come up with anything appropriate. Still, a few men kept working on ideas, and reports had it that they were eventually successful. It made for an interesting wait in the dark. Only those few smiling knew of the surprise that awaited the blacks.

Some of the Logan men had been in touch with their families, and the fear that was prevalent when they first heard of the move had been eased somewhat by assurances from Col. Stout, the commander of the post. The imposing colonel said that the blacks would be restricted to the rearmost area and would not have access to the main gate. He also made it known that the 24th's Third Battalion would be, to use his term, *low-key* during arrival and were expected to maintain that presence throughout their stay. The colonel was unable to say how long the assignment would last, since he hadn't been informed. But time and again he assured city officials, along with the concerned and grumbling citizens of Houston, that the Army was fully aware of the colored soldier's troubled past in Texas. But as commander of the post he was authorized to take bold new measures which would prevent any recurrence of past hostilities. Anyone listening to the drawling colonel, however, should not have been misled, whether about the black presence on post or about his stated concerns for the people of Houston. While he was a southerner and it sounded as if his views ran parallel to those of the average white commander, Col. Bradford Stout was not the man everyone thought he was, as his former aide, Maj. Perrett, could have attested. Earlier, when Perrett delivered the Special Order from Headquarters assigning the black troops to Logan, he had referred to them as *a gang of niggers.*

Two hours later Perrett was on a train heading for a southern command. Smoothly and without fanfare, Stout had the man reassigned to Fort Benning, Georgia.

In coming on Post, *low-key* was a long way from what First Sgt. McClellan had in mind. As the rehearsals had shown while they awaited the trucks back in Columbus, he aimed to march out of the Houston city limits and through the Logan gate proudly. But now that the first part had been eliminated and the company reduced to entering the post via the rear gate, it was in his mind to let it rest. But he couldn't. As he saw fragments of L Company on the road ahead in what he thought were ragged, unsoldierlike columns, his mind never left the issue. Front, side, or rear, he knew what was important.

From the moment they received the news of transfer, the First had wanted to present the blacks in the best light; to present the best they had to offer. He knew it would have been good for his men, that it would have been a morale booster. He knew that a good, soldierly entrance would have been good for the whites at Logan as well. After all, most — if not all — had never seen a black in uniform. Some didn't know that the Army would allow blacks in its ranks. They had to be shown. And what better way for the man who had achieved the distinction of being in the service of his country to show himself? What better way for the man denied the right to fight for his country to exhibit himself? Marching. They could do nothing else. Marching showed precision, order, discipline, unity — all the things that strengthen man and elevate the race. Marching would show pride, purpose and confidence. It would show the whites that they didn't have to worry about sharing or, as fear was sure to have it, losing their post to a bunch of incompetent ignoramuses; that the talked-of slowness, shallowness, and disunity were not the true culture, only the perpetuation of a small mind's hope, that the colored soldier was as dependable and as proud and as respectful of the uniform as any white man, that the nation was wrong in not using the marching man to his fullest, that something was wrong somewhere, but that there was still time to rectify the wrong, and that if you could goosebump the sideliner, you could trenchwhip the foe. Order, pride, and discipline could do it. King Company *would* do it. The First could not control the battalion, but he could control the company and the company could change minds. That's what the people needed. They needed a mind change.

They needed to change their minds about the coloreds. They needed to erase negativity and doubt. They needed what King Company had to offer. Marching would have helped.

Headquarters and I Company had passed through the rear Logan gate, and Company L was nearing it. From King's position, fourth in the line of march, the First couldn't tell if there had been an earlier reaction. But at a certain spot, a loud, profane commotion rose from the ranks of L Company. Capt. Reed kept his men moving.

Soon King Company was at the same spot that had caused L Company's outbursts. What the men saw was unforgettable. Soldiers from Logan were scurrying away, having held their surprises in check so that they couldn't be seen by the staff cars, but back — *away* back — in the unattended fields, lit by hugely growing bonfires and beyond the ill-scrawled and barely-seen signs advising the niggers to go back to where they came from, big, black homemade scarecrows dotted a rotting fence that backdropped cotton-picking, watermelon-eating, cardboard characters capped with red bandannas. Overlooking them and footed by more bonfires, a series of crosses led to a cluster of trees with low-hanging branches. Swinging from the lowest branches were uniformed blacks, tarred and feathered and, much like the one seen near the station, hanging in effigy. Capt. Farrell, who saw it first, was shocked.

When McClellan, a few paces back, saw the field, he acted quickly and decisively. Without warning — without a word to the captain — he halted the column and sent Simms to the head of the company. He ordered the men to their regular marching positions. Capt. Farrell said something, but it was too late. The company was tight and rigid, and McClellan, with Dukes enthusiastically repeating, was already into another series of commands.

"King Company! Eyes straight ahead!" bellowed the First.

"What're we gonna do?!"

"Soldier!"

"I can't hear you, Troopers!"

"Soldier!"

"Louder!"

"We can do better!"

"*Soldier!*"

"Well, alright," shouted the First. "How're we gonna soldier?!"

"Together!"

"*How're we gonna soldier?!*"

"Together!"

"I can't hear you!"

"*Together!*"

"Say it again!"

"Tooogetttherrrr!"

"Stony the road we trod!"

"Bitter the chast'ning rod!"

"But we keep on....?!"

"S-s-s-soldieringg!"

"We keep on *what?*"

"*S-s-s-s-soldierrringg!*"

"Guidon!" called the First.

Simms shot the banner up, waited for the next order, then armed it smartly out front. He was moving like a drum major. "Alright! Lemme hear you! Delayed cadence," shouted the First. "Count!"

In tight *sound-off* precision, the company responded. "One! Two! Three! Four! One-Two-Three-Four! Onetwothreefour! *Onetwothreefour! Onetwothreefour!*"

"Break it down, Black Lightning!"

Simms snapped the guidon to the upright position, and in the same instant the company slowed to the half-step.

"Nigeral O. Carter! Yancy! Roosevelt! Menyard!" Sgt. Dukes called, sending the drummers' hands into a flurry of motion. Carter was a born African, and he led the others in sweating and beating the drums as if they all had come from the Congo. Dukes called,

"Andrews, John Chin, Carlos Rodriquez! Find something to work with. Everybody workin'!"

Harmonicas and Jew's-harps sprung out.

"Alright. Let's stir it up! Get set!" McClellan bellowed.

"Set!" Dukes yelled.

"Stomach in, chest out! Heads held high!"

"Stomach in, chest out! Y'heads held high!"

"*Who are you?!*"

"King Company!"

"Say it like you mean it!"

"*Kingggg Commmpannny!*"

"Alright! Ignoring the ignorance that surrounds us! Let 'em hear you! Let 'em hear your anthem, King Company! Sing your song, Black Lightning! *Sing a song!*"

SING A SONG, FULL OF THE FAITH
THAT THE DARK PAST HAS TAUGHT US.
SING A SONG FULL OF THE HOPE
THAT THE PRESENT HAS BROUGHT US.
FACING THE RISING SUN —
OF OUR NEW DAY BEGUN,
LET US MARCH ON 'TIL VICTORY IS WON."

"Second stanza, King Company! McClellan called. "Second stanza, Black Lightning! Second stanza! *'Stony The Road We Trod....'*"

The boots bit the dust in unmatched exactness. With the drums kicking to fever pitch, the voices rang out louder and stronger than ever before:

"*STONY THE ROAD WE TROD,*
BITTER THE CHAST'NING ROD,
FELT IN THE DAYS
WHEN HOPE HAD DIED.

YET, WITH A STEADY BEAT,
HAVE NOT OUR WEARY FEET
COME TO THE PLACE FOR WHICH
OUR FATHERS SIGHED,
WE HAVE COME OVER A WAY WITH
TEARS THAT HAVE BEEN WATERED,
WE HAVE COME, TREADING OUR PATH
THRO' THE BLOOD
OF THE SLAUGHTERED."

"Out Of The Gloomy Past!'"

"OUT OF THE GLOOMY PAST,
TILL NOW WE STAND AT LAST
WHERE THE WHITE GLEAM
OF OUR BRIGHT STAR IS CAST."

When the troops passed through the gate, they hit the half-step and continued magically into the night. They were electrifying. With rousing syncopation, they melted into the darkness, singing and hitting steps and moves as if all of Texas were watching. All of Texas wasn't, of course. But the soldiers of Logan were watching. And in the end they were applauding fervently.

Indistinctly, both colonels heard the company when it arrived. It would have been far better if one had not.

Chapter 9

Because of a return wire from Lt. Col. Briggs, Col. Stout, the post commander, had made no welcoming address to the troops. While it was not a military requirement, on many occasions when a unit was transferred to another post, there would be a speech or two, sometimes followed by a *passing in review*. The troop review was done mostly as a courtesy, ostensibly to give the host commander an opportunity to view the transferring unit in full. Sometimes it would take place on arrival. Col. Stout, sensitive to the Houston whites, didn't know if there should be a formal welcoming of the black troops or not. Not wishing to offend the blacks — which some thought was strange in itself — the post commander had wired the battalion commander for advice long before the battalion left Columbus. Briggs's wire back to Stout did not mince words. It read: *No parade. No trouble.*

The wire got the point across. It also put the Camp Logan commander on alert.

Col. Bradford Stout was a full bird colonel, outranking Lt. Col. Heinrich Briggs by one rank. What bothered him most was that after 27 years of service he had no medals of significance to pin on a puffed chest. He had not fought in a war.

The colonel was a large, muscular man with an iron face under a head of splendidly silver hair. He was from the South, but he was an odd man for a southerner — particularly a man from the deep South. When he was a child, his father had captained one of the first three steamers ever to traverse the Mississippi. It was presumed that the boy would follow in the father's footsteps or widen his interest to include a life at sea. Few knew it, but he would have done anything to distance himself from the father he so despised. The hatred had been long-standing.

As a child, Bradford Stout was terrified by the father's callous, endless talks of hanging a man, and by the sheer glee he derived from the telling. It was not all talk. The father had been a staunch defender of the Confederacy; he was mean, crude, and had participated in the lynching of any number of blacks. Worse, he was always detailed in the telling. He would spend hours describing how they, the garrote-minded justice-seekers — defenders of the American way — would grab the nigger, any nigger, and bind his wrists so tight that if not for the blood the gristle would show. With the nigger kicking and screaming, they would find a tree, the right tree with the right branch, and throw the rope over it. With one end, they would secure the kicker and screamer, who by now had screamed and moaned himself almost to the point of exhaustion. Still they had to be careful, the father always told the terrified young boy, because though the nigger had his arms tied behind his back, he still had the will to live. Sometimes they had to punch him and beat him. If that didn't do, they would have to interrupt the act and go out of their way to find a stick or a rock to beat the nigger over the head, putting the brave defenders of the American way at risk. The hands that were to hold the rope's other end could become bloody. They didn't like that. Blood made the rope slippery. If all went well, and it usually did, the defenders and justice-seekers would give the rope a yank, pulling on it until the nigger's body lifted from the ground. With the neck straining and stretching grotesquely from a tree limb, the eyes gave the first signal that things were going well. The eyes would bulge — not too much, just enough to let the legs know that it was time to stop their fitful air-dance and sway to a halt because the rope had gouged and tightened around the neck as far as it could go — that the sounds that once emanated from the throat had now stopped — and that, up and down, in and out; the esophagus — the trachea — from the larynx to the bronchi, all systems were down; functionally void; everything — choked, blocked — cut off, ended; and that the air — all life-sustaining things — was no more; everything was at a stand-still. Another nigger was dead. Another nigger was dead, dead, dead. He was dead, and this filthy, wasted, black, gutter-born, son-of-a-slob, kin-of-a-pig was so dead that his black skin became wan, and a defunct abdomen, trying to stay rigor mortis, recoiled, swelled, and tried to vomit its innards upwards but could only succeed in purging itself through rectal discharge. Indeed, another nigger was gone.

Most times the defenders of the American way would remain on site. Other times the odor that drifted from the anal discharge would drive them home. As they left, they shared a collective thought: the nigger looked almost like a human being hanging there. Maybe he was. He couldn't have been much of one, though. He wasn't white.

And true to the end, the nigger stank to the end.

•
•
•

Col. Bradford Stout envied Infantry. Following the *no parade, no trouble* wire sent by the Infantry commander, he had decided on a small reception for the officers of the Third Battalion. When the staff cars and entourage arrived on post, beating the arrival of the troops by some 40 minutes, they went directly to the reception at Post Headquarters. Col. Stout, after describing the post and talking about where everyone would be quartered, spent most of the time talking about the war with the lesser-ranked officers of the Third Battalion. At the same time he was ruing the fact that he was in command of a post that did nothing but construction. Later, with the far-away sound of King Company seeping in, Col. Stout wended his way over to Briggs for a getting-to-know-you chat. He started off by lightly complimenting the battalion commander on the brevity of his wire, then followed up by saying he was surprised that the lieutenant colonel had given what amounted to a speech at the station after wiring him that there should be none. The commander of the post also expressed surprise at the contents of the speech and said it seemed a mite rude and heavyhanded. Briggs accepted the complaint without comment. Continuing, and admitting he had never commanded black troops, the senior colonel said that he was also surprised that the battalion commander didn't want to show the blacks off, since they were so orderly and professional and certainly not what some of the people in Houston had expected. To this, Briggs, either jokingly or sarcastically, said that he had personally trained the troops and schooled them in discipline, but that after such an arduous task he was now ready to relax by assuming command over a post of whites. The post commander responded by saying that any time he was ready, he could take over Logan. He wanted to go to Europe. Briggs told him he wasn't alone in wanting to go. The post commander poured a drink and said, "But I'm not Infantry. I just have to wait my turn."

With the faint sound of King still filtering in, and the officers seemingly too engaged to notice, Briggs sensed that the colonel had gotten the wrong interpretation. Attempting to make his position clear, he said, "When I said you weren't alone in wanting to go to Europe, Colonel Stout, I wasn't speaking for — or of — myself."

"Oh?" The post commander's voice indicated that he had misinterpreted.

"I was speaking of the coloreds," Briggs said.

"Well, seeing those boys I can imagine how bad they want to go. They certainly seem fit," Col. Stout responded. "But, as we all know, it's not going to happen any time soon. If it happens at all. Unfortunately."

"Unfortunately?"

"Why, yes, Colonel. Not allowing the Negro to fight is most unfortunate. It's wasteful and ridiculous. You do agree?"

It was the first time the battalion commander had had the chance to voice his opinion to someone whose rank was not beneath his. His position had not changed, and his voice and content was strong enough to silence all the other officers in the room. "I think the coloreds on the front would be a goddamned disaster."

"The disaster," Col. Stout countered, "is in not letting the Negro function like everyone else in this country."

Briggs looked at the colonel and poured himself another drink.

"Maybe the solution is in sending them all to the front."

"As long as they are fighting, Colonel."

"I don't mean to fight, Colonel."

"Well, what do you mean?" Stout asked. "They're soldiers."

"No. They're in uniform," Briggs countered.

"Which means they're soldiers."

"Which means they're in the *uniform* of soldiers. Being in uniform doesn't mean they're capable, Colonel."

"Well, then, Colonel Briggs, perhaps I'd better ask what you meant when you said 'send them all to the front'?"

"Troops and civilians. Simple. Send the whole race to the front. Use 'em for target practice," Briggs said. He tried to cover up with a small chuckle.

"I don't find that amusing at all, Colonel."

"It was a bit harsh, I'll admit. But it was not said solely to amuse, Sir," Briggs said. "Colonel, you're not Infantry. I can understand if you don't realize what takes place in war. The front lines are where soldiers are killed. The more coloreds up front, the less casualties the whites will suffer. It seems to me to be a matter of clear logic."

"It's not logic at all, Colonel," Stout said. "It's pathetic."

"Call it what you will, Colonel. But, as a soldier who's been in combat, I'm inclined to agree with my superiors and yours in Washington, who, I believe, have a far better understanding of the situation than you or I. I also believe in the well-held position of the American people. The colored man is not equal. By any standard, he is incapable. In most instances, a dunce. And to have a dunce serving on the front or representing this country abroad is sheer folly. It's foolhardy."

Except for the two commanders, the room was in total silence.

The post commander set his glass down and spoke evenly. "Lieutenant Colonel Briggs, Sir. I am very much tempted to call you a goddamned ass, but I pride myself on being an officer and a gentleman, and I do not like speaking to a senior officer in such a manner and in front of other officers, particularly those of lesser rank. But my disgust can hardly be contained. As my staff already knows, I am a firm believer in the Negro — and a *most* firm believer that the Negro is as much a part of this country as you and I. I do not agree with Washington, which is why I'm here in command of a construction brigade that's doing nothing but wasting my time and the government's money. I would give everything I've ever owned to be in your shoes — to command a battalion of Infantry. *Negro* Infantry. I don't think there's a more capable people, and I don't think there's a more glorious unit in the Army than Infantry. Infantry, Negro, and Stout. Put us together, and I'll show you who the dunces are. Then send us to the front; let us fight your goddamned Germans, and then bring us back. We'll come home and really kick some ass. Yours first, Colonel."

The Third Battalion commander stiffened as tightly as if a live grenade had been tossed at him. He glared at the colonel, slammed his glass down, and stormed out the door.

Chapter 10

The next morning Col. Briggs was still on fire. Warrant Officer Froelich made the situation worse when he met the colonel in front of what was to become their Headquarters building and asked him if he had heard K Company when they marched onto post last night. In the same breath, he reminded him that they had shown a blatant and utter disregard for orders by marching on post with drums beating, sounding-off, singing, calling cadence, and doing everything he had ordered them not to do.

The battalion commander didn't need the reminder. He was already fire-eating mad on two fronts — and on both, he was stuck. The K Company violation was flagrant enough to warrant at least a summary court-martial, and he felt like charging the entire company. That had its problems, and the natural choice boiled down to reprimanding the C.O., particularly since he had been marching with the company. But Farrell, the colonel knew, didn't cause the problem. He was in charge, but the problem was with the first sergeant. The battalion commander decided to go after them both, and, at the same time, he would not let the company off without punishment. This created a problem as well, since an infraction they were not directly responsible for would normally call for punishment along the lines of pass restrictions and an early curfew. But, as he had discussed on the train, such restrictions would be in effect, anyway. Still something had to be done. As a matter of principle, it had to be far-reaching enough to be seen by Companies I and L, as well as the Camp Logan men.

Froelich was dismissed, and the colonel went to what amounted to his new office and spent time juggling a number of ideas. He came up with several, but the most effective one required the cooperation of Col. Stout.

Briggs detested the idea that he had to go to someone he so readily despised, but Stout was the commander of the post. He was an idiot. But he was still commander of the post, and the punishment Briggs had settled on involved the post. He would make it clear to the colonel that, as commander of the Third Battalion, he was supreme commander of the black troops, and, as such, was in Stout's office seeking only cooperation, not anybody's permission.

A half hour later Briggs was in the office. Though it was obviously on both men's minds, neither made mention of the previous night's dispute. With no exchange of greetings, Briggs waded right in. He told the post commander of the K Company violations and stated that he needed his assistance in meting out punishment. Stout, like Briggs, had heard traces of the company when they marched on post and agreed that if they had violated orders, they rightly deserved disciplinary action. He asked the battalion commander what he had in mind, knowing that whatever it was had to involve the post. He wouldn't have been there otherwise.

"I want as much paint as you have on post."

"Why, Colonel?" Stout asked. "Are you going to have them paint their tents? They haven't had time to pitch them yet."

"They will be pitched," Briggs said with force. "And after they're pitched, I'm going to have them paint every damned building on post. Those that can't be painted, they'll scrub. When that's done, they're going to go into your kitchens, your motorpool — anywhere and everywhere — to do the same. And after that, I'm going to have them build some new crap houses —"

Stout interrupted. "I believe what you're suggesting is excessive, Colonel. I might also add I think you're going about this in a most petulant way."

"Then there is no point in my continuing."

"I don't believe so, Colonel," concluded Stout. "I've had my say. You're the commanding officer of the battalion. Those are your troops. I'd rather not hear of anything you have in mind."

• • •

By noon, while Companies I and L were still busy at the rear of the post, digging holes, pitching tents, and doing everything required to settle in, the members of King Company were nowhere to be seen. The crates, bags and gear were at the assigned area, but the men were not. Nor were their tents up. They were carrying out disciplinary orders the colonel had dispatched via Froelich.

Camp Logan was a smaller but far better-looking post than was the 24th's home base, back in Columbus. The company streets were wide, and the men were billeted in clean, white barracks instead of tents. The one thing the barracks or anything else on post did not need was a fresh coat of paint or scrubbing. Obviously Lt. Col. Briggs thought otherwise.

His orders were effective and immediate.

Training was automatically suspended for all three companies. Companies I and L were to carry out guard assignments. With only the shortest time off to pitch tents and set the company up, after the first day, K Company, in addition to servicing, was to be broken down into sections and, as the order flatly stated, they were to "renew the post."

Capt. Farrell did not know exactly what renewing the post meant, but at the colonel's office he soon found out, not from the colonel, who refused to see him, but from another directive that was hand-delivered by Warrant Officer Froelich.

The directive, procedurally odd, was more of a reprimand, and the damaging remarks had been entered into the captain's 201 (personnel) file. In addition, the K Company commander was given a poor efficiency rating that augured transfer. Worst of all, according to Farrell, in the same directive he was ordered to prepare papers reducing his first sergeant's rank. And he would no longer assume the position of First.

In the captain's mind the matter was terribly unfair. Of course McClellan had been wrong. The colonel's orders were violated, and as the commanding officer — right there when it occurred — he had been wrong in not stopping him. But there was a reason for it. What they had seen en route to the post was obnoxious and hateful. Reason or not, though, the punishment far exceeded the crime. Farrell thought about appealing the case to the post commander, but he immediately abandoned the idea because he didn't know the man, it violated chain of command, and in the long run it would work against the company, particularly if the post commander weren't sympathetic to the appeal.

Farrell decided to wait.

A routine was established and the days sailed by.

Stout, like Farrell, McClellan, and the company, knew that the battalion commander had been excessive in dealing with them, yet 11 days later under his disapproving eye just about everything on the grounds of Camp Logan had been painted or repainted. Anything that could not be painted was washed, polished or greased. Without bothering to inspect anything, but still not satisfied, Briggs ordered more punishment. And though it seemed like the Company had been disassembled, the Company NCO's were still in charge, and as if to confound the Battalion Commander, they pushed even harder than required. Night and day the members of King found themselves hammering, patching, scrubbing mess halls, digging and working the grounds.

The whites would eventually benefit from cleared fields, scrubbed trucks, new ditches and walkways, resurfaced company streets, new latrines and cleaned-out backhouses.

Farrell felt helpless. The captain knew the assignments that denigrated and demoralized his company and pushed his First into a strange silence were taking their toll.

On the mornings that followed Farrell made reveille, but he rarely left the company area to see if the orders were being carried out efficiently. Only once did he go near Headquarters, and that was to make an uninvolved, face-saving visit with the other officers at the new Officers' Club. He had selected a time when he knew Froelich or the battalion commander wouldn't be around.

It was a Friday afternoon when Farrell moped in and saw Whitney and Reed. When asked, he talked a little about the company and tried to keep the conversation away from himself. But when questioned by Whitney and Reed about his punishment, he dismissed the subject. That caused both C.O.'s to push harder, as they were more than surprised that the K Company commander showed such little concern over his punishment. They were wrong. Farrell showed no concern over his punishment. In answer to the push, he explained that he didn't care about a poor rating and cared even less about what had been entered into his 201 file. "And as far as the reprimand," he said, "I think it's a waste of ink."

"You say that now," said Reed, "but what about promotion? What if you're ever considered for major?"

"Don't make me laugh," said Farrell.

"They would never do it now," said Whitney. "But let's say you were offered a promotion, would you accept it if offered?"

"Are you kidding?"

"Why wouldn't you?"

"For starters, I won't be here."

Whitney and Reed took the statement to mean that the K Company commander would no longer be in the 24th's Third Battalion. Farrell meant something else. He had made up his mind days ago that he was on his way out of service altogether, despite what would be said at home. The scholarly looking, sandy-haired captain didn't relish the idea of being labeled a slacker and the other names associated with it. The type of discharge the Army would grant him now was sure to be less than honorable. But even if the papers did not actually use the term *dishonorable*, early discharge would create suspicion. Treatment would be harsh and would, of course, have an immense if not irreparable effect on his family and everyone he came in contact with, particularly those having to do with his military-loving father-in-law and the business involving the engineering contracts. But it was set. He would wait until the transfer papers came in, then he would go through the process of claiming Conscientious Objector status, and that would be that. With nothing else to say, he delivered a quiet "see you later" to the two company commanders.

As the disturbed captain was leaving, Warrant Officer Froelich was coming in. Neither man spoke to the other.

Although he was no longer concerned about his own well-being since he had a clear plan of action in mind, on the way back to the company area Farrell again gave thought to his company. He hadn't been with them long enough to even begin to know them as well as he would have liked to, but still they would be missed. McClellan came to mind again. The captain was not secure in his thoughts. Deliberately he had avoided preparing the papers calling for the First's reduction in rank. Time had passed and he still hadn't done anything towards carrying out the demotion order. He didn't know why. He and McClellan had never been close. Company commanders and first sergeants, while they were not even close to being on each other's level, did find it important to maintain a relatively good working relationship. But not so with them. Their relationship was strained from the start. On that very first day when he was assigned to the company — from the moment the captain had walked onto the field — something was there. And for the few short months they had known each other, attitudes hadn't improved. There would be no words, of course. McClellan wouldn't have gone that far, and Farrell would not have allowed it. As a man he was insecure, and as an officer he was unprepared; he knew little or nothing about coloreds and even less about commanding a company of coloreds, but he was still a captain in the Army of the United States. Was he afraid of the coloreds? He wouldn't say; he didn't know. He did know that he felt a hell of a lot better being with the officers at the all-white Officers' Club. Though they would never reveal why, all officers felt better being away from the blacks. Farrell knew it went beyond simply wanting to be with someone of their own stature.

Whether racial or not, a mistrust clearly existed between Farrell and his First that went beyond the norm. From day one, they had made a point of avoiding each other whenever possible. A part of Farrell's problem was that his perception of the first sergeant had a great deal to do with his single-minded and militantly arrogant control over the company.

It was no secret that the first sergeant wallowed in the military. Worse, as the captain had come to discern, was his over-devotion to blackness. It led the captain to believe that the First wouldn't have been in favor of any white's being in command of the company. Yet, the First never thought, or more accurately, he never pictured, how it would have been had a black been the company's C.O. In fairness to the sergeant, however, with fewer than a half dozen black officers in the entire U.S. Army, and with most of them being chaplains, it would have been difficult to picture a black officer standing in front of the formation giving orders. In fact, as the Captain had overheard Sgt. Dukes commenting one day, in over 35 years of service he had never seen — nor had he ever had the occasion to even salute a black officer.

Farrell knew that McClellan's troubles or at least his concerns went beyond having a black in charge of blacks. Underneath, he thought, the first sergeant was mysterious and dangerous, and he held the Army responsible. He believed that at one time long before the military — whenever that was, and since it appeared that he was hiding something, *whoever* he was — the First had had all the makings of a good man, but he chose to be a soldier. To the captain's way of thinking, however, there was no virtue in being an excellent soldier. Excellence in soldiering was a waste; an exercise in breast-beating bravado. Moreover, it was against the will of God. In its truest sense, the sole purpose of a soldier's existence was to destroy what God had created. And that was not good. It was obvious that the soldier was called upon to do other things, to defend and service, but the ultimate purpose was to destroy. From day one, the soldier was trained to fight — to destroy. Helping mankind was last on the agenda. Not only was it last, it sometimes didn't exist. A soldier was trained to kill — to destroy. Battles were won by killing — by destroying. The soldier was promoted for knowing how to kill — how to destroy; he was praised and awarded medals for killing — for destroying. He was welcomed home and celebrated for winning — for destroying; for killing. The killer was the Army's best.

Excellent soldiers and their myopic, Pied Piper ways of following had always been blinded by the military. Killing had always been depersonalized, the sanctity of life meant nothing. And though he had not been in combat, thought Farrell, the First had all the makings of being one of the Army's best. With his streak of militaristic sightlessness, if sent to the front he would set records. Given the opportunity to fight in the Great War, First Sgt. Obie McClellan would have been a hero, because he was the type who would shell, shoot, grenade, gas and bayonet with impunity and, pitifully, he would have thought he was in the right.

War and the military aside though, something told the captain there was a more immediate and tyrannical danger that lurked beneath the mysterious surface of this aloof black who didn't socialize at all, who never revealed anything about himself even to his men, and who spent his nights alone reading in his tent. The captain also knew — and feared — that his First was becoming obsessively race-conscious, fanatic to a degree. His last speech to the company in Columbus, which Farrell didn't hear in its entirety but knew would contain elements of that embittered tone of racial inequality, was, in his view, excessive. It was no secret the man wanted the best for his race. The captain knew this, because he paid close attention to a speech the sergeant had made a few months earlier. It was laced with racial overtones. What interested him most, though, was that the First had addressed the men as though they were the most intelligent and literate bunch who ever wore a uniform. He was lofty, perhaps even didactic; sermonic — again. Obviously the aim was to get the men to strive higher; to get them to enjoy the beauty of the spoken word rather than to remain in the pig sty of illiteracy. But they couldn't possibly have understood all that he was saying. The Colonel said that the illiteracy rate in the battalion exceeded 70 percent. Going beyond those pathetically alarming numbers, it caused the captain to wonder: if the troops couldn't fully understand all that was being said, what really was the aim? Was this a trait of Negro leadership? — compensating by being excessive? He had no answer. Despite wildly differing claims from the likes of Briggs, Whitney, Froelich and others he had met, he didn't know the blacks. He would never know them. Like any other white, he had no reason or incentive ever to know them. In spite of the standard beliefs, presumptions and assumptions, he didn't *know* them. It wasn't necessary to know them. They were Negroes. Coloreds. Blacks. *Blanks.* And no matter how many name changes they went through during their history, to him, at least, they would have remained *blanks* had he not left home and received the K Company assignment. Until then, the blanks didn't warrant knowing. They were on one side of the ledger; the other, a credit. They were a debit; the other, a credit.

On the now compelling and discomforting question of race, apart from the speech, there was another instance that the captain found disturbing. About a week after he arrived at the company, in the Orderly Room he saw the First filling out an application for some new organization called the National Association For The Advancement of Colored People. Next to it were pamphlets describing the virtues of something called the Urban League. Curious, he waited a day or two and asked Simms, the part-time company clerk, about them. Simms wasn't entirely familiar with the new organizations, but told the captain enough to start him wondering. The next day while the company was on the field the captain returned to the company area and spent time combing through the many books that lined the first sergeant's tent, which had been pitched next to the Orderly Room and positioned just about as it had been back in Columbus.

Being in the first sergeant's tent was an eye-opener. He knew it would be stern, but the sheltered white captain from St. Agatha, Maine had never known there were that many black books, that many black voices — *revolutionary* black voices — all calling for a change in America. They wanted change *now* — and by any means necessary. It was the theme of almost everything he put his hands on: *Change. Change — by any means necessary.*

Farrell remembered shuddering at the phrase *by any means necessary.* Whether he knew the blacks or not, whether the First was within his rights as a soldier to even think about joining them, the captain could only hope that the new organizations would exercise patience and restraint. Whatever they were up to, they obviously had captured a thinking man's attention.

Now there was the other matter before the company commander, and it was pressing. He had to prepare the papers. Twice before he had gotten close. On those occasions, he had done nothing but sit in the Orderly Room and manufacture excuses for not carrying out the order for demotion.

Once, unwilling to do it himself, he got as far as having Simms read the manual for procedure. Again he allowed the results to fall by the wayside, and for three additional days he continued to sit in his office in the Orderly Room tent and do nothing but think. Any minute now, he knew, Briggs was going to be on him like a hawk.

If the captain was looking for help by seeing his First, he wasn't getting it. Other than for making roll call at reveille and a few other formations, the First wasn't seen much.

• • •

The days came and went, and it seemed like the proud company's will had been crushed. Yet, with Dukes and Poole, and sometimes with Mess Sgt. Willie Powell, the King Company NCO's were still in charge. And, as if to confound the battalion commander and lift the first sergeant's questionable spirits, they pushed on with the added work. They did it swiftly and without noticeable complaint. They were derided by the whites and made fun of by Companies I and L, but they pushed on.

Again, First Sgt. McClellan wasn't with the three NCO's when they made their rounds, checking up on the various work details on the morning of the second week of August. The First didn't let it show, but King's hard labor and humiliation were taking their toll even more now. Lately he was even less visible and, for the most part, the unimposing man remained quiet and alone in his tent. Out of respect, the cadre didn't approach him. Neither did the captain.

Cpl. Poole had taken the inspecting lead that morning. The first stop they made in the white area on the Camp Logan grounds was at C Company. There they were assailed by the stench as they watched three of their men sweating and pulling on ropes that eventually revealed containers loaded with dripping human waste from the C Company latrine. With the help of Carter, Yancy and Boland, the rank waste was poured into a large vat and muscled away on a cart that didn't get far before it tilted over and browned-out the ground.

Poole, already the angriest of the group and ready to explode at any moment, tightened his jaw and moved off. Sgt. Dukes and Mess Sgt. Willie Powell followed.

In time, they stopped at another latrine. This was B Company's. As with all the rest, it was set far back from the barracks. It had already been cleaned. Moving on, the three NCO's went to F Company, where they saw more of their men washing windows, removing trash, and doing general household chores. A few white soldiers, apparently off duty, sat comfortably in the shade reading, talking, and making the most of an uninvolved day. Paralleling the barracks was a stable. Working inside with the horses were Pete, Jody, and Puerto Rico. Actually, Jody and Puerto Rico were doing the work. Pete was stretched out on the high point of the hay, sleeping like a newborn. He would have remained that way had Jody not awakened him when the trio of noncoms approached. Despite Jody's urging him to get up, Pete couldn't bring himself to get to his feet. He decided he would make the most of the situation by cracking open an eye.

"Mornin', Sarge," the scamp of a soldier said. He made no attempt to move from the curled position. "S'cuse me for not gettin' up, but I have to keep layin' on this hay to keep it warm for the horses."

Sgt. Dukes said patiently, "It's eighty-sumthin' degrees out there, Pete."

"An' headin' for a hundred an' one," Poole added.

"It is?" Pete asked, opening both eyes in mock amazement.

"Yeah, Pete. S'bout the same as it's been every day since we been here. They say it's one of the hottest summers ever. S'prised you haven't noticed."

"Well, now, how 'bout that? One'a them white boys just came by here an' told me it just got cold out there."

"Not likely, Pete," Dukes said. "It seldom gets cold in Texas."

"Specially durin' the month of August," Poole added.

"Well, spank me with a whiskbroom an' set my behind in motion," Pete responded, trying to act surprised, but not surprised enough to move from the curled position. "I was concerned b'cause these is warm-weather horses. I should'a checked for myself. That's what happens when you tryin' to do too much, like I been doin'."

"What have you been doin' too much of, Pete?" Dukes asked.

"Just too many things to count, Sarge."

"Like what, Pete? Gimme an example."

"Milkin'."

"Milkin' what?"

"A horse."

"No, Pete," Jody cut in. "You can't milk a horse."

"Quiet, Jody," Sgt. Dukes said. "I'd like to hear what farmer Curry has to say. Now, Pete, you say you was milkin' a horse?"

"Er, um, like Jody was tryin' to say, it must'a not been a horse," said Pete. "I'm so tired, I get them things mixed up. Er — Sarge, actually, I was over on one side lookin' at the horse. An' then I was on the other side milkin' a cow. An' then I came back over here to give the horse some of the cow's milk — to go with the hay. Like when I used to eat cereal? Horses like their hay with milk."

The boy from Wyoming was pained. "No, they don't, Pete."

"Yeah, they do. Horses like milk. It's good for their teeth. Especially the big ones in the back. An' they prefers buttermilk because its chewable."

Even Jody knew it was best to leave the subject alone.

Sgt. Dukes shifted gears. "How come you so sleepy all the time, Pete? Ever since we been here, I notice you can hardly keep your eyes open."

"I been concentratin' on my work, Sarge. An' I been doin' a lot of readin' at night. Workin' on Texas history."

They all knew that was a lie, too. As did most of the men in the company, at his very best Pete had only minimal reading skills. He even had trouble with the address Nell had given him when they arrived.

Like the others, Pete's last lie was not only unworkable, it didn't even sound workable, but only Jody and Mess Sgt. Willie Powell knew why he was lying. Jody knew because of their last-name initials. The two bunked next to each other, and every night since being there, Pvt. Curry, Peter P. would steal away and a wide-awake Pvt. Cunningham, Jody was left to cover for his friend. Mess Sgt. Willie Powell knew Pete was lying because he would be in the mess tent, cranking up the kitchen at around 0400. At 0545 he could count on watching Pete climb back over the fence at the rear of camp. Pete would make it back just in time to catch the 0600 reveille. Going or coming, though, he was always careful scaling the fence. He didn't want to hurt his hands.

Pete had found a midnight home with Nellie Moore, the big hippo of a woman he had met in front of the train station upon arrival. Nell treated him like royalty. Every night she closed the house of prostitution early, dusted and powdered herself, and waited at the door shortly after midnight with a freely parted, fuzzy-collared lavender nightgown that exposed rippled thighs and generous hips.

When they were together, Nell wanted an unhampered run of the house, and of late it seemed that everything she did was in exclusive honor of her AWOL little soldier from camp. She had even moved the furniture around.

Although Nell preferred her runt in the nude, she loved the uniform. She thought the hats with the four dimples, the tight-fitting tunics, hip-hugging pants, and firm leggings highlighted a young man's body and made him look tight, vigorous and sturdy. It made him look as though he could last a night, come back for more in the morning, and have a woman screaming and reaching for the chandeliers throughout the rest of the day. Nell loved black soldiers without hats even more. With their dark skin blending beautifully with the woolen olive-drab uniforms — when they marched, to her they looked like a body of moving peters.

Nellie Moore was one of the few in the San Felipe district who had never seen a black soldier before. Not flesh and blood, however. He was in one of the catalogues she had ordered from Sears, Roebuck & Co. in Chicago. She kept the big book on display to impress her waiting customers from Logan. Most of them never knew there were any blacks in uniform until they saw the picture. Even at that, some of them weren't convinced. Fewer were impressed.

From the moment Nell laid eyes on her doughboy, he reminded her of her picture-book soldier. There was a difference, of course. The picture-book doughboy stood strong and erect and looked wonderful in his uniform. Pete was short — only about a foot taller than Jody, and his body was almost lost in his uniform. But on that first night visit with the woman, he didn't disappoint in the area she was most interested in. In bed. And on that first night, Pete worked wonders. On subsequent nights, he did even more — so much more that it caused a change in the big woman. By week's end she was saving herself for her scrawny beloved.

Pete, though, was a long way from being Nell's first experience with a man in uniform. Her first, indeed her second, third, fourth, fifth, six, seventh, eighth and all the way up to uncounted numbers, had been white.

Before the arrival of the blacks, Nell's clientele listed about two dozen Camp Logan whites. It was tricky because her clients included NCO's and a number of officers as well. It placed a strain on her operation, because neither group wanted to be seen by the other. In the officers' case, they didn't even want to be seen by each other. After many backdoor and cellar-creeping episodes which in the main did not work too effectively a Capt. Slodenhower, the officer in charge of the post's communications, came up with a solution. In exchange for free sessions, Nell would be provided with something few blacks in the area had ever seen. A telephone. The officers could make appointments. But the *parvenu* side of Nell loved it even more, because the instrument gave her status beyond the snobby "Red Book" blacks who didn't care for her or her occupation, so when she first got the telephone, she kept it in a tin tub by the window. She wanted her detractors to hear it when it rang.

Nobody — officers, NCO's, or regular troops — was overly fond of going into the Fourth Ward's San Felipe district, and rarely would one be seen in the area at night. But in terms of time off post, the Logan personnel never spent much at Nell's, anyway. Most of their time was spent in saloons and gambling halls and houses far away from the district. The whites ventured into the district and to Nell's for one thing and one thing only: to unload in a black gal. Thus the sessions were short and to the point. But they were not always appreciated by the working girls. Most of the girls felt that they were no more than objects of the white man's curiosity. In most cases that was true. Most of the whites never engaged in any sort of conversation, never fully removed their clothing, and sought to get the act over with as quickly as possible. When they were through, they never said anything. When they left, they never said goodbye. And through it all, there would be no kissing. The girls knew the whites found it repugnant.

The lack of anything but intercourse between Nell's girls and the bunny-rabbit whites of Logan had its roots in several emotions. Sometimes shyness was a factor. Some men simply didn't know what to say to a woman, black or white, prostitute or prude. Other times, loneliness in the barracks played havoc with the mind, and with faulty imaginations working overtime, back-home wives and sweethearts became suspects of infidelity. When the always-dangerous *what's-the-use?* attitude linked up with an angry *getting-even* attitude, the combination would, more often than not, escort them to the Nells of the world.

Though rarely, warmer emotions sometimes were touched, and a white would get carried away with one of the girls. Most times the attraction didn't amount to much and was broken off. Then there was the never-to-be-discussed time when a Maj. Hap Arden, the post adjutant, unloaded his heart on another young girl, felt guilty over the association, and decided to end it all by putting a bullet through his temple about 100 yards in front of the main gate. Fortunately for Nell, the suicide occurred while Arden was returning to post. She was spared vigorous investigation, but the policeman Quackenbush still had his suspicions as to the cause.

The large lady's house of prostitution was a solo act. It was located in the center of the San Felipe district, about a mile north of the police station. Too large for the area, the tri-storied affair without much yard was situated diagonally across the street from Verl's, the storefront tavern that was not suffering from a lack of business. At first glance, laying gaudiness aside, one was hit with the thought that the big place was a funeral parlor.

The house had two large bay windows with valances that draped down thick, lavender curtains fringed with gilt-covered balls. Riding from the windows was a large porch that Nell had seen fit to overload with flowers, plants and wicker chairs. Except for the flowers, all had been painted in various shades of purple.

Inside, the living room was large and clumpy with heavy, dark-brown beams that threatened from above. Two overstuffed velvet, doily-draped sofas faced each other. They were deep purple. In the center was the coffee table. The glass was flecked with gold and inlaid with violets. The end chairs were the same, but were spotted with huge appliquéd lavenders. Like the purple outfit Nell was wearing at the train station the evening the troops arrived, this was not a scheme to lift a decorator's spirits.

Upstairs, the reign of purple, lavender, fuchsia and violet continued to assault. The colors ran the length of the long, flocked hallway and sprouted bold new birth in six bedrooms.

Pete loved the place. His nightly AWOL escapades had him and the big woman who had a smidge of hair that grew from the fold of her chin applying their brand of eroticism in every room. Nell was a machine. Pete wasn't. Nor was Pete the durable gymnastic expert he claimed to be, and lately the machine had begun to have him on the run. For the first week he had risen wonderfully to the woman's challenges, but not so in the days that followed. Pete was beginning to have second thoughts. He couldn't help it. He was drained. He was beginning to show wear and tear. Now when they settled back into her room, having taken the tour of the house in the nude, Nell would have him huffing and puffing in the purple-covered canopied bed like a train heading uphill. Once, to get away from the amorously aggressive partner, he tried climbing on top of the canopy and promptly fell through, landing faceup on the bed. It was a mistake. Aroused again, the big woman, easily 20 years older than the runt, rolled out of bed, reared back — spread-eagle-like — and with her buttocks hanging like two overstuffed sandbags, charged forward and pounced.

That morning, it took every ounce of strength Pete could muster to make haste back to camp. If the fence had been a foot higher, he would have been in more trouble. Huffing and puffing and wrapped in a purple-embroidered muslin sheet, Nell was right on his heels. Fortunately for Pete, the woman couldn't scale the fence. She tried, though. If daylight hadn't been close, she would have kept on trying.

Although Nell had an insatiable appetite, she soon learned to pace herself, because she liked the runted soldier for what he was, and not for his claimed endurance. When not coitally dissipated, Pete was fun, cheerful, and for that first week or so, coitally inventive.

From the northern part of Philadelphia, Pennsylvania Pete Curry had been with King Company for a little over two years. As with a lot of the men in the company, he came from a broken home. As contrary as it might have seemed, Pete was raised in church. His father, Bladen Curry, had been a roustabout, one of only four blacks ever allowed to do such work. But working on the docks got to the man, so he quit and took up a life of gambling. Around the neighborhood he was known as a chronic loser. It didn't sit well with anybody, particularly his wife. Oddly enough, his wife, Pete's mother, had been a minister with great hopes for her little one. But the valiant lady had to close her tiny, struggling, store-front church because the money she collected on Sundays was always missing on Mondays. Actually Bladen would take the money the night before, but his wife never checked.

In time, there was the inevitable breakup with the Currys, and Pete, the one-time avid church-goer, found himself drifting to the other side of the tracks and hanging around the local barber shop. Watching the barber rhythmically slicing and snipping the air with the long, elegant scissors was always impressive to Pete, which was another reason he would sometimes talk with an extended pinkie while allowing the forefinger to gently touch the thumb. From those days to the present, there was almost artistry in the way he moved his fingers.

At 18, Pete enlisted in the Army because one day a man came into the shop "wearing these funny clothes." It was an unusual outfit for a black. Pete thought the man was on his way to something like a Halloween party and actually tried to wangle an invitation from him. The man explained that he was a soldier in the Army of the United States, got a haircut — the 20-cent special — and generously tipped the barber 10 cents. Pete saw the transaction and jumped so high his head almost got caught in the ceiling fan. He particularly liked what the man in the funny suit had said to the barber in giving him the tip.

"An' there's plenty mo' where that come from."

"An' where's that?" The question wasn't as obtuse as it might have sounded.

"The Uninny Stakes Army."

Two days later, Peter P. Curry had talked his way into becoming a private in that same Uninny Stakes Army.

Chapter 11

As the days passed, and although there were no outright hostile acts committed by either the whites or the blacks at the Camp Logan post, tension was mounting and talk indicated that something was in the air. The black troops from Companies I and L were having meetings outside of the presence of their NCO's. Unknown to them, their cadre were also having furtive meetings. The meeting was all in response to a belief that the whites were going to set fire to their tents. They had gotten word from P.K., the dim-witted truck driver. Although P.K. was a civilian, he knew the post, and by alternately driving the poultry and vegetable trucks, he had gotten to know a few of the blacks by virtue of their having to do the unloading. It was not at all as Clay Tanner had said when the troops were arriving. The white gate guard had said at the time, *"One of 'em's gotta see how to drive your truck."* Not true at all. Except for Boland and perhaps one or two others, none of the blacks had ever been behind the wheel of a motor vehicle, and even if so, the Army would not have allowed them to drive — trucks or automobiles.

Although P.K. would not overly extend himself, he sometimes helped the blacks with the unloading. At the same time, he would engage the men in conversation, often telling them how much they were disliked by the whites. He was subtle and always smiling. With the smile and his engaging personality, the blacks couldn't help but count him as a friend, and they soon valued anything he had to say. It was a mistake. What the blacks didn't know or didn't take time to evaluate was that P.K. was an out-and-out liar and troublemaker. He'd tell the blacks one thing, then drive to the front of the post and tell the whites another. As demonstrated on the evening when the blacks first arrived on post, he had difficulty in not referring to blacks as niggers when he was not in their presence. Sometimes he had difficulty in not using the term while he was in their presence, but he would laugh the oversight off. Often some of the blacks would laugh with him.

When P.K. drove away from the blacks and landed with the whites, and knowing most of them were from the deep South, his face would change. It would droop. Always with the engine running, he'd climb down from the truck, shake his head, and say in a heavy voice, referring to the back of the post where the blacks were stationed, "Well, I was just back in the jungle." He'd let it drop for a moment, then say in a sing-song way, "I was listenin' to the niggers agin. They plottin'." Plotting what, P.K. never said. Then the little canker-faced man would go on to somberly say how he was becoming afraid to drive the delivery truck to the back of the post because the blacks "was becomin' more an' more h'stility." He would add, "Y'all be careful, y'hear? 'Cause the niggers ain't playin'." They plottin'." Gloomily, he would drive off.

Tension was mounting.

• • •

Since the disciplinary assignment melded into one of seeing

permanence and took them away from the rest of the battalion, the men of King Company had little knowledge of what amounted to growing tremors. Occasionally they would hear a word or two, but nothing was given weight. They remained practically oblivious, working up front, servicing the whites in daylight and being virtually isolated at night. This was because another line of punishment Lt. Col. Briggs handed down had restricted them to the company area during all off-duty hours.

Added rumors mixed with growing uneasiness and landed squarely at the feet of the post commander. He feared an outbreak of some sort. This notion was fed by the news that in East St. Louis, Illinois another riot between blacks and whites had just broken out. With 39 dead and hundreds wounded, it was deemed one of the country's worst.

Col. Stout purposely had not seen the battalion commander, a man he obviously wished he had never met in the first place. Surely on such a small post, he undoubtedly would run into him at some point. Their meeting was certain to be unpleasant, but there was trouble afoot, and personalities had to be laid aside.

After several meetings with his executives, all dealing with measures to relieve tensions, the post commander took the unusual step of calling upon the battalion commander at his headquarters. It was a brief meeting that took place on August 24. It was Friday.

By Saturday morning, owing to Col. Stout's having to pull rank over the vehemently resisting Lt. Col. Briggs who had also heard rumors, but had declined to act, a change had been effected. Neither the watermelon party nor the kind gesture from the — to use Briggs' term — "*flat-assed*" president of the Houston Tea and Sewing Club — was ever mentioned again, but the good news was that the men of the battalion were going to be allowed passes. King Company was included.

And there was more good news.

The day had started out with Capt. Farrell's summoning of First Sgt. McClellan to the Orderly Room for a meeting that lasted for about 10 minutes. The captain explained that the paymaster would be arriving at noon, and that after the men received their pay, which had been delayed since long before leaving Columbus, most of the men would be allowed to go on pass. Exactly who was selected to go was, as usual, discretionary. The passes along with the pay were a big surprise, but McClellan did not have much to say. His only question to the captain dealt with a police presence in the San Felipe district. The captain told him that some members of I and L had been drafted as military policemen, and that they would be stationed along the road to town and throughout the district. When McClellan left the captain, he went to the First Platoon tent and ordered Sgt. Dukes to sound a delayed reveille.

At 0710 the company was in full formation. Capt. Farrell and First Sgt. McClellan were in their regular positions. Sgt. Dukes was calling the roll. It was odd to have a late reveille, but the larger irregularity was that, unlike the way it had been before arriving in Houston, every man in formation was fully uniformed. And every man, for the first time, had a weapon at his side. And Poole was smiling. It was evident that along with a few helpers, the corporal had had many busy nights since arriving at Logan. It brought to mind something he had said on the train: "*Stealin' from white folks ain't no trouble. It's an art.*"

There was strength in Sgt. Dukes's voice. "Akahito!"
"Here, Sir!"
"Auer!"
"Here, Suh!"
"Boland?!"
"Here, Sir!"
"Boyd, Babe!"
"Here, Sir!"
"Cannon!"
"Here, Suh!"
"Carter!"

"Here, Suh!"

"Chin?!"

"Here, Sir!"

"Crawford!"

"Here, Sir!"

"Cunningham!"

"Here, Sir!"

"Curry?!"

There was no response.

Sgt. Dukes looked up from his clipboard. "Curry, Peter P!!"

He still didn't get a response.

"*PRIVATE PETER P. CURRY!*"

"On my way, Sir!" The voice escaping from the First Platoon tent was making a mad dash to the formation. "Comin', Sarge!" McClellan waited until the disheveled Pete had almost reached the assembly. "Where were you, Trooper?!"

"Oh, er — um — I was oversleepin'," Pete said, weak after another of those excessively rough nights with Nell and sliding in next to the fearful Jody. "See, Sir, I was havin' this dream. An' it was a deep dream. The deepest I done had since I been here. You can even ask Jody stannin' here. He was innit. See, I was bein' attack'd by all'a these Germans and they was with these white folks who had these pointy white hoods and sheets on. An' I was askin' 'em what they wanted, but they didn't speak no English. So they started burnin' these crosses, and they had these ropes. So I start'd runnin'. They was chasin' me, an' there you was, comin' to the rescue. Chargin' to save me from — "

"Finish your dream in a six-by!"

"But, Sarge, please, before you make me do any diggin'," Pete said, clutching his stomach, "I was just tellin' you that because I'm too scared to tell you the real reason why I'm late."

"And — ?"

"And what, Sarge?"

"Why are you late for my formation this morning, Trooper? Why were you late yesterday morning? And the morning before? And the morning before that, and just about every morning since we've been here in Houston, Texas?"

"I didn't realize I been that bad off. I'm sorry I'm gonna have to tell you this, Sarge," Pete said with a groan. "It's my health. But don't you go worrin' 'bout it none, 'cause with a lil' rest I think I might make it."

"What about your health?!"

"Oh, you don't know?"

"No, I don't know," McClellan challenged, and waited to see what else Pete would come up with.

"See, Sir, if you r'member, before we went to work on the horses, me an' Jody was on one'a the details cleanin'. Y'kno' the backhouses? An' y'know how all the stuff in there floats? Well, every night I been dreamin' about fallin' into one. An' when I starts swimmin' around in all'a that stuff, an' I starts inhalin' an' breathin', it starts chokin' an' stranglin' me. An' my health is been fallin' ever since. An' y'kno' we don't get to see no doctors. So lately —"

"Double the six-by!"

"Aw, Sarge, damn."

"Make it a twelve-by-twelve!"

"Oh, please, don't, Sarge —"

"And dig it with a spoon!"

"But, Sarge —"

"And after that, report to Mess Sergeant Willie Powell for sixteen straight hours of K.P.!!"

Pete had to give it one more shot. "Since I might not live, Sarge, can Jody come an' stand by?"

"Git!" McClellan shouted, sending a groaning, hunched-over Pete on his way.

The captain got McClellan's attention and low-toned, "The passes, Sergeant."

McClellan took a moment and said to the company, "At noon, for half of the company, there will be passes."

It was totally unexpected. When they were positive of what they had heard, the men started hollering and cheering.

Crawford who was from Beaumont, Texas yelled, "San Felipe, here we come!"

"There's gonna be a hot time in the old town t'night!" commented Yancy.

Puerto Rico said, "Poontang time!"

"Hallelujah," said John Chin.

Pepe de Anda looked at Boland and said, "Now, maybe you an' Simms can stop sleepin' t'gether."

The trio — Roosevelt, Menyard and Andrews — looked at Boland, hugged each other, gagged and began to rhyme.

"Sleepin'? Sleepin'? Sleepin'???
— You been sleepin' in y'cot
with'a boy that's not
as firm an' sweet — as a she?
— Better let it get aroun'
that'cha goin' into town
Y'gonna change yo' ways
      — maybe???"

McClellan was about to call for silence when the captain got his attention.

"Tell them about the other matter, Sergeant."

"I think that should wait until they return from pass, Sir. It'll be less trouble."

Farrell was firm. "The other matter, Sergeant."

McClellan, though hesitant, called for silence, then spoke. "As I said, there will be passes for half of the company, to include those of you who wish to attend Seventh-day Adventist services, since today is Saturday. For those of you remaining on post, there will be a picture show. Now, for you men going on pass — and I will make that determination as you line up — you will remember what you were taught about hygiene, and about venereal diseases. You will not bring a venereal or any other kind of disease back to garrison. Is that understood?"

"Yes, Sergeant."

"I can't hear you!"

"Yes! Sergeant!"

He waited until they had completely settled and said, "Now, I want you to remember what you were told before you left Columbus. Despite what you are reduced to doing, I will brook no bad reports. In San Felipe, you will find a number of MP's on duty. They will be augmented by members of I and L. Obey them; treat them with respect. At all times you will conduct yourselves as King Company soldiers. As King Company soldiers of the Third Battalion, 24th U. S. Colored Infantry Regiment, willing to lay down your lives for the cause of freedom, you will obey all Jim Crow laws. You are not to go into any establishment where there are signs reading 'for whites only' — although I have always found it difficult to understand how you are to obey something you cannot read. But, as that is the white man's way of doing things, it is useless to argue. I've been told — never argue with a fool, people might not know who's who."

The first sergeant was about to discharge them when the captain again got his attention.

"The other matter, Sergeant," Capt. Farrell repeated, wanting to show who was really in command.

"Other news that might interest you — and, same as with the passes, lineup will be in front of the Orderly Room tent for your signatures — for the few of you who can write. For the others, you will write your normal x's." As the first sergeant held for a moment, someone in the formation broke silence. Others followed.

"Can't we just get our passes?"

"At ease in ranks!" the First commanded. "Make another remark in my formation, and I'll keep your behinds on post 'til Christmas! An' I don't give a damn *who says otherwise!*"

No comment came from the captain, who knew the strength of the remark had been directed at him.

The formation was silent. "Now, as I said, lineup will be in front of the Orderly Room. Your delayed pay arrived late last night."

Jubilation ruled the ranks. Interestingly, the First didn't even try to stop it.

McClellan had been a bit harsh, but he still wasn't the same old leader. For the first time, he failed to dismiss the company. Instead, he walked away without even a takeover order or nod to Dukes. Something was missing, and Sgt. Dukes knew it.

Taking it upon himself to dismiss the company, Dukes started to go to the First's tent to talk to him. After a few steps, he changed direction and headed for the Orderly Room. Sending Jody home was back on his mind. With the pay having arrived, he was now able to buy the boy a ticket. Like McClellan, because of rank and time in service, the veteran sergeant would be receiving well over a hundred dollars — enough to give the boy a little something so that he could enjoy himself with the boys before leaving, and enough, too, to help his mother when he returned home. Dukes knew he could count on McClellan's assistance with the first part of his plan. The other part, dealing with the boy's departure, he wouldn't dare mention. It was going to create a terribly serious problem with the First — and the captain, but Dukes decided he wouldn't worry about it until the boy was gone.

Noon blistered the camp. After standing in the long line in front of the Orderly Room x'ing and signing for the two months' back pay which amounted to 42 dollars in most cases, the men were still jubilant.

Later, the beaming hot sun found more than half the men speedwalking and dancing out the back gate, around the fencing, and down the long, dusty road to the San Felipe district. The road separated weeded fields that were occasionally dotted with a few houses along with one or two roadside stores that displayed fresh "Whites Only" signs. None of the blacks on pass had been to the district, before, but they followed along as if they were trailing a homing device.

With dollars held high, the rhyming trio of Roosevelt, Menyard and Andrews set the tone.

"Money? Money?? Money???
There's nuttin' like money
on a good Sat-ur-daaayyy;
An' since we soldiers in the Army,
We'll go in any ol' plaaaze."

The mercury pushed higher and the humidity soared in the city that was home to 30,000 blacks, though fewer than a quarter of them were in the San Felipe district. To be accurate, the district was the Fourth Ward, but by tradition it was called San Felipe. Whatever it was called, the road was packed and the troops could easily see that it was the place to be. The Fourth Ward — or the San Felipe district — was ripe for fun and rowdiness. Even the trio, having rapidly tested their theory of going into any ol' plaze, was back to cheerful clowning. En route to the district, they had merrily entered two white-owned establishments; they had been promptly bounced from two white-owned establishments. One never would have known it, though. They danced and clowned all the way to town.

The trio, indeed all the men, had good reason to be bright and spirited when they arrived. A panorama of excitement flooded the area, the core of which covered about 4½ blocks. More than half the members of all three companies of the black battalion were on pass, and they converged on the district as if they were a plague of locusts. Soldiers were everywhere. Greeting them were trolley cars, ox-carts, and horse-drawn wagons loaded with men, women, and children who had come to Houston from as far away as Tyler and

Waco, and points in between. They all were there to gape, ogle, and mingle with the oddity of their kind in the uniform of soldiers in the Army of the United States.

It was a great day. A normal, lazy, heat-ridden Saturday afternoon had turned into an unofficial holiday. It was throbbing. Bright and festive. The lone icehouse was busy, supplying the picnics that sprang up everywhere. At the south end, children happily played in the little patch of greenery that passed for a park.

Even the heart of Houston's white section, distant and normally oblivious to the goings-on of blacks, felt something. It was all positive. The fear that had lain quietly underneath had been pushed further back by news that there had been no serious trouble on post since the arrival of the blacks. Through some of the white soldiers, to include family and friends, the whites learned that the blacks had earned the right to taste freedom on the other side of the Camp Logan gates. They would be in the city for the first time, but they were not expected to invade the whole of Houston. They were expected to remain in the Fourth Ward's San Felipe.

All the news was good.

The sun was overly generous. It powered from an unclouded sky and bathed the dusty section in an ethereal hue that lent added significance to the normally dull and lackluster-brown uniforms. Wilson Street, intersected by Main, was the hub of the action. Looking north, it curved a bit, but not before showing off a dozen one- and two-story houses and storefronts that flanked the road.

Busiest of all was Verl's, the saloon diagonally across from Nell's house. To greet the troops, it had been open since early morning. By midafternoon, as someone aptly noted, *"the joint was jumpin'."* Outside, the morning drunks who had beaten the sun and the clock weaved in front of the one-story, glass-front building, hoisted more bottles, crooned out-of-tune melodies, and added to the merriment. Even the alley and the stable next to the saloon became arenas of lusty action.

The narrow, drab tavern, poor by any standard, was jammed to all four corners with energetic revelers. The entire place was thick with the odors of legal and bathtub whiskey, new perspiration, old sweat, cheap perfume and clouds of smoke. Flab, rolling and jolly, bounced from a derby-wearing gent who pounded the thumbtacked piano from a tiny stool that bent and moaned for help.

The syncopated rhythms of Joplin, Sissle and Nickerson were the favorites, as everyone tried to outsing the others. The songs were played over and over. The lyrics, if any, were of no importance to the singers except when they all jumped and joined in with the spirited minstrel *Jump, Jim Crow, Jump.* It was their way of parodying the white man.

After the parody the revelers would segue into the more refined *The Darktown Strutter's Ball,* and then bring it back up with Eubie Blake's *There'll Be A Hot Time In The Old Town Tonight.*

Women, young and old, were everywhere. Hands, frisky and determined, were everywhere. Hands that hadn't touched female softness in what seemed like ages went on patrol and didn't stop until they hit the sunlight of happiness. Propositions were made; propositions were accepted. Some couldn't wait. The money flowed. The tight alley on the west side between the saloon and the stable became a virtual bedroom. Not a position was spared.

After the brief talk he had with McClellan concerning the favor for Jody — that of seeing that he, too, was paid, Sgt. Dukes reached town early, went to the train station and quietly made arrangement for the youngster to leave on Monday — though something did tell the old field sergeant it would be best to collar the boy and send him on his way now. But a day or two longer with the boys couldn't hurt, concluded Dukes. In fact he might even learn something, and it would give him a chance to talk to the boy about the possibilities of going to school when he returned home. He thought that with the proper schooling, the youngster could grow up to be as smart as McClellan.

Feeling particularly good over the thought, and because the boy could actually get to Chugwater without any problem, Dukes paid for the ticket, and not wanting to lose it, left it at the depot for the Monday morning pickup. He returned to the center of the district and joined the NCO's Odums and Williams of Companies I and L in the saloon.

The three noncoms had gotten off to a good start. Armed with the third or fourth round of drinks that came in half-pint bottles and peach jars, they were elbowing their way back from the bar to reclaim their seats in the corner. They had engaged in friendly, boastful chatter since leaving camp, and neither Odums nor Williams wanted to let the King Company field sergeant off the hook. At the table, and talking over the noise and around a leggy woman who was drinking heavily and wore a short, dark-green silk dress that rose higher with every sip, the L Company NCO again chided Dukes about King Company's fall from soldiering grace. He sat the woman on his knee and said, "Bye-bye, King Company."

"We'll be back," roared Dukes. He hoisted his drink and took a futile shot at the woman. "An' I'm gonna say it again and again, we'll be back.'"

Odums's big voice boomed through the noise. "The hell you will."

"Tell you what," Dukes yelled back. He dug for his watch. "This here pocket watch is the most valuables' thing I ever owned. My daddy gave me this watch before I left home over thirty-five years ago. Now, I'll bet either one of you this watch, we'll be back. An' we'll be back, stronger'n ever. King Company can still — an' *will* — outsoldier any unit in the history of the world."

"You can't prove it by cleanin' them white boys' crap-houses an' slop-buckets," Sgt. Williams said. He again prepared to match Dukes drink for drink. "An' keep the watch. Maybe you'll learn how to tell time with it one day."

"When he do," Odums said, laughing, "it'll be too late."

"Is that all y'all doin' here?" the woman asked. "Cleanin' for the white boys?" Though sitting on Williams's knee, she was crinkling her nose at Odums.

"That's what they doin'," Honeychile. Cleanin' crap-houses an' slop-buckets," chortled the sergeant from L Company. "King Company — the King o' the slops."

"An' cleanin' slop-buckets ain't all they doin'," Odums added with a laugh. "Washin' windows, cleanin' stables, an' all. Is y'all soldiers or wimmins, Dukes?"

"Wimmins," Williams ventured. "Like my lil' sweetie here."

Her dress riding higher, the woman went for the bottle. "I don't do no cleanin'."

"With these big ol' hairy legs, you won't have to — not long's I'm aroun'," said Williams, giving one of the exposed thighs a pinch and an inviting pat.

"Or me, either," said Dukes.

"Don't listen to him, Baby Girl. He's too old, an' he ain't gonna have no time. Stay away from anybody in King Company, they ain't soldiers. They doin' old maids' work."

"The hell we is."

"You ain't doin' no soldierin'," responded Williams. "You doin' wimmins' work."

"Y'all ain't allowed to do no soldierin'," said Odums.

"Y'all ain't doin' much better," answered Dukes to both of them.

"All y'all doin' is guardin'."

"Yeah, but that's what we came here for. Least we ain't nurse-maidin' white boys."

"An' go fight your way over to that window up front an' take look outside," said Sgt. Odums. "You'll see we even got some of our boys out there servin' as MP's — just to keep an eye on y'all."

"Yeah," said Williams laughing, "the colonel wanna make sure y'all come back. We need some cookin' an' cleanin' done."

"An' I might want my boots shined," Odums said, joining the laughter. "Ooops, I forgot. They got a bootblack shop at camp."

"An' guess who they got shinin' boots in there now?"

The two NCO's said in deriding unison: "*KING COMPANY!*"

"Y'all keep it up," said Dukes. "You'll find out who ends up on top."

"Sho' ain't gonna be y'all."

"Like I said, we'll be back. An' we'll be back stronger'n ever."

"Not as long as Briggs is battalion commander, you won't," said Williams.

"Who's Briggs? Is he with Quackenbush?" asked the near-drunk woman, now straddling Williams's knee but brushing a leg against Odums. One of the largest and blackest men in the battalion, Odums had a voice that was thick and hands like anvils.

"Who's Quackenbush?" Williams asked, trying to reclaim the woman's look.

"The poe'lice."

"Honeychile, if it was the police, they wouldn't mind. But Briggs is our battalion commander, and they scared as all hell of him."

"You better be scared of Quackenbush," hiccuped the woman. "He don't like no colored folks."

"Neither do Briggs," said Odums.

"But Quackenbush'll do somethin' about it," responded the woman.

"What can he do?"

"He'll beat the livin' daylights outta you with them cycle chains, that's what. Cross him one time an' y'all will see what I mean. He don't care nothin' 'bout y'all bein' no soldiers."

"Darlin'," said Dukes, "I'm from King Company. We ain't scared of nobody. We ain't scared of Briggs or this Quackenbush. An' he better not put his hands on this uniform. Now, let's talk about somethin' sweet."

"Did'ja say sweet or *weak*, Dukes?" Williams asked.

"I said *sweet*," Dukes said, leaning over to touch the woman. "Like this lil' thang here."

"I thought you said *weak*," returned Odums. "Like your C.O."

"No, I said *sweet*," Dukes said, withdrawing. "An' my C.O. ain't weak."

"Captain Farrell *is* weak, an' he jus' might be a lil' sweet, too."

"Watch what you sayin', Odums," Williams cautioned. "You implyin' somethin'. An' you implyin' it about an officer."

"You better watch it. An' for your information Farrell is all man," Dukes said. "But I'll tell you this: as far as I'm concerned he can be anything he wants to be as long as he ain't as narrow-minded as that peckerwood of yours, Odums."

The woman, still brushing a leg against Odums, didn't like being ignored. "Listen, if all y'all gonna do is stay here an' talk about the Army, I'm goin' to talk to somebody who 'preaciates me."

Williams released his hold on her waist and patted the woman on her behind. "What's your name, Suga-pie?"

"Josephine."

"Bye, Josephine."

"You gon' let me go just like that?"

"Honeychile, let me tell you somethin'," Dukes answered. "When we talkin' serious 'bout the Army, we don't talk about it in front of no civilians."

The woman took Williams's drink and left.

They watched her get lost in the crowd. Odums got up, nudged his way back to the bar, and reordered. Returning to the table with three half pints, he said, "I didn't want to say this in front of that hen, 'cause to let our coloreds know we got troubles with our officers ain't good."

"Ain't good for nonna us," agreed Dukes.

"But," Odums continued, "like I was sayin'," Captain Whitney ain't no peckerwood. He just don't like colored folks."

"Then he's a peckerwood," Williams said.

"If that makes him a peckerwood," said Odums, "then every officer in the Army is a peckerwood."

"All of 'em ain't bad," Sgt. Dukes said.

"Show me one that ain't," said Williams.

"Captain Farrell," Dukes said, again defending his commander.

"He's a good man."

"Your C.O. is like all the rest," Williams said.

Dukes came back, "No, he ain't."

"The hell he ain't," Odums said, sounding like Williams. "He white, ain't he?"

"Of course, he's white. That's why he's an officer."

"Then if he's an officer, an' he's in the Army, then he's a peckerwood. He's a redneck, nigger-hatin' peckerwood. An' I don't care how you slice it," Williams said. "That's the only kind they put in charge of us."

"Williams, you don't have the slightes' damn idea what you're talkin' about," Sgt. Dukes said.

"The hell, I don't. The only kind of officer the Army puts in charge of coloreds is a nigger-hatin' redneck. All of 'em ain't nothin' but a bunch'a peckerwoods."

"An' if they was any good a'tall, they'd be commandin' white boys," Odums's big voice added.

"Sho' would," Williams agreed. "It's for sure they wouldn't be commandin' no coloreds."

"Both of y'all talkin' like jackasses," Dukes said.

"I am?" Williams retorted. "You been in the Army over thirty years. Show me — or *name* me — *one* officer who didn't treat you like you was a monkey tied on the end of a organ grinder's string. Thirty-some years in the Army, Dukes —"

"Goin on thirty-six," corrected Dukes.

"Alright, almos' thirty-six years," Williams reinforced. "You done seen everything. You was learnin' the Field Manual when most of these peckerwoods was still in diapers. You know how to train, march, count cadence, conduct drills, teach skirmishin', an' all'a that other stuff, an' I betcha every nickel you done ever earned that not one — not a *single* one — of them white, nasty-faced sonsabitches ever give you the respect you due. I betcha not a single one of 'em ever come to you an' said, 'Sergeant Dukes, what's the best way of doin' this? How do we go about doin' that?' An' not a one ever said to you, 'You're a smart man, Sergeant, you got expe- rience, I wanna take a'vantage of that experience. Let me ask you this — let me pick your brain on somethin'.' I bet'cha in all'a your years in service that ain't never happened to you. An' you wanna know why it ain't happened? Cause the white man don't think you got no brain. In his eyes you ain't nothin'."

"He ain't s'pose to come to me for nuthin'," Sgt. Dukes responded. "I'm supposed to go to him. That's why he's an officer."

"He's an officer 'cause he white," Odums said. "Ain't no other reason."

"An' a man is s'posed to go anywheres he can go to get some learnin'," Williams added. "Officer or no officer."

"It'll be a sad day in the Army when the officer is got to go to the noncom to find out what he's s'posed to do," Dukes said, hoping the conversation would end.

"I ain't sayin' he's got to come to us," continued Williams. "I'm sayin' all he's got to do is look at us like we got some sense. Like we know what we doin'. I'm sayin' take a'vantage of what we know."

"Williams, that is got to be one of the most stupidest things I ever heard of," said Dukes. "You sayin' you want the white man to come to you so's he can take advantage of what you know?"

"You damn'd right. That's exactly what I'm sayin'. Treat me like I know somethin'. Don't treat me like I'm a damn stone."

"Both of y'all sound just like my Corporal Poole. Now, lemme tell you what's so stupid about what you sayin'," Sgt. Dukes said testily. "That's what's wrong with the colored man now, sittin' there waitin' for the white man to take a'vantage of 'im. If the white man wanna think we're a stone, let 'im. If he wanna think that we don't know a damn'd thing, then let him. We don't have to prove nothin' to him. He's a man just like me. His callin' ain't no higher'n mine."

"If the white man's callin' ain't no higher," countered Sgt. Williams, "then why's he over you?"

"Whoa, now, that's where you wrong," said Sgt. Odums, suddenly switching sides, his big voice rumbling. "The white man ain't over me. He thinks he over me."

"Think, my ass," countered Williams. "He is over you. An' he's gonna always *be* over you. He's always gonna get r'spect, an' you always ain't. Why? Because he's over you."

"Like hell he is," Odums said.

"Well, then, lemme put it this way," Williams argued. "If you walk into a bank an' the white man walks into a bank or any other important place, which one of you gennemens is the man behind the counter or runnin' the place is gonna call '*Sir*'?"

"The white man," said the big black man from I Company as he prepared to take another drink.

"That's my point."

"But it ain't mine," Odums responded before he could get the drink completely down. "Now, before I got in the Army, I was a prizefighter —"

"I know that," Williams said, sleeving his lips. "But that ain't got nothin' to do 'bout what we talkin' about."

"Oh, yes, 'tis. S'got plenty to do with it," Odums responded. "Just listen to me for a minnit. Now, the ring was my territory. Know what I'm sayin'? The ring was *my* territory —"

"Who'd you fight, Odums?" Sgt. Dukes interrupted.

"I fought Jack Johnson before he became champ."

"You lie," Williams said. "I knowed you was a fighter. You done told me a hunnert times, but you ain't fought no Jack Johnson."

"I ain't lyin'. I fought 'im in oh four. Thirteen years ago, two years 'fo I got in the Army."

"An' he became champ when?" Williams asked.

"Oh eight. He beat Tommy Burns in Australia."

"He wudda been too old then," said Williams.

"No, he wont. He was thirty-nine," said the big I Company sergeant. "An' he'd still be champ if he hadn't made a fool of the white man and married them three white women."

"That sho' was a mistake," commented Dukes. He tapped out the remaining light on the tip his cigar. "Marryin' *one* white woman could'a got 'im killed."

"It almost did. An' he almost got killed in the ring. The wimmins sapped his strength. He ain' had no business losin' to Willard," the I Company sergeant said. "But, like I started to say, in the ring is where I functions best. Now, Williams, if you take that same bankerman you was talkin' about, put me an' that same som'bit in the same ring, an' I whup his ass, who's gonna be the *Sir*?"

"You."

"Damn right, I will," Sgt. Odums said, rearing back contentedly.

"For the moment," Williams added with delay.

"Oh, I'll agree it'll only be for a moment," Odums said.

"Why only for the moment?" Sgt. Dukes asked. "If you done beat 'im, that's it."

"I can tell you what he's drivin' at," Williams said.

"No, lemme tell 'im," Odums said, "I got the experience. It done happened to me. Now, r'member I done fought an' beat a whole slew of the sonsabitches to git to be where I was. The white man you done beat in the ring can call you *Sir, Champ* — or any damn'd thing you want him to call you. He'll do that while you lookin' at 'im. But the minute you turn your back on him — or any one — an' I mean *any one* of them suckers, you know what you gonna be? Another nigger. An' if you was champ? Just'a nother nigger that got lucky. An' if you think you done truly beat that sorry sumbitch at any time, you a fool for life. An' I ain't just talkin' 'bout in no ring. Here, there, everywhere, the white man is the most snakiest sunovabitch the Lord ever put on this earth. An' his woman ain't no better. The only thing worse than both of'em is they corny-ass jokes about colored folks."

"Oh, now," sang Williams, who had an undying affinity for something he'd never had. "I ain't so sure 'bout that."

"The white woman is just as bad as the white man."

"No, she ain't."

"The hell she ain't. He got y'all thinkin' that pasty-faced thing'a his is the most precious thing that ever walked the earth, an she's just as bad as he is. An' she hates you just as much. An' you better b'leev it."

The big first sergeant soaked for a while, caught his breath, and recharged. "Don't none of 'em like you, me, your daddy, your momma, or your daddy's momma's momma. An' it ain't gonna change. An' another reason I don't like 'em. There ain't a white man alive who's taken twenty seconds out'a his life to know a dam'd thing about you, but when it comes to talkin' about you or talkin' about what you want, where you from, where you goin', or what you're thinkin', don't you say nothin', not a damn' word, 'cause he ain't gonna hear it. He's gotta do the talkin', 'cause he knows everythin' about everythin' there is to know. An' above all, he's a expert in niggerology. An' the worst of all'a them sonsabitches is in this goddam'd Army. I hate every one'a them skunks."

The dialogue died for a moment. When Dukes was asked for his comment, he said nothing. He didn't agree, but he no longer wanted to be a part of the conversation. He was disturbed because he had known both Odums and Williams for quite a while, and he never realized they had so much hostility in them. Often when they had gotten together in the past, Odums would lead Williams in talking about how great everything was, and how fortunate they were to be in the Army. The subject of race and the white man rarely came up — if ever.

The old King Company field sergeant removed from his shirt pocket the nub of a cigar that he had tapped out, and started to relight it. Instead, he tucked it back into his pocket and sent his disappointed eyes scanning the room. The drinks were flowing; the blacks were happy, but Dukes didn't hear them or see them. He was too upset. His mind wandered back to First Sgt. McClellan. Not that McClellan would ever have been in that position, he was too smart, much too smart to even be in the company of these two — or anybody like these two — nor, for that matter, would he even be in the saloon since he was never known to take a drink, but he wondered if the First had been there, what would he have said to the pair. That had the old field sergeant thinking about Jody. He hoped the boy would never hear such things. More than likely he wouldn't. Come Monday at 0700, he would be on his way back to the clean environs of Wyoming.

With the conversation on hold, another woman wandered over to the table. She was quickly followed by the woman in the dark-green dress. They didn't like each other. It was quite alright with Sgt. Williams, because the other woman was younger and appeared to be cheaper. She was also a lot quicker. Her wee-size breasts jiggling for freedom in a low-cut dress, she bent over and huskily whispered something into William's ear. He grinned, dug into his pocket, and squeezed three quarters into her hand. Together they romanced out to the alleyway, leaving the woman in the dark-green dress with Odums and Dukes. She was interested, but Dukes was not. He was too old to handle a woman.

And now even the fun of pretense was gone.

Pouring in from the rear of the saloon were whoops, hoots, and hollers. Every sound imaginable exploded from three crap games taking place outside. The main game, closest to the saloon's back door, was surrounded by a thick crowd of eager-eyed participants who held dollars high and shouted out numbers while pushing and shoving with every roll. Never was a crowd more boisterous and raucous. Gleefully mixed in with the soldiers were any number of civilians who, like the soldiers, held dollars high and acted as though they had been given instructions to invest in the future. There hadn't been a good game of crap-shooting in the San Felipe district in years, and the local hustlers weren't about to let the moment with fresh-paid soldiers pass by.

It was no match, but the last reasonably good game that had taken place in back of the saloon was some years ago when the Daughters of the Mission held a raffle to build a new church. One of the church elders got hold of the funds and started a new game. Word went out, and the locals came by the wagonload.

There was no happy ending. The police won. The church was never built.

But bygones were bygones, and on this Saturday it seemed that every man who had even thought about gambling came to the game. It looked as if they all had searched every nook and cranny, raided every tin can, dug under every mattress, plowed up every jar, cracked open every piggybank, and rolled back every mat to find every dollar they could. It was all in the name of gambling, and the participants couldn't have been happier. The money, crumpled, stretched and rolled, flowed to what was euphemistically called the *pot*. Actually it was a spot on the left side of the brick wall, and from the gnarled hands of workers to the slick hands of the hustlers, the money came. Since it was the main game it was played on a blanket, and it was a crapshooter's paradise. With every roll of the dice, the dark, steady hands of the kneeling *houseman* scooped and raked the money into a high mound just off from the center, then quickly fingered the dice back to the shooter, who would blow on them as though they were piping hot coals. Sometimes holding them as though they were too hot to handle, and at other times holding them up to an ear as if they either clicked out a sweet melody or were letting the holder in on a secret, the shooter would either grin or fix his face in determination and get set to underhand the dice to the wall. Coming out for the point, there would be yelling; crapping out, there would be yelling; making the point, there would be thunder. Happy hands swooped down from every angle.

Standing outside the larger circle and soaking in the fun-filled commotion was Jody. Lost and bewildered, he was grinning from ear to ear. He was at the soul of the action. The nice little underage draftee from Chugwater, Wyoming would like to have seen what was going on, but he couldn't. The circle was too thick with bodies. Yet he couldn't stop standing there and being bumped to and fro, his mouth open in glee. But his hands were jammed firmly in his pocket, protecting the money Sgt. Dukes said he had earned.

Boyish Jody Cunningham had never seen such excitement. Except for when the battalion had assembled at the depot, he had never seen so many people. In fact, Jody Cunningham had never seen so many black people in his life. Not that he had ever thought about it, but he never knew there were so many black people in the world. He had never seen his father, so his mother and aunt were the only people of true color he had ever seen. There were several Indians in and around Chugwater, but they were quiet and there wasn't the mixture of color as they generally remained with their own.

Sometimes, though, the Indians would come by the farm for a friendly chat, and when his mother fell ill and was no longer able to work, a lot of them came with porridge and offers of help. Several even offered him and his mother a place to stay.

The Chugwater Indians were like a lot of Indians when it came to dealing with black Americans. At times there was a great deal of suspicion, with some even regarding the *buffalo hair*, as they called them, a natural enemy in the early years. Some even held blacks as slaves. Such occurrences were few and far between, and in the country as a whole, most Indians and blacks melded together and any number of marital unions emerged. A number of people in Chugwater thought Jody Cunningham had Indian blood in him, but it wasn't true. He had the best of Indian features, but he neither looked Indian nor was he ever in the company of Indians, except for the times when they happened to drop by.

It was easy to understand the Indian connection, however. Jody's mother, a beautiful but sickly, coal-black woman with soft, pliant skin that yielded quiet eyes, eyes made all the more mysterious by thick, silky hair that, when untied, flowed down past her waist, could have had a bit of Indian blood in her. If so, no one in Chugwater would have known. Cunningham was the maiden name, and some thought it was Irish. Maybe so, but it was taken from an Indian.

The mother never talked about her parents, nor would she ever talk about young Jody's father. A few thought the father of the boy could have been her employer, Mr. Buttercup, but that was highly doubtful. As best anyone knew, Jody's mother had never met the man before going to work for him. Besides, Mr. Buttercup was not the sort to liaison with a woman to whom he had not been properly wedded. Yet, the old Dutchman's concern for morality and women went only so far. Three women worked on his ranch, and none of them were paid. As far as the old miser was concerned, room and board was sufficient. It was a take-it-or-leave-it offer.

Jody's mother had to take it. Before Mr. Buttercup, she was homeless. She became that way shortly after Jody was born. At the time, the pretty young mother had lived with her stepparents in the town that neighbored Chugwater, and they were not at all pleased with the birth of the boy. Feeling that they would forever be disgraced, once the infant was out of danger the stepparents severed all ties by pinning a note on her bedroom door, giving her one day to leave the house. Chugwater became the obvious place to settle, but the trouble was that the young mother had nothing to settle with. She was penniless in a backward little burg that offered nothing but wide skies and spacious lands. And it was a place where people were not bound in closeness. The people were not hostile to the young woman of a different color, but no one came to her immediate aid. She was not totally ignored, and from a few she received handouts. In the main, though, with the baby strapped to her back, papoose-like, she found herself roaming the back streets and roads, pilfering and scratching for whatever sustenance she could find. The condition would remain until she was discovered sleeping in the back of Trinity Church one evening. By morning the pastor of the church had gotten in touch with Mr. Buttercup, who agreed to take in both mother and boy for a six-month stay. The stay stretched into years. They slept on the floor, but at least they had a home.

Because of the excitement, Jody would like to have stayed at the game, but he couldn't. He was supposed to have been at Nell's. Before leaving camp, he had gone around to where Pete was supposed to be carrying out the disciplinary digging to tell him the good news. And good news it was. Not only was the raw recruit going on pass with the rest of the company, but he had actually x'd a piece of paper and gotten money for doing it. He hadn't received as much as the others since he had only been in the Army for less than a month, but they were still nice enough to pay him. Combined with the unknown generosity of Sgt. McClellan and Sgt. Dukes, he managed to amass 13 dollars — which was only five dollars less than a first-period private earned. It was more money than he had ever seen.

The news was so good, Pete almost fainted.

"Say it again," he said.

"We goin' on pass."

Pete cupped his hand to an ear. "Say it — sloooooly."

"We goin' on pass."

"One mo' time."

"We. Is. Goin'. On. Pass."

"Loveszit," Pete said melodiously. He then jumped up and screamed. "*Iloveszzzit!* So that's what all'a that yellin' an' screamin' was all about. An' the money? Did I hear you say our mun-mun's done come in?"

"Umhum. I got thirteen dollars," Jody dug into his pocket and showed his friend a corner of the money. "I even signed for it."

"You done just got in the Army — an' ain't hardly a first-period private or 6th Grade Specialists — an' they done gave you *thirteen* dollars?"

"Umhuh," Jody said, not realizing what either term meant, or that the First and Sgt. Dukes had been responsible for his bounty. Dukes had him put his mark on the payroll sheet only to make him feel important.

Pete's patriotism took over. "I loves this country."

"I do, too," Jody said, getting ready to leave. "Want me to see you when I come back?"

"Oh, no. But here's wha'cha gotta do first. You r'member the love of my life I met at the train station?"

"Umhum. Her name is Nell."

"How you know what her name is?"

"You talk about her in your sleep, the few times you make it back in time to go to sleep."

"True love is like that, M'boy. Now, I want you to go aroun' to her house, which is right across the street from a saloon called Verl's. Got that?"

"Yep."

"The house is got a lot of purple on it. You can't miss it. Tell Nell that I done been helt up for a few minutes, but I'll be by."

"How you gonna do that, Pete? The sarge said you gotta dig a hole two times bigger'n the one we was s'pose to dig back in Columbus. An' he said you had to dig it with a spoon. An' looks like you ain't been doin' nothin' but sleepin' back here."

"I've been med'tatin'."

"But you ain't been diggin'."

"A good med'tator ain't s'posed to be diggin'. He's s'pose to be thinkin'. An' that, my good man, is why I'm gonna be meetin' up with you later."

"How you gonna do that?"

"Unbeknownst to the sarge, I'm gonna be extendin' my disciplinary area to the fair territory of San Felipe. I shalst conclude my thinkin' there."

"Great, Pete!"

"A masterful stroke, if I must say so m'self."

"Want me to go an' tell the sarge?"

"Er, no. He an' me will be confabin' about it a lil' later, that is, after I chat with the colonel. You just go an' tell Nell what I said. If you play your cards right, I might line up a lil' nooky for you."

"Nooky?"

"You don't know what that is?"

It was obvious the boy didn't have the slightest clue.

"Oooooh, my gooood-neezzz," said Pete. "A real, live *cherry*. An'

I'm sendin' you to a sin den."

With its purple-green trim running through the porch's banister and landing harshly on the painted cane furniture that matched purple curtains and everything else, Nell's house by daylight was even more gaudy, and no one with a semblance of taste could have thought otherwise. But Jody did. He thought the big New Orleans-inspired mass of planks, with its pointed gables and multiple projecting bays, was the prettiest thing he had ever seen. He stood on the porch a full five minutes admiring and touching the wonder of it all. He thought about his mother and hoped that one day she, too, would enjoy something so lavish and pretty. A few more paydays, and maybe she would.

Jody would have stayed on the porch longer had Nell not come out.

At first Nell thought the youngster with the high-riding eyebrows was a delivery boy, but her sense of business crept in. The customers are getting younger, she thought.

"Ummmm," she said, sizing him up. "You're kinda cute. Young, but still sorta cute. An' not a bad lookin' lil' outfit you done made for yourself. Gonna be a soldier when you grows up?"

His uniform fitting only because of the generous use of safety pins, Jody said, proudly, "I'm a soldier already."

"You in the Army?"

"Yes, Ma'am."

"Lord a'mercy. Which one?"

"Sergeant McClellan's."

"Whoever he is. An' what'chu here for?"

"You."

"Think again, Honey."

"Ain't you the one Pete like?"

"How you know Pete?"

"He's my buddy. We in the same platoon."

"So, that really ain't no made up outfit you wearin'? You really in the Army?"

"Yes, Ma'am."

"I thought the Army was doin' bad enough when they let him in, but you — " Nell laughed. "How old you have to be to be in the Army?"

"I dunno."

"An' where's Pete?"

"Still at camp."

"When's he comin'?"

"He told me to tell you he'll be comin' by soon."

"Why's it takin' him longer than anybody else? Seem's like every one of y'all in uniform is in town. But not him."

Jody attempted to make his friend look good. "He's doin' somethin' for the battalion commander, Colonel Briggs."

"It's just like that lil' sweet-thing, workin' for the higher-ups. Well, come on in. Might as well get you started."

Jody didn't know what she meant by getting him started. He was all the more baffled when she took him into the living room and plopped him down on the overstuffed purple sofa amid three scantily clad young women.

"Treat 'im good. An' I means *real* good," Nell said. She collected the six other girls and pointed them upstairs. Leaving, she said, "He's special. He's a friend of my honey-hun's." She closed the two living-room doors that separated the room from the corridor and staircase.

Fearing the police, Nell had set up a new rule. She saw to it that the soul of the action always took place upstairs, because she had been raided more times than she cared to remember. The last time, about a month before the arrival of the black troops, the police had been excessively brutal and reckless. They broke down doors, smashed windows, and sent two of her girls to the hospital. The next time, she vowed, she would go down fighting.

Over the years Nell had tried everything to keep the business going. Owning the only brothel in the area, she went from paying off Quackenbush to virtually servicing the entire department. Still the police came, and each time it became costlier. What it amounted to, she concluded, was that the police would never get enough — of her, her money, or her women. One day she decided that she would stop giving. Not a smart move, she was told. With the warning, she knew the police would try every trick in the book. To counter them, she didn't like what she had to do, not that it would hurt business that much, but no longer would she allow her girls to entertain any white man out of military uniform. She had Clara, the one white girl working for her, but that would be alright. White men never came to see her, anyway. Clara was the busiest of all the girls, but not because of white men. The whites didn't want her, and she didn't want them. She was the busiest because of the local blacks. Because of threats, she had grown afraid of the whites, and despite the separate entrance reserved for them, whenever one came in, she would remain out of sight.

In the past weeks Nell had gotten so cautious that she would not even allow money to exchange hands downstairs. When the customers came in, they would be allowed a quick peek into the living room to see the variety, and then she would guide them all to the big staircase just off to the right of the living room.

With Jody she was a lot different. Not that she would have charged Pete's friend anything, but he was allowed to be alone with the girls in the living room. That was an honor. Only Nell and Pete were allowed to dally there. Different or not, though, even before Nell had closed the door the upstairs bumping, grinding, and groaning had the lad sitting there looking as though he had been frozen by a new ice age. He was scared to death.

Young Jody Cunningham had never been close to a woman; he had never laid eyes on the curvaceousness that lay beneath the frocks, ruffles and petticoats that most times dragged the ground, acting as though their sole purpose was to cover the better mysteries of life. The youngster had never given thought to a kiss, intimacy, a sexual relationship, or even artificial gratification. He had never heard of prostitution or a house of prostitution. Following the natural order of growing, of course, his tubes had bounced and pulsated at some unknown thoughts that swept the mind and stirred the lower part of the body, but, again, that was a passable unknown. It was one of those indefinable nudges that was attributable to nothing and couldn't be directed or pinpointed. That is, until now.

Saying nothing, one of the girls threw a well-defined leg across his. The young soldier instantly forgot about his mother, the beauty of the place, Pete, and everything else. He broke out into a cold sweat. His eyebrows rose higher, his hands became clammy, and all he could do was sit there, patting his feet and rubbing his hands on his knees. The second girl, as wordless as the first, dismissed the little clothing she had on and bounced a breast in his face. Jody froze. Draping an arm around his neck, the fetching young miss nudged his stiff head closer and slipped a wet tongue in his ear. Up and down went the feet, patting rapidly. Then he started shaking. He didn't know what was happening. The third girl cooed a bit and stared him directly in the eyes as she directed her fingers skillfully around his loin. Now Jody was patting his feet heel to toe. He was also sweating. This was no longer a nudge. This was all of creation knocking.

Taking her sweet time, the second girl unbuttoned the little soldier's trousers and began massaging his groin as the first girl slowly unbuttoned his shirt and mouthed his stomach. She lubricated the navel. Now Jody was patting his feet, shaking, panting, fighting the nudge, and feeling the urge. He started humming. With his eyebrows at maximum height, his eyes danced to the ceiling, and there they stayed. Twirling. But the body had no compliance. On a smooth move, the second girl sent her tongue working. The stiff body yielded a bit and was eventually coaxed to the supine position, where it lay as unbending as concrete. The female tongue darted again. With his breeches tucked into his leggings and boots, the boy soldier's feet started moving. Another dart, and the legs went straight up, the booted feet tickling the air with short rapid strokes. The eyes were no longer dancing. Like his eyebrows, they were stuck. Supple and sweet little bites on the nipples, and the feet started moving as if he were pedaling an upside-down bicycle. The girl nibbled a little more. Now, it seemed, the pedals of the bicycle were too slow. The eyes were again twirling. There was a marathon up ahead, and, and, if he could see, he had to catch it. He started running and humming on his own. The breeches came all the way down to the leggings. The third girl was working her magic. The boy's mind swirled, the eyes spun and surged forward. Girl two alternated with girl three. The boy's legs pumped faster and the body shook as though caught in a vortex. The eyes went blank and the boy-soldier felt the wonderment of the heavens on the move. The girls kept working — constant, true, physical. Vibrantly precious it was. And when all vibrancy and preciousness were ready, girl three stopped his airy run for the roses and climbed on top of him. She closed his stiff legs and parted hers. She made sure that there was penetration. There was. It was unctuous and good. She began to ride him like a pony.

The sensation, the passion, the awe — everything coming from all corners. Every muscle working, now; urgent, driving, uncontrollable. It was new, raw, right, belonging. Eyes blank. Eyes closed. Eyes gone. Body lifting. Head swimming. He, encapsulated in flashes, lightning, colors, rainbows; violet doilies rising; lavender appliqués weightless in air, the purple sofa suspended in air —swirling, he, on it — floating, soaring, gone; a star-crossed world dipped from its axis, ready to burst into a million pieces of kaleidoscopic wonder. Nudge gone, urge here; unbridled; demanding — driving, pushing, forcing. He wanted to jump up and reach out and grab and hold onto and cling to all the light that had ever existed in the universe, but in the heat of the fast-coming moment, all the boy-soldier was able to do was moan, "I gotta pee! I gotta peeee! I gotta peeeee!"

He detonated. He screamed.

"I'mmmmmmm P-p-p-eeeeeeennnn!!!"

Chapter 12

With most of the black battalion and practically all the whites on weekend pass, most of the activity at Camp Logan came to a halt. Stout, the post commander, lived on post with his wife and two daughters but was never expected to be around on Saturday afternoons. Lt. Col. Briggs had located an old Houston acquaintance he knew during his teaching days at the Point and was paying him and his wife a visit. The only official activity that had something of an unusual note was that the mail had caught up with the battalion. It was processed and dispatched to the various companies.

Simms, because Boland hadn't been selected, elected not to go on pass even though he had First Sgt. McClellan's permission to go. The part-time company clerk and guidon bearer was approaching the Orderly Room to catch up with some typing chores when the cyclist sped into the King company area and dropped the mail pouch at his feet. Before entering the Orderly Room, Simms checked to see if his mate, Boland, had received mail. There was a letter from his family, but there was none from the young lady he had spoken of. Her name was Colette. Simms was smiling when he went into the Orderly Room tent. Boland and Colette were going to marry once his tour of duty was over.

"Mail call, Sergeant," Simms said, handing the subdued First a letter from the pouch. When the sergeant looked at the envelope, his face registered a huge and delighted surprise at the return address. The letter was from Sgt. Jim Newton. He was in Europe. The sergeant decided he would wait and read the letter in his tent.

McClellan hadn't moved from the Orderly Room tent since overseeing the payroll and issuing the company passes. He sat in a distant quiet at the same table. He was sullen, thought the captain, who sat sluggishly at his desk at the rear of the tent. He had delayed going up to the Officers' Club at Battalion Headquarters because he wasn't certain as to the colonel's whereabouts.

Contrary to what the captain thought, McClellan's look was not sullen. He was phlegmatic, impassive. But it was easy to see why the captain would come to that conclusion.

Farrell had never informed his First of the impending demotion, but he assumed — correctly — that McClellan knew. The order was not a closely guarded secret. Even if it had been, it would not have worked. Simms, as the company clerk, had access to all company papers and was sure to tell him, which he eventually did. But Simms was also concerned enough to tell his First how the captain had been agonizing over writing the order.

McClellan, peculiarly, was almost matter-of-fact in his reaction. He had none of the gloom that had enveloped Simms, though he did show a great deal of concern over who was going to take over the company. It was only later that the concern had grown into worry.

A new First, McClellan believed, would probably have to come from another battalion or regiment, maybe even from as far away as the unappreciated 9th or 10th Cavalry. It was highly unlikely that Odums or Williams of I and L would be transferred to King. With his attitude toward the company, it was certain that Col. Briggs wouldn't allow promotion from within the ranks. Besides, Dukes was too old and would retire before accepting the duty. Poole was too irresponsible and hot-headed, and Mess Sgt. Willie Powell knew nothing of the field.

The captain was equally aware of the problems, which could have been one reason he was so reluctant to carry out that part of the battalion commander's orders. No matter what, though, Farrell knew that Briggs wasn't going to wait much longer for him to act. And so that Saturday afternoon he made up his mind to have the order for demotion on the battalion commander's desk Monday at 0700.

Sunday was to be the last day Obie O. McClellan would be first sergeant of King Company.

Chapter 13

"So, what do you think of Texas, Heinrich?"

Lt. Col. Briggs felt like guffawing at the question from the chatty wife of his old friend Del, with whom he had attended West Point.

"Do you want the truth?"

"Knowing you, maybe we don't," answered the woman.

Located just outside of the Houston city limits, the one-story beige house looked as though it were made of shutters and screens. The three friends were sitting in rocking chairs on the veranda, overlooking a plain, spacious view. Mixed drinks for the two men had been prepared and served by a butler. Priscilla Rideout, the wife, was sipping tea. Nearing 60, she had sparkling eyes and silver, wavy hair tied in a loose bun. Aging gracefully, she was a genteel woman with the kind of face that said she had been a stellar beauty in her earlier years.

"Priscilla, maybe you'd better ask me something a little less incriminating. Like when am I going to do as Del has done.

Retire."

"I'll do one better. What do you think of Logan?"

"Pardon my French, dear lady, but Logan is the worse goddamned post I've ever served on."

"I deplore course language, but I've heard the word before, Colonel," the lady said, sewing as she sipped her tea. "But I'm sure you've served at worse camps, Heinrich."

"I don't know where all you two have served. Remember we lost touch for about ten or fifteen years, but Logan takes the cake."

"Oh, Henrich, you must be joshing. The boys at camp are so sweet. I wish we'd had sons like that. Don't you, Del?"

"Next life, M'love," the retired colonel with the thinning hair said, finally joining the conversation. "Why are you so down on Logan, Heinrich?"

"Have you ever met that idiot in command?"

"Colonel Stout? Of course."

"We've had him here for dinner," his wife said. "Any number of times. He's a lovely man. Isn't he, Dear?"

"I find him quite honorable. I can't vouch for him as an officer," said the host, "which is what I gather you're talking about, Heinrich."

"As an officer — as a human being, I think he stinks," the Third Battalion commander said, fanning at the lazing heat that pushed through the screens. He raised his arm and motioned for the black servant to refill the 8-oz glass. "And go easy on the seltzer."

Before moving off, the butler refilled the woman's cup. She thanked him, snipped at a thread, and said to Briggs, "Heinrich, how can you say such things about a fellow officer?"

"Priscilla," Briggs said, comfortably going back to the early years, "I've known you and Del since we were young Turks at the Point —"

"You introduced us. And at the wedding, you were our best man."

"Best' is right. You were the prettiest, the loveliest thing around.

I should have kept you for myself," Briggs joked.

"How could you?" responded the host. "She preferred intelligence, remember?"

"Boys, boys, boys. Now, Heinrich, what's the problem between you and Colonel Stout?"

The retired colonel looked at his wife. "Priscilla, dear, I think that's a military matter. Perhaps you should leave us alone for a moment."

"I'll do no such thing. And you're no longer in the military, unfortunately. Now, I'd like to hear what the colonel has to say about the commander."

Briggs swatted at a fly that arrived with the butler, caught it, and crushed it underfoot. "For my money, Stout's a first-class idiot."

"Heinrich. How can you be so cruel?"

"I can assure you that's not cruelty," Briggs responded. "How the U.S. Army can put a moron like that in charge of a military encampment is beyond me."

"Well, it's only a labor post, Heinrich," said his host. "It's not designed for the things you and I are accustomed to."

"Doesn't make any difference. It's still a U.S. Army post. And he's still in command of it." Lt. Col. Briggs said, leaning back in his chair. "Del, if I told you Stout is one of the most incompetent sons-a-bitches —"

"Heinrich."

"Sorry, Priscilla. My language has slipped since I last saw you."

"Now, you're not going to blame that on Colonel Stout, are you?"

"No. You can blame that on the coloreds. I've been commanding those S.O.B.'s too long. I'm losing decency."

"Any excuse will do," she chided.

"By the way, Heinrich," the retired colonel asked, apparently not giving weight to what his visitor had just said, "how do you like commanding the coloreds?"

"Del, I can't tell you how bad it is. It's an embarrassment. An out-and-out embarrassment. Assignments don't get any worse. And these troops of mine are the worst bunch of pea-brained simpletons you're ever likely to find. I've never seen a more rowdy and worthless bunch. It's my second go-around with these people, and I'm still mystified over their ignorance. They're terrible. Uncontrollable. Most of them don't even deserve citizenship, let alone being in service. And I've got a first sergeant at one of my companies who clearly belongs in the Belgian Congo."

"My God, Heinrich," expostulated Mrs. Rideout. "That's obscene. It's deplorable."

"You don't know these birds, Priscilla."

"That sounds very much like a Simon Legree mentality."

"You're going a little far afield there, Dear," Col. Rideout cautioned.

"Well it does sound like a cruel, slave overseer," the wife responded. "But I'll reserve judgement."

"Thank you," Briggs said bogusly.

Mrs. Rideout gave the matter more thought. "Henrich, are you meaning to say the men aren't disciplined?"

"They don't know the meaning of the word."

"If they're that bad, why are they in the Army?"

"Priscilla, my dear, I've asked myself that same question more times than I'd care to remember." Col. Briggs replied. He steered the conversation in a different direction. "Del, how long have you been retired?"

"It'll be two years, this coming January," the wife answered for him.

"But you two are from the East. Why Texas? And Houston, at that?"

"Well, oddly enough, I was assigned here," said the host before the wife could answer. "Before retirement I was going to take over Logan. I took one look around and said to hell with it."

"You were going to take command of Logan?"

"Yes, and I thought it would have been ideal," the wife answered. "But you know Del. Never satisfied. But, Heinrich, about the colored — "

"And Del never would have been satisfied," the retired colonel said of himself. "The Army doesn't want you to be satisfied."

"But, Dear, it's such a nice, clean little post. It's ideally situated, and there wouldn't have been that many demands placed on you. Certainly not like some of the others."

"Priscilla, we've gone over this a hundred times — "

"More like three or four, Dear."

"It feels like a hundred. But we could have gone over it a thousand times. What you and the Army fail to understand is that I could have been best suited working for somebody like Billy Mitchell."

"Aeroplanes?" Briggs asked.

"Aeroplanes. Precisely."

"Nonsense."

"I told him that, too, Heinrich. But he wouldn't listen to me."

"That's pure nonsense, Del. I know Mitchell — "

"We know him, too," Mrs. Rideout said. "Before coming here, Colonel Mitchell and Del corresponded all the time."

"What were you two writing about, Del? Couldn't have been wasting your energies on this silly notion of air warfare he's been crying about."

"That is precisely what it was about," answered the wife.

"Humgh. That's about as senseless as using the colored man to fight."

"I don't know about the Negro," Col. Rideout answered, "but in the future, wars will be won, not solely on the field of battle, but in the air. That's what the Army should be thinking about. And Mitchell is right in speaking out, no matter what the cost. The country should be thinking about aeroplanes. And the aeroplane — or airplane — flyers should have their own branch of service. Call it the Aero Corps, Wings, call it any damn thing, but that's what has to happen. One of these days some country is going to realize that whoever controls the air has the advantage of whatever is on the ground."

"Heinrich, does that answer the question as to why he's retired?"

"I'm retired because for me to come here and serve as a commander for some useless and inconsequential thing called a construction post is a waste of my time and the government's money."

"I'm sure this is all very interesting," the lady said, "but, Heinrich, I want to know about the coloreds. I want to know why you think of them the way you do."

The husband pleaded. "Priscilla, please."

Before she could respond, Col. Briggs said, "Del, you and I went to the Point together —"

"Before you start," said the retired host, "I'm not saying de-emphasize Army or anything that was taught at West Point. I'm not saying that Infantry, Artillery, Cavalry, Engineering, or any branch should be devalued. Nor am I saying we should ease up on the commitment to have a strong naval force. But along with everything else we've got, we must start creating a presence in the air. England is doing it. And so are the Germans. Look at what their flyers are doing. They've got an ace over there called the Red Baron, who trained under Volker —"

"Who the hell is Volker?"

"Germany's best, until he got shot down."

"That just goes to show you how vulnerable those flying things can be," Briggs assessed. "And if I recall correctly, didn't I read where the Germans shot down over a third of the British flying corps a few months ago?"

"It's war, Heinrich," the colonel responded succinctly.

His wife asked, "What were you saying about this baron chap, Dear?"

"He's not an actual baron, Priscilla. He's known as the Red Baron. He's a captain who flies a red aeroplane. His name is Richthofen."

"I'd like to get back to the coloreds, but isn't a red aeroplane a bit much?"

"I was thinking the same thing, Priscilla," Briggs said. "He sounds too much like a hotshot, if you ask me. Next you'll be telling me they've got someone over there who flies a pink one."

The lady laughed. "Oh, dear, that would sound attractive to the ladies. Do you think women will be able to fly those things one day?" she asked her husband.

"You can't be serious, Priscilla," Briggs answered. He swallowed a drink, and said, "A woman flying? That would be the joke of the century. Women have no mechanical skills. They're a lot like the coloreds in that regard. Besides, women can't stand the altitude."

"That's where you're wrong again, Heinrich," said Rideout. "Baroness de la Roche has been flying since 1910. That woman Harriet Quimby has already flown across the English Channel."

"I think women flying is an outrage," Briggs snorted.

"Outrage or not, they're still doing it. And doing it well," the retired colonel said. "And hotshot or not, Heinrich, we need people like Von Richthofen. This young man is not twenty-five yet and he's already shot down over two dozen planes and was given command of his own fighter squadron. If we don't get men like that, and commit fully to men like that, the country is going to be in trouble. In the eyes of the world, we'll be dinosaurs — if we survive at all."

"Poppycock," Lt. Col. Briggs responded. "Pure poppycock."

"Isn't he sounding more and more like Colonel Mitchell?"

"Worse," said Briggs to the retired colonel's wife. "And the way Mitchell's been talking lately, I wouldn't be surprised if they run him out of the Army."

The wife asked, "Is he in trouble, Heinrich?"

"Damned right he is. He's been going around the country, speaking to groups and newspapers and doing nothing but bad-mouthing the military, all because of air power. All because nobody's fool enough to see things his way."

"But you're bad-mouthing the coloreds, Heinrich."

"Priscilla, if you don't mind, Dear," said the retired colonel to his wife, then switched back to Briggs before she could say anything. "Mitchell should be bad-mouthing the idiots. He's a visionary."

"Del, use some common sense, will you? Any way you look at it, Colonel Billy Mitchell is nothing but a crackpot."

"Because he's speaking out for what's right for the country? Because he's willing to prove bombs can be dropped from aeroplanes?"

"You can drop anything you want out of aeroplanes. But where the hell is it going to land? That's the question. I'd hate like hell to be within fifty miles of the one that makes the drop. And can you imagine what would happen if somebody was up there in one of those fancy new things and dropped a bomb near a company or a battalion of troops? Total disaster. And Mitchell is going even further than that. He's talking about launching planes from ships! And he's talking about dropping bombs to sink ships! That's insanity. Pure insanity. It's downright disgraceful."

"I've thought about it many times," the retired colonel said. "Colonel Mitchell is right. Dead right. And to question him is disgraceful."

"How can you be so sure he's right, Dear?"

"Priscilla, please stay out of this."

"I will not," retorted his wife. She calmly inspected the item she was working on.

"It's a military matter, Dear."

"Delbert Rideout, the country is at war. You're no longer in the military. And that's beyond disgraceful."

"Do you see what I have to put up with, Heinrich?"

"That's why I'm not married," Briggs said smugly. "But, Del, think about this for a second: I don't know a damned thing about aerodynamics, but common sense tells me one thing — the same as it should be telling that bunch back in Washington — to include Wilson —"

"The president?" asked the wife interestedly.

"If you want to call him that. Personally I have few other choice names for him."

"And what have you got against the President of the United States?"

"Everything," said Briggs, directing his attention back to the colonel. "Now, Del, Mitchell may have a point. As I said before, you can drop anything you damned well please out of this aeroplane thing, but the chances of hitting anything with any degree of accuracy are nil. It'd be almost like dropping a feather from a roof. You don't have the slightest idea where it's going to fall, except down. And as far as a ship is concerned, if a bomb or a missile should defy the laws of gravity and hit the goddamed thing, it still wouldn't be able to penetrate the armor."

"Colonel Mitchell is planning on giving the Army a demonstration to support every claim he's made."

"How?"

"The Army is putting an old tanker at sea. He and some of his men are going to bomb it."

"Giving that lunatic that much credence is stupid. Absolutely stupid. And I hope right after that fiasco is done with, the Army carries out its plan to court-martial the sonovabitch."

"Heinrich, your language is deplorable."

Her husband responded, "I'd asked you before to go inside, Dear."

"I would have. But I had asked a question and you two have chosen to go into something totally irrelevant."

"Anything having to do with war can't be irrelevant, Dear. But what was the question?"

"I wanted to know more about the coloreds. And I want to know why Heinrich thinks so little of them."

"Because they are inferior," Briggs stated, without the slightest hint of equivocation.

"Obviously he doesn't like them, Dear," said Rideout.

"But I gather you do, Priscilla," Briggs said.

"I obviously do, Colonel," the refined woman responded sweetly. She patiently squinted to rethread the needle. "Otherwise, as president of the Houston Tea and Sewing Club, I wouldn't have asked Colonel Stout to invite them to my home."

Chapter 14

The Camp Logan Officers' Club was much like the Officers' Club back at Columbus. The only difference was that here the entrance to the club was a few steps below ground level.

Walking down to the door, Capt. Farrell still criticized himself for going there just to break the Saturday afternoon monotony. He figured Col. Briggs would be gone, and he knew what to expect. Whitney, Reed and Froelich were sure to be the same. Only now, the tired conversation would likely be aided by the Logan officers.

Going inside, he was stopped by Froelich, who was coming out.

"Where you goin'?" the warrant officer asked, unnecessarily.

It was the first time they had spoken to each other since the Officers' Club back in Columbus. In Farrell's mind it registered as the back-stabbing incident, and he had vowed not to speak to him again. "I'm going inside. Seems kind of obvious," Farrell said curtly.

He started to move past Froelich.

"None of our guys are in there."

Farrell didn't comment.

"In case you're interested, they're in town. Some of the guys who live off post invited them to a Brunswick stew."

"What's a 'Brunswick stew'?"

"That's where they put everything that can walk, crawl or slide into a big pot, throw in some vegetables and cook it. S'like a cookout."

"How do I get there?"

"I don't know. And I don't care," the warrant officer said glumly. Farrell started to turn around. He stopped. "Froelich, how come you didn't go with them?"

"No Jews."

Farrell almost winced. Had the statement come from anyone else, he would have.

Froelich had to be burning inside, thought the captain as he walked away. He gave the warrant officer more thought. His mind flashed back to the attitude Froelich had always shown around the race-baiting Capt. Lloyd Whitney. In Farrell's opinion it had always been cowardly and embarrassing. One way or another, Whitney would always find a way to make his anti-Semitic feelings known, and always Froelich sat there and took it. Even Reed, far more sensitive, got in a jab or two. But it was the captain from New York who assailed him at every turn, and each time the dumpy little warrant officer did nothing but make an ineffectual pretense of jabbing back. At first, Farrell thought it was because the commander of I Company outranked the warrant officer by two positions. But that wasn't it. And what was more troubling, as he thought about the conversations led by Whitney and witnessed by Froelich, was that whenever Whitney got around to excoriating the blacks, Froelich was in full agreement. It didn't make sense. Here was a Jew, an unappreciated Jew, who in the eyes of a purebred white like Capt. Lloyd Whitney was looked upon with virtually the same level of disdain as that reserved for the blacks. Yet this same unappreciated man didn't hesitate to contribute to the castigation of blacks. Surely, thought Farrell, the former clothier

from New Jersey had to know that despite all his attempts to ingratiate himself with people like Whitney, he would never belong.
He would never be accepted as an equal. Like the blacks, he continued thinking, the Jew would remain socially unacceptable. It
was beyond comprehension; it was dripping with disgust. The man
might achieve great heights and lay claim to whiteness, but to the
Whitneys of the world he was still a Jew, hardly a cut above the
colored man.

More troubling to the captain was what Whitney once said before the warrant officer arrived at the club back in Columbus. He
said that the Jew was worse than a black. He could hide — and he
often did. But one day — somewhere — the Germanic-thinking
captain chillingly predicted, the Jew wouldn't be able to hide.
Whitney had family living in Berlin.

Chapter 15

"Thank you, Lord Jesus."

The voices rang out, rich with fervency and reverence.

"Thank you, Jesus."

"Thank God A'mighty."

"Amen."

Saturday was the Sabbath, the day to give praise and thanks to a great and giving God, as far as the Seventh-day Adventists were concerned. The church was clean, small, homely, and located in a pasture-like setting, comfortably away from the other churches. Most of the San Felipe blacks didn't understand the tenets of the Seventh-day Adventist religion, or that their Saturday worship had actually stemmed from an interpretation of the Bible. Except for a sometimes feeling of being different and at times isolated, mostly by the children, it really didn't matter that much.

The people's firm belief made for a happy church. On this Saturday, it was an unusually joyful church. Never had it seen so many faces. Soldiers from the black battalion were everywhere.

The pastor and the regular congregation sweltered in the smallish enclosure, swatting at the heat by pumping fans donated by Bullock's, the local funeral parlor. But they treated the visitors like national heroes. Hardly a soldier in attendance was a member of the sect, but they all were there to receive the Word. Baptists, Methodists, Episcopalians — it didn't make any difference. They were in uniform, in church, standing and holding hands in an act of spiritual kinship, receiving the Word and giving testament to what was important to them and to black life. Those who did not understand or have the slightest pretense of procedure — people like John Hong Kong Chin, who was a Shintoist, and Pepe de Anda, who was Catholic, simply followed the lead of others.

Earlier, a welcoming speech was given by an engaging and erudite pastor. After a chorus of Amens, a soloist stood and gave a magnificent rendition of the old hymn *Near The Cross*. The choir, 16 in number, followed with the touching *Take Me To The Water*. When they had finished, there was hardly a dry eye in the house. The pastor was so inspired he had the choir sing it again and opened "the doors to baptismal." He had dedicated the service to the troops and told them that he understood they couldn't wear the traditional white for the occasion, but that the uniform and the cause and the honor they brought to the race were as pure and as glorious as any color and that God would understand. He told them that, much as he wanted their membership, he understood they were transients and could not pledge themselves to the church — that even if they couldn't be baptized, they were to consider this their home away from home anyway. The pastor didn't know anything about the military, nor were he and the rest of the congregation mindful of the country's policy of not allowing the blacks to go overseas to fight. If anything, he and all the rest of the blacks thought the battalion was in Houston as a precursor to their move to Europe. The notion caused him to speak briefly about the war, saying how wrong Germany was and how right was the cause of America. To those who harbored fears about having to go overseas for the purpose of taking a life, he told them that it was all right in God's eyes. It was right because Germany was the enemy of all things Godly. It was right because David slew his enemies. And, he said, it was right because if Germany won the war in France they would sweep through all of Europe and eventually come over here and kill or enslave every black in America. He said they wouldn't hesitate to do that because the Germans were an evil people, unmerciful and unsparing, and that one day the world would know that in their quest for ethnic purity they would be a murderous people.

How the pastor knew this, no one knew. It was, however, food for thought.

• • •

Food for thought was the last thing on anyone's mind back in the center of town. The streets were flooded, the saloon was still jammed with wall-to-wall people, and across the street at Nell's house of prostitution business had gotten so good, an anxious line had formed outside.

Inside, the big woman with a touch of hair under her chin and considerably more under her oleaginous arms was searching the pantry just off the kitchen when she heard someone jiggling the back door. Nell knew it was the police. She rumbled to the kitchen and came back with a rolling pin firmly in one hand and a huge cast-iron pot swinging from the other. She stood behind the door with sweaty raised arms, ready to do battle. When a head slipped inside, she was about to crash it with the pot and follow up with the rolling pin. Fortunately for the head, it was kinky, so she held up. Then, seeing who it was, she screamed, "Lover-boy!" "Jelly-jam!"

It had only been since dawn, but Pete and the woman embraced as though they hadn't seen each other in months. In her excitement, she told her happy-eyed lover that his buddy had shown up, and that she had seen to it that he was well taken care of. She tried to tell him that his friend had gotten a *Nellie Moore special* and that the only trouble now was that he had fallen in love with not one but all three of the girls. She couldn't complete telling him all that had happened, because Pete had darted up front.

When he slid into the living room, Jody was stretched out on the sofa with a smile on his face that matched daylight.

"Well, look who ain't feelin' no pain."

"Pete! Hi'ya doin'?"

"Looks like you done left earth an' come back again. What all's done happened to you?"

"He been baptized," said one of the girls.

Pete did a little jig. "Baptized and sermonized; pipes cleaned an' lookin' mean."

Jody laughed sheepishly.

"Howz it feel to donate yo' cherry to charity?"

"Pete, leave him alone," said Nell.

"Leave him alone? I'm proud of 'im. Who did the honors?"

"Mable, Hattie, and Coralee," Nell said.

At first the numbers slipped by, then Pete gasped, "Tha — tha — tha'reee? The mascot is done had *THA'REEE* girls?"

"Umhummm."

"Hoooly smooookes!"

Pete didn't waste another second. He grabbed Jody by the hand.

"C'mon, Boy. Anybody as lucky as you is got to go across the street. You is got to get your hands on them lil' cubies! Can you walk?"

Nell put her hands on her hips. "You ain't goin' over there behind no Verl's to play no dice."

"Oh, yes, I am, Hun-Bun," Pete said. Before Nell could say anything else, he and Jody were on their way to the rear of the saloon. John Hong Kong Chin, who left church early, had been entertained upstairs. Through the window he could see Pete leading Jody to the alley. Grabbing his clothes, he dashed down the stairs and sailed outside to join them.

At the game, Pete pushed his way through the crowd and to the front. He saw the bouncing red dice and beamed. "A reg'lar Juneteenth in August. Freedom day! I luvszit." He waited for Jody. "C'mon, Lil' Mascot."

Jody came through just as the dice were being handed off to another shooter. Pete leaned into his ear. "All you gotta do is watch for a while an' listen to me. If you is able to stand up."

"I'm stannin'."

"I don't see how," said Pete. "Three girls. Wow! Okay, now, we gon' get the dice. I'm gonna give 'em to you, an' you is gonna follow my other lead."

"But I ain't never done this here kinda stuff b'fore."

"You ain't never had a woman before, but you learned, didn't you? An' I'm gonna tell you somethin'. When word gets aroun' that you done what you done done, the rest of the boys is gonna give you a parade. In fact, if I had a spare medal on me, I'd pin it on your chest right now. On second thought, maybe I should pin it on the fly of your underwear. 'Cause you is a legend. I wanna hear all about it, but first, 'bout this game. I want you to have the same good time as you had with them honeys."

"Yeah, but —"

"Was the wimmins good?"

"Great."

"Well, dice ain't nothin' but wimmins reduced in size. All you gotta do is gettum hot, an' they yours for life. An' ain't nothin' both of 'em likes better than a fresh, new honest face."

"Pete —"

"Ssssh, don't say nothin'. I know you don't know nothin' 'bout them sweet lil' things. But all you gotta do is listen. Okay. Now, when I gives you the dice — cup y'hands like this. Just like you was holdin' corn kernels with mittens on. Then you take them lil' ol' babies, cuddle 'em like you did with the girls, an' roll 'em. Roool-l-l 'em aroun' like you rollin' them lil' cubie-woobies in butter. Then you shake 'em real good. An' when them ol' kernels get hot, let 'em pop. 'Cause you is got —?"

"Popcorn!"

"That's all it is! You is shakin' up popcorn."

The houseman handed the dice off.

"Can I get faded for forty?" bumped Cpl. Calvin Jackson, a seldom-seem member of I Company. He took the dice and prepared to shoot.

The money floated down. Pete poked his partner. "Lemme have five o' them thirteen you said my Uncle Sam done paid you." Jody unenthusiastically went into his pocket and held out the money. Pete selected a five and shouted, "Five he's right!"

"You're on!"

Cpl. Jackson crapped out — again. This time, he folded his remaining two dollars and headed for Nell's.

"By my count you should have eight mo' dollars," Pete said to Jody.

"I guess."

"Lemme have 'em."

"But, Pete —"

The next shooter passed. "Quick, quick, quick," Pete said, "lemme have them dollars." As Jody dug for the money, another shooter in line reached for the dice. Pete grabbed them, took Jody's money and plopped the dice into his hands. Jody didn't have the slightest clue as to what to do with them. Pete cupped his hands and said, "Now, if you can handle three girls, two little dices should be a snap."

"But with the girls at least I was gettin' somethin'."

"Just as you will be gettin' here, M'boy. All you gotta do is listen. 'Member what I told you — the dice just luvs a fresh new honest face. Lettum see your face. With that peach fuzz, you look mo' honest than Honest Abe Lincoln. Now, close your hands an' mother an' smother them lil' cubie-cubes, an' then shake 'em like the kernels you use to make popcorn. An' when they get hot, let 'em pop."

As the onlookers yelled and demanded action, Jody started shaking the dice clumsily but excitedly.

"I'm doin' O.K., Pete?"

"Spectac-u-larrr. A lil' more now. Put some butter on 'em."

"Like this, Pete?" Jody asked, rolling his hands around.

"That's it, M'lad," Pete said to the crowd. "How much is we bein' faded?"

"How much you got down there?"

"As much as you want," Pete said, nodding for Jody to keep shaking.

"I don't see nothin' down there."

"How 'bout a hunnert an' five, for starters. An' then I might have a change of heart an' get serious."

"Put'cha money in the pot, Soldier Boy," the houseman said, his head sweating and thick with a pomade stronger than axle grease.

Pete smoothed out Jody's five-dollar bill and did a sleight of hand with the three remaining singles, folding them so that only the tip of the green would show. "I see a few dishonest faces in the crowd. I'm nervous. An' I'm new to these parts. I don't know y'all, so I might just bet this one lump an' leave." He gave Jody a quick wink. "I hardly know this here young fella here. What's your name, Son?"

"Jody," said the little soldier. He was still clumsily shaking the dice.

"Jody. What a nice, lil 'homey' name! Now, Jody, if you was to win a lil' sumthin' here, what would you do with the money?"

"Send it home."

"To whommmm? Notice I said, to whoooommm-mah-mah."

"Well, I'd send some of it to whoooommm if you want," Jody said, catching the cue, "but I'd send most of it to my *momma* so's she could buy a sleepin' bed."

"Did you hear that, Folks?" Pete asked, making room and hopping around like a carnival barker. "He is going to send his winnin's home to his momma. Pardon me while I brush away a tear! He's gonna send his winnin's home to his *momma* so's she can buy a bed. See, Folks, that's why I likes this boy. An' that's why I select'd him. I trust an honest face, and that's why I'm willin' to bankroll him to the hilt. An' I just might be tempted to unload this other lump you see in my other pocket on all'a y'all — "

"Shuddup an' let's play!" said a voice that was joined by a chorus.

"Okay, I'm layin' down five, an' I'm gonna hold on to these other three hundred-dollar bills 'til my man gets a point. After that, the sky's the limit. They don't call me Payroll Pete for nothin'."

"Who you?" a weaving drunk asked.

"Payroll Pete."

"You're on for twenty-five."

"That ain't enough," said John Hong Kong Chin in a confident voice. Well aware of what Pete was doing, he cooly threw a month's salary onto the blanket and, like sheep, they all started betting. Pepe de Anda, who like Hong Kong, was fresh from church, emptied his pockets. Money poured in from everywhere. When it had built to a sizable mound, Pete looked at Jody. "Is them ol' kernels hot enough?"

"They burnin', Payroll Pete!"

"Then let 'em poprooollll!! Oh, an' Jody? Don't f'get that bed for your dear ol' mammy. An' while you shoppin', get her a pillow too."

"Furniture an' covers too, Pete?"

"Furniture, covers, an' anythin' else to make a body happy! Now, roll 'em!"

"Popcorn!" Jody yelled. He released the dice with a scooped, two-handed, jerked, sand-in-the-air, first-time-playing motion. When the dice finally came down, they hit the wall and bounced back. Pete took one look and jumped higher than a rainbow. Hong Kong Chin tried to match him. Seven and one read the dice. Beginners' luck worked its magic, and when it sought rest by producing snake eyes, Jody didn't lose his turn with the dice. Fate stepped in and smiled on the eager little soldier as it had never done before. He couldn't miss. With every roll of the wayward, lively little cubes, Pete would shout to the heavens, fall to his knees, then roll down to wallow in the money. And then he would start collecting, his arms flying in every direction.

• • •

It was 1420 when Quackenbush grunted into the police station with his assistant, Ananias Blanchard. They were reporting in almost three hours before schedule. Quackenbush was not at all happy. Watching his Saturday afternoon baseball game had been interrupted. Worse, his favorite team was on the verge of winning their first game of the season and he wouldn't be there to see it.

Elmore Quackenbush was a sluggish, slow-walking man. His feet had bunions on the toes, calluses on the bottom, and arches that ached under his massive weight. His jowels hung low, and gave him a sad, puppy-dog look. He was a plain-clothes sergeant who frequently wore a dark-brown, tilted fedora. He made it a habit of wearing the same dark-gray, food-stained necktie every day. He had been with the Houston Police Department for almost 18 years. Seventeen of those years had been spent in and around the Fourth Ward, which included San Felipe.

Quackenbush considered himself a law-and-order man, but he wasn't. He took bribes, drank corn liquor by the jarful, sponged meals, and shopped without paying. Early in his career he convinced blacks that he was not afraid of them by blackjacking one of the local saloon regulars to death in broad daylight, and in full view of the patrons of Verl's.

The black man's death was ruled a justifiable death.

The big policeman had been at the train station when the black battalion arrived. He was off duty, but he wouldn't have missed it for the world. Like the other members of the department, at the request of Col. Stout, he followed the department's orders and remained out of sight. It was clear, however, that the policeman was angered. He was yanked even more because the local blacks made such a fuss over the arriving black troops.

Typically, the big man didn't have much to say when he reported for duty the following day, grunting only to his co-worker, Blanchard, that they would have to do something in the Fourth Ward's San Felipe to show the niggers in uniform who was in charge.

Quackenbush was wrong about the time, but it was in his mind that it had been almost a month since he conducted the last raid on Nell's. Now that the soldiers were on pass and in his town, it was time to do it again. The fat man had planned on raiding the house of prostitution the day after the troops arrived. Blanchard agreed that something should be done but counseled that to get maximum exposure it would be best to wait until they had been given word that the announced period of acclamation was over and passes for the black battalion had been granted. He recalled that Col. Stout had promised the city fathers that the police would be notified when the time came.

Despite his confrontation with Briggs, Col. Stout had made up his mind early on Friday that he was going to relieve on-post tension by seeing to it that Saturday passes were issued. By an oversight, the police had not been notified. Blanchard found out anyway and reported the decision to Quackenbush. Feeling that a good many of the troops would be either in Nell's or in the saloon, along with others, the two policeman spent that Friday evening plotting Saturday's strategy.

The raid on Nell's was supposed to take place at 5 p.m., but the seething big man was reporting in hours early because he had been summoned. There were several crap games going on at the rear of Verl's. Reports had it that all of them were getting out of hand.

• • •

At the main game, Jody was still yelling popcorn. The slap-happy trio of Roosevelt, Menyard and Andrews had shown up after taking another tour outside the San Felipe district again. They were bounced out of every white establishment they entered. But they were on site, happy, and deep into rhyming their contribution.

"There's nuttin' like bein'
in your own neighborhood —
An' shootin' dice in the Army
Makes us all feel good."

Jody scored another point. The trio sprang back into action. They clowned around the outer circle, then pushed their way back to the center and continued having fun.

"Put'cha money in the pot
We don't want no ex'cuuuse —
We likes the way the boy
is handlin' them cuuubes."

The little soldier kept on winning. There was nothing but hap-piness among Pete and Jody and the trio, who had now elbowed their way into the inner circle and dropped a dollar or two on be-half of their company member.

"We bettin' with our boy
from King Kumpa'neee —
Cause we likes the smell
of y'alls mon-n-neee."

To cap it off, Jody made another point. The trio went wild. Jody still didn't know the mechanics of the game, but he knew he was winning. Pete's pockets were overloaded. He had crammed so much money inside his shirt, he had gone beyond looking pregnant. Except for color and uniform, he looked like a stunted Saint Nick.

Later, beginners' luck was still holding. All the onlookers and participants who hadn't bet with the clumsy little shooter had been financially hurt. It was apparent the next roll of the dice could clean them out entirely. Pete, fearing that Jody's streak would come to an end, decided to bet the pot. It would be the last roll, and he was sweating, yelling and encouraging.

"All right, Baby Boy, this is it. This is it. This one is for all the marbles. Ready?"

"Yeah!" Jody said, his hands cupped around the dice.

"They hot?"

"Yeah, Pete."

"They real, real hot?"

"Really hot."

"Then blow on 'em an' cool 'em down."

"I'm blowin', Pete."

"Okay, then. Gettum hot again. Treat 'em like you done treated them three honeys you had earlier. Luv them lil' cubie-woobies. Butter up them kernels."

"I'm butterin' an' lovin' 'em, Pete."

"An' they luvs you. Open your hands so they can see y'face."

"They lookin', Pete."

"Good," Pete encouraged. "Member what I told you. Dice is like wimmins. They luvs a fresh, new, honest face. Peach fuzz!"

"An' my momma's sleepin' bed."

"A dozen of 'em!"

"An' the covers?"

"Quilts! An' furniture, too! Just like Nell's."

"Oooh, boy-y-y-y!"

"Is them ol' kernels gittin' hot again?"

"Almost!"

"Got wimmins on y'mind?"

"Mostly popcorn!"

"An' don't forget the butter!" Pete said, his fingers combing the air. "Git them lil' cubie-woobies kernels jus' a lil' bit hotter 'cause it's house-cleanin' time.

The rhyming trio chipped in.

"S'time to hit the big one,
We don't want no duds —
'Cause we goin' in the bar
We needs money for the suds."

"Y'ready???"

"The kernels is ready, Pete!" Jody said, shaking with all the vigor he could muster.

"O-o-o-k-k-a-a-y-y-y!" said Pete. *Lettum rooool-l-l!!!"*

"Popcorn!!!" Jody yelled.

The dice went high into the air, came down, and bounced crookedly to the cement wall. They spun erratically and settled at the edge of the blanket. Pete slumped to his knees, held his breath, and crawled forward to take his look.

The trio did the honors.

*From where we stands
It ain't no seven —
But we don't mind
Cause the dice say....
'LEVEN!!!"*

Six and five were the numbers. The crowd exploded. The trio was already dancing. Pete had already jumped up and started dancing with them. Suddenly he thought about the money and gave Jody a joyous hug. Together they fell deliriously onto the pile.

After they rolled around a bit, Pete swept his arms out to rake it all in, skirting enough for the trio who picked up theirs — and more. They danced away grinning and rhyming. John Hong Kong Chin and Pepe de Anda, happy with their winnings, danced away behind them.

He hadn't heard the approach, but as Pete happily sent his fingers reaching out for the money that had spread to the other side of the blanket, a foot, big, slow and deliberate, powered down on his wrist and knuckles. It held for a moment, and then the hulking figure attached to the foot lowered his body down for a face-to-face confrontation. The gamblers at all three games were too stunned to move, and those who were inclined to run were unable to because they were surrounded by gun-toting police. They were backed by an unobtrusive black paddy wagon thought to be loaded with more police.

It was a powerful presence facing Pete, still paining under a massive and bunioned foot. The big man said it in a nice, unintimidating sort of way: "The name is Quackenbush. An' I been waitin' on you."

As the moment crested, one of the miscreants on the outside of the circle started to inch back. The houseman started to move with him.

"Hold it!" said Blanchard, leveling his gun from behind the fender of the paddy wagon.

Quackenbush turned to look, and the moment he made the move, the crowd scattered. Pete pushed the big man viciously off balance, collected more of the money, and started to run. Jody, bewildered as ever, hesitated for a fraction of a second and started to go for the dollars that remained.

"C'mon, Jody! Run! We got enough money! C'mon, we got enough!"

Quackenbush rolled over, saw the little soldier stuffing his pockets, and collared him. He gave three blasts on his whistle, emptying the paddy wagon, and then took out his weapon and pistol-whacked the little soldier. Pete, looking back, saw what was going on and ran back for assistance. Running past the onrushing police, he pounced on the fat man and started biting him on the ear. Jody scrambled to his feet and ran. Pete gave the big man a going-away kick and caught up with Jody, now clearing the alley between the saloon and stable.

"Across the street!" Pete hollered. Running past the still-scattering soldiers and swarming policemen, he yelled, "Nell's! Go to Nell's!"

A shot rang out. The big man was back on his feet, rumbling through the alley, shouting and firing wildly.

Adding to the confusion, the bar was spewing patrons, among them Sgts. Dukes, Odums and Williams. Directed by Blanchard, most of the uniformed policeman had gone inside the bar. With nightsticks swinging freely they began to clean house. Outside, almost from nowhere, three black MP's appeared and started shouting for order. Quackenbush, almost to the front of the bar, was accosted by one of the MP's, a Cpl. Baltimore, from Company L. "What's goin' on?" he demanded.

Quackenbush, huffing and puffing with a pistol in one hand and a nightstick in the other, fired back. "What'd you say, Nigger?"

"I'm a military policeman, an' I want to know what goin' on?!"

Quackenbush diverted his attention. "You see that over there?" The instant the MP turned his head, the civilian policeman cracked him over the head. Baltimore went down, and Quackenbush began clubbing and pistol-whipping him. A few civilians saw the incident and shouted to some of the soldiers to take a look. When they did, there was an explosion of action. Soon the street was thick with angry, defiant blacks ready to do combat. Dukes, Odums, Williams and several other noncoms circled the area, trying to get the men to head back in the direction of camp. The trio was first to leave.

Sgt. Dukes spotted Carter and yelled, "Go back to camp! Get McClellan!"

Carter took off, running as fast as he could.

Across the street at Nell's, Pete and Jody had already crashed through the door and, along with others, were trying to push the big purple sofa against the door. It was too late. The police were in hot pursuit, and when the out-of-breath Quackenbush rumbled past the bar and arrived on the porch, the detail of men was already making entry. Cpl. Jackson of I Company saw them crashing in and dove out of the window.

Once inside, it was a case of police brutality versus black violence. With Nell screaming and shouting invectives, and with partially clothed prostitutes and customers scurrying around and trying to flee, it was a madhouse. Several made the attempt to escape out of the windows and back door. It didn't work. Blanchard had positioned two baton-wielding men in back with the clear-cut instructions to crack any head — male or female — that came out either a door or a window.

Back in the living room, in the thick of things, Pete was fighting viciously. He had already been clubbed, and a policeman was hanging on his back. Jody helped him shake the man, and instead of trying to leave, the soldier with the money still falling from his pockets and out of his shirt grabbed the stove poker and creamed Quackenbush with a behind-the-neck haymaker. The big man with the pained face stumbled forward and hit his head on the fireplace. He was out for about two minutes. Pete filled the minutes swinging the poker at anyone he even thought was a policeman. There were no black policemen in the San Felipe district, but one would have thought there were. A well-dressed black emerged from the bathroom, buttoning his fly. He came Pete's way and was immediately knocked in the head. Nell was crying for the soldier-gone-berserk to come back to sanity. He wouldn't. Jody, trying to help, leaped on his friend's back. It was a costly move. The policemen moved in.

When Quackenbush regained consciousness, Pete was almost out on his feet. Blanchard had led three policemen in beating him nearly senseless. Pete was staggering around the room, bleeding profusely. He would have been out, but something told a tearful Jody to keep his friend moving on his feet. Even that wouldn't have been allowed had Blanchard not heard two shots ring out from upstairs. Racing up the stairs and into the first room, he found the partially clothed body of a bleeding white girl slumped over a dead Carlos Rodriquez. Blanchard looked at them briefly and began to toe to toe at them when he was called to another room by the policeman who had done the firing. Pompa, the policeman, had discovered Clara, the white prostitute, nude, and hiding in the closet with two black soldiers. They, too, were nude. All three were seized in fear as Blanchard raised his gun and got set to do the honors.

Blam! Blam! Blam! Blam! Blam! barked the gun of the derby-wearing policeman. He reloaded and went to another room. He was disappointed. There was no one in there. He returned to the original room and emptied his weapon at the nude bodies.

. . .

First Sgt. Obie McClellan's Saturday afternoon had been quiet and uneventful, except for the first-time letter he received from Sgt. Newton, the old friend of many years standing. Newton, the name they had gotten used to using, was a friend of Sgt. Dukes as well. He had spoken of him on the train.

Obviously affected by the contents of the letter, McClellan read it over and over. When he'd read it the last time, he gave a look of depletion, placed the letter back in the envelope, and carefully folded it into his shirt pocket. As he was putting the envelope away, he happened to look down at his sergeant's stripes. He thought of the impending demotion. He remembered the day he had gotten the sixth stripe that framed the diamond in the middle. He remembered how quick and easy it was to move up through the ranks, from private to private first class, to corporal, to buck, to staff, to tech, to master, all in less than three and a half years.

For some reason, perhaps because of who wrote the letter, his mind settled on how he had pulled Field Sgt. Dukes up along with him. It would have been tough running a company without his trusted old friend.

Drifting back to the premonition that had plagued him, McClellan slowly removed his eyeglasses and pressed hard at his temples as though trying to assuage stress. Brownsville came to mind again. He stood and rested a foot on the cot, trying to push the memory away. It didn't work. Moving away, he gave a cursory glance at his makeshift bookshelf that topped the right side of the tent and continued to the doorway. There he remained, staring absently out at the company grounds. Only a few troops were milling around. From his vantage point, he could see a few of the men on the side of the First Platoon tent as they rehearsed a song he had never heard. It could have been a modern tune, still he wouldn't have recognized it. The sergeant knew little about what was popular and what was not. Interestingly, his favorite song was *The Battle Hymn of the Republic*. As he had once told Carter, the company drummer — or company musician as he had begun to think of him — he had never understood why it was called the Battle Hymn of the Republic, since, if listened to closely, the title didn't fit the song. But he liked it anyway. It was an interesting sentiment. He felt that it was a perfect blend of melody and lyric.

McClellan didn't know anything about the picture show he had OK'd for a later viewing by the men who had not been allowed to go on pass. It was. D. W. Griffith's *Birth Of A Nation* — a controversial film that did much to foster the unsavoriness of blacks. Had he known anything at all about it, he wouldn't have allowed the showing, and he certainly wouldn't have planned on seeing it. Simms, knowing that the First would probably be attending the outdoor showing, had requested something made by a forerunner of the black filmmaker Oscar Micheaux. But the whites in charge had never heard of a black film producer or even a black actor, for that matter, so they sent what they thought would be appropriate.

Perhaps it was to get a rise out of the troops.

Far down in the company area, beside the Supply Tent, Poole had fashioned himself a shower by hoisting an overhead bucket with holes in the bottom. From his position in the tent's doorway, the First could see that the corporal was getting a late start into town.

Poole was getting the late start because he had taken time out to draw a birthday card to send to one his three children.

That was the one domestic thing the lanky corporal could be counted on to do, remember the birthdays of his children. He had two boys and a girl, ranging in age from eight to 12, and in the six years he had been away, never had he forgotten to send them a card or letter and seal it with a kiss drawn on the envelope. He would also write his wife a brief note — nothing loving, just a word saying that he was okay and to take care of the children. Along with the note he would include most of his monthly salary, something he never would have done had he remained in civilian life.

From Mississippi, Cpl. Theolonius Poole had been a terrible husband. He constantly fought with his wife, went out and drank, and would pick fights with others. Invariably he ended up in jail for an overnight stay. Mentally bruised, he would return home and start with his wife all over again. It was only after the children saw him strike the woman that he decided to change. But he couldn't do it alone. He needed help. He joined the Army.

Over at the Mess Tent, just beyond a group who was trying to get a game of *catch* with a frayed baseball going, Junius Rochester and three or four others were circled around three pots, chatting and peeling spuds. The question of Sgt. Willie Powell's whereabouts was answered when he emerged from the tent with a saliva-stained, hand-rolled cigarette dangling from his mouth. He was emptying a hot, greasy pail of water on another thick trail of ants that had crept under the tent and traveled up the legs of a table, rounded the stew pot, turned west, and made their way along a ladle and over to a shelf. The ants did all that in order to conduct an assault on the syrup that oozed down from one of the cans.

Sgt. Powell went back inside. The first sergeant was about to step next door to the Orderly Room when he saw Carter breathlessly sprinting into the company area.

"Sarge! Sarge!" he called as he raced past the platoon tents. The first sergeant held his position. It was almost as if he knew what was coming.

Carter was almost in front of him now. "Sarge, they's fightin' an' shootin' in town!"

Surprisingly, the First didn't say anything.

"Sarge! Sarge! The white police an' our boys is fightin'!" McClellan remained oddly quiet, as if his mind had been sealed, and he wasn't going to allow anything else in or out. The young soldier with the heavy African features knew that he had been heard. It was impossible not to have been heard. He was standing directly in front of the man's face.

"Sarge, Sarge! Somma our boys is fightin' with the police in town!!" When McClellan still didn't respond, Carter spoke even louder. "Sarge, y'hear? The police an' our boys is fightin' in town. An' there's shootin' and killin'. Y'hear, Sarge? Y'hear?? Sarge — ?"

The breathless young soldier waited but still didn't get the expected reaction from his First.

Carter pushed. "Sarge, did'ja hear me, Sarge? Our boys an' the polices —"

Pressing the point again, Carter tugged at the sergeant's sleeve, as if to make sure he was being fully heard. In the Army — in King Company — one did not touch an NCO, especially the first sergeant. Few things warranted swifter punishment. But McClellan did nothing. Timidly the young soldier tried touching his First again. Again there was no reaction. Puzzled, shaken, the company drummer gave it a second or two longer, then lowered his head and walked away. At midfield he stopped, turned to give the First another look, and resumed walking away. He had tears in his eyes.

He simply couldn't understand his leader.

The first sergeant watched the dejected young soldier as he crossed the field and went into the First Platoon tent. Looking at nothing in particular, and after a moment or two longer in the doorway, the first sergeant retired back into his tent. He sat on the cot with a strange, far-away look in his eyes. He did nothing for a long while, then dug for Newton's letter again.

• • •

At Nell's, the outburst hadn't subsided. Sgt. Dukes had entered the house and been struck by a policeman. Bleeding, he sought to fight back. Jody set Pete down, then he, along with Boot and Dow Lee, tried to go to the old sergeant's aid. Before they could get to him, Quackenbush smacked him in the teeth with the butt of his pistol. The sergeant capped his mouth with both hands and went down. Had it not been for Jody and Boot's interference, he would have been pistol-whipped to death.

It is not known how Col. Stout, the commander of the post, or Col. Briggs got word of the conflict. Briggs had extended his visit with Del and Priscilla Rideout on the outskirts of the city, and Stout had been at his home on post, but the two Army staff cars skidded to a halt in front of the house of prostitution almost at the same time. A third car — a civilian's — arrived seconds later. In it were Captains Farrell and Whitney, along with Warrant Officer Froelich and three other unidentified officers from Logan. Capt. Reed, of Company L, could not be found.

The street was still crowded, and Nell's house, inside and out, looked like a combat zone. The porch, the living room, the kitchen, the pantry, upstairs, everywhere one looked were signs of combat. The fighting was still going on inside when the officers entered. Froelich had called *attention* — several times — and had assumed that would do. Briggs supported him by acting as though his presence alone should have been sufficient to bring about order. He ducked for cover as a flying purple-shaded lamp missed him by inches. Safe, he yelled to Froelich. "The Anthem! The National Anthem! Sing it!"

It took a while, but Froelich got the meaning. He felt stupid, but he started: *"Oh, Say, Can You See...."*

Farrell and Whitney joined in. The three officers felt equally stupid, but it was beginning to work.

Briggs knew it would work. The battalion commander knew that any soldier in or out of his right mind would instinctively stop whatever he was doing and respond to The Star-Spangled Banner.

At first one black, then two, and then three. Soon a group of soldiers was standing at attention.

The fighting had at last ceased.

Briggs emerged from his cover and circled the room, shaking his head in disbelief. "Animals," he said. "A bunch of goddamned, low-down, good-for-nothing, pick-a-ninny, black, crow animals."

Whitney eased over and whispered to Farrell, reminding him of something he had said in the Officers' Club back in Columbus. "You find your understanding yet?"

It had been so long since Farrell had said it, he had forgotten what Whitney was referring to.

"Take a look around, Mister," Quackenbush said to Stout.

"I'm a colonel in the United States Army."

"That don't make a damn bit of difference to me. Your boys are responsible for this."

Col. Stout started to counter him, then thought better of it and dismissed the man with a look.

Lt. Col. Briggs, attempting to take over, said to his officers, "Let's get the hell out of here."

Farrell asked, "What about the soldiers, Sir?"

"Do you see any goddamned soldiers around here?" Briggs said scornfully. Without waiting for an answer, he stepped outside. Froelich followed him out.

Col. Stout, who had been looking around, went to where Pete was groaning. He then saw the injured Sgt. Dukes and bent down for a closer look.

"Aaawp," Quackenbush said. "Don't go near 'em. He's my prisoner."

"Your prisoner?"

"*My prisoner*," Quackenbush repeated firmly. "Him, an' all the rest of 'em in here. You're on civilian grounds, Mister."

Stout knew that the policeman was right about the civilian-grounds precept. With what looked like a final survey, he inquired, "Will the injured receive medical attention?"

"There's a dead policeman across the street. An' likely some injured ones upstairs, and in the back. Will they be gettin' any?"

The colonel ignored the policeman and instructed Farrell to march all those who hadn't been involved in the melee back to camp. He then stepped away. Capt. Whitney accompanied him.

Outside, with Briggs and the other officers gone, the post commander folded his arms behind him and quietly watched as Capt. Farrell rounded up every man in uniform who had not been involved in the fracas and ordered them all into a quick formation. With Capt. Whitney, a few other officers, some MP's, and Sgts. Williams and Odums assisting, Farrell took a head count and was preparing to march the men back to camp when Cpl. Poole sprinted into the area.

"What's goin' on?" Poole asked, flicking his head around.

"Get in formation, Poole," ordered Farrell.

The corporal stopped in the middle of the street, fixed his gaze on the black civilians milling around, the formation, and the house. "What's been goin' on here?"

"I said get into formation, Corporal!"

Reluctantly Poole complied. Capt. Farrell then gave the order to move out, and farther down the road he ordered the men into a *double-time*.

Col. Stout waited for a moment, took a last look around, and walked down off the porch to his car. The waiting driver saluted him, and they were off.

Whether deliberately or not, Quackenbush came out to the porch and stood there, but the prisoners didn't come out until Col. Stout had left the area. A large number of black civilians were still milling about when the troops came out.

The fat policeman remained on the porch while his men filed the men down the steps. Once they were in position in the middle of the street, he instructed Blanchard to face them toward the porch so that he could address them.

With effort, the big man put his bunioned foot up on the banister and said, "A lil' later on, I'm gonna see just how bad you animals are." He didn't know rank, but it was obvious Sgt. Dukes would have been the senior. He looked at the bleeding man who was barely able to stand and said, "You, Head Nigger, march these here boys to the station house." He pointed east. "It's up the road, that a'way."

An three-inch gash near the old soldier's mouth matched another on his forehead.

Dukes was about out of it. His eyes blinked almost uncontrollably, and he couldn't stop bleeding from the mouth. One of the policeman told Quackenbush he thought some of the men were too hurt to walk to the police station and suggested that the sergeant, along with a few of the others, would be better off riding in the paddy wagon.

"An' smell up my vehicles?" Quackenbush responded.

He ordered the policemen to surround the detail with guns drawn. When that was done, he said, "Straighten up there, Head Nigger, an' get 'em movin'!"

Dukes was unable to comply, and the policeman bore down.

"Move 'em, dammit!"

Holding on to an equally mindless Pete, Jody whispered to the sergeant, "Sarge. Sarge, he want you to march us, Sarge."

Quackenbush snatched a blackjack from the hands of one of his policemen and started to move off the porch.

"Please, Sarge," Jody continued, "you gotta march us — "

Rhythmically slapping the blackjack in the palm of one of his hands, the policeman continued to move forward.

It is not known how Pete did it, but he did. Wounded and deflated, and certainly no longer the same ol' Pete, he struggled limply forward to face the 30 or so black soldiers from the Third Battalion. He did something that roughly resembled an *about face*.

"Detail," he said in a voice without energy. "A'tention. Right face."

One or two men tried to give the *one-two* movement count.

"Forward, march," said Pete.

Under the eyes of the black civilians, the ragged columns moved away.

Forty minutes later the row of cell doors at the police station slid open. Thirty-three members of the Third Battalion had found a new home.

The men were processed in, and when Quackenbush was leaving for an early dinner, he returned to the main cell and said, "A lil' later on, I'm gonna see just how bad you niggers is gonna get."

Shortly over an hour later he was back. He had a bicycle chain swinging in his hand.

Chapter 16

The day was dying in the City of Houston; the crowd that had flooded the streets of the San Felipe district had dissipated, but there was a feeling of combustible tension in the air that remained. The explosive sense that something was going to happen settled over the quieted grounds of Camp Logan as well. The feeling also reached out and had spread to all the white companies, covered the Third Battalion, and nested on the grounds of King Company. There, nothing nor no one moved. It was as if more than the day was dying. It was as if a way of life had ended; a tradition was no more, like hope and glory had died.

In Col. Stout's office, the quiet went far beyond that of the normal Saturday evening. He was sitting with a cadre of his officers, all quietly assessing the implications of the day.

Over in Lt. Col. Briggs's office there was an equal quiet. Except for Capt. Farrell, all of the battalion officers were there. None of them was contributing very much. They didn't know how.

The same could have been said about Farrell at that moment. He was still at the company, not knowing what to do. He had spent all of his time in his tent, pacing back and forth in deep worry.

The captain had reason to worry. The quiet at his company was different. It was more combustible, more eruptive. And in that quiet, the captain assessed, something was going to happen. He didn't know what, he didn't know when. He might have been distant from the coloreds as a people; as a man he might have been bland and uninspiring and not the leader his troops deserved; and in the eyes of the colonel and the other officers he might have been unsoldierly, a neophyte, weak, and all the things that were said about him even before he left home, but he had grown to know something of this company.

Something was going to happen.

A handful of men had remained in their tents. Most, however, chose to attend a meeting that had been called in the First Platoon tent. It was never made clear who called the meeting, and it was for volunteers only.

The meeting was still going on when full darkness came.

A black hand reached up and turned on the single bulb that illuminated the tent's interior, revealing almost a quarter of the company jammed inside. Sitting on the cots farthest to the rear were Sgts. Odums and Williams, along with several members of their companies. Positioned on the corner of a cot midway of the tent was First Sgt. McClellan. Poole, standing, showed signs he was ready to move out at any moment. Although no one spoke immediately after the light came on, a great deal of tension was stirring. Earlier the hushed and darkened conversations had centered around the telling and retelling of what had happened in town and more importantly, as far as Cpl. Poole was concerned, what they were going to do about it. Then, with Poole taking the lead, the talk grew louder.

Three times Poole had asked the close-mouthed McClellan about arming themselves, marching on Houston, freeing the men, and taking care of Quackenbush. Three times McClellan hadn't responded. Most telling, though, was that the First never expressed outright opposition to the move, nor was he critical of Poole or Poole's suggestions. The fiery corporal was about to ask the same question again when Capt. Farrell poked his head through the tent door. His eyes scanned the interior of the cluttered tent, and he didn't appreciate the look he was getting in return.

"May I see you for a moment, Sergeant?" the captain asked.

McClellan rose slowly.

Not backing off from what he thought was the best course of action, Poole ignored the captain and again asked his question.

"Do we get an answer, Sergeant?"

McClellan looked at him, and then at the men. He cleared his way down the aisle without a word.

"Over thirty-some coloreds done already been lynched this year, Sarge," Poole challenged. "An' this is just August."

McClellan didn't say anything.

Poole called after him again. "An' this is the only country on earth where they still burnin' people at the stake. Over twenty of us in four years, Sarge."

The First still didn't respond.

"An' before that, thirteen of 'em was burned where they s'pose to love colored folks — where we ain't *s'pose* to have no problems, Sarge. *New York!*"

Poole continued hotly as McClellan was clearing the door, "An' we still bein' tarred an' feathered around the country, Sergeant. Some even wearin' the uniform of a United States soldier!"

The last statement was particularly stinging to the first sergeant. His back had a twitch to it, and he looked as if he were going to stop. He didn't. Poole hollered something else, but McClellan was already outside.

Walking swiftly to the convertible car the driver had parked on the side of the Orderly Room, the captain queried, "What was Poole talking about?"

"You heard some of it, Captain. For the rest, you'll have to ask him."

"I'm asking you. You're the first sergeant."

"I won't be First for long," McClellan said quietly.

"None of us is going to be anything for long. Now, I'm asking you again, what was Corporal Poole talking about?"

"A sorry state of affairs."

"That doesn't tell me much."

The captain could tell something extremely serious was going on even before he had stuck his head inside the tent. The company had been too quiet, and now the first sergeant's evasiveness only increased his concern, but he was in a rush and didn't have time to pursue the matter. They stopped at the car, the driver hopped out and cranked up. "I've just been summoned to Battalion Headquarters. I hope that when I return I'll still be company commander. But whether I'm C.O. or not, I want you to make absolutely certain that nothing else goes wrong. And I want that meeting broken up. I'm ordering a *total* restriction to quarters. And I want the men to return to their tents immediately — and they are not to leave their tents, let alone the company area. And under *no* circumstances will anyone be allowed arms or access to the Supply Tent, particularly Corporal Poole. So take the keys from him. Bed check will be at 2100 hours, one hour from now. Is that clear?"

"Very clear, Captain."

The captain didn't like the way McClellan said it, but he didn't have time to go into it. He hopped into the convertible. "Now there's a possibility the colonel will want to talk to you. If he does, he'll send a driver. So make yourself available, and come as quickly as possible."

"Who do I leave in charge?"

"To repeat," the captain said, motioning to the driver to pull out, "bed check will be within the hour."

McClellan watched the headlights disappear, and instead of

returning to the gathering he went to his tent.

While McClellan was apparently mulling things over in his tent, Poole had blistered the air in the First Platoon tent by saying they should march on Houston — with or without the First.

Sgt. Williams again said that he was wrong — dead wrong — and that he was crazy for even thinking of such a thing. He added, "An' you must be a damn' fool to think these boys will do anything without McClellan."

Sgt. Odums supported Williams. "You'd do better waitin'," he said.

"Wait for what?" Poole demanded. "We ain't got time to wait. If they can rope off a bunch of innocent civilians doin' nothin' but waitin' at a train station, what'n hell do you think they'll do to a nigger in jail — and in uniform?"

Boland said, "I agree with Sergeant Odums. We ought'a at least wait 'til the sarge comes back. He might have a plan."

"Plan my ass!" Poole fired. "Didn' he just walk outta here with the white man? You think the white man's gonna let him do what ought'a be done? If he wanted to do somethin', he'd a' said so while he was sittin' here."

"Yeah," said Williams, "but you don't know what he was thinkin'."

"I don't give a damn 'bout what he was thinkin'. All I know is what I think. An' I'm thinkin' I'll be damned if I sit here an' let these crackers get away with this crap. I'm sick an' tired of all of 'em! Sick an' tired of lettin' the white man walk all over me. An' I'm thinkin' the time to do somethin' about it is right now. Sergeant Odums, you was a fighter. You know what we ought'a be doin'."

The big black First with the rumbling voice and hands like anvils looked at the corporal and said, "I was a fighter in the *ring*. This ain't no ring. An' I say before anybody do anything, you ought'a wait."

"An' I still say, wait for what? You think the police is waitin'?

You think that bastid Quacken-whatever-the-hell-his-name-is is waitin'? Hell no, he ain't waitin'. He probably done already beat hell out'a Dukes an' them. I heard how he uses bicycle chains to beat people. An' he'll do it because they know us niggers ain't gonna do a damn thing but talk, just like the first sergeant. An' if you waitin' for him to do somethin', you might as well forget it. You might just as well forget about Dukes an' all our boys, 'cause the First ain't gonna do nothin'! All he want to do is run up an' down the field, actin' like some war-crazy maniac, yellin' and makin' everybody sweat — for nuthin'."

"It ain't for nothing," Simms said, surprising everyone by showing strength. "It's to make us look good. It's to make us proud, to show everybody that the colored man is as good as the white man."

Poole gave him a dismissing look. "Shut up, you faggot, an' sit down."

A steaming Boland scrambled to his feet with clenched fists. "Don't you talk to him like that! I'll knock your block off!"

Poole looked at the beefy soldier. He would have taken him on had not Sgt. Odums tactfully diverted his attention.

"Poole, you're talking about going into town an' knocking over a whole police station?"

"That is *precisely* what I'm talkin' about."

"Do you have any *idea* what that would mean?"

"It means our boys will be free. It means we won't be layin' down lettin' the white man run us aroun' no more. It's time for us to run *him* aroun'."

"How?"

"By showin' him we ain't afraid of him. By showing him we got some spine. By showing him an' everybody else we got backbone," Poole said. "An' we got somethin' else. We got guns. I'm the Supply corporal. I got the keys."

Mess Sgt. Willie Powell, who had been sitting next to Cpl. Jackson of I Company, had heard enough. It had gotten far too dangerous for him. He finished packing a cigarette he had been rolling, ran his tongue along the side of the gummed paper, and started out. "S'time for me to get back to my kitchen. I'm a cook, not a fighter. Anybody wanna volunteer for K.P., follow me. It's a heap a'lot safer in my Mess Tent than in here. An' I'm thinkin', you gonna live a whole lot longer."

About three or four men trailed Powell up the aisle. Poole became even angrier. "That's it, run! Run!" No one turned around. In a huff he returned to the others. "Let me tell the rest of you dumb, black sonovabitches somethin'. That's the very reason y'all ain't got nothin' now — you too scared to fight for what you believe in. Look at'cha. You call yourselves soldiers. An' *King* Company soldiers — 24th *Infantry soldiers* — on top of that! Well, if you're soldiers, Lord help what they call them other people. But wait a minnit, maybe I know what kind of soldiers you are. Maybe I know somethin' about you, after all. You these same ignant sonsabitches that come runnin' to the Army because somebody told you a nigger could *be* somebody here, that you could prove your manhood here. But that same somebody forgot to tell you that we ain't got half the equipment them white boys got. They got beds an' we got cots. They got pillows an' we got air. They even got Springfields an' what do we got? Junk — an' even half of them won't fire. An' them same sonsabitches forgot to tell you that their corporal of Supply don't have to go aroun' sneakin' an' stealin' to make ends meet, like I do. They forgot to tell you that ol' Joe Nigger breaks down sometimes an' could use a little medical attention, that he's sick and tired of eatin' a bunch of garbage even the rats don't want. Yet you bitch an' moan 'cause they won't send you overseas 'cause you're colored. You done fought — and *died* — in every war and skirmish this country's done ever had. Now, they don't want you in Europe to fight another white man, but you still wanna go so's you can serve in a labor battalion an' end up workin' in sanitary squads, cleanin' crap-houses for the white boys. An' then maybe — *maybe* the good ol' U.S. Government'll give you *permission* to go over an' lay in some muddy, stinking, rat-loaded trenches to face a German, a sunovabitch you ain't never seen before an'a sunovabitch that ain't never done you no harm. Over there you ain't wanted, and over here you ain't nothin'. Even the American Red Cross won't have nothin' to do with you. You can't even go to them for somethin' as simple as a stick of gum, or a cigarette, or a chaw of tobacco. But yet you wanna go fight."

"Check yourself, Poole," said Sgt. Odums. "The Germans would'a done you some harm if they could'a got to you,"

"An' you better b'lieve it," Sgt. Williams added. "Didn't they kill a hundred thousand natives in Southwest Africa?"

"An' in Brookhaven, Mississippi where I was born, they lynched a boy, an' twenty thousand crackers showed up just to enjoy the crime," countered Poole hotly. "An' it wasn't too long before that when the KKK alone flogged, burned, and murdered some two thousand coloreds in Louisiana. An' they still doin' it! You can't count all the coloreds the white man's done killed in this country."

"So wha'chu sayin'?" Sgt. Odums asked.

"I'm sayin' the white man is here; our war is here. An' it's gonna be here for the next nine hunnert an' ninety-nine years, that is if he don't find new ways to kill you all off first while you grinnin' in his face. I'm sayin', as long as there's a white man an'a black face on this earth there's gonna be somethin' to war about, 'cause he's always gonna think you're a horse's ass an' want to get rid of you, one way or another. An' if you're still around, the best he wants you to do is clean up after him, to be his servant. An' I'm sayin' I didn'leave no wife an'three kids to come in the Army to be nobody's lackey. An' I'm sayin' to all'a you dumb, black asses to go on over there an' fight — or clean toilets or white behinds like the Army want you to do — an' if you lucky enough to get back, I want you to walk up into some cracker's face like that Quackensunovabitch, talkin' 'bout how you fought for this country, so's he can knock the livin' daylights outta you. An' I'm sayin' one more thing: when the war over there is over, ain't a damn thing changin'. We win, they lose, an' you'll still be a nigger. On top of that, all of 'em you didn't kill over there will get on the boat, come over here, join the rest of these white sonsabitches, an' you'll be a nigger all over again. You're home, he'll be from Europe, you'll still be a nigger, an' with his no-English-speakin' ass, it'll be his country."

Fired by his own words, Poole was ready to go. "Who's marchin' with me?!"

Puerto Rico, a lone company member, stood. And then there was Pedro, and then one other.

Boland looked at Puerto Rico. "Puerto Rico Hicks, why don't you sit yo' pink-lookin' self back down. You know the sarge ain't gonna like what you doin'."

Puerto Rico remained standing.

Sgts. Odums and Williams stood, but not for the same reason. They were leaving.

"You boys from Companies I and L, let's get back to our areas."

Only a few men stood to follow them out.

"Okay," said Odums. "The choice is yours. Y'all don't know what you're lettin' yourselves in for. But, again, the choice is yours."

Seconds after the eight men left through the rear of the tent, McClellan returned. He saw that Poole was ready to make a move. "What are you doing?" he asked. His voice was not nearly as rigid and demanding as it should have been.

"We're on our way to free Sergeant Dukes an' them."

It didn't draw the expected reaction from the First. Taking a long look at the three men standing with Poole, and much to everybody's surprise, he said quietly, "To march on Houston is not the thing to do."

McClellan should have been staunchly against the move, but his manner and tone of voice said otherwise.

Poole was thrown off guard, but he pushed on. "King Company lives are at stake, Sergeant," he said, but not harshly. "And Sergeant, you have faced a similar situation before."

It was indicting. McClellan quickly looked at him and then at the men. He knew exactly what the corporal was referring to, yet he was still taken by surprise. "How would you know what I've faced before?"

"I've known it all along. Sergeant Dukes told me."

McClellan fell silent. He mulled the guarded secret he and Dukes had shared for 10 years, looked at the puzzled faces of the men again, and settled back on the corporal. "And you told who?"

In a quiet, respectful voice, Poole said, "Nobody, Sir."

The First lapsed into another silence. Whether he was thinking about revealing all in the moments that followed couldn't be determined, though it looked as if he were about to say something significant to the men when a white soldier stuck a fearful head through the door.

Breaking the quiet and addressing no one in particular, the soldier timidly asked, "First Sergeant McClellan? Is he in here?"

The First nodded. "I'm McClellan."

"I'm to take you up to Battalion Headquarters right away. The wheeler's waitin'."

The head ducked back out. McClellan started to leave.

Poole started again. "Do we march, Sergeant?"

McClellan didn't say anything. He didn't want to say anything. Poole wanted an answer. "Do we march, Sergeant? We can't talk our boys outta jail."

McClellan stopped for a long moment without looking around. Then, as he had done before, he exited quietly.

• • •

When the wheeler arrived at Battalion Headquarters, McClellan got out quickly. He had never been to Battalion Headquarters at Logan. It had been different back in Columbus. Back there he found himself making at least biweekly or bimonthly trips. There were always some reports he had to deliver, requisitions to be filled, schedules to be O.K.'d—any number of things had to be done. But not so at Camp Logan. Here, he was a stranger.

Warrant Officer Froelich emerged from an office down from the corridor's entrance. When the first sergeant saw him, he saluted as required by regulations. Ignoring the salute, Froelich led him past a few doors and on to what amounted to a conference room. It was roomy and stark, and the lighting was insufficient.

Lt. Col. Briggs flanked one side of a long table, and Col. Stout, the other. Surrounding them were any number of officers, with Capt. Farrell seated about midway. Present also were seven important-looking civilians.

The King Company first sergeant entered the room with stern deliberateness. He clicked his heels and saluted his battalion commander. "First Sergeant/Master Sergeant Obie O. McClellan, reporting as ordered, Sir."

Briggs didn't waste a moment. He shoved aside a folder that Froelich had placed before him. "You are a career soldier with a number of years of service, are you not?"

"I am, Sir."

"As a career soldier, do you recall violating marching orders and demonstrating obstreperous arrogance when you arrived on post?"

"I recall violating orders given to me by my commanding officer, Captain Farrell, Sir."

"For which charges should have been filed by now."

"We received disciplinary action, Sir."

"For which *charges* should have been filed?" Briggs demanded harshly.

"Charges could've been filed, Sir."

"But they were not?"

"Not to my knowledge, Sir."

"You're still wearing chevrons and rockers. You were to be reduced in rank and position. You knew that?"

"I had heard about it, Sir."

"Did you *know* that, Sergeant?!"

"I knew it, Sir."

"Knowing you were to be demoted, you still took charge of K Company?"

"Because I read nothing official, Sir."

"*Did you — and are you not — taking charge of Company K?!*"

"I did. And I am, Sir."

"You're still assuming the position of First?"

"Yes, Sir. But only because I've received no orders."

"You've received no written orders, and you were never told anything verbally?"

McClellan didn't respond. Briggs asked more heatedly, "I'm asking you, Sergeant. Your company commander never told you that you were — or you were to *be* — the subject of demotion?"

"Captain Farrell told me he was cutting demotion orders."

"*That isn't true, Sergeant,*" Capt. Farrell said, trying vainly to protect his First, as the First had been trying to protect him. "I never told you I was — "

"Shut up, Captain!" Briggs said.

"Colonel, what the sergeant is saying is not true. He was never informed he was to be demoted, verbally or otherwise."

"*Shut up, Captain!!*"

The captain reluctantly did as ordered, not realizing — or perhaps not caring — what Briggs was trying to do.

The battalion commander knew that it would be better to say to a board of inquiry that was sure to be convened that whatever happened in the San Felipe district was strictly because of the natural unruliness of blacks and black leadership. He wanted nothing to point to officer's — or, more important, *officers'* — dereliction.

"Continue, Sergeant."

"Before he continues, Sir, I'd like to say something."

"If you do it'll be the last word you'll ever say," the colonel threatened. "And I mean every goddamned word of it, Captain."

McClellan, feeling freer, continued on his own.

"As I said, Sir, Captain Farrell said that he was cutting orders for demotion and I was to no longer assume the duties of first sergeant."

"And when did he tell you that?"

"At the time we were put on disciplinary action, Sir."

"With that in mind, I will be brief and direct. The seriousness of this afternoon's occurrence cannot be overstressed. To be perfectly blunt, it was a goddamned disgrace. *Sickening.* And there is going to be hell to pay. I've been informed most of these people in town have been armed since you people arrived and I can damn well understand why. Now, in addition to my concern and the people of Houston's concern, not to mention what is sure to be the concern of people of the country over, the Army has dispatched ranking officers from both the inspector general's office and the judge advocate's office to conduct a full inquiry. Before they arrive, I feel it imperative to get all the information I can, to include colored input. Particularly from you."

"As Captain Farrell has probably told you, I was not in town, Sir."

"But most — if not all — of the guilty were your men."

"Guilty, Sir?" McClellan asked. His brow showed a mixture of incredulity and anger. Even the deflated Capt. Farrell caught the implication. McClellan tossed a look at all the stone-faced officers. They gave nothing in return. Neither did the important-looking civilians.

The First could hardly form his question. "How can the troops be guilty, Colonel? There's been no trial yet."

"*Trial?!* For these Bolshevistic anarchists, you're talking about a *trial?!*"

"Yes, Sir."

"Well, you keep on thinking that way, Mister. I hope the sons-a-bitches are shot before sunrise."

"*Shot* — before sunrise,' Sir?"

"Shot *dead* before sunrise! And if I had my way, that is precisely what would happen. The courts be damned."

The first sergeant's mind raced back to that earlier point in his life when he had always been plagued by the bad dream. As it had been just a few hours before, the dream — or nightmare — was becoming all too true.

Said the Sergeant to the Colonel, "I have no colored input, Sir."

Chapter 17

The lights of the returning motorcycle with the sidecar came to a sudden stop at the edge of the King Company area. McClellan hopped out and headed directly for the First Platoon tent. The motorcycle sped away. With the colonel's words echoing in his mind, the First was calling as he moved. *"King Company! Volunteers only!"*

From the front of the tent, Poole's voice responded. "Volunteers —armed, ready, and waiting, Sergeant!"

Poole knew the first sergeant would be treated roughly at Battalion Headquarters. He knew it because he prided himself on knowing the white man. He knew that for the first sergeant it would be decision-making time.

King Company would march.

In the First's absence, the lanky, kinky-haired corporal of Supply had entered the armory and had put several *stacked arms* collections at the company's midpoint. He told every man who wanted a weapon to take one, but only a few did. Most returned to their tents, as did practically all the members of companies I and L. Babe Boyd and about a half-dozen others, fearful of what was taking place, and not knowing if the first sergeant would be returning, left the company area altogether. They wanted no part of marching on Houston under Cpl. Poole.

When McClellan appeared, or when they heard his voice, just about every man who had returned to his tent came out to retrieve a weapon from one of the stacks. As they would have done on a normal march, they fell into formation.

Simms and Boland, who had left the platoon during the sergeant's absence, looked on from the safety of the Orderly Room tent. When they saw the returning sergeant moving to the formation, Simms quietly got the company guidon. The two followed the hurrying First to the assembly. Others came out as well. Even Mess Sgt. Willie Powell, apparently with a change of heart, sauntered to the formation.

As McClellan closed in he was surprised that a small portion of the company had been formed with full gear on, but he said nothing. Poole, soldierly erect, saluted and said, "King Company. Armed, ready, an' waitin', Sergeant. An' when we get to town, we ready to shoot anything that moves. We gonna blast the whole city of Houston. It's gonna be a war."

"There will be no such thing. And you will do no such thing. Assume your normal position, Corporal," McClellan said, sending the man moving to the end of the formation. His voice had lost some of the tautness and he sounded almost matter-of-fact. "Tonight we march on Houston. We will march in order so as not to arouse suspicion. You will fire only if fired upon. The purpose of the march is to free our troops who have already been adjudged guilty. Expect trouble. I have knowledge that some of the white civilians have been armed since our arrival here at Logan. What we are doing, and what we are about to do, is illegal and is contrary to every law known to man or the military. But it must be done. The consequences will be severe. Most of us will not live after it is over. Anyone want out, say so. I will not hold it against you. If you do not want out, hold your positions. I take notice of you few men from Companies I and L. It is nice to have you with us, but I ask you to realize what you are doing. I ask you, as I ask my men, to consider the consequences. After you've done so, you are free to leave."

No one moved.

"I say again: We are marching. It is *not* lawful. It will be a high cost for a short step. After we are done, most of us will not live. Reconsider what you're doing, and feel free to leave."

Still no one moved.

"Alright, then, Corporal Poole, Mess Sergeant Willie Powell, bring up the rear. If anybody falls out, shoot them. Detail, sling arms! Right, face! Forward, march!"

Deep, sober, grimly silent, they moved away. Prominent among the 52 were John Hong Kong Chin, Puerto Rico, Pepe de Anda, and Boland. There, too, and as determined as all the others, was the trio of Roosevelt, Andrews, and Menyard. There were no rhymes in their minds.

As the tail end of the company cleared the Supply Tent and angled off to the rear gate, bringing up the rear with Poole was Mess Sgt. Willie Powell. He took a few steps with the detail, then broke formation and ran for the Mess Tent. Poole yelled, *"Powell!"*

The mess sergeant didn't stop. Poole then spun around, dropped to the prone position, and fired. The scrambling Powell wasn't hit, but just as Poole releveled, the headlights of a vehicle swung along the front side of the Orderly Room tent. Being driven back to the company area, Capt. Farrell heard the shot and stood in the convertible, attempting to trace the sound. Because of darkness and distance, he couldn't see what was taking place, but bolstered by the earlier thought that something was bound to happen, he hollered, "What the hell's going on?!"

"We're marching, Captain!"

"You're *what?!*"

"The company is *marching*. And we're *armed*," Poole hollered clearly.

"Have you people gone mad?!" the captain yelled. He hopped out of the vehicle and cleared his way almost to the front of the Orderly Room.

"That's far enough!" Poole hollered.

Farrell moved in closer.

Poole slammed the rifle's bolt forward and fired off a warning shot.

"Poole! Put the rifle down and return to your tent!"

"It's too late, Cap."

"Lay your weapon down, Corporal! *Poole!! Put the weapon down and return to your tent.*"

The captain still didn't know Poole was alone. He called out to the empty company area. *"Sergeant McClellan?! First Sergeant McClellan?!!"*

Although the captain didn't know it, it would do no good to call the First. He was moving the remnants of the company down the road without looking back. Rochester, on guard duty in the shack, saw the company as they approached. He automatically left his post and joined the departing men.

Back at the Orderly Room tent, the scared driver saw the captain's predicament, hopped out of the vehicle with the crank, and started cranking furiously.

"Don't you dare move that vehicle!"

"But, Sir!"

"Don't move!" the captain yelled. He directed his attention back to the area from where Poole's fire and voice had come. He took another step and called, *"Poole!"*

Poole answered by shooting out one of the vehicle's lights. Unafraid, the captain glanced back at the vehicle, then started walking forward.

"That's far enough, Captain!"

"Poole, put the rifle down!"

"Hold it right there, Cap."

"Put the weapon down, Poole, or you'll find yourself before a court-martial!"

"One more step and I'll fire!"

The step was taken. Poole fired three rounds and said, "I been missin' on purpose, Captain. The next one will be your throat."

The driver started to crank up again.

"I'll skin you alive if you move that thing!" Farrell yelled back as he continued to move in Poole's direction.

The captain had reached a point where he could see the symmetry of one of the *stacked arms* collections. Most of the rifles were missing. Now he knew with full certainty what was going on. There were no signs of life coming from any of the tents, and if McClellan were still there, he would have at least responded to the shots. Quickly the captain decided to get help from Battalion Headquarters. As he turned to head back to vehicle, Poole took aim, fired two shots, and took off for the formation. One of the shots flattened a tire, the other hit the driver. The captain raced back to offer assistance. One look and he knew there was nothing he could do. The driver was dead.

There was no time left. The captain sprinted out of the area. While he was sprinting to Battalion Headquarters, McClellan and his men were double-timing to Houston.

Chapter 18

The Houston Police station was a horror. The old two-story brick building, built to hold no more than 20 to 25 prisoners at a time, was naturally segregated, and tradition had seen to it that all the blacks were imprisoned in the rear. The cells were dank, and even on a good day one was apt to gag from the stench. Normally most of the cells would be filled with weekend drunks, gamblers, wife-beaters, and assorted miscreants who — black or white — thought nothing of puking or relieving themselves in whatever spot that was convenient.

On this Saturday night in August, steamily hot and active, seven black civilian prisoners had been held over from previous arrests. Together with the day's haul, they took up all the space. The three up-front cells, nearest the front door and desk, were reserved for whites. One cell, midway of the corridor, benefited from a window that was barred but did permit a welcome passage of air. In it was P.K., the trouble-making truck driver. He had again gotten drunk and been arrested earlier in the day. Scared and knowing that the blacks were going on pass, he was trying to leave town by driving his truck from Houston to Amarillo on the railroad tracks. Even at that, he was driving with the brakes on.

Sixteen of the 33 troops had been crammed into the sweltering segregated cells. Those who couldn't fit were placed in the *backroom*, even though they would have had far more room up front. The *backroom*, as the police called it, was wire-caged and was for emergency purposes only. Dark, dingy, and hose-drenched, it measured an inadequate 19 by 27 feet. Unlike the cells, it had a heavily stained commode in the far corner. There were no bunks, and a wire-protected light hung from the ceiling. Two wire-meshed windows permitted vague light from the city to beam through.

With his mouth still hurting along with the rest of his body, Sgt. Dukes was resting in the corner opposite the commode. Jody was constantly at his side, doing much to comfort the ancient soldier. Seeming to work against restoration of health, however, he was using a filthy, blood-stained handkerchief.

Also getting Jody's attention was Pete. He was sitting fairly close to the sergeant, and it appeared he was getting ready for another relapse. Seeing this, Jody again stepped over the sergeant and began mopping his friend's brow. It helped.

All the men in the backroom, drenched and weary, looked as though they had been through the mill. Some, admittedly, looked much better than others, but, in the main, they were a nauseating sight.

The men could hear a lot of what was going on up front, and they could also hear P.K. occasionally throwing up while drunkenly making the attempt to croon *Old Black Joe*. Knowing he could be heard by the blacks, he replaced the words *gentle voices* with *gentle darkies* and lingered on the note. When Quackenbush passed by his cell on the way to the backroom, P.K was still lingering.

"Gonna whack 'em with the cycle chains this time, Quack?" he asked.

"I'm gonna whack you if you don't shut up," the fat man said, bypassing the bulk of the black troops and continuing toward the 12 or 13 in back.

"Alright, Boys," the policeman said when he got there. His voice was relaxed and pleasant. "I'm gettin' ready to tuck it in for tonight. Anything I can do b'fore I go?"

"What about some food and water?"

"I thought y'all had enough water." With concern in his manner, he called up front and told Blanchard the men needed water.

"It'll take a minnit", responded Blanchard.

Actually it was going to take longer.

While Capt. Farrell was still laboring up to Headquarters, McClellan and his men were making telling progress on the main road leading to the city. They still had a long way to go before reaching the outskirts.

It was a long, dark road now, far different from earlier when it was clogged with the men going on pass. The troops were determined but quiet, and only managed to collect curious stares from the very few whites and even fewer blacks whom they passed. No one said anything. They thought that the troops were in training.

The men moved on without event, alternately double-timing and speed-walking. Their grim eyes remained planted dead ahead. They would have no trouble with directions to the police station, because one of the men from King and two of the men from L Company lived in Houston and were familiar with all routes.

"You 'bout ready with that water, Blanchard?" Quackenbush called back.

"Another sec."

"K."

The fat man leaned against the bars. "How long y'all gonna be in town?"

No one said anything.

"Cat got'cha tongue?"

He still didn't get a response.

"Well, I can understan' it if y'all don't wanna be sociable. An' that's the way it should be in a white man's presence. Can't fault you for that. But I'm gonna tell you somethin', Boys. Y'all in some pretty deep do-do." He waited and casually asked, "Y'all like sports?"

Someone answered, "No."

Whoever said it wished he hadn't.

"I love sports," the policeman said, then was quiet.

The commotion started as an outer door opened. "Comin' thru," said Blanchard. He was leading two policemen as they dragged a thick hose that had been attached to a fire hydrant.

Blanchard aimed the nozzle and hollered something to the man outside. Instantly the water powered through the hose and tossed bodies around like straws. Some men were riveted against the wall, unable to say anything. Others screamed and yelled as they slipped and slid from corner to corner.

Finally, Quackenbush had seen enough. He told Blanchard to cut the water off. When Blanchard complied, the big policeman, appearing like a blur to the men as he moved to the bars, said, "Now, am I gonna have any more trouble out of you people?"

The answer was slow. "No."

"Now, say it like you s'pose to. Say it like niggers — all of you."

One of the men said, "We can't do that 'cause the sarge told us the word nigger is only used by a nigger."

Quackenbush didn't know who said it, but it made no difference. "What'd you say, Nigger?"

Pete hadn't said it. The water had pinned him in the corner. But, hurt even more, he managed to crawl to the cell door and lifted himself up so that Quackenbush could fully hear what he had to say.

His voice raspy, he faced the man and said, "Listen to me careful: The soldier said our sergeant always told us 'the word nigger is only used by a nigger.' So guess what you is? A fat, slop-eatin', pig-faced nigger. You white, but you ain't nothin' but a pig-faced nigger all the same. An' you hurt my woman, Mr. Nigger. An' I ain't gonna forget that. When I get outta here, I'm gonna find out just how much sports you like. I'm gonna get me a baseball bat an' I'm gonna beat your head 'til it turns to mush. An' then I'm gonna kick your fat —"

Pete was unable to finish. Knuckles exposed, his hands were wrapped around the bars. Quackenbush, almost in a sleight-of-hand move, slipped his blackjack out of his pocket and came down on the knuckles with all his weight. Pete was hit so hard the knuckles and tissues nearly fused in place. He screamed in agony. Jody sailed over to help. He tried to pry the fingers away, but he got no help from Pete, who was out like a light. The body slid down. By Quackenbush dropped to his knees and pounded him again. By the time Jody and the others pulled the body away from the bars, Pete's wrists and fingers were nothing but blood, bones, and dangling skin. Still not satisfied, the fat man fumed for the hose. When it was turned on, he kept it blasting for so long that even the policemen who had accompanied Blanchard felt sorry and ran outside in panic to cut the water off.

"When that bastard wakes up, he's dead," Quackenbush said. "Y'all hear me? He's dead. An' the rest of you niggers, if you even think of actin' up again I'll kill every single one of you black sunovabitches. You hear me?"

"Yessuh," a lone voice said, which could have been Jody's.

"Yes, Suh', *what?*"

"Yessuh, Mr. Quackenbush." It was Jody's voice.

"Now, I'm gonna ask you again. An' you better answer like you 'spose to. Am I gonna have any more trouble outta y'all black sonsabitches?"

"Nosuh."

"All of you say it."

"Nosuh," they said in unison.

"Agin. All of you niggers. Say it agin. And say it like you s'posed to."

In poor, weak, broken unison, they said, "You ain't gonna have no more trouble out of us, Mr. Quackenbush, Suh."

The fat man ended his visit.

On the way home, Blanchard remembered that Nell hadn't yet been arrested. And so the two policemen went there.

It was a fruitless trip.

Nellie Moore died as a result of Ananias Blanchard's pistol blow to her head. She had already been moved to Bullock's funeral home with the others.

• • •

Two hours and thirty-two minutes after the start of the discussion about the march to the police station, the troops arrived at the police station. McClellan halted his men directly in front of the already opened door, which permitted light to bathe the brick stairs and spread a few yards beyond. Militarily he ordered Simms to plant the guidon and strategically deployed Poole and five others to cover the rear. The other men, strangely quiet, remained standing at attention. Before going inside, the First quietly designated four 12-member squads, and said, "If shots are fired, I want the First Squad to come running. Second and Third, cover the flanks and assist Poole in the rear. Fourth, stand guard."

Inside, McClellan walked directly up to the high desk and saluted the desk sergeant. What he said could have sounded self-serving, but in his state of mind, it was not.

"My name is Obie O. McClellan, Master Sergeant, First Sergeant, King Company, Third Battalion, 24th Infantry, Army of the United States. I'm here to see about my men."

The desk sergeant, a thin man, frowned. Stealthily he sent his fingers sliding to his side for his pistol. The last move was jerked and obvious. It sent McClellan digging for his weapon. The policeman successfully fired a shot, but he missed his target. The first sergeant didn't miss. Almost without aiming, he fired. The bullet penetrated the chin, and the desk sergeant's head hit the desk. Blood gushed from his nose and mouth.

The shots created a commotion inside and out.

The First Squad raced inside. Three upstairs policemen raced downstairs, firing. Charles Johnson and Rufus Cannon from Company I broke and ran like cowards. LeRoy Johnson went down, as did Hong Kong Chin. Pepe de Anda was hit. Johnny Auer and Peter Brown from Company L spun around and fired at the policemen at the same time. Down they went.

By now, McClellan had rushed midway to the rear of the corridor. "Dukes! Dukes! Where are you, Dukes?!"

"Back here, Sergeant!" answered Henry Crawford.

Leaving a few men covering the desk, the first sergeant quickly collected a detail and rushed to the back.

Outside, toward the rear, another shot rang out. In the second floor window of a house across from the station, a man leveled his rifle at one of the men with Poole. Poole returned the fire, hitting the man. More fire came from downstairs. Eugene Hutchinson, another of Poole's men, was hit. Angry, Poole grabbed the downed soldier's rifle, and together with his own, he blasted the entire house, hitting an elderly man. A younger figure was also hit. There was no more fire coming from the house, but Poole reloaded and fired again. This time he aimed at a silhouette leaning out of the third-floor window. Loading and reloading, he tried to saw the head off with bullets. Another figure, smaller, poked a frightened head out of the window. Poole leveled and fired. A 16-year-old girl fell from the window, hit the second landing, and crushed her skull on the cement below.

Inside, McClellan had blasted all cell locks and swung open all the doors. The prisoners, whites and blacks, civilians as well as soldiers, poured for freedom. P.K. stumbled out of his cell and consumed time generously thanking the sergeant for his efforts. Still drunk, he was so grateful he was at the point of trying to hug the black man. McClellan shook him off. P.K. ran to the front door. Before dashing out, he turned and yelled to the sergeant, "You still a nigger, I don't care wha'cha do!"

Moving up from the rear was Dukes, hanging onto Jody and barely able to make it. He was delighted to see his old friend, and as he came forward, he tried to force a smile from his aching mouth. He caught his breath and said, "Thank you, Mac. They'd a killed us."

"Not as long as I'm around, old friend," McClellan said, taking a moment to look the old-timer over.

"I could use a good cigar right bout now, if my mouth would let me smoke one," Dukes said, in pain.

"I'll get you a box if I ever get out of this mess."

Sounding doubtful, Dukes asked, "You think you will?"

"Not a chance, my friend. Not a chance," McClellan answered. He then directed his attention to a couple of men rushing by. "Some of you men help Sergeant Dukes and our wounded get back to camp."

"I ain't leavin', Mac."

"You've got to."

"I can't leave, Mac. I ain't gonna do it."

"Dukes, the end is closer than you think."

"S'alright with me."

"But not with me. It'd be better if you left now. At least there'll be something left of the company. This young fella will help you, won't you, Son?"

"Yes, Sir," Jody said eagerly. "An' I'll take Pete, too." Dukes looked at Jody. "Why on God's earth didn' I do what somethin' told me to do when I was down at that station. I should'a put you on that train today, 'stead of waitin' on Monday. *Damn, damn, damn,* that hurts me."

Neither Jody nor the First knew what he was referring to.

"C'mon, Dukes, you've got to go."

"I ain't gonna go, Mac. Maybe later. Not now."

"You've got to, Dukes. So far, you haven't done anything serious. The Army can't charge you with anything. With us, those who marched, well, it's just about over."

"Say wha'cha want, Mac. I ain't leavin' — 'least 'til we get further down the road. An' nonna our boys is gonna leave, either."

The first sergeant didn't force it.

With everybody hustled out, the formation had been re-formed. While waiting for Poole to return from the rear, McClellan told the men from Companies I and L to return to their respective companies. Six of them did. Dow Lee left with them.

The first sergeant again tried to get Sgt. Dukes to leave.

"Mac," said Dukes with finality, "you wastin' your breath."

• • •

It was a safe bet that Col. Stout would still be on post, thought an alternately running, walking and panting Capt. Farrell. After the meeting earlier, he had overheard the post commander say that he'd be stopping by the Officers' Club to have a word with all of his officers not off post for the weekend. Because of the enmity that existed between the two, and the hard feelings that had erupted again during the meeting, Lt. Col. Briggs was sure to be in his quarters.

The club and Col. Briggs's quarters were about equidistant. Deep down, Farrell knew he would be better off if he followed his instincts and took his case to Stout first. But he followed the chain of command and veered off to his battalion commander. He was nearly out of breath when he got there, but he had enough left in him to explain fully and clearly what was taking place with his company.

Though not exactly casual, Lt. Col. Briggs didn't attach the necessary urgency to the situation and spent far too much time questioning the K Company commander. For reasons known only to himself, Briggs engaged the protesting captain in conversation a full 22 minutes before letting him leave to contact the post commander. Even then, instead of summoning a car or letting him use the car that was there, Briggs made the captain walk to the Officers' Club. In the meantime, the colonel said with damning casualness, he would dispatch a detail to head McClellan off.

When Farrell finally arrived at the club and related the events to Col. Stout, the post commander reacted with rage. Common sense took over, and he acted swiftly and decisively. Stout immediately had all the officers in the club assemble whatever troops they could find and ready them for an urgent move to the Fourth Ward's San Felipe district. He told his officers to find all Supply sergeants, and if they couldn't be found, he ordered them to break open the armories and Supply Rooms and get weapons. He contacted the Motor Pool and had every truck available put on standby. Unwilling to wait for troops and trucks, he placed his adjutant, Maj. Edward Tilque, in charge of the post, gathered whatever staff officers he could find, and loaded them into four staff cars. In less than 18 minutes, the cars were racing off post. Lt. Col. Briggs, the Third Battalion commander, was not with them.

McClellan and his men were now in formation preparing to march. Before leaving, and unknown to the First, Poole had sneaked across the street that ran in back of the station, where he shot and killed another man and his wife. Now, back in front of the formation, he wanted to riddle the station and send it up in flames, but McClellan wouldn't allow it. The corporal argued that it would prevent Quackenbush and his men from returning from Battalion Headquarters and gunning for them. It was at that point that McClellan again started looking strange, a bit disconnected. It was a look that had progressed from the look he had when Carter first told him about the fracas in town.

Steely-eyed, his voice low, the First asked Poole how he knew that Quackenbush went to Battalion Headquarters.

"When I was in back, I overheard one'a the policeman ringin' there," Poole said. "That's why I started shootin', after he started shootin' at me. They was talkin' slaughter. Then the policeman saw me listenin' through the window, an' he started shootin'."

Poole was lying. There wasn't an ounce — not an *iota* — of truth to anything he said, yet it had the first sergeant thinking. Perhaps had he been in another frame of mind, he would have done something different. Trying to make a quick assessment, he asked, "Are you sure, Poole?"

"Yessir. I swear they was."

"I want you to be sure. Very sure," McClellan said, his voice still low, and still tainted by strangeness.

"I'm positive, Sarge. I heard 'em."

"And they were talking about slaughtering us?"

"Ever last one of us," Poole added to the fabrication. "The policeman on this end of the line told 'em we was here an' what we'd done."

McClellan's mind was racing; he appeared even more peculiar. "Everything okay, Sarge?"

"Yes."

"We wastin' a lotta time," Poole said. "We gotta do somethin'. An' we gotta do it now."

"If they're coming from Battalion Headquarters —"

"That's where they comin' from. Camp."

"We'll meet them on the road." McClellan said.

"And do what?"

"Plant the guidon."

It was like declaring war.

•   •   •

There were no street lights on the long dirt road that led from camp. When the staff cars' lights cut through the darkness, from a distance they looked like a short string of jewelry shimmering through velvet. Col. Stout occupied the passenger's seat of the first car. Capt. Reed was behind the wheel, with Warrant Officer Froelich and others in the rear seat. Close on their tails were three other cars, two of them convertibles. Guns pointed from all sides of the cars. They were carried by officers who were tucked inside and jammed the running boards and wrapped their free arms around window posts and whatever else would secure them.

When the cars left the gate, they were moving with speed but fearful of ambush, and not one hundred percent sure the troops would actually go all the way into town, Stout decided to move with caution along the road. Several times they stopped, searched the fields, and continued to inch along.

What Col. Stout and the gun-bearers didn't know was that the troops had done what they had set out to do and that soon the convoy would be crawling into a trap.

The first thing that would greet them, although because of darkness it couldn't be seen, was the K Company guidon. It didn't fly or wave with snap, rather the dark-blue banner with the white lettering hung limp in a muggy heat that hadn't eased up even in the night.

McClellan had divided the detail into two groups. He led the smaller body away from the others. They were several hundred yards away, and like the others they were still catching their breath after the long run. Yet, they were silent and waiting. Some were still pairing from the afternoon's fray and Quackenbush's later treatment, but no one spoke. From a strategic point of view, the second group was in what appeared to be a holding pattern, standing far back in the weeded fields. They were loose, but still in formation.

The first group — the firing party, as it turned out — was spread 12 to 15 feet behind the guidon and lined along the road's ditch, awaiting the enemy. Except for McClellan, standing to give the order to fire, they were all in the prone position. Among them were the injured Sgt. Dukes, the mindless Pete Curry, Cpl. Poole, Simms, Boland, the rhyming trio of Roosevelt, Andrews, and Menyard,

Crawford, Boot, Pedro, Yancy, and several others.

The one person McClellan wouldn't allow to be in the firing party was Pvt. Jody Cunningham. He was in the holding position far back in the field with the others. He had tried to accompany Pete and Sgt. Dukes to the ditch, but neither McClellan nor Dukes would allow it.

Shortly the beads of lights were seen. The convoy had picked up speed.

The ambush was set. All rifles were at the ready.

"Get ready!" First Sgt. McClellan yelled, and then waited until the cars came in closer. As they did, judging by their headlights, the First called out, "Range 400. Range 300. Range 200. Range 100." The cars were easily within rifle range.

The engines roared in closer. McClellan waited a second or two longer, and called, "Ready!" He paused, then said, "Aim!" He waited — and waited — and waited. Then it was clear. He didn't give the expected follow-up order. Instead, he bellowed, *"HOLD YOUR FIRE!"*

A volley of shots rang out.

"HOLD YOUR FIRE!!!" the first sergeant yelled hysterically, *"THEY'RE ARMY! CEASE FIRE!! DON'T SHOOT! THEY ARE NOT POLICE VEHICLES! CEASE FIRING!!! DON'T SHOOT! THEY'RE ARMY! THEY ARE ARMY!!"*

It was too late. Capt. Reed, standing on the running board, was hit in the chest. The driver was hit. Warrant Officer Froelich stood, ready to jump from the car that now spun erratically out of the wounded driver's control. Both he and another officer were hit by a new volley of shots. The car tilted over into the ditch. Col. Stout was thrown free, and Capt. Whitney, in the second car, leaped to save him. The third car tried to brake to a stop, but failed. The .03's barked off another volley and sent the car careening off the road, where it burst into flames. The cars that were still able to move picked up the injured and U-turned back for assistance. McClellan was still shouting, *Cease fire! Cease fire! Hold your fire!*

Don't Shoot! Hold your fire! They're not police! They're Army!" Uncharacteristically, he had lost control. Almost berserk, he was yelling and screaming, frantically moving up and down the line, wrestling and kicking rifles out of stubborn hands. And then, like everything else around him, he fell quiet.

But the damage had been done.

Chapter 19

Under a clearing moon, the road and everything that surrounded the road to camp was strangely silent. The smell of gunpowder and smoke still hung heavy but there was no wind; no nature's call. Nothing.

The bespectacled first sergeant was alone. He had sent the men who were with him in the ditch to join the others. They moved away stiffly, like zombies, not talking to each other, not really understanding what had happened. The first sergeant understood, but only for a short while. For a moment he knew that everything he had ever known in life was over; that everything he had worked for, sweated over, taught, learned, and believed in was over. No matter what was to come, it was over and nothing was going to change.

For what seemed like an eternity, the first sergeant stood there, molded by the strange look that had grown and, for a time, paralyzed him. He was saying nothing, doing nothing. Darkness couldn't be used as a cover-up or as an excuse to deny or lessen the impact of what had been done, because now that the clearing moon glinted a little brighter, he could see. Perhaps he couldn't see all the carnage, but he could see something, and he could hear something. The barrage of shots again echoed in his mind, but there was no outward reaction. There was no look of sorrow, no feeling of remorse; nothing. There was no look of disbelief that cut through the strangeness and had settled in the eyes; there was no refusal in face or mind. It could not have been that the ordinary senses discredited anything because it was all too real, the bodies that had been riddled with bullets — one still pinned under the overturned vehicle, were all too dead. Dead soldiers.

There was a growing deadness about him as well.

First Sgt. Obie McClellan's eyes were dead. Though he was standing motionless and indurative, still on the forward side of the ditch, it was clear that his mind had slipped into its own abyss. The ditch became trenches. Only in the fields and trenches of Europe were there supposed to be dead soldiers. Soldiers die at the hands of the enemy. These people were not enemy.

The mind plunged deeper. Now he didn't know why they died; why they were there.

Unlike moments ago, he stood there now not knowing what he was doing; not knowing where he was. He was not fighting for an answer, but one came. *War*. A war was raging here. Everything that had happened here happened in war.

In time of war.

Strangely now, the First was enveloped in a far-away look that differed from the other which had been displayed in his eyes.

First Sgt. Obie McClellan was glad the Army had changed its views about the blacks and had allowed them to come here to France.

The battlefields were dark and brooding, but combat was not what he thought it would be. War was not the hell everyone said it would be; it was not the hell he had trained his troops to face. The hardship wasn't as long; death was quicker. Even seeing the dead was not rooted. It did not cut to the core. Nothing did. Death was detached and the dead were depersonalized. He didn't understand it at first, but death and the dead rose up and spoke to him. They told him they worked for war. One said they worked *for* war, the other said they worked *with* the mind. And then they spoke as one. As one they said that in war the mind allowed immunity to the physical and sent signal that it shielded against the personal, thus the living wasn't immobilized by a loss. Hurt, but not immobilized. And together they said that in war if the cause was just, so too, was the journey; so, too, was everything that would happen *on the journey.*

The King Company First Sergeant was sorry — though not deeply because he had been shielded — but he was sorry that in the first skirmish the company had lost Capt. Farrell. He was not among the dead here, but the First knew he must have gotten it somewhere. Perhaps he had gotten it back in the village. Maybe at that station — at that German stronghold Poole had wanted to level.

It was odd for the First to think of his corporal at that moment. It was too bad he had had gotten it. Belligerent and racially militant Poole. He had been right all along about the enemy. Back in the States — at their home base he had been right. And he had been right when they landed in Europe — at the train station when they disembarked and the captain gathered them aside and told them something about the enemy, when he said that *silence was the order of the day.*

And giving his corporal added benefit of the doubt, he was right when he made the statement: *we can't talk the prisoners out of there.* He was right even when he said *we ready to shoot anything that moves.* His anger was justified. The Germans were a cruel people, heartless and merciless. Even at the start, before even engaging in combat, they built bonfires so that all could see that they had burned crosses and had hanged Negroes in effigy. And they had done so without shame or remorse. The Americans would never think to do a thing like that. But the Germans were not Americans. The Americans were the standards of decency. They were everything the Germans weren't. Always America — *always* Americans were fair, charitable, humane, compassionate — believers in democracy, justice and equality. They were not barbarians. And they lived up to the rules of war.

America. *Sweet Land of Liberty.* America. *Her truth keeps marching on.*

He was moving now. Over and over the first sergeant with the wounded and knotted mind wandered up and down the outer edge of the road under that full and unstreaked moon, viewing what the barbarous enemy had done. His mind stayed on fairness as he studied the remaining bodies that had been shot and burned and were now charred and sprawling grotesquely on the ground, pinned under a still smoldering car. The bodies could have been Captain Whitney's and Warrant Officer Froelich's, he didn't know. But there was no question about it, the Americans would not have killed in such fashion. And the Americans would not have allowed the bodies to remain atop the ground in such sobering disrespect, either. If only — the far-away eyes said — if only King had not spent so much time freeing the prisoners of war, they could have arrived earlier and prevented the atrocity; they could have gotten here to this French field and every one of the Americans who had been killed could have been saved. What a pity. What a shame. If only he could have arrived earlier. He was wrong, and he deserved to be criticized, because it was he who was in charge, and it was he who had not moved with resolve. He hadn't responded as a leader.

Now the First was beginning to feel terrible; worthless over the failure. To his way of thinking now, as one of the first blacks to lead blacks in combat, not only had he failed, but by being so derelict and negligent he and he alone had been responsible for a most disgusting and egregious act of criminality. His act — or lack of action, he no longer knew which — but his misdeed had been the worst ever committed by a Negro. The crime was compounded because of all the books he had read; to think of all the Negro lives, the black organizations he had studied — he had failed. To think of all the people and associations who inspired racially; people who spoke of hope, pride, dignity and leadership, it was he who had not acted responsibly. Add to that the many hours spent alone, doing nothing but thinking about ordinary responsibility and black leadership, and then when the time came — when that responsibility and leadership were needed most — what did he do? *He* failed. First Sgt./Master Sgt. Obie O. McClellan *failed*. Here, in Europe, on the field of battle, he had been presented with one of the greatest opportunities in the world; *opportunity*, the one thing that blacks will be struggling and fighting and agonizing over for as long as there will be an America — here, it had been laid directly at his feet — and he *failed*. Obie McClellan had let his race down, his country down, and he had let the Army down; and having done so, once again — *once again* — it gave the white man the right to question the black man and the black man's ability to lead.

First Sgt./Master Sgt. Obie O. McClellan of King Company would leave the military as soon as he returned to the United States and papers could be processed. His only hope was that the Army and the Negro race would never see his likes again.

"Mac, are you alright?"

The two were alone. Sgt. Dukes, still weakened, but now able to move on his own, had walked the First far away from the ditch and the bodies, and where they couldn't be seen from the road. He and two of the men had come over with canteens of water taken from the men who were in full gear and doused the man's face. Dukes sent the men back to the formation to tell Poole where they were, as he continued dabbing the sergeant with his handkerchief. He had been walking and talking to his friend for a full six minutes before the First even recognized him.

The field sergeant walked his First a bit more and then again asked if he were alright.

This time the first sergeant was close to understanding, but not fully. He mumbled something about the company and burying the bodies, and lapsed back into silence. Dukes continued to walk him around.

A curious Poole, anxious to get moving entirely out of the area, came over. Dukes told him that the First had been hit by a ricochet and that it would take a little more time for him to come around. Reluctantly, Poole went back and stayed with the men. Dukes waited, then tried it again. "Are you all right, Mac?"

The First was not alright. The old sergeant walked him some more, and then set him down and started dabbing his face with water from the canteen again.

A few minutes later, the first sergeant started to talk. He wanted to know what had happened. Dukes told him, and during the telling it all came back.

McClellan's sorrow had grown. He spoke for a long while and became so deeply anguished that Dukes was fearful of relapse. After a few more minutes, the First assured the older sergeant that there was nothing to worry about, that the shock of what had happened was over and that his mind was back to where it should be. He stood under his own power and gazed across the darkened field, then his eyes returned to Dukes. "I'm okay," he said.

The old soldier wanted reassurance.

"Dukes, you know me better than any man who has ever lived. Have I ever told you anything that wasn't true?"

"Not yet."

"Then if I say I'm okay, I'm okay."

"We're talking about the mind, Mac."

"I know."

"It can be tricky."

"I know that, Dukes."

"I know what you're trying to say. But I'm alright." McClellan looked at him in a way that said there was something deeper. "How is your mind doing?"

"Not so hot."

"What's that mean?"

"It means it's the end of the road for me. I didn't want to say it back at the station, but it's all over for me. It's time."

For the implications, it was all so casual. They stood quiet for a moment, almost not looking at each other. Sgt. Dukes then looked at his friend and spoke as if reminding himself. "We killed soldiers, Mac," he said. He lowered his head, then brought it back up again. He was about to carry the conversation into an area they had discussed long before, but he saw Poole coming back. McClellan knew what the older sergeant wanted to say, so they both waited.

Poole was in a hurry. "Y'kno, Sarge, I was over there thinkin'. Instead of us just headin' nowhere, we could strike out for Mexico. On a forced march, it won't take us too long to reach the border. Them Mexicans is mad at the Army, anyway. They still mad because of what the Army did to 'em, an' for tryin' to capture Pancho Villa an' stickin' it to him. They'll be glad to help us out."

"The order of march will be as it has always been, back to garrison," McClellan said.

"Sarge, that ricochet musta done somethin' to your head. They'll lynch us if we go back to camp."

"We can expect something like that."

"*An' you still want us to go back?*"

"We're still Army, Poole. We're soldiers, and we will do what soldiers are supposed to do. And we will do it to the very end."

"But, Sarge, that's crazy. We better be tryin' to get as far away from the Army as we can. An' we better start doin' it now. I done already heard some'a them trucks speedin' by back over there. Next they gonna come back and start combing the fields. Then when all'a them people in Houston hears about what we done, there's gonna be hell to pay with them, too. Them crackers ain't gonna be playin'. They don't give a damn about us bein' soldiers or anything else."

"Form the company, Poole," McClellan said. "Right or wrong,

we're going back."

"But, Sarge — !"

"*Form* the company. And form it *now*," McClellan said forcefully. "The order of march will be back to garrison. There will be no further questions."

Poole gave the First a sobering look and stalked off. Sgt. Dukes was pleased. McClellan was back, alright. Now the old sergeant could do what he had to do without worry.

McClellan started to walk off in the direction of the troops. Noticing Dukes had not moved, he stopped and turned. "Dukes?"

Dukes was slow and hesitant. "No, Mac. I can't. I hate not goin' with you, but I can't."

From the look on the field sergeant's face under the moonlight, and knowing what he'd wanted to go into before Poole's interruption, the First could tell that the end was near. Very respectful of the older sergeant, he turned back to him and said, "Please come, Dukes."

"You don't say 'please' to nobody, Mac, so I know what you're feelin'. But after near 'bout thirty-six years, it's all over for me. Addin' 'em all up, it's prob'bly more'n that. It's got to end sometime."

"It doesn't have to be now."

"Now would be a better time than most. I'd do anythin' in the world for you, Mac. You know that. But I'm too old and tired to carry on. Now I'm hurt. An' I'm hurt in more places than one. The man done even knocked the last few teeth out of my mouth. I can't even eat no more. Even if I could, I wouldn't be doin' nothin' but slowin' you down."

"We're not escaping."

"An' you better not," Dukes admonished. "I know you wouldn't do nothin' like that."

"No, I wouldn't. But it doesn't change the fact that I still need you. The men need you."

"But the Army don't. Y'hear what I'm sayin', Mac? The Army

don't."

"I hate to pull rank on you, Dukes, but I can order you to the formation."

"But you wouldn't do that."

"No," McClellan said. "No, I wouldn't."

"An' you gotta remember, Mac, the Army's done changed too much for me, anyhow. It ain't the Army we used to know. S'been a long time since I had that real, good soldierin' feelin'. Today the Army is for kids an' motors an' machines an' things. An' it's for a bunch'a officers that don't know nuthin'. That ain't soldierin'."

"It might not be, but it's still Army."

Dukes took his time, then asked, "R'member what me, you, and Field Sergeant Newton used to say?"

"I remember."

"An' you r'member the promise we made to each other?"

"I remember," the First said, reflecting with his old friend. "It was more like a vow."

"Then you know I gotta do what I gotta do. Am I right?"

"You're right."

"Because it was a promise. The promise that said the first one of us who got the feelin' we could no longer soldier, then the closest one around's gotta help the other end it."

"I remember."

"Then gimme your sidearm," Dukes said, extending his hand. "I can't soldier no more."

"I'll give it to you. But before I do — " McClellan dug into his shirt pocket for the letter that had never left him. "I'd like for you to know I received this from Newton today."

"My God, did you really? How is the ol' dawg?"

"He's doing well. And he's a sergeant."

"Well, I'll be. An' so he made it back."

"Like us, he's back in."

"That's just great. I wonder how many others got back in?"

"I have no way of knowing."

"Me neither. But we made it," Dukes said with a small, satisfied smile. "An' notice how I r'membered the name? It was hard, but I never went back to the old ones. His, mine, or yours."

"Let me read you what the letter says."

"No. No, don't read it to me, Mac. I know it's somethin' that ought'a be heard, but do me a favor. Save it, an' read it for the troops. An' pick a good time to do it, Mac. I know it's a good letter, 'cause he was a good man." Dukes's mind raced back to the old days as he said, "McCall, Creek and Pulham. What a team we used to be."

"Those were the days."

"Where is he now?"

"In Europe."

"*You're kiddin'.*"

"He writes of how well he is."

"God bless 'im. I knew one of us would make it! I knew it! Don't tell me he's with the Infantry, or one of the fightin' units?"

"He's —"

"No, don't tell me. Don't tell me, Mac. When I get to where I'm goin', I wanna be able to look down an' be s'prised." The older sergeant looked away for a moment. He brushed away the years and said, "Army. It's been a good life."

"Yes, it has."

"But you be sure an' read that thing for the boys. An' let 'em know what we been through."

"I will."

"An' Mac; Mac, this time you know what the penalty is gonna be, don't you?"

"Every step of the way. Fortunately, though, there'll be a trial. Or at least a pretense of one."

"As long as it's somethin'. Maybe you'll get the chance to say a few things that need to be said, even though I know it ain't gonna do no good. The white man ain't gonna never hear what people like you have to say."

McClellan didn't say anything.

Dukes waited, then said, "It's a shame. A damn'd shame. It was a good company. Some damn fine boys."

With no boast in his voice, the first sergeant said, "Best in the Army."

"A lot of it had to do with you."

"Not really. They would have been good with or without me. We were just fortunate to have them."

"Houston," Dukes said thoughtfully. "Well, anyway, the savin' grace is, you didn't cause it. You tried to do somethin' about it. An' no matter how you look at it, it was somethin' we needed to do. An' I hope that one day the coloreds will get to know about this company. And you. And when they do, somebody's gonna be thankin' you, because, Mac, you're rare. You was a leader; a good and decent man — on and off the field."

"I'm not so certain about that. Not in the slightest. But thank you, my old friend."

"I gotta go."

"I wish you'd be there with us at the end."

"Naw, I'm too old to be with 'em up there. I could hardly keep the cadence. In fact, I don't think I could even make it up the stairs. But when they get up there on that thing, Mac, that's when they gotta look their best."

"We'd be a helluva lot better with you."

"Get Poole on the ball. Make him help out. Oh, an' Mac, do what you can for the boy. All he was doing was taggin' along."

"I know. And that really hurts me. I'll try and speak with someone, but I know it's not going to work."

"*Damn* I wished I'd sent that boy home like somethin' told me to, 'stead of waitin' on Monday," Dukes lamented. "Anyway, see what you can do. An' for the end, get Poole on the ball. He can soldier when he want to. But whatever happens, Mac, take 'em out the way the colored soldier is s'posed to go: strong. Proud an' strong. Show 'em all what we made of. Promise me that."

"You have my promise."

"I'm gonna be watchin'." "Now, lemme have it." Time seemed to stand still. Then Dukes braced himself. "Now, lemme have it."

McClellan would have preferred taking his own life. He simply did not want to give the old soldier the sidearm.

"C'mon, lemme have it, Mac," the old soldier insisted.

McClellan did something strange even for him. He gave the man a strong embrace, stepped back, and saluted him. Dukes returned the salute. McClellan, choosing not to delay, dug into his holster and gave him the gun. It was a .38. In exchange, Sgt. Dukes removed his watch and gave up his most prized possession. Instead of saying goodbye, they saluted each other again.

Walking away, since he could not see the face of the watch, the First held it up to his ear.

It didn't keep time. It never did.

With his back to the man, the first sergeant was still walking towards the formation some distance away when it came.

The shot cracked through one side of the old sergeant's temple, spun partway around the skull, and exited gruesomely.

McClellan didn't turn at the sound of the shot. His back twitched a little but he walked on, his mind peeling back the years.

McCall, Creek and Pulham — three soldiers who had an unmatched love for the military and for each other. They were going to be soldiers until the end. Early on, when they were younger, they had made a theme of the old saying *You can run me around the Army, but you'll never run me out.* They were wrong. The Army did run them out, as McClellan had alluded to several times.

Because of the uprising in Brownsville, Texas, the Army ran the entire 1st Battalion of the 25th Infantry Regiment (Colored) out of military service. They were banned for life. Among the banished, and under their original names, were Carey McCall, Joshua Creek, and Oliver B. Pulham — *Jim Newton, Abraham Dukes,* and *Obie McClellan*. McClellan and Dukes had been corporals then.

The three had taken no part in the Brownsville disturbance that caused the action by the President. They hadn't taken up arms and hadn't been among those who encouraged firing on the civilians, nor had they been seen along the corridor that separated the city of Brownsville from Camp Brown. Fate had them paying the price.

McCall, Creek and Pulham knew what it was to see a group of soldiers run amok and strike terror in the whites, and they were soon to learn, too, what it was to be charged falsely, and how swift and exact the punishment could be.

As shown by his speech to the troops before leaving Columbus, Brownsville never left the first sergeant's mind. It is doubtful if what happened there ever left Sgt. Dukes's or Sgt. Jim Newton's mind, either. What was clear was that they had never been seized by it, as had McClellan. It concerned them, but they didn't wallow in it, nor did it haunt them.

None of the three had been involved in the conflagration, but over the years McClellan tossed the event over in his mind a thousand and one times. Innocent though he had been at the time, perhaps Field Sgt. Dukes knew his friend was haunted and tortured by Brownsville. Maybe that was why the old sergeant showed so much concern when he moved him away from the ditch where the remaining bodies were. What Dukes did not know was that the mind-leaving episode in the field had not been a first for his friend. The night after they re-entered the military under aliases and reported to camp, McClellan started having problems with nightmares that recurred over several months. It bothered him that he was living a lie.

Mercifully, the nightmares stopped. And for about seven or eight years the first sergeant's nights were essentially trouble-free. Before that, however, he would wake up in a cold sweat. Mornings would find him sitting on his cot, trembling, his eyes glazed.

Many nights he tried not to sleep at all. He would lie on top of the cot, and the moment he found himself drifting off he would get up and go outside. It was a useless move, because eventually he would tire and have to go to sleep. Sometimes he'd sleep at the back of the tent, too fearful to go back inside

Always the theme would start with the experience in Brownsville. More troubling was that the torment would often carry over until the daylight hours. Sometimes it wouldn't leave until well after reveille. The worst thing was that the nightmare — or premonition, as he had begun to term it — would always end in an execution. Whose execution was never made clear.

The only thing he did know was that in the end he was standing on a high platform, surrounded by guards, and there were 13 strands of rope dangling before his eyes.

He was not allowed — nor did he want to be allowed — full recall, but the last premonition was vivid enough. The platform was a scaffold. It was a frighteningly massive creation, woefully out of place in an area calmed by mesquite trees, plant life, and the nobility of God's ceaseless and unerring hand. To anyone standing on it looking down or anyone standing below and looking up, the structure was ghastly. It was ugly in design, and hideous in purpose. Two lines of rope riggings, thickly knotted, hung with chilling straightness over two rows of holes that allowed the trampled ground to be seen 13 feet below. It was mesmerizing. The guards tried for detachment but failed. Even the late-arriving whites, many still tainted with revenge, were overwhelmed by the grotesqueness of it all. Some came to the site, took one look, and returned to camp. Those who remained stood motionless at the area's perimeter, their mouths ajar. They stared up silently at the structure that had come alive with black faces and weary bodies in frayed, unkempt uniforms.

The troubled first sergeant was standing in front. And always he was giving orders to the faceless.

Chapter 20

It was the first time King Company had ever marched back in the direction of any camp without cadence or song. The imagery was strange. Moonlight made it haunting.

First Sgt. McClellan was in an unusual placement. He was in front of the formation rather than in the flanking position. Next to him was Simms, carrying the guidon. Poole was in the command position, and for protection, the First had placed Jody in the rear. He was still lugging Pete. When the company appeared out of the silhouetting darkness on that last part of the gloomy road that led to camp, they looked like POWs on the move. They were tired and ready for surrender.

They had no weapons. McClellan had given the *stack arms* order way back in the fields. They had been so deep in the fields after the shooting that they could not be seen by the trucks that were still zooming and searching along the road. They still had some distance to go, and the First knew that the post would be surrounded by a strong gun-wielding contingent. He also knew that arriving with weapons would only lead to slaughter.

In leaving the weapons in the field, the First had told the men that it was not likely but there was a possibility that they would be fired upon once they were seen by the whites. In that event, he said, they were not to panic or disperse, and that even though it was dark, he would wave a white handkerchief — signaling surrender — and everything should be all right. He would wave the handkerchief, he said, until touched or ordered to drop it by some-one from Logan. In the event he was shot, he ordered, under the direction of Poole they were to continue marching to and through the gate. After that was made expressly clear to Poole, he briefly mentioned that Sgt. Dukes wouldn't be accompanying them. It was no surprise to most of the men, since the field sergeant had not been seen since they heard the single shot.

The First then ordered his men into a formal marching formation. There would be no audible commands, he said, and no matter what, they were to appear orderly and fearless. If fired upon, he stressed again, they were not to break ranks, disperse, or run under any circumstance, rather they were to continue marching until shot or until inside of the post compound. There they would surrender. He told them that they would probably spend the night in the company area, surrounded by guards. He almost pleaded with them to be on their best behavior, because the white troops of Logan, along with the police and untold numbers of gun-bearing civilians, would be their guards. They would understandably be ablaze with anger, and if provoked, no matter how slightly, they would shoot to kill. He said that revenge would come from every quarter, that all the guards were sure to be abusive, and that they would be spat upon and called every name in the book. Still, he said, they were to hold themselves in check. Probably at about 0500, he believed, they would be hauled away in trucks and shipped back to Columbus. "And there —" He halted midsentence.

It was almost as if the First had been revisited by the night-mare. He wanted to get to a feeding schedule and reassure them on other matters, but he couldn't do it. Instead he told them to *take ten*. Those who smoked he told to light up. He wanted everyone to stop and take a breather.

When they slumped to the ground, he himself moved away and found a quiet thinking spot.

It had all happened so incredibly fast. Everything that had happened since Columbus had whipped by like a blur. Now the last part of the nightmare was fitting into place like the last few cuts of a puzzle. That is what had stopped him.

Sitting in the dark with his back nestled against a tree that had been stripped of leaves and life, First Sgt. McClellan let his mind — fully back and working fine — push back a few years. It was almost as if he were testing it. Taking the trip back, he likened everything that had happened since leaving Columbus to two words, and to those two big black bolts of lightning that dominated the regimental sign. He recalled that many yards forward of the company tents, it was paralleled by rusted barbed wire and the long red-and-white pole that stretched across the dusty roadway represented the gate. *Black Lightning*, said the words. Past and present thoughts mingled, and he wondered what would happen to *Black Lightning*. Would the Army disband the regiment? The battalion? King Company? Masterful, masterful King Company. Would it be banished? No, he concluded. In time the Army would forget the incident, or the mutiny or insurrection, as they were sure to term it, and someday there would be another King Company in the Third Battalion of the 24th Infantry Regiment (Colored) of the Army of the United States. Perhaps the Army would grow and wouldn't even single out the word *colored*.

King, he concluded, would always be under a dark cloud of censure, always evoking controversy and disdain, but in time there would be another King Company.

He thought again about the term *Black Lightning*.

As he had wondered when he first arrived at the gate and saw the boldly painted sign, he wondered again what would happen if lightning really were black? It was just a word, a metaphor, he thought, then as now. Still, going back years ago, now to the day when he and the newly-named Abraham Dukes had first arrived on post, a sense of peaceful joy crossed his face. Except for the deception, it really was a happy day in both their lives. Dukes couldn't stop laughing and doing the *jig*. Certainly the two weren't the same as they had been for the few months they were without the Army. Those days had been disastrous, and there could be only one conclusion. They couldn't make it without Army life. It was not simply a matter of the work in civilian life, though, even at that, they tried everything. They soon learned that work was hard to find, and that for the dishonorably discharged, finding decent work was virtually impossible. And so they spent a good portion of the time applying for work at menial jobs and suffering the indignity of feeling useless and out of touch.

Pulham and Creek. They didn't even look like civilians; they couldn't relate to civilian life. They couldn't adjust — which was the real reason for their dismay. At one job, hopping bells in a hotel, it didn't take long for them to come up with a plan. They thought it was bold and daring at the time. Looking back, it wasn't really bold *or* daring. There weren't that many blacks in the Army, and records were never checked very closely, if at all. And because they knew the routine and one of them could read and write, when they showed up at the recruiting station they were accepted without question. And so with falsified records under the names of Obie O. McClellan and Abraham Dukes, and with only minor concern that their pasts would catch up with them, they were accepted in the United States Army. Since it was a Regular Army unit, they were assigned to the 24th — *the Deuce-Four,* as it was affectionately called.

McClellan wrote to McCall and told him what they had done. He re-enlisted and moved up in the ranks under the alias of Jim Newton. He had been assigned to Camp Dix in Wrightstown, New Jersey. They had heard it was not an Infantry encampment. Until the letter, McClellan always thought his friend had not been touched by good fortune.

The First couldn't shake the thoughts of that first day. Again and again he thought of the pride he felt in looking up at the big sign that served as the archway back in Columbus. Again he came back to the notion that it was an 18-footer, boldly lettered, and framed by two bolts of black lightning outlined in crimson. Again he remembered the big, bold wording that centered the sign: Home of the Twenty-Fourth United States Infantry. Then came the word *Colored* — always written in parentheses. The Army wanted it that way. It indicated separation.

The First remembered how Columbus, New Mexico rounded off the bottom, and how the colorful insignias and campaign awards denoting outstanding service in the Spanish American War were neatly positioned on the side. *Awards for war*, McClellan thought at the time. *Progress.*

One look and he and Dukes were convinced they had found a home. It was Infantry, and it was great. Better than great really, because there was nothing about the 24th that would throw them into the flatness and dubiousness of the three other Negro units, particularly the 10th Cavalry. Here, in the Infantry, soldiering involved men, not horses. Even when he was a boy, playing at war games back in Rhode Island, it involved running and jumping and firing on foot. Great battles and wars were won on horseback, but since the beginning of man, the greater glory had always been attributed to the man on foot. Thor, the god of lightning and thunder, might have ridden the heavens in a chariot drawn by goats, but his greatest feats were achieved on foot.

He had never thought about it — perhaps he wouldn't even have admitted it — but there was a time when it appeared young McClellan (again, Oliver B. Pulham) wouldn't live long enough to join the Army. At age 10, a strain of consumption claimed both his mother and his father, and later the dreaded virus settled in his lung. Weak and feverish, he was quarantined for the better part of a year. When he didn't heal, a lobectomy, virtually unheard of at the time, was performed by a forward-thinking white doctor who was determined that someone in the family he once called friends should survive. The upper right lobe of a lung was removed. The boy survived the exploratory operation with damaged ribs and a partially sunken shoulder. The disfigurement couldn't be seen through the shirt, but during his school years it was never far from his mind. As a boy bent on perfection, he was bothered that he wasn't physically perfect, that he wasn't even able to compete athletically. It bothered him so much during those years, particularly the two years spent in college back in Tuskegee, that it had him shying away from serious female companionship. Getting married was out of the question, although for a brief spell a young lady almost had him slipping from that position. Flora Pound was her name, and she almost made him change his mind about the military.

The First did not like being reminded of her, but Flora was a grade school teacher's aide and part-time typist at the recruiting station at Belton Street. From the moment young Pulham walked through the door, he and the young lady could not for a moment keep their eyes off each other. Getting together was inevitable. After being sworn into service, the young soldier promised the young lady he would never forget her, and that as soon as he had a permanent assignment and was able to be furloughed, he would return. Time passed. The adage worked. Absence and the letters did indeed make the heart grow fonder, so much so that young Pulham almost had second thoughts about the military. Before the 25th and, at the time, assigned to a Company in the 10th Cavalry on temporary duty in Washington, he would spend his days and nights thinking about the lovely young miss he had left back in Rhode Island. She thought of him just as often, and, since she had attended Howard University in Washington, D.C. for a short spell, she was thinking about resuming her studies there. Then one day he came home. Flora was there at the station to greet him. They spent the night holding hands and talking about a possible future. It could have been a nice union, but two things worked against them. Although she worked for the military, Flora didn't fully like the idea of committing to someone who, as she understood it, would be unable to commit to a stable home life. It wasn't an insurmountable problem, because they were beyond the verge of meeting each other halfway. And, as he told her, he loved the Army but it didn't have to be for life — if he could spend it with her. The other problem, however, was exceedingly serious and was something that had rocked the senses.

It was the young lady's mother.

Flora Pound was adorably petite, with eyes like a fawn. She had fairly light skin and came from an elitist family. Her father, a prominent doctor in the community, didn't mind it quite as much, but the mother, exceptionally snobbish and class-conscious, simply didn't believe that a dark-skinned man would make a suitable companion. In fact, she was so against the darker shade that when Flora invited the young soldier to her house, Mrs. Pound, planted in the window since noon, saw the uniform coming. Before he even got to the porch's first step that evening, she stepped outside and told the visitor he had to enter the house through the rear door.

Hurt, the young soldier turned around and started running. It was the evening he McClellan remembered that evening. It was the evening he tried his best to run from Rhode Island to Washington.

He was dark, but the mother was darker.

Chapter 21

The company break that was supposed to be for 10 minutes lasted for more than 20. It was deliberate. Had it not been for the anxiety-ridden Poole, the break would have lasted longer.

When the First reassembled the men, he spoke at length of the court-martial that would ensue, probably back in Columbus. He talked of how disgraceful it was going to be to arrive back at their home base, chained and under guard by the whites. But, he said, it was better to go back to Columbus and face a court than to remain at Logan. He pulled no punches and said that the people in Houston would not sit still for a court-martial to convene. Recalling Brownsville, where there had been no trial, he said there was no question that the townspeople would be so filled with outrage and revenge they would take the law into their own hands. Not a single member of the company would be spared, he said. He went on to say that Battalion Commander Briggs would side with the citizenry and they would end up like ducks in a shooting gallery. Every white in Houston — civilians and soldiers alike — would likely be armed to the teeth, and one night they would likely storm the Logan post. If they did, they wouldn't stop shooting until whole-sale slaughter had been achieved.

Poole simply couldn't understand it. "If things can get that out of hand," he fumed, "then why'n the hell are we going back, Sergeant? Why?"

"We are soldiers, Poole," the sergeant said. "We are going back because it is the honorable thing to do. We revolted. We were not the first to do so, nor will we be the last. Throughout our history in this country we have revolted and fought. From the two million slaves that were smuggled onto these shores to the present, we have fought. In 1822, Denmark Vesey, a freed slave, planned revolt and died with thirty-four other Negroes. They didn't run. Nine years later, Nat Turner led a revolt that caused the deaths of something like sixty whites. He was fighting for justice; he knew what the end was going to be, and he faced it bravely. Gabriel Prosser did the same. L'Ouverture of Haiti, who spent time here, went back and united his people and fought both the Spanish and the French. He didn't run. There have been many, many others. And before all of them, there could have been more. If the wide river of the Congo hadn't been blockaded by dead bodies, there would have been more. *Thousands upon thousands* more. They would not have run. Neither will we. We will face what is coming to us without fear, whine or shame; we will face it without pity or sorrow. We will face it with backbone — with courage and conviction. And no matter what penalty is imposed upon us, we will accept it bravely, and we will give all there is to give. We *have* to. It is our character that is at stake here. We are not what they think we are. We are soldiers. Negro soldiers. We are something only a few of our race are so honored to be. We were not right in doing what we did. I will never say we were. I will never say it because we were not right. We were wrong. *I* was wrong. But in that wrong, our presence was felt. And for us to diminish the importance of our actions by going out like sniveling dogs only serves the white man's point.

Run if you wish, but these soldiers will not run with you."

Seventeen minutes later none of them could run. They were under guard.

• • •

The only decision the First had to make beforehand was whether to bring the troops in at the front of the post or at the rear. Symbolically, he led the men to the front. Before they got even close to the gate, they were surrounded and arrested by the Logan troops. Civilians were there as well, but the thick of their venom was in Houston.

Still outraged that the Army had again assigned blacks to the area, many citizens had converged on City Hall and demanded action even before they learned of the ambush that took place in the field, far away from city limits. They would learn of that attack later.

A number of people had heard the shots that were fired at the station, and to quote the writer C. D. Waide, "word spread by mouth and by telephone within minutes of the outbreak."

Rumors fed rumors, and most of the citizens didn't know if 50 or 150 or 550 black troops were in on the march. Many whites assumed that the local blacks were in on taking over the city as well, and in the Fourth Ward's San Felipe district, houses were fired upon. Acting fast, and well before midnight, the governor declared martial law and pressed the commander of the Texas National Guard into service. He swiftly issued the following edict:

All citizens will remain in their homes or
usual places of business. No citizen will
appear on the street with arms.
Saloons will not be permitted to open.
Places of business where arms and
ammunition are sold will remain closed.

Securing more help, the State's governor put in a call for federal troops. Three trains left San Antonio that night carrying a battalion of the 19th Infantry. Another special train brought up three companies of the Coast Guard, and again from the regular Army, another train came in from Galveston. Word spread wider. Texas was under siege. The Illinois National Guard, on duty near Houston, was mobilized and arrived under cover of darkness. By 3 a.m., a citizen's committee had been formed and 500 of the town's leading citizens were selected to serve as a *posse comitatus* to act under the sheriff's department with the powers of sheriff. By 6 a.m., 499 of the 500 men had reported for duty.

The streets of Houston would be patrolled for 48 solid hours by white men of every stature. Ranchers, mill workers, farmers, doctors, bankers, lawyers, and what-have-you did the work of a disorganized police force and bumped into each other with cocked rifles and loaded pistols.

Fear was everywhere. And everywhere the talk of revenge grew louder. The Army had to move. It did.

Rather than to go for an orderly departure, the entire black battalion was ordered to leave without fully breaking down tents or securing equipment. Within hours, two trains hissed and rumbled into the Southern-Pacific station. The engineers were set to fire them away on short order.

When the big canvas-backed trucks rumbled up the road and zoomed through town, escorted by an almost equal number of gunpointing troops of the Nineteenth Infantry, members of the posse comitatus fled to the train station with fire in their eyes. Some went to make sure that the troops were leaving, others went with the clear and unmistakable intent of taking revenge. Because of the presence of the Nineteenth Infantry no hostile acts were carried out, but through it all, left to worry and wonder and wonder and worry, were the black civilians. There was fear of reprisals. The few blacks who dared to show up at the station didn't give the troops outward support. But hidden signals said it was a job well done.

Again recalling Brownsville, and fearing that the Army would be as lenient with these black soldiers as it had been with the dishonorably discharged 25th 10 years earlier, Houston authorities demanded that the Army turn over the lawbreakers to the civilian courts. It made no difference that the troops had already departed. To provide some satisfaction, and to contest the notion of leniency and indifference, Col. Stout, the Logan post commander, became the temporary scapegoat. He elected to retire. Col. Delbert Rideout, Lt. Col. Briggs's retired Houston acquaintance, was again asked to take command. He declined. Forty-eight hours later, a new commander, Col. Lonnie Childress, was installed at Logan. A Briggs sound-alike, he immediately acknowledged the mistake of sending blacks to Houston. To satisfy immediate concerns, he publicly assured the citizenry that the Army was a firm believer in the death penalty and went on to cite examples. To further placate them, the former commander of the 15th National Guard of New York flatly promised that there would be executions in the case. He repeated the statement and unmistakably added "executions — regardless of the degree of guilt."

Executions — regardless of the degree of guilt.

From all indications, it was to be a terrifying assault on justice. Washington was no better. Similar sentiments were voiced there, and they would be voiced there again.

Days later, the hearing room of the office of military affairs in Washington was packed with high-ranking personnel, mostly military. The chairman, a civilian, sat facing two tables, one for the military, and one for the civilian officials.

A major general was the spokesman for the military. Dennis Fredrickson was the intelligent, beleaguered Secretary of War. He had already heard scores of condemnation speeches that morning alone. He was braced for more.

"The chair recognizes the Senator from Alabama," said the chairman.

The Senator stood. "Mr. Chairman, the Senator from Alabama would like nothing more than to speak out at this time, to speak on the blackest of all black issues. However under the circumstances, I feel it is more than right for this committee to hear from the Senator from Texas. Alabama yields."

"Thank you, Senator," the chairman said. "The Chair recognizes the senator from Texas."

Senator Orville Huyler was his name. Old, hardened, and crafty, he had a voice that carried weight with quiet indignation. "Mr. Chairman, it grieves me to no small extent to have to address this hearing in the aftermath of a great tragedy. A tragedy, I am sorry to say, that surely could have been prevented had the Army exercised any degree of foresight. It is a tragedy, I need not remind you, that shall long stain the pages of American history, and surely, the minds of those poor people of Houston, whom I am privileged to represent.

"As most of you know, I have long opposed the idea of indiscriminately arming colored boys. You know, as well, that I have long opposed the idea of arming and sending colored boys to train in any of our southern States. And most of you know, too, that my opposition has not been based upon a personal dislike of the coloreds serving in the Army, for I quite firmly believe that if the Niggra folks are to continue to sup the fruits of this great and bountiful nation, then surely — except for serving in our naval force — their boys must share some of the burdens of this dark and restless hour. This war, Gentlemen, has placed great demands upon us, and indeed, upon our regular troops. And while I am forced to admit that due to the very nature of the race I have always harbored grave doubts as to the colored man's soldiering capabilities, and they, I'm sure you will admit, have done nothing to convince me — or anyone else — otherwise, I have somehow managed to swallow my personal beliefs and have supported the secretary of war each time he has appeared before committee requesting to open the ranks for additional coloreds in the military. A check of the records will reveal I have always asked the secretary exactly what the coloreds were going to be used for, and the secretary has always indicated they were going to be used for the more menial tasks, thereby relieving our regular troops for the more important assignments. I construed this, as I am sure many of you did, to mean that no armed colored boys would ever be in the South. Then, according to the secretary, it somehow became necessary to *train* troops in the South, *but* the secretary said this training — this measure of *military necessity* — would take place only in *select* areas of the South, the more *receptive* areas. And we permitted it. We permitted it, and by so doing we permitted one of the worst outrages in the pages of American history to take place. It cannot happen again. I will not allow it to happen again. And that is why I speak today. I stand before you demanding that no more of these Niggra boys be sent south of the Mason-Dixon. And I come before you, lastly, hoping that the secretary will find it in his heart to resign his post."

Most were taken aback by the Senator's final remark, but not the secretary. He looked at the old Texan without comment.

"Mr. Secretary?" the chairman inquired. "Mr. Secretary, do you have a comment you wish to make?"

"Mr. Chairman," the pleasant, round-face man said, "I do not feel it necessary to respond to the Senator's statement, at least in its entirety. I also do not feel it necessary to defend my record, nor the Army's record. I would like to say, however, that my actions have never been independent of the President's wishes, and not without some measure of approval from this committee as a whole. The decision to send Negro troops to Houston was not mine alone, although honesty compels me to say that if anything in that regard had been my decision to make, Negro troops would not only be in Texas, but, just as it is with the whites, scattered all over the nation."

"Does that include the South?"

"All over the nation, Sir."

"Mr. Fredrickson," the chairman asked sternly, "do I understand you correctly? In the light of all that has happened, you have the audacity to appear before this committee with the inflammatory idea of stationing more of these people in the South?"

"You understand me perfectly, Sir. There must be an increased utilization of the Negro. May I remind you, the Negro quota in the military is no longer limited to the prewar need of 10,000. Selective Service has, on the first draft alone, called more than 75,000 Negroes to arms. At the rate the Great War is going, we are going to have to have numbers far greater to that, and we cannot run the risk of concentrating these people into one area."

"And the country, Mr. Secretary, cannot run the risk of having these people run a course of lawlessness. I recognize the need for an increased quota of coloreds, but, in full agreement with the distinguished Senator from Texas, I fail to recognize why the Army doesn't act sensibly and restrict these people to the unarmed areas of supply and servicing."

"That was acceptable *prior* to the war, Mr. Chairman. But as I have stated any number of times before, we either increase, arm and train these people for combat, or permit the burden of battle to rest solely on the shoulders of the white troops."

There were murmurs of agreement from the witnesses seated around the room. The chairman pounded the gavel and returned to the issue that had caused the meeting. "What about Houston?"

"The Army has already taken the matter into account, and is at this very moment taking the necessary steps to effect a speedy court-martial. In order that the outbreak will serve as a deterrent to others, you can expect maximum punishment for the guilty."

"Where are the prisoners being held now?"

"At their home base in Columbus, New Mexico. Awaiting charges."

"I am inclined to think that is another blatant mistake on the Army's part. Proceedings should have already started, Mr. Secretary. An entire battalion of coloreds were involved in the attack on Houston —"

"Not true, Sir," the secretary interrupted. "Only *some* of the men from a Company K with perhaps a few members from the Companies I and L were involved."

"I was told that it was a battalion of troops."

"No, Sir. That is an unfortunate exaggeration, Senator."

"In terms of a count, how many coloreds were there?"

"Trial will probably involve more than half a company."

"Mr. Secretary, have you ever heard of the city of Brownsville in my State? And what took place there in my State?"

"Of course, I have, Sir."

"Do you realize there was no trial for the crimes committed in Brownsville?"

"I am more than fully aware of that, Senator."

"And are you *fully aware* that there were only two deaths in the Brownsville fray, and a battalion of coloreds was dishonorably discharged from the service? And here we're talking about a number of deaths that could possibly exceed eighteen or nineteen people — along with a goodly number of crippled and wounded — and you're saying that only *half* of a *company* of coloreds will be tried?"

"That is what we're certain of at the moment, Sir. But what would you recommend, Senator, that we again forgo due process and dishonorably discharge the entire battalion?"

"No, that is not what I would recommend, Mr. Secretary. But I will tell you this: with nineteen of my constituents confirmed dead, if you have a trial, you — or somebody — had better make goddamned sure that the death penalty is spread around just as liberally."

Chapter 22

In 1619 a Dutch ship brought 20 Negroes to the English colony of Virginia. They were not slaves. But they were not free. They were indentured servants. Later some were granted freedom, but, still later, the principle of slavery had taken hold in America. The indentured servants lost their indentured status and were held as slaves. They were confused.

At the close of August 1917, blacks were equally confused. When word filtered out about what the black soldiers had done in Houston, blacks the nation over were confused and concerned. Soldiers and civilians alike didn't know what to think. Without question it was wrong to revolt and kill. And what the troops had done in Houston was sure to damage the cause of all blacks in the military. Many blacks were angry. Black newspapers and organizations around the country were bombarded with letters of protest. But there was, too, an absolute feeling of empathy in many black communities. There were similar feelings in the black camps. Like the civilians, law and recriminations aside, they knew what it was to be pushed and goaded and treated with ill respect and, when outside of camp, to suffer at the hands of the police.

Washington particularly knew about some of the conditions at camp. Any number of reports had been submitted by Emmet Scott, the black special assistant to the Secretary of War. Appointed shortly before the outbreak of war — and at first thought to be a sellout by some blacks — Scott did his job. He discovered — and to the surprise of many actually reported — that food was a problem, that there was a frequent lack of medical attention for the black troops; that they had practically no sanitary conveniences, or bathing facilities; that the whites were given barracks while all too frequently the blacks were assigned to tent camps; that during the winter, hard and grueling, they had insufficient clothing; that there was a shortage of overcoats and adequate bedding for the men; that the tents were without flooring and often were situated in wet places where ice formed in winter and malaria flourished at other times. Scott saw to it that Washington knew that in Camp Alexander, Virginia and in other places, during the winter men died like sheep, and it became a common occurrence to drag men frozen to death out of their tents. So, in the main, and because of the special assistant, blacks in uniform around the country did not condemn the explosion created by the 24th's King Company.

• • •

When the prisoners arrived back on post in Columbus from Houston, now under guard by C Company of the Nineteenth Infantry, a number of blacks stood silently on the side of the road and gave the prisoners *thumbs up*. Some even saluted them.

But there would be no thumbs up or salutes for the insurrectionists coming from the hierarchy of the military. The Army was preparing for the largest trial ever to be held in the United States. Boards of high-ranking officers were formed to investigate the participants and all aspects of the uprising.

Four weeks later, the investigators had amassed a mountain of evidence, which was turned over to the judge advocate general's office. There was more work to be done, but since there was enough evidence to go to trial, in the interest of speed it was decided to try 63 men. They would constitute the first wave. A defense team was assembled and the troops went through a series of interviews conducted by Capt. Donald Thoren, an insecure aide of the chief defender.

The only question that remained for the military was where to hold the court-martial. Columbus, the home base of the troops, was deemed inappropriate.

With the death penalty firmly in mind, authorities recommended Fort Bliss, at El Paso, Texas. It was appropriate to mete out maximum punishment in the State where the offenses had occurred. The post, however, was found to be not acceptable.

Fort Sam Houston in San Antonio, Texas was suggested. It sounded ideal, but there was a concern that there wasn't a building on post big enough to accommodate a large trial. In checking, the trial board and the trial judge advocate were assured that there was indeed a building large enough to hold court. Two days later it was announced that court would convene at 0700 on the morning of November 1. It would be held in the post's chapel.

When the 63 prisoners heard that trial was going to be held in a chapel, they felt relieved. The Army of the United States wouldn't dare sentence a man to death in the House of God.

First Sgt. McClellan thought otherwise.

So did Capt. Thoren, aide to the chief defender.

Chapter 23

It was mid-October when the King Company convoy pulled onto post at Fort Sam Houston, in San Antonio, Texas to await trial. Although late at night, the arrival still attracted considerable attention, which was surprising. The post wasn't large, and there weren't supposed to be many troops there. Orders had come for the unit to join a contingent that was headed overseas. Because of the impending arrival of the prisoners, the Army had apparently delayed departure.

Not only was Fort Sam Houston smaller than expected, but it was not an impressive post. The barracks and tents appeared tired and faded, and the old post left an overall impression that a cavalry unit had been stationed there. As had been the case at Camp Logan, there were no blacks. None had ever been there.

Word about the Houston uprising and the expected results settled heavily over the camp, and troops with fixed bayonets were everywhere. The added security was unnecessary. The 63 blacks to be tried — tired and hungry and still shackled — were still under heavy guard. They had been driven directly onto the stockade yard, and though—except for Poole—none of the prisoners thought about it, there was no chance for escape. The Fort Sam Houston stockade was one of the most secure in the whole of the western United States, having once been the final place of imprisonment for members of Mexico's Federal Army who had surrendered to the U.S. Cavalry in 1914.

If he had ever been caught, it would have also been the home of the Mexican outlaw, Pancho Villa.

The stockade was indeed secure. Four big arc lights powered down from the four corners and criss-crossed stationary lights that beamed down on an old one-story brick building and swept along the space between the double line of barbed-wire fencing and an outer wall of cement. Troops with fixed bayonets patrolled the area between the wall and fence. They were supported by guards who walked around on elevated platforms. The 15-foot inner fence had been reinforced. Now swung up and coiled, it hung over the edge of the spacious prison yard like a line of giant dinosaurs.

First Sgt. McClellan, his wrists and legs shackled, had been riding in the third truck. Cpl. Poole, saddled with the idea that there was no way to escape, rode in the second truck. Sgt. Corey Yeager, the bullish Irishman, was the noncom in charge. The commissioned officer was a wiry first lieutenant by the name of Alfonse Davies.

It was he to whom McClellan went.

"Lieutenant, I'm First Sergeant Obie McClellan. A few things, Sir. Back in Columbus, I'd asked to talk with a member of the prosecution team concerning Private Jody Cunningham, one of my men who shouldn't be here. Next, I'd like to see about getting food for the men. No one has seen to it that we've had any since yesterday." He felt strange, not because he had to ask for food or that he was still shackled. It was the first time in both his careers he had ever addressed an officer without saluting.

The lieutenant looked over at Sgt. Yeager, who was busy helping Jody climb down from the second truck with the terribly wounded Pete. "Sergeant Yeager, is there any chance of food for these people?"

"Not at this hour, Sir."

"The mess hall is closed," the lieutenant said to the First. "The request to speak with the prosecution will be passed through proper channels."

"I've already gone through proper channels. Twice."

"That's the best I can tell you, Sergeant."

"Since the mess hall is closed," Poole asked testily, "what about some water? Is the well or the pipes closed, too?"

The lieutenant looked at him quietly. "For you, they are."

McClellan interceded. "Another one of my men could use some medical attention. Last night I was told he would be getting some help here. Is there a doctor on post?"

McClellan had reason to be concerned about Pete. While the wounds the other men had received at the hands of Quackenbush had long since healed, Pete was still mindless and weaving. He hadn't been able to utter a coherent word since being hit in the cell. Along with his mental state, his hands were still a serious problem.

Without looking at the injured soldier, both the lieutenant and the sergeant gave the K Company First Sergeant a look and walked away without saying anything. Poole watched them exit the gate. He turned back to McClellan. "You still think I'm wrong, huh?"

"About what?"

"Wantin' to kill crackers."

Chapter 24

Time passed, the prisoners were secure, and another night was crawling along. It was not the best time or place to be interviewed. The building at the south end of the post was old and, for the military, oddly shaped. It was not square; yet it wasn't round. Inside, the main room was small and uncomfortable with no table and only two chairs under a lonely, monotonous ceiling light. Following a written order, Capt. Farrell had reported on time. The officer he was supposed to meet was late.

The captain had arrived at the San Antonio post from Columbus only the night before. He hadn't been seen much since Houston. After the troops were returned to the home base in New Mexico, he went through a series of harsh question-and-answer sessions and was told to do nothing else but await orders. He filled most of the time fighting depression, wondering about his future, and writing letters. Strain had marked his face.

Farrell hadn't had a decent conversation with anyone since he left home, and he was lonely for his wife. A beautiful and gentle woman, he missed holding her, talking with her, reassuring her, and being comforted by her. And he missed his children more and more. He thought about them daily, and for the first time since being in the company of the blacks he began to wonder if any of them had children. He wasn't supposed to, as it somehow seemed to violate a societal or ethical code, but he wondered about the men's families, their mothers and fathers, wives, sweethearts, friends, and children, and in light of what the Army had in store for the men, if any of them would ever see their family or loved ones again. In that connection, the captain thought about something that, deep down, he wished he could have stayed away from.

It came strictly from the halls of the unknown, but Farrell wondered if it were possible that the coloreds could have the same feelings and regards for their loved ones as the whites did for theirs. It was no doubt a witless thought but, after all, standards were different, and no one knew how far, how wide, or how deep they went or how many nerves those differences in standards touched. To get away from that thought and other thoughts about the personal lives of blacks, he went back to letter-writing. One of the letters he wrote was to the wife of Capt. Reed. It was a very sensitive letter that he spent hours composing. His major concern was for the captain's four children. He also wrote a letter to Warrant Officer Froelich's family. In it, almost as he had written to Reed's wife, he said the warrant officer had been a commendable officer and a friend, and that he had died nobly.

The officer who came through the door 28 minutes late offered no apology.

"Captain Farrell?"

Farrell stood stressfully. He had expected someone older. "I'm Captain Farrell."

The man extended his hand for a short, insincere handshake. He was younger than Farrell, but Farrell knew that the younger man had held his rank longer.

"Captain Theodore Algonquins, assistant to the trial judge advocate," he said officiously. "Welcome to San Antonio." He gave Farrell another brief look, sat, pried open his briefcase, and started scanning several official documents.

Farrell sat, saying nothing, but knowing it was going to be a grinding session.

"When did you get in?"

"Last night. Late."

"Glad you're here." The officer looked up from the documents. "As a member of the prosecution, you can understand we've been somewhat deluged. I also hope you can understand I'm in somewhat of a rush, Captain. So just a few questions, if you don't mind."

"Certainly. But may I ask why you're in a rush?"

The captain looked surprised. He removed his glasses and wiped them. "The country is at war, Captain."

"Yes, but the war is over there. Some men are on trial — here — in San Antonio."

"And it is our intention not to allow that trial to be a distraction — here — in San Antonio. We do not intend for the trial to be a distraction through length or otherwise, Captain." The assistant paused long enough to make sure his point was clearly understood. Neither of them was sure that it was. Algonquins started for his briefcase, then stopped and asked, "By the way, Captain, you haven't been in contact with any of your men, have you?"

"No. The troops have been here since September, and, as I said, I've just arrived from Columbus late last night. Anyway, after my first series of interviews back in Columbus, I was told not to have any contact with the men."

"Good. We prefer it that way," the assistant TJA said. "Now, Captain, preliminary investigations indicate that on 25 August, you had ample reason to believe your troops were plotting an uprising. True?"

"Plotting an uprising? No, that is not true."

"You didn't know your troops were plotting an uprising?"

"No. I've said it before, and I'll say it again. I still don't believe there was an actual conspiracy, as some have said."

"Forget anything anyone has said regarding this case, Captain. I also strongly advise that you forget anything you have said in the past, to include any and all written statements. Is that clear?"

Farrell hesitated. "Yes. But may I ask why?"

"We've had a shift in direction," Algonquins said without clarifying. "Now, you say you didn't know your troops were plotting an uprising?"

"No, they were not. In the main, I'd say my troops were as contented as any troops I've ever commanded."

"Contented troops don't mutiny, Captain," Algonquins said, his voice a monotone. "How long have you been commanding troops?" Farrell didn't say anything.

Algonquins looked at the document he was holding and said, "You haven't been commanding very long."

"No, not very long. I haven't been in active service that long."

"Which means you really haven't had much experience commanding anyone, let alone coloreds."

"I suppose you could say that."

"And in not having that much experience in dealing with the coloreds, it is quite logical to assume they could have been plotting without your knowledge, true?"

"I'm not going to agree with that. To make an admission of that sort would indicate I didn't know my men. It would also indicate there was dissension in the ranks, or that they were possibly dissatisfied with my leadership."

"On the contrary," Capt. Algonquins said curtly. "To make such an admission would only serve to exonerate you."

"*Exonerate* me?" Farrell repeated, startled. "I haven't done anything."

"That could be a very interesting play on words, Captain. Keep in mind, we would like for the public to think you haven't done anything — negatively, that is."

Farrell caught the implications. "You would like the public to think I haven't done anything — '*negatively?*'"

"Yes. We wouldn't want that."

"And the *we being — ?*" Farrell said, after struggling with a series of thoughts.

"The United States of America. The Army of the United States of America. The division commander. The commanding officer of the 24th United States Infantry, the trial judge advocate who will prosecute, and me, assistant to the prosecution."

"I'm telling the Army, I'm telling you and anyone else who happens to be interested, I haven't done anything. I was not involved in the uprising."

The visiting captain, deciding to say nothing, pulled another paper from his briefcase. Farrell looked at him, as if bothered. Algonquins returned the look. "Question, Captain?"

"I'm bothered by this 'exonerate' me statement, and this idea you don't want the public to *think* I haven't done anything."

"So, I haven't made myself clear?"

"In that regard, I'm afraid you haven't. Frankly, I'm still missing something."

"Captain Farrell, we don't want the Army to go on trial."

"The Army is not going on trial," Farrell said. "Some soldiers are."

"I'm afraid you don't understand."

"I'm afraid you're right. I don't understand."

"You do understand you represent the Army of the United States?"

"Yes, I do."

"The coloreds don't."

Farrell looked at him. Again he didn't like what he heard. Algonquins went on. "To place you on trial would be indicting the Army. To place the coloreds on trial would be responding to the insurrection."

"What do you mean '*place me on trial'?*"

"Would you care for me to repeat the statement?"

"You can repeat any damned thing that you please. But I sure as hell don't have to agree with something that sounds fairly preposterous to me."

Algonquins stared him directly in the eye. "It's not your position to agree or disagree. And I can assure you, there is nothing 'fairly preposterous' about it."

"Place me on trial for what? What would I be charged with?"

"Violation of the 95th, the 89th, and the 67th Articles of War."

"You can't be serious."

"I couldn't be more serious, Captain," Algonquins said. He quoted from memory. "The 95th, the 89th, the 67th. For starters, failing to maintain good order; conduct unbecoming an officer; and failing to suppress a mutiny."

"You can't be serious."

"You've already said that once, Captain, and I've already told you how serious I am. And how serious the Army can be."

"This is ridiculous. It's ludicrous."

"Call it what you will, Captain, but facts are facts."

"Conduct unbecoming an officer? Failing to suppress a mutiny? You couldn't possibly think — ?"

"It isn't a matter of what I think," Capt. Algonquins said flatly. "And, to be frank, it is no longer a matter of what you think. It is a matter of the evidence we've amassed against you."

"The 'evidence' you've amassed against me?" Now Farrell was about to explode. Thinking better of it, he stood and paced the room.

"Problems, Captain?"

"You're damned right there are problems. I don't think I'm hearing you correctly. If I am, what you're saying is ridiculous. And you know it."

"Your battalion commander doesn't seem to think so."

"My ba — ? Colonel Briggs? You mean to say Colonel Briggs had something to do with those allegations?"

"Let's put it this way: your battalion commander has graciously come up with what the trial judge advocate would like to refer to as *possibilities* — depending, of course, on your cooperation."

Still standing, Farrell threw his head back against the brick wall.

"And those possibilities, Captain," Algonquins filled in, "those *possibilities* would accompany other possibilities. As an example, I believe you told your fellow officers, even before going to Houston, you would desert rather than go overseas and fight?"

"I never said that."

"The record states otherwise," Algonquins said, looking at the file.

"This is an outrage."

"And according to your 201 file here — your personnel file? — you've said worse. But that's not Colonel Boatner's concern, for the moment, that is. Colonel Boatner is from the judge advocate's office. He's the prosecutor, in case you're wondering."

"I don't need you to tell me what a TJA is. I'm not stupid. And I'll tell you as I've told the officers from the IG's office, the people from Division, and every —"

"Excuse me, Captain. We've agreed we wouldn't discuss any statements you've made previously — and that includes statements you've presumably made to personnel from the inspector general's office."

"How the hell can you say that when you've been telling me about evidence you've 'amassed' against me, and then sit there and quote Colonel Briggs? And speaking of my battalion commander, did he say anything else? Did he tell you what I did that night? That I actually *ran* all the way from my company area to Battalion Headquarters to see him *before* the troops marched on Houston? Did he tell you I told him there was going to be trouble? That the troops were marching? Did he tell you how he held me up with unnecessary conversation? — which I now believe was deliberate. Did he tell you he didn't want me to go to Colonel Stout? Did he tell you that I asked him to send out the white troops? Did he tell you his response to me? Did he tell you that it was me who *ran* from his quarters to Battalion Headquarters to find Colonel Stout while he did nothing? Did he tell you that it was me and Colonel Sto —"

"Captain, what you're saying makes for interesting drama and some rather serious accusations against a battalion commander should it get beyond this room. And I warn you, it had better not. Do I make myself clear?"

Farrell returned to his chair. "You got it wrong, Captain. The question is, do I make *myself clear*?"

"We'll see just how clear in a moment, Captain Farrell."

Farrell recognized the threat. He didn't know what the captain had up his sleeve, but he couldn't chance going further.

"You started to mention Colonel Stout. Be advised, the colonel has retired. In his retirement from service, the former commanding officer of Camp Logan has publicly acknowledged that he had grossly overestimated the behavior of the colored troops and was severely disappointed that they betrayed his trust and confidence."

"I don't believe that, and you don't either. The colonel might have retired — or been forced out — but he wouldn't have said what you've just quoted. Furthermore, I read the papers. I've never seen any statement that he's publicly made."

"Perhaps it's because you've been in Columbus and not in Houston."

"Columbus is not an island, Captain. And it's not a separate country. Listen, Colonel Stout was in definite favor of the troops. Of course he was disappointed by what happened in Houston. Any sane man would be. But he wouldn't have said any of that garbage you're now saying."

"Just as I've asked you to control your accusations, Captain, I ask that you control your language as well. Now, you can believe as you wish, but I thought I made it sufficiently clear in my earlier statement that the trial judge advocate doesn't expect to put the

Army on trial. That includes Army officers. And I ask again that you not do the same."

"Oh, the prosecution doesn't want to put the Army on trial, but yet you have these charges against me."

"You continue to *erroneously* refer to them as charges. They are not charges, Captain. They are *possibilities*. And those possibilities are contingent upon your answer to certain questions."

After a long, soul-searching moment, Farrell surrendered. "What is it you're trying to get to?"

"I shall say again. Preliminary investigations indicate that on 25 August, you had ample reason to believe your troops were plotting an uprising. Is that not correct?"

He tried, but Farrell couldn't force himself to agree.

"You're wasting time, Captain," Algonquins advised. "And there is something else you might consider. You're an officer of the United States Army. It is my understanding that you and Captain Reed were friends. He was an officer of the Army of the United States. That officer — your friend — is dead, Captain. He was killed by your troops. *Colored* troops. That doesn't seem to mean anything to you."

"Captain Reed and I were not that friendly. We talked, but we were never what one would call close friends. We never knew each other that well. Outside of the Officers' Clubs at Logan and Columbus, we never saw each other that much."

"And so his death means nothing to you?"

Farrell thought about it, but chose not to mention the caring, sensitive letters he had written to Reed's wife and Froelich's family. "Of course the captain's death meant something to me."

"It doesn't sound like it. It sounds as if you're only concerned with yourself."

"I'm sorry you have that impression. Captain Reed's death meant a lot to me, as did Warrant Officer Froelich's. Anybody's death would mean something to me. I'm bothered by all the fatalities connected with this thing. But I can't just go along with saying anything you want me to say. Then I really would be wrong."

"To begin with, you're not just 'going along.' We're not fools, either, Captain. We know for a fact the coloreds were huddled in the First Platoon tent, conducting a meeting prior to the march on Houston. We have a sworn statement from a white soldier — a rider — who witnessed it. He saw the men assembled in the First Platoon tent. We also have sworn statements from two of the coloreds who were present at the time. And I can assure you we will have more in due time. Most importantly, Captain Farrell, we know that somewhere between 1940 and 2025 hours, the approximate time of the start of the conspiracy, you entered into the First Platoon tent to summon your first sergeant. Now, from your mouth, did you or did you not enter the tent at or around the stated time?"

"What I did was stick my head in the tent — briefly," Farrell said reluctantly.

"Is that your normal procedure? — to just 'briefly stick your head' into your troops' tent?"

"No, it isn't."

"Normally you would have fully entered the tent?"

"Yes."

"Why didn't you follow your normal procedure, Captain?"

"Because I knew it was a tense situation."

"So, then, you did have the feeling something was going on?"

"Obviously. As I just said, I had a feeling that everything wasn't as it should have been."

"Because — ?"

"Because of the trouble that had occurred in the Fourth Ward that afternoon."

"Meaning the Fourth Ward's San Felipe district?"

"Yes. Because of the fighting. And because some of the men had been jailed."

"And when you *stuck* your head inside the tent — *briefly* — did you hear anything? Meaning, were there any words spoken?"

"No."

"You heard nothing?"

"Nothing."

The assistant prosecutor took a brief look at one of the papers.

"You did not hear Corporal Thelonius Poole of your company say to First Sergeant Obie McClellan of your company as he was leaving to join you outside the tent, 'Do we get an answer, Sergeant?' — or words to that effect?"

Farrell was again slow. "Yes. I heard that."

"And so you did hear something?"

"Yes. I heard what you've just stated."

"And what else did you hear?"

"Nothing."

"Meaning you did not hear Corporal Poole say — and I quote: 'Over thirty-some colored peoples is done already been lynched this year. And this is just August'?"

"Yes, I heard it."

"And what else did you hear, Captain?"

"Poole said something else to the First —"

"By 'First' you mean First Sergeant Obie O. McClellan of K Company?"

"Yes," Farrell said wearily. "But, Captain, you have said nothing — and there is nothing I heard that evening — that would indicate a conspiracy."

"I strongly suggest you let the trial judge advocate be the judge of that, Captain. The troops were furtively gathered in the tent, at first speaking in hushed tones, so much so that it halted your normal actions, and, by your own admission, you knew it was a tense situation. As the commanding officer you aren't normally found in a platoon tent at that hour on a Saturday evening. Even at that, you would have fully entered. It was only after you 'stuck' your head in the tent — briefly — that Corporal Poole became threatening, and his demeanor, belligerent. Is that, or is that not, true?"

"It could be interpreted that way."

"It is not an interpretation, Captain Farrell. It is fact. And we can substantiate it. Now, what else did you hear Corporal Poole say?"

"As the first sergeant cleared the door, Poole said something like, 'This is the only country where we're still bein' tarred an' feathered. Some even wearing the uniform.'"

"And what was Corporal Poole's tone of voice, Captain?"

"Understandably angry."

"Why 'understandably'?"

"Excuse me. Corporal Poole wears two chevrons — stripes. He is a noncom, a noncommissioned officer in your company. It is a position of leadership and trust. Why is it you've never cared for him?"

"I've just never cared for him," Farrell said. Fearful he was being led into a trap, he added, "Listen, I don't want to be in a position of defending the corporal, but even he had the right to be upset over what happened earlier that day."

"Captain Farrell, you don't know everything that happened earlier that day. You weren't there."

"And neither were you, Captain."

"But witnesses favoring the prosecution were. Try not to forget that. Now, while the corporal was in the tent, did he appear angry enough to want to do something about a country that he thinks is — and I quote — 'still tarring and feathering coloreds'?"

Farrell didn't want to answer.

The assistant trial judge advocate was firm. "I am not going to ask the question again, Captain. And let me remind you, we are talking about a conspiracy against the good and lawful order of the United States."

Farrell sighed, but he still wouldn't commit.

"Captain, your reluctance to cooperate is not at all commendable. Might I remind you of your wife and two little girls back home in St. Agatha, Maine — 94 Glastonbury Road — I believe?"

His jaw tightened, Farrell glared at the man.

"I'm sorry, Captain, I didn't get your response. That is the right address, is it not? At least that's what you have in your 201. And that is the address where someone from the trial judge's office might be going, should the need arise."

It was more than a veiled threat, and Farrell got every ounce of it. His face was taut and red. He started to exploded, but he held up. Through clenched teeth he said, "You bastard."

Farrell had never used the word before. He couldn't remember being that angry before. "You rotten bastard," he said again.

Algonquins pretended he hadn't heard either of the responses. Importantly looking through the file and extracting another paper, he continued. "And there's more. According to what I'm now reading, Captain, your father-in-law — whom you worked for and with — is a retired major who served this country honorably. He has an engineering firm now, and he is doing business with the military. Even more now that there's a war going on. And I note, too, he did quite well for you — government contracts and all — something I presume you're going back to once the war is over and you are *honorably* discharged like the rest of those desiring to go back to civilian life. But enough about your family and future, Captain," the assistant trial judge advocate said, putting the papers away. "I want to go back to those possibilities I spoke of — possibilities that with the stroke of a pen can be turned into charges. We wouldn't want that, would we?"

Farrell was still too angry to comment. Algonquins wouldn't be stopped. "Oh, and by the way, Captain, you were ordered by your battalion commander to prepare papers reducing your first sergeant in rank. Which, if it wasn't done — and if I am correct — could be classed as dereliction of duty, and which — if I am again correct — could amount to another severe charge for a loving family to hear, wouldn't you say?"

Farrell was burning inside. He took his time and said, "You're a blackmailing sonofabitch."

Perhaps for the first time in his life, he would have said more, but flashing through Farrell's mind was the beautiful home in St. Agatha, Maine. He saw the U.S. Army staff car pulling up to the front of the house, he saw the two officers getting out and walking up the sidewalk to the door, he saw his beautiful wife as she opened the door. He heard the escaping squeaks and giggles of his two little girls playing with the loving grandfather in the background. He heard the officers say something. He heard —

"Captain — ? Captain Farrell — ?" Algonquins said, knowing he had him. "You're delaying the process, Captain. The question I wanted to get back to, was Corporal Poole — the person whom you did not like in the first place — was he a naturally hostile person?"

It was a losing battle. The torn captain could do nothing but shrug.

"Presuming the answer was in the affirmative, tell me this: at the time in question, was the corporal angry enough to want to do something about a country he thinks, and I quote: 'is still tarring and feathering coloreds'?"

"I believe he was," Farrell said almost inaudibly, and after taking a long time.

"I couldn't hear you, Captain."

"I said I believe Poole was hostile! At the time in question, Corporal Thelonious Poole of Company K was hostile! At the time in question, Corporal Thelonious Poole of Company K was angry enough to want to carry out his hostilities! He was going to carry them out against the country, against the military, against the whites of Houston, and every white in Texas, and every white in America! Is that good enough for you?"

"Certainly," Algonquins said, unruffled. "And now, Captain, did you have the occasion to observe First Sergeant McClellan when he met with you outside of the tent?"

"Yes, I did."

"And his demeanor?"

"His demeanor was fine."

"And his demeanor, Captain?"

Farrell didn't want to repeat what he had said.

Algonquins pushed. "What was the first sergeant's demeanor, Captain?"

In exasperation, Farrell finally said, "The first sergeant is a very calm and aloof man."

"The first sergeant also led the march on Houston," Capt. Algonquins retorted. "Now, what did you say to First Sergeant McClellan when he came out of the tent?"

"I asked him a question."

"And the nature of that question?"

"I asked him what the men were doing inside," Farrell said, again reluctant. "And I asked him what Poole was talking about."

"To which the first sergeant replied?"

The captain simply didn't want to say. Again he sighed heavily.

"He said Poole was talking about a sorry state of affairs."

"A sorry state of affairs?'"

"Yes."

"A sorry state of affairs — *where*?"

"In the Army. But remember, I didn't hear McClellan say anything in the tent."

The trial judge advocate's assistant overlooked the second part of the response. "So, First Sergeant Obie O. McClellan and Corporal Theolonius Poole, the one who believes the country is tarring and feathering coloreds, were angrily talking about a sorry state of affairs in the United States Army and in the United States of America?"

Farrell had sunk to rock bottom and could only manage a feeble, "If that's what you want it to be." He no longer knew what to say and almost mumbled the last response. But at least his family was safe.

"And together McClellan and or Poole, two leaders — NCO's of K Company — wanted to do something about the sorry state of affairs that they believed exists in the United States Army, and in the country itself?"

Farrell nodded.

"Please voice your reply, Captain."

"In the Army; in the United States. They didn't like the conditions."

"And they wanted to do something about it?"

"And they wanted to do something about it."

"Captain Farrell, that sounds like the makings of conspiracy." Farrell remained quiet.

"On the subject of weapons," Algonquins continued, "were they under lock and key at any time during the evening in question?"

"They were supposed to be."

"*Supposed* to be?"

"When I returned from Battalion Headquarters after the meeting with Colonel Briggs and the post commander that evening, the rifles were not in the Supply Tent where they were supposed to be at that hour. And where they were before I left."

"Where were they?"

"Some of them were at stacked-arms in front of the tents."

"And not authorized by you?"

"No."

"You said 'some of the rifles.' Do you have any idea why all the rifles weren't at stacked-arms?"

"I presume they were in the hands of the detail who marched on Houston."

"Is there any way any of that can be substantiated? Without presumption?"

"Yes."

"How so?"

"When I returned from Headquarters, I saw Poole. He was armed. He was ordered to lay down his arms, and he — "

"Yes."

"*He*' — meaning Corporal Poole — was armed?"

"Yes."

"And he was ordered to lay down his arms by whom?"

"By me."

"How?"

"By verbal order."

"And the corporal responded by — ?"

"He responded by firing his weapon several times. They were warning shots. Then he hollered something and fired again, at first hitting the vehicle that brought me back from Headquarters, then he fired and killed the driver."

"Corporal Poole actually fired a weapon at you — an officer in the United States Army — and he eventually fired at — and killed — a soldier in the United States Army?"

"Yes."

"And you actually saw Poole when he fired his weapon?"

"It was dark, but there is no question he fired the shots."

"And where was First Sergeant/Master Sergeant Obie O. McClellan and the remaining men of the company at the time?"

"Marching to Houston."

"And how do you know that?"

"Poole said so."

"How did Poole say so?"

"After firing, he said in a loud voice, 'We're marching, Captain.'"

"Poole actually said the words, 'we're marching, Captain'?"

"Yes."

The trial judge advocate's associate had heard enough. He started writing. "For the record, now, Captain, and as you will testify. From the top: Preliminary investigations indicate that on 25 August, 1917 you, as company commander of Company K, had ample reason to believe your troops were plotting an uprising. Is that true?"

The captain reluctantly nodded.

"For the record, Captain, please vocalize your reply."

"They could have been plotting."

"Not 'could have been,' Captain."

"Alright, the troops were plotting."

Algonquins stopped writing for a second. "Is that your reply to me or to the question?"

"To the question."

Satisfied, the advocate's assistant started writing again. "And the full answer to the question is —?"

"I had ample reason to believe my troops were plotting an uprising."

"And you obtained that information —?"

"By observation and ensuing statements."

"You observed your troops conspiring?"

"I observed the troops in conspiracy."

"When was this? And where was this?"

"Shortly before the march on Houston —"

"Meaning on the evening of August 25, at around 1920 hours? Be specific, Captain."

An exhausted Farrell replied, "On the evening of August 25th, 1917 at about 1920 hours, I had occasion to enter the First Platoon tent of my company. Corporal Poole, the company's Corporal of Supply, was speaking —"

"Conspiratorially?"

"As if in conspiracy."

"Not in *as if*, Captain. Now you say again?"

"The troops were speaking in conspiracy."

The interview lasted another hour.

Capt. Farrell's home in St. Agatha, Maine never left his mind.

Chapter 25

The sign above the door read "R&R." In the military it meant rest and relaxation, but it was just another Officers' Club. The profile seemed lower, but it really was no different from any of the other post clubs. Drab and sparse, it was located well away from the barracks and the B.O.Q. — the Bachelor Officers' Quarters.

Receiving neither rest nor relaxation was Maj. DeBerg. Old, alone, and grumpily independent, he was sitting in a dark corner in the windowless place, nursing the gout and sipping on a drink. Severely overweight, DeBerg didn't look like an officer. He had a round face, slouched a lot, and didn't look well in the uniform. He had a naturally commanding presence, but he had the look of a man who had never been happy, always troubled. For a man leading the defense, and for as much work as there was to do, he hadn't done much since arriving in San Antonio. It wasn't that he was disabled by his long-time illness, or that he wasn't capable. DeBerg was tired. And he was not pleased. In the few weeks he had been on the post, the North Carolinian spent most of his time in his quarters, thinking about the heretical oddity of using the chapel as a court. It was pure blasphemy, and he was a part of it — a major part of it. At a time when he should have been getting closer to God, here he was adding distance through sacrilege.

The major had been in the club for an hour or more, and he was three quarters through a drink he hadn't been enjoying when Lt. Col. Briggs came in talking and scanning the room. He saw the old form he thought was familiar. Cutting off the conversation with the officers he entered with, the lieutenant colonel veered around the tables and over to the major. His first glance had landed on the major's profile, so Briggs wanted to make sure. He stood back a few feet, scratched at his horseshoe hairline, and gave the quiet man a long look. It was Maj. DeBerg, alright. They hadn't seen each other in years. Briggs smiled, moved in closer, and said, "P.D. DeBerg! You ol' son-of-a-gun." He slapped the man's back.

"How are things back at where the big boys play?"

"Heinrich, I'd thank you to keep your damned hands off my back."

"Oh-oh. I can tell by that, Pee, you haven't changed a peg, except for that spare tire around your belly," Briggs bantered. "Still crusty and ornery."

"And you're still full of crap. Still bluffing your way around."

"Now, that's no way to talk to an old friend you haven't seen in ages."

"We were never that friendly. If I remember, there was a small problem with my ancestry."

"Well, it might have come up once or twice. But it never stopped me from liking you. And it never stopped me from speaking up for you. You know, you and I have always had a lot in common."

"I've never needed you to speak up for me. And I'll be damned if I can remember anything we ever had in common."

Briggs laughed off the grumpiness. "Maybe it was our high I.Q.'s. Maybe it was our concern for our fellow man."

"You're b.s.'ing again, Heinrich. And distastefully so. What is it these Texans say about people like you? All hat and no cattle?"

"You know, P.D., in all these years I'd forgotten what a bitter man you are. I'd really forgotten that. With your attitude, I'm surprised to see you've made major."

"I'm surprised you've made light colonel."

"I should be a full bird by now."

"I thought the Army was overdoing it when you made second lieutenant."

"Thanks for your confidence. If you hadn't been so damned indecisive about everything and played your cards right, maybe you'd be a colonel by now. With a command."

"I'm happy being what I am, where I am."

"You don't believe that, and neither do I," Briggs said, "But as an old friend, I'll tell you this. When I heard they put you on this thing, I said to myself, with your concerns, the Army couldn't have picked a better man."

"You lied to yourself again, Heinrich. But, as I've tried to get across before, there's nothing new there."

"Pee, if I didn't know you better, I'd swear you didn't like me," Briggs said. "But, seriously, does the Army have your cooperation on this thing?"

"Are you asking how relaxed my defense will be, Colonel?"

"Oh, c'mon, now. Don't get sanctimonious on me. It isn't a matter of defending; this is a case of representing. How the hell can that bunch not be guilty?"

"If they're guilty, why have a trial?"

"You're from Division Headquarters, you know the answer to that better than I do. It's a formality. Give the people a show. Send a message for a couple of weeks. That's what the Army wants. We do what the Army pays us for."

"You know something, Heinrich, I've known you for what? — twenty, thirty years?"

"Well before I went to the Point."

"And since your unceremonious departure, you've always done

what was convenient."

"I'm a career soldier."

"You're a survivor. Admit it."

"You're damned right, I am. You can be a survivor, too, if you'd ever wise up," Briggs started to sit but remained standing. "Listen, I've just thought of something. Between you, me, and the gatepost, there's a command opening up. Of course, being from Division, you probably know that already."

"I don't stick my nose into places it doesn't belong."

"Well, you should know something about that. You might be just the man for it. They need a permanent replacement for Lonnie Childress. You remember him? C.O. of the 15th National Guard unit out of New York."

"I don't remember him, and I have no interest in the 15th or any other unit."

"Don't kid me, Pee. I know you. When we were younger, we used to talk. It might've gotten strained a few times, but we still talked. And I can tell you've still got the old fire in you. I know you'd like to have one more shot at it before it's over. Lose some of that frontage, and commit to it. Go for a command."

"Weight is the least of my problems, Heinrich. The vicissitudes of time has bowed me. I've got the gout, arthritis and practically anything else you can name is killing me. I've got one more case pending back east. After that, I'm out the door."

"You're going to tell me you'd rather spend your last days in service running around the country defending lost causes than have a command? Keep that up and you're going to end up like Del Rideout. You remember him? I saw him when I was out in Houston this summer. That flat-assed wife of his has got him out to pasture."

"Weren't you after Priscilla at one time, Heinrich?"

"Couldn't stand her."

"You're lying again, Briggs. She wore a dress."

"Not nice, Major. Not nice. Anyway, marriage was the worst

thing that could've happened to him. It could've been me. I'm telling you, Pee, Del's losing his mind. He's not able to do a damned thing but sit in a rocking chair, drink, look feeble, be bossed around by a woman, and come up with these crazy notions about bombing boats with planes — some launched from ships, mind you. He's pathetic. Don't wind up like him. Find a command. Put in for Lonnie's old job. Shake a few pounds and I'll vouch for you. Stay there for a while, and you might get lucky. Remember, Lonnie started off with the Guard and now he's the commander of Logan. And you know how he got it? He replaced that idiot, Stout."

"From what I'm told, Heinrich, it wasn't Bradford Stout who was the idiot. And he wasn't responsible for what happened in Houston."

Briggs stiffened. "I don't care what you were told. If Stout hadn't been so damned derelict and ineffectual in command, the incident in Houston never would have occurred. Talk to Del. Ask Priscilla. I spent that entire Saturday afternoon telling them about the coloreds. I predicted trouble."

"If you spent a Saturday afternoon predicting trouble, why in the hell didn't you do something to stop it?"

"I tried to. Stout wouldn't listen. If anything, he made matters worse."

"Once again, Heinrich, that's not what I heard."

"Well, you take it from me, if there were no Stout, there would have been no Houston — starting with his insistence that those people should have been allowed to go on pass earlier that day. I fought him at every turn, but he was in command of the post, and as a bird he outranked me. But I'll tell you one thing, Pee, everything that egotistical sonovabitch did there was wrong. And he knows it. Why the hell do you think he chickened out and retired so damned quickly?"

"Since I'd like to get his testimony, I don't think I'm able to discuss the matter."

"You'd bring him back and put him on the stand?"

"If he'd change his mind and cooperate, I damned sure would. That is, if the Army would allow it."

"And they shouldn't. But it probably wouldn't do you any good anyway. He'd be a hostile witness."

"What's so different about that? The whole atmosphere around here is hostile. And not only would I bring him back, Heinrich, I might even put you on the stand and subject you to a heavy cross."

Briggs was taken aback. "I think you're going a little too far, P.D. I'd seriously think about that, if I were you. Remember this trial is supposed to be swift and decisive."

"Concerned that it won't be, Colonel?"

"Yes. But not for myself. For you."

"Easy, Heinrich, easy. Don't lose your sense of humor. And don't worry about me. The gloves are not going to come off. It was just a little flight of fantasy on my part. I'm not going much beyond name, rank and serial number. But let me tell you, if I were younger or healthier, I damned sure would give it a shot. I'd come out with guns blazing."

"If you were younger and healthier and defending coloreds for rioting and murder, and word got out that you were even thinking about coming down heavy on a battalion commander, the Army would have your head. And you know it. This is not a democracy, P.D. This is the Army of the United States."

"And what a tragedy that is, Colonel. What a tragedy," said the major. He emptied his glass as though the subject had exhausted itself.

Briggs picked up with the earlier thought of conciliation. "What about that command position?"

"Don't be ridiculous."

"There's nothing ridiculous about it at all. You can handle a command. I want you to go out living your dream."

"Living a dream at my age? What a joke," the major said. Suddenly he was tired. "Heinrich, I'm a lawyer. I'm just a tired old North Carolina lawyer who many years ago made the mistake of thinking he could be a soldier. It's a pity I'll go to my grave knowing I've failed in both."

"If you're going to take that attitude, there's not a damned thing I can do about it. Just try not to kick the bucket until after trial."

"The Germans have a phrase for that: Macht nichts — or something like that."

"Well, don't nix it until after trial."

"Why so much concern, Heinrich? You're afraid I'm not going to lie down and play dead in court?"

"That's not my worry. But, off the record, what are you going to do?"

"I don't know what I'm going to do. I just said the gloves aren't going to come off. The only thing I've done thus far is conduct a few interviews in Houston and send word to the accused not to say a damned word to anybody, to keep their mouths shut, before, during and after trial. If they're guilty, they're guilty. If they're not, they're not. Let the Army prove what they've got on 'em. It's not going to be all that hard to do, considering what happened. But then again, when the troops were in the field and ambushed the military vehicles, maybe some things will be hard to prove. It was dark, no witnesses. Only those who actually did the firing know exactly what happened. The way I understand it, half of the sixty-three on trial didn't participate in the final assault. Same as the others to be tried. They were way off in another part of the field."

"We don't know that for certain, and naturally those birds are going to lie. What about the officers who were fired upon?"

"What did they see? What could they see? Stout was in the lead vehicle, but now that all of you have managed to get him pissed, you think he's going to cooperate? Hell, no. If he testified under subpoena, would that make things any better? And I'm not at all certain he can provide any more information than anyone else. Did he or the other officers actually *see* anything? Did they see *any-body?* Can anyone point to a specific individual and say that he did this or that? Can you make out an individual black face from a vehicle — at night — dressed in an olive drab uniform and lying in the prone position in a ditch? You tell me."

"Who do you have assisting you?"

"In the preliminaries I had a Captain — ? I forgot his name. Anyway, he submitted his reports and dropped out. Career move, I guess. Maybe he thought the case was hopeless. I don't know. But to answer your question, I've got a Lieutenant Jennings. She becomes my second. You wouldn't know her."

"She — ? Her? Come again. Did you say *her?*"

"*Her.* Denoting female."

"A *woman?*"

"A woman."

"You're kidding."

"I'm in failing health, God is so close I can smell His breath, and I'm preparing for a trial that's going to take place in a church, Heinrich. I'm not exactly in a kidding mood."

"But a *woman?* In the bona fide Army?"

"The 'bona fide' U.S. Army."

The Third Battalion commander guffawed, then grew serious.

"A woman in the Army? And in court?"

"And if she doesn't talk too much, she'll be fine."

"I've never seen a woman in a court before, let alone at an Army court-martial."

"Well, now you have something to look forward to."

"In fact," Briggs said more seriously, "I'm going to be honest about this thing. I didn't know they'd let a women come even close to the Army."

"Your ignorance is showing again, Briggs. It's interesting because you fancy yourself as some sort of military historian. Women have been hanging in and around the Army since the revolution. Of course, most of them were nurses. But who cares?"

"I care. This is a man's Army."

"That may be, but if you want to get specific about it, women have been spies, saboteurs, water-bearers, launderers, cooks and practically everything else you can name. And they've been on the battlefield. They haven't all been on the payroll, but they've been around."

"The hell, you say."

"And if it makes you feel any better, Briggsy, ol' boy," the major said loosely, "one of them was even awarded the Congressional Medal of Honor."

"Impossible."

"Look it up."

"Well, I'll be damned." Briggs huffed and snorted.

"But don't lose any sleep over it. They took it back from her."

"As they rightly should have," responded Briggs. "Why'd you pick this bird? A little action going on under the covers?"

"I'm like you, Heinrich. I couldn't get it up with helium."

"Yeah, but you've stopped trying. I haven't. But why'd you pick her?"

"I didn't pick her. Washington sent her, and I accepted her. I don't know why. And I don't care."

Briggs laughed, then settled back to ponder the surprise. "A damn woman in the Army of The United States — and *serving* at a court-martial! No wonder this Army is falling apart. Why the hell did you accept a woman?"

"You've just asked me that," DeBerg said. "She showed up and I went along with it. It's no skin off my back. And besides, in a case like this, what difference does it make?"

Briggs couldn't get over it. "A woman in the real Army."

"And if it makes you feel any better, she's English."

"Oh, come now. That's going just a little too far. What the hell would an English woman know about American law?"

"Our laws came from England, Heinrich."

"Which is where they should have stayed," commented Briggs. "What was she, one of those suffragettes stirring up trouble over there and they kicked her out of the country?"

"I have no way of knowing."

"What a joke this thing's going to be. During trial, where's she staying?"

"Why do you need to know that?"

"I might have a bone to pick with her," said the colonel in a joking but prurient fashion.

DeBerg was not amused. "She sleeps in her own quarters, Heinrich. And I hope like hell the Army's put a guard on the door. Two of 'em, with you around."

Briggs forced a laugh and, despite his carnal interest, shook it off. "Women in the Army. What's next, children?"

"Well, you might as well get used to 'em. A few years ago, the Army established a women's corps. They're here to stay."

"Like the goddamned coloreds, I guess," the battalion commander said. "And look what a fiasco that's turned out to be."

"Speaking of the coloreds, what's your present status with the 24th?"

"The minute trial is over, I'm out," Briggs answered. "And I wouldn't command another goddamned colored unit if my life depended on it. From here on out, I'm dealing with the top of the deck. It's whites only. I might even do myself a favor and look for those women you're talking about."

"It's the Army Nurse Corps, Heinrich."

"Makes no difference. Maybe the Army's got a point, after all."

"So now you're accepting."

"It's beginning to make sense."

"How so?"

"We can command them all day, and screw 'em all night."

"Heinrich, isn't there anything beneath you?"

"Maybe it's not nice, but there sure is a lot of truth to it," Briggs said, preparing to leave. "Anyway, good luck to you, Pee. And personally, I'm glad you've got that woman as an assistant. Makes me feel a whole lot better."

"Why?"

"Now I know the niggers are gonna hang."

Chapter 26

"You have heard the charges," said the brigadier general and President of the Court, his bulldog face set for action. "How do you plead?"

And so with the war thundering on, and after all the investigations, queries, charges, back-stage maneuverings, pressures, and fears — and slackness from the defense — the court-martial of the first contingent of blacks from Company K of the 24th United States Infantry (Colored) was finally under way in Fort Sam Houston's Gift Chapel, in San Antonio, Texas. It was November 1, 1917, a day which had begun with a frost — and a mere 65 days since the uprising in Houston on a hot and muggy Saturday in August.

In many ways the trial could have appeared to be a classic case of rushing to judgement, but not to the military, and not, apparently, to those who sat stone-faced in the pews of the chapel, certain of guilt and wondering only what the punishment would be. Clues couldn't be found in body language or faces, unless absolute stillness counted. Only the 63 blacks sitting in the roped-off area of the chapel showed any signs of life. They didn't know it at the time, but they were to be the first wave. The second wave, consisting of 40 men, would be tried later. And yet to be scheduled was a third wave. None of those eventualities, however, could be read on the attending faces. Everyone in the chapel was focused on the job at hand.

First Sgt. McClellan, legs crossed and arms folded, his mind having returned from the long, memory-filled journey, showed no emotion. Like everyone else in the court, he waited for the woman who would formally respond to the general's request for a plea to the charges and to the specifications.

McClellan was still holding the letter he had received from his old friend back in August. Occasionally he'd look thoughtfully at the envelope and think about Sgt. Dukes. He would think about his old friend throughout trial. Oddly, Maj. DeBerg of the defense would be thinking and glancing at McClellan all through trial. Others would relent and look at him as well, but not for the same reasons.

Serenely competent and poised, the lieutenant slid her chair back and stood. Except for DeBerg, all eyes in the packed courtroom withdrew from the 13 high-ranking trial officers and swung to her when she answered the brigadier in that clipped, British accent. "Not guilty," said Lt. Wilmona Jennings, her large eyes unmoving.

"Not guilty, *Sir*," Brig. Gen. Hawley corrected sternly.

The lieutenant was so intense, she had made a mistake. She registered the oversight in her mind. It wouldn't happen again.

"I beg the court's pardon, Sir," she said deferentially yet with style and strength. "Not guilty, *Sir*."

"Noted," the brigadier said. "And to the specification of the charges." The words weren't framed as questions.

The woman with the face that suppressed her attractiveness and displayed nothing but the job at hand stood again. "Not guilty, Sir."

"The trial judge advocate's opening statement," called the brigadier.

Capt. Algonquins, who had read the charges, gave way to his superior.

His bearing erect, his thick mustache neatly trimmed, Col. Paul A. Boatner was an elegant man. From San Francisco, he was paced and eloquent. He was no stranger to either law or the court. His grandfather had once served as a justice of the U. S. Supreme Court and wanted his grandson to follow in his footsteps. As had his father, young Boatner chose the military.

"History makes an uncertain prophet," the colonel began, his prosecutorial voice low but penetrating, causing the prisoners to stiffen and the spectators to squirm. "One would think that in opening your doors and bidding the criers of oppression to enter, a rare thing called gratitude would be in evidence. Perhaps if not gratitude — something — something of value. Unfortunately there are those among us much too primitive and vulgar to understand this, and that is why we are here in this court today. We are here today because savagery and rot exist in certain human beings, and, despite all, it is much too deep-rooted to ever hope to conquer. The Army of the Army has learned this, and the Army has suffered. The Army of the United States has suffered because it extended its arms and tried to instill the decency of mankind into the veins of the unworthy, those over there in the darkened corner of this room. I ask this court to consider the even darker charges leveled against them, the 64th Article of War, disobeying lawful orders; the 66th, mutiny; the 92nd, murder. Crimes, gentlemen, that even the jungle, the very roots whence they came, would not tolerate.

"The trial judge advocate can quite readily prove that even before that disgracefully tragic night — and afternoon — of August 25th, these so-called *troops* had already entered into a conspiracy. Houston only served as an excuse. The prosecution can show that without the slightest bit of the alleged provocation, the accused entered into a mutinous pact, disobeyed their commanding officer, unlawfully armed themselves, marched on the city of Houston, and primitively murdered at will. Their defense will undoubtedly run along the tired old lines that have always shielded the Negro from responsibility. It will be that of the racially deprived; the cry of the downtrodden, the oppressed, the unequaled — the denied. Such ignorance will not be accepted here. Though we have the right to be and do otherwise, though sanctioned by law and by custom — de jure and de facto — the military has chosen to be the very epitome of equality for the colored man. That is why their uniforms are the same as ours.

"The prosecution will be able to strike down every single claim that will falsely umbrella these people, these sixty-three and the many others to follow. But that is not our purpose, nor is it the purpose of this assembly. The government's purpose — *our* purpose is to remember that the very posture of the military, and indeed that of the nation as a whole, has been affected by these scabs masquerading as soldiers, and to even have a trial for them is, by far, many times over what they deserve. Even so, we must remember that we are not here to become enmeshed in the rigors of legality. We are not here to test law or its jurisprudence, to burden ourselves with trundles of evidence, to recreate those awful horrors in the minds of the already grieving. Our purpose is to prove to the American people that the Army will not — and cannot — tolerate the awful shame these unquestionably Kaiser-leaning and no-doubt Bolshevik-inspired people have brought down upon us. They are not Americans; they do not believe in the American way. They have stained our flag. The eagle, our symbol of courage and conviction has been ravaged by crows and pretenders — those in the darkened corner of this room. Look at them. *Soldiers*, you say? I think not. *Mockingbirds* is what they are — *Mimus polyglottos* — mimics; pretenders. Ours is to get rid of them.

"Ours is to prove to them and all the other coloreds that you cannot run a course of lawlessness in this country. Most importantly, Gentlemen, ours is to put the American people at rest. And the only way we can do that is to take full refuge in the Articles of War, wherein the maximum penalty for such offenders is death. Since civil law was violated, our law prescribes death by hanging. Let us exercise that maximum, remembering that the cowardice of a black in uniform is all too obvious, all too odious, and, as has been proven before, all too dangerous. Fired by the riots in East St. Louis, Illinois, and in other places where many innocents were slaughtered and wounded, again this disease of society has run amok and struck terror in the hearts of the citizenry. Perhaps it could be argued they were not quite as bestial and monstrous as these here before us today, but they were, I need not remind you, of this ilk — members of the Tenth Cavalry; members of the Twenty-Fifth Infantry. *Soldiers* they were; and the Army showed them mercy. Again and again this great institution has been lenient and satisfied itself with the mere and meager act of discharging *colored soldiers — mimics —* without honor, and without trial. Gentlemen, let us err no more — knowing well that a monster of unspeakable hell broke out on that night of August 25th, and for three and three quarters hours there raged a riot. A riot fired by the morally corrupt and intellectually inferior. Soldiers. Pretenders. *Colored soldiers.* And when the colored soldier was through on that night of August 25th, what did he leave in his wake? Death and destruction. What did he leave in East St. Louis just a month or two ago? Death and destruction. What did he leave in Brownsville, Texas, just a few years ago? Death and destruction. What did he leave in other places? Death and destruction. And it mattered not who the targets were. When the colored soldier had done what he wanted to do in Houston on that horrifying night of August 25th — when nearly one third — over 200 of 645 enlisted men marched through the streets of Houston, shooting and bayoneting in abandonment, a sixteen-year-old little girl lay dead. A *woman* and eleven other civilians, including ten police — *ten officers of the law* — lost their lives, and even more were wounded. The *military* death toll was five, including a captain — a *captain* in the

Army of the United States. Gentlemen, as members of that same Army, sworn to do our duty for God and Country — let us — if we are to do nothing else for as long as we are in the military, if we are to do nothing else for as long as we are members of the human race, let us for once satisfy justice. Let us not disappoint the American people who now demand the full measure of justice; let us not disappoint our American Expeditionary Forces, those brave and courageous young hearts now engaged in the honorable and noble task of defending this great country on foreign soil under the command of our great general, General John J. "Black Jack" Pershing, hero of the Indian Wars and the Mexican Expedition. And isn't it ironic, isn't it the height of irony that just a few days ago — October 27, to be specific — it was formally announced that our troops abroad had just fired their first shots in the great war? The beasts with the incorrigible, medusoidlike brains before you had already fired their shots — at home; at unarmed civilians, at innocents. It is remarkable; the timing, all too saddening. For the grieving, on behalf of the Army of the United States I offer the deepest of sympathy. I promise you and the nation that we shall not allow such horrors to ever take place again. It stuns credulity what the depraved will do. But as guardians of the American way, we will put a stop to it. We will start with this court. We cannot allow that when the French troops mutinied a few months ago after hearing about the losses sustained on the eastern front, it became contagious. The uprising swept through 16 corps. We cannot allow that to happen here. The French executed the 23 socialist and pacifist agitators. In that regard, it is incumbent upon us to do no less.

"Gentlemen, you who sit in judgement are required by law to be swift and decisive in your renderings. May I remind you that at this very moment the gallows are being constructed at Fort Sam Houston. They are being readied for the depraved. I ask you not to waste the time or the effort. The *mockingbirds* — those in the darkened corner of this room — must die. It is in our national interest."

The prosecutor returned to his seat amid a concrete silence. He had scored heavily with the speech. Few expected the refined man to be so damning or lengthy. No one in the court moved.

Brig. Gen. Hawley looked at the defense's table. DeBerg, having spent most of his time studying First Sgt. McClellan, would say nothing. Neither would Lt. Wilmona Jennings.

The prisoners, having listened attentively, were now smoldering in distress. The prosecutor's words had cut deeply. The words were even more sobering because they had been spoken in a chapel.

To everyone's surprise, First Sgt. McClellan breached silence by standing. He had risen slowly. Thoughts of his men and the gallows were on his mind. "May I address the court, Sir?"

Brig. Gen. Hawley was as surprised as everyone else. "You may not," he said flatly.

Col. Boatner disagreed. He thought it would be to the prosecution's advantage to allow the first sergeant to speak. Though he wasn't supposed to, he had tried on two or three occasions to get McClellan and Poole to give statements. Following orders from Maj. DeBerg of the defense, the two NCO's, leaders of the insurrection, had declined to say anything.

Neither DeBerg nor Jennings had actually spoken with the first sergeant. All contact had been done through Capt. Donald Thoren, the wavering aide, who, after conducting the last series of interviews with the troops and anticipating the trial's outcome, had himself removed from the case.

But it didn't matter that the First and DeBerg hadn't talked. Knowing that he would be questioned about his past, it is doubtful McClellan would have said very much to the defender anyway. The First, however, did try to again get word to the prosecution that he wanted to talk about letting Jody go. The prosecution wasn't interested.

Col. Boatner was standing. "Mr. President, the trial judge advocate recognizes the impropriety of the disgraced first sergeant's request. However, in view of the strict pretrial silence practiced by the accused, and as no doubt advised by Major DeBerg and this woman on the defense, the prosecution is in favor of hearing the prime leader of the mutineers in the hope that his statement will shed additional light on the subject, as well as possibly leading us to an even swifter trial conclusion."

"Objection, Major DeBerg?" asked Brig. Gen. Hawley. Jennings leaned over to the quiet man. "Sir, surely we're not going to allow the sergeant to speak."

"Why not?" DeBerg replied, not fully in the form of a question. "If he wishes to hang himself, that's his choice. Before trial, it was made clear to all the coloreds they were to maintain silence."

"I prefer the term *Negroes*, Sir."

"Negroes, mulattos, coloreds, blacks, or anything else, it isn't going to change anything, Lieutenant."

"Except the degree of respect, Sir," Jennings whispered in return.

"And the point you were trying to get to?"

"To allow the first sergeant to say anything could be self-incriminating."

"I'm sure it will be. But that's his choice, Lieutenant," DeBerg said, fully realizing that it was not lawful for the sergeant to make a statement. As he ended the conversation by pulling back, he sounded as if there were animosity in his voice. That wasn't the case. The old defender was more thoughtful than anything else, his mind having flashed back to the *"executions regardless of the degree of guilt"* statement the Army had made to the citizens of Houston back in August. He evaluated the implications further and went back to studying the black man standing erect in court. Jennings took it upon herself to stand. "If it please the court, to allow the first sergeant to speak at this time confronts this tribunal with a violation of a most fundamental issue."

"I think not, Lieutenant," Brig. Gen. Hawley said. "But out of curiosity, what is that fundamental issue?"

"The Fifth Amendment to the Constitution, Sir. It prohibits self-incrimination."

"I presume you know what the prisoner is going to say?"

"No, I don't, Sir."

The President of the Court stared at her for a moment and asked, "How familiar with the Constitution are you, Lieutenant?"

"I know it well, Sir."

"You can assume the court knows as much," said the brigadier. "Now, be seated."

Her look to DeBerg, the defender, wasn't returned. Judging from the way the lieutenant was being stared at by Hawley of the prosecution and the court as a whole she knew it was best to hold herself in check. The lieutenant sat, as ordered.

The brigadier nodded for the sergeant to speak.

"I would just like to say, Sir, that it was me and me alone responsible for the march on Houston. I, and I alone, was responsible for the ambush that was set up. I gave the orders to fire. I bear full and absolute responsibility for every single thing that happened, going to — in — and coming from, Houston. I gave the orders, and my *men*, not *rot*, not *scabs*, not *murderers*, not *depraved*, not people from the jungle; not crows or mimics, and surely not cowards nor beasts — not anything but *soldiers* — Army of the United States *soldiers*, Mr. Prosecutor, and the Army of the United States soldiers responded as they had been trained to respond. And let me add, Sir, they bayoneted no one. The troops had been trained for war, and pushed to the boiling point, I led them to a war. And a number of them were killed and wounded, which you did not mention. Now, if anybody is guilty of anything, save for the attitude of the country and its treatment of the Negro and the Negro soldier, I, and I alone am guilty. And I am willing to accept the consequences."

"The country notwithstanding," the brigadier general said with tepid patience, and seeming as surprised as everyone else that the colored man sounded literate. "Excuse me — the *attitude* — of the country notwithstanding, did you pull all the triggers, Sergeant?"

"I gave all the orders, General."

"And for that, I can assure you, you will pay."

The first sergeant started to sit back down without comment.

"Just a minute." Speaking was Col. Ballentenkoff, the old, intellectual-looking officer who sat on the bulldog general's immediate right. "Sergeant, you said you led your men to war?"

"I did, Sir."

"That statement alone bespeaks volumes, regrettably. I find it incredible. Now, I ask, who was with you when you gave the orders to fire on the vehicles containing the military officers?"

The First didn't say anything.

"I say again, who was with you, Sergeant?" Col. Ballentenkoff asked, his voice sharp. "You've acknowledged you were there?"

"I did, Sir. And I say again, I was in charge," McClellan answered. "Some of my troops were unfairly arrested, beaten with cycle chains, and drenched with hoses earlier that day. At the police station, I was personally fired upon *first* by the officer who sat at the desk in the police station that night."

Boatner, the trial judge advocate, stood. "Colonel, I believe there will be ample testimony substantiating the fact that the sergeant had no way of knowing what had transpired in the police station earlier that day. His knowledge could have come only after the march, and from the prisoners whom he illegally freed. The first sergeant and his band of lawbreakers sat in conspiracy and marched on the Fourth Ward's San Felipe district in the city of Houston without provocation. The prosecution will prove it."

"It was not necessary for me to have been at the police station, Mr. Prosecutor," returned the First. "My men are Negroes. They were in the hands of an angry police. It's no secret what that combination means in this country. And, as I said, when I entered the police station, I was fired upon first."

"But you would not have been fired upon first had you not been there illegally," Col. Ballentenkoff stated.

"That is correct, Sir. I am not trying to excuse any of my actions, to include returning the policeman's fire or setting the prisoners free. They, and those who were with the column en route back to camp, were under my direct command and influence. They were following orders. Orders given by me and me alone. I set up the ambush. I *ordered* the men to do everything that was done. The killing of good and decent Army of the United States officers will always be inexcusable and goes far beyond regret. I say — and feel — the same about the civilians. For giving the orders, as wrong and hurtful as they turned out to be, I deserve maximum punishment. I am guilty. And I alone am guilty."

Anxious to get the proceedings under way, Hawley, the President of the Court, addressed the trial judge advocate. "Who is your first witness?"

"Captain Lloyd Whitney, company commander of I Company."

"Sit down, Sergeant," Hawley interrupted.

McClellan sat. The clerk stood and belted out the name of the first witness. "Captain Lloyd Whitney! Company Commander, Item Company."

The prosecution had sprung a surprise. It was thought that Lt. Col. Briggs, the battalion commander, would have been first to be called, followed by Farrell, the K Company commander.

Whitney, like Lt. Col. Briggs, should not have been sitting in the court. It didn't matter. He kneed his way out of the section and went up front for the oath. In the witness chair, and as he had done since Houston, he avoided looking in the direction of Capt. Farrell. Whether consciously or not, Farrell avoided looking in his direction. Keeping in mind the vitriol Whitney had spewed at the club, Farrell had long since made up his mind not to be surprised by anything Whitney said when and if called to the stand.

The I Company commander was presented with a series of questions that appeared to be innocuous. Then the prosecution asked, "Captain, when your men received the Houston orders, as you've testified, were they disturbed in any way?"

It is safe to say that had Col. Boatner not asked the question, Brig. Gen. Hawley, cutting to the core, would have. He disliked courtroom peripherals, and he clearly wanted to establish a hastened pace.

"My men weren't all that happy."

"Did this mood prevail all the way to Houston?"

"Yes, Sir."

"And while in Houston?"

"Yes, Sir."

"Up to and including the 25th of August?"

"Yes, Sir."

"And, generally speaking, what was the cause of this mood?"

"They didn't want to be in Houston. They wanted to go overseas and fight."

"But they held their emotions in check."

"Oh, absolutely, Sir."

"Speaking of August 25th, there was a skirmish with the police earlier that day, allegedly precipitating the K Company uprising. Were any of your men involved?"

"Yes, Sir."

"How many were there?"

"Eight, Sir. As best as I've been able to determine."

"And those eight were actually involved with the police? And the policeman Quackenbush?"

"They were, Sir."

"So, then, it is true that from Columbus to Houston to the encounter with the police, your men were subjected to the same treatment as the accused?"

"Yes, Sir."

"And, Captain, how many of your men are on trial here?"

"Three, Sir. Five were found to have been wrongly charged." The President of the Court interceded. "Captain, how many men are here from L Company?"

"I believe there are four from the late Captain Reed's Company

L, General."

Col. Boatner picked up. "So there are 63 men on trial here, and only three are from your company, and only four from Company L. Does that tell you or this court anything, Captain?"

"A lot."

Jennings stood with an objection, but she was overlooked by the court. Boatner was allowed to continue.

"By the way, Captain, as a result of the fight in the bordello earlier that day of August 25th, were any of your men arrested?"

"Just a handful, Sir. Because, again, the house was taken over by K Company."

"And those few men from your company were taken to the police station along with the K Company men?"

"Yes, Sir."

"And later that evening, those same men of yours were illegally freed by McClellan and his men?"

"Yes, Sir."

"And when they were illegally freed, what did they do?"

"They returned to the company."

"How do you know that?"

"Before leaving to go to Battalion Headquarters, I ordered the men into formation and took a head count."

"Did you get the opportunity to talk with the men who had been in confinement there at the Houston police station?"

"Yes, I did, Sir."

"And what did they say?"

"Calls for hearsay," Jennings said, to no avail.

"More specifically, Captain," Boatner continued, "I am interested in hearing why your men returned to the company."

"They felt they were in enough trouble without following Sergeant McClellan to do whatever else he was going to do."

"In other words, they knew McClellan had not finished with his assault? He was going on to kill more people?"

"Objection."

"Rephrase."

"Your men were fearful of McClellan and wanted no part of whatever else he was going to do?"

"That was what I was going to do?"

"Did you talk with any of the men from Company L — Captain Reed's company — who had been illegally freed from confinement there in Houston?"

"None, Sir."

"But the men from your company — I Company — those who had returned reported back because they knew McClellan had intentions of doing something else?"

"That. And because they were scared?"

"Scared of — ?"

"First Sergeant McClellan."

"Why?"

"Well, they knew of McClellan's reputation. And they knew he and his men had just shot up the police station."

"And they knew that other criminal and hostile acts were to follow?"

"Yes, Sir."

"And they knew some policemen had been killed at that time?" Jennings interrupted. "As with the previous mind-reading question, the witness can't testify to that. It's beyond his scope of knowledge."

"Lieutenant," Boatner said calmly, "the policemen are dead. They can't come in to testify."

"Did the witness see who killed them?" Jennings asked.

Boatner looked to Hawley for support.

"Ask your next question," the president said to the prosecutor.

"The policemen were dead, your men were free, and they returned to camp? Is that not correct, Captain Whitney?"

"I believe that was the sequence."

"So, now, jumping ahead, five of your men were wrongly charged. Three are on trial. Four, you believe, are from L Company. Why is that, Captain? Why aren't there more? You've testified that your men were somewhat disgruntled when they arrived in Houston. And since being in Houston, and subsequently going on pass, all of your men were subjected to the same as K Company. L Company members were subjected to the same as K Company, yet there are only seven men from I and L combined. If math serves me correctly, I am led to conclude that the overwhelming number of the 63 on trial here are from K Company. Why? Why aren't there larger numbers from companies I and L?"

"Objection," said Lt. Jennings.

"Quiet, Lieutenant," said the court. "Continue, Captain."

"There are perhaps many reasons why there are so few men from the other companies. My troops were disappointed. They grumbled a bit, but they didn't act with rage. A soldier goes where a soldier is ordered. And I can only tell you that in my company I have always stressed military discipline, obeying orders, and a strict adherence to law. Other factors could possibly include —"

"Excuse me, Captain," Col. Ballentenkoff of the board interrupted, "*you* stress obeying orders, military discipline, and an adherence to law and order in your company, and not your first sergeant?"

"Colonel, Sir, my first sergeant, Sergeant Odell Odums, is not in command of I Company," Whitney said. He looked beyond the rows of spectators and for the first time gave the irritated Capt. Farrell an implicating look. "I am the commanding officer. We do things by the book; I do what is required by military regulations. My First is only a go-between between me and the troops. I am in total control of the company. Sergeant Odums and I have a clear understanding on that. It is an absolute *must*. The men were not trained or encouraged to practice blind, puppy-dog allegiance to my First. I might add that the same was true with the late Captain Reed and his first sergeant, Sergeant Williams —"

"I object to this entire response," Lt. Jennings said, looking to DeBerg. Seeing that he wasn't going to say anything, she followed up. "It is self-serving, and pure speculation."

The president of the court gave the woman defender a hard look but said nothing. He nodded for Whitney to continue.

"As I started to say, the late Captain Reed had the same relationship with his first sergeant. We kept them in check."

"And this was done because —?"

"The colored NCO is not capable of running a company, and to allow him to impose his will over a company of men is fraught with danger and is contrary to Army regulations."

"And to your knowledge, did that occur with K Company?"

"I believe it did. I know it did."

"And lawlessness prevailed," Boatner said.

"Indeed, it did, Sir," Whitney said. "Lawlessness prevailed."

The prosecutor looked at the court and repeated the statement with finality. "*Lawlessness prevailed.*" He then turned to the defender's table. "Your witness."

The major didn't stand for the cross examination. "One question. Captain, in the battalion, better yet, in the 24th Infantry Regiment, Colored — or the Deuce-Four, as some of you call it — what company was referred to as the *soldiering company?*"

"K Company."

"And how does a company attain that distinction?"

"By being the best in the battalion. Supposedly."

"I think it is more like *factually*. Wouldn't you agree?"

"Yes, but —"

"Thank you, Captain. I have no more questions."

Boatner eyed the defender, who was busy looking beyond the unlit stove, trying to read McClellan's reaction to the brief cross. Neither of them received anything in return.

When Hawley dismissed the captain, Cpl. Jackson of I Company was next to take the stand. Like most of the witnesses he had been called in from the battalion's home base in Columbus. Calling Jackson seemed out of sequence, but unknown to the black prisoners or DeBerg, the wide-nosed, thick-faced corporal had slipped a note to a prosecution member, stating that he would testify in exchange for leniency. That occurred after Capt. Thoren had left the case and after all the official pretrial interviews were over. What Jackson did wasn't necessary. Since he had only been in Nell's house and had jumped out of the window before the fracas started, he wouldn't have been charged with anything.

Midway through the Jackson testimony Boatner asked, "And as a member of I Company did you sometimes get the chance to associate with the members of Company K?"

"Yassuh."

"Now, will you tell the court the last time you were with anyone from Company K."

"The 25th of August."

Col. Ballentenkoff of the board leaned forward in his chair and looked to his left. "I presume you're talking about August 25th of this year, Corporal? 1917?"

"Yessir," replied Jackson. "Twas in the afternoon."

Boatner continued. "And whereabouts were you on that stated date and time?"

"In Houston. San F'leepee Street."

"What was the occasion?"

"Beg y'pardon?"

"Why were you there?"

"We was on pass. An' we was at this house, an' the police come. That's when I got hit."

"What kind of house was it?"

"A fun house."

"Was it a brothel?"

"A who?"

"A house of prostitution."

"Yeah, but I ain't never bought no wimmins. I wont doin' no nothin' wrong."

"And I don't believe you would, Corporal Jackson. But what were you doing in the house?"

"Sittin' down talkin' an' laughin'. Me, a few of the boys from King, and a few ladies."

"Can you identify the boys from Company K?"

"Not by name."

"Can you point them out?"

"Yassir."

"Well, then, do that. Go over there and point them out."

Reluctantly Jackson did as ordered, singling out Pete, Jody, Yancy and Crawford, then continued on incorrectly to point out Roosevelt, Menyard, Andrews and a few others who were not in the house. He received hard glares from the prisoners. He returned to his seat, and though the witness chair was well away from the prisoners and they were partially blocked from view, he tried not to look in their direction again.

"You were in the house, and they were in the house during the major part of the conflict, let's say during the shooting?"

"And you were hit by the police?"

"Sho' was."

"Yassuh."

"Where?"

"On my shoulder and neck."

"What were you hit with?"

"A stick. An' I think with the end of a gun, one time."

"Were the blows hard?"

"Knocked me down."

"In other words, you were provoked and had *reason* to seek revenge, but you didn't take part in the uprising later that evening?"

"Oh, no Suh."

"Why didn't you?"

"Wont no need."

"Were you in on the meeting that took place in the K Company tent that evening?"

"Yassuh."

"Were there any K Company NCO's in attendance?"

"Yassuh. They was all there."

"Did you hear any of them speak?"

"Corporal Poole. He was doing all the talkin'."

"What was he talking about?"

"Goin' inta town an' shootin' the place up."

"And you're sure of this?"

"Pos'tive."

"Goin' into town and shooting the place up'."

"Yassuh."

"Do you have any idea what place Corporal Poole was talking about?"

"The police station."

"The police station," Boatner echoed. "Corporal Jackson, was First Sergeant McClellan in the tent when Corporal Poole advanced the idea of going into town to 'shoot the place up'?"

"Yassuh."

"Did the first sergeant voice any objection to the plan?"

"No, Suh."

"He never dissented? He never said anything, such as 'Corporal Poole this is wrong; this is something we should not be doing; this is against the law; this is against all the rules and regulations of the military'?"

"I never heard it."

"Did he ever say, 'this is something we shouldn't even be *think-ing* about doing'?"

"No, Suh. Not even when Captain Farrell poked his head in the tent. He didn' say nothin' like that."

"And after the captain withdrew, Poole continued urging the men on?"

"Yassuh."

"And his voice became loud enough to be heard outside of the tent, didn't it?"

"Yassuh."

"Perhaps even loud enough to be heard by the company commander and the first sergeant, who were standing just outside of the tent?"

"Yassuh."

"Were any of the men now seated in the roped area of this court there?"

"Yassuh."

"Would you mind telling us who?"

"All of 'em sittin' over there. An' more."

"*And more*," the prosecutor reaffirmed. "I can assure you we will be getting to them. But the question, Corporal, and to make certain we're absolutely clear about this, you are speaking of the prisoners?"

"Yassuh."

"And all the prisoners over there were inside the tent that evening of August 25th? And they were all in a position where they could clearly hear every word the corporal was speaking?"

"Yassuh. Everybody could hear everythin'."

"And none of them voiced any objections with regard to illegally marching, did they?"

"Nosuh. Not a single one."

"Thank you," said Col. Boatner. He marched back to his seat.

"Your witness, Counselor."

The chief defender looked at McClellan and for the first time approached the witness chair. He was slow and old. "Corporal, I was very much interested in your testimony. As a matter of fact, I am still very much interested in your testimony, particularly your affirmative reply to the question relating to your association with the boys from Company K."

"Beg y'pardon?"

"Oh, come, now. How many times have you actually been in the company of the men from Company K?"

"Quite a few times."

"So many times, you can't even remember their names. You had to go over there and point to them. You couldn't name them.

Now, Corporal Jackson, isn't it a fact that there was so much jealousy among the three companies you rarely associated with each other?"

"I done ain't never heard nothin' 'bout it."

"I don't suppose you would have," DeBerg said. "Now, you've testified that you were 'sittin' down talkin' an' laughing' when the police arrived at this house of prostitution. Is that correct?"

"Yassir."

"And when the police first entered the house in question, what did you do?"

"Nothin'."

"You did nothing?"

"S'right."

"If you did nothing, why were you hit?"

Jackson didn't have an answer. DeBerg took it in stride.

"Did you — or anyone — have a weapon?"

"Nosuh. Why would we be needin' a gun in a ho'house?"

"I'll ask the questions, if you don't mind. Now, you say you saw everything that took place in the house?" the major asked.

"Yassuh."

"And before the police came, you were there?"

"Since almos' noon."

"Which means you, as indicated by statements I have in my possession, were not shooting dice at the rear of Verl's saloon."

"I won't there."

"You were in Nellie Moore's house."

"Whose?"

"You were in the house of prostitution across the street from Verl's saloon," the old major said impatiently.

"Yassuh."

"Which means you were there when Jody Cunningham showed up."

"Who?"

"*Private* Jody Cunningham."

"I don't know who that is,"
DeBerg pointed to the little soldier. "That's him. Were you there
when he arrived at the house?"

"Yassuh."

"And, later," DeBerg said, pointing, "when Private Pete Curry
showed up?"

"Yassuh."

"And you were there when the first shot was fired?"

"Yassuh."

"Who fired the shot?"

"One of the soldiers."

"One of the soldiers'?" DeBerg asked with interest. "Corporal
Jackson, I find that extraordinary. And I hope the court finds likewise. How could one of the soldiers have fired if they didn't have
any weapons, as you have just testified?"

"I dunno."

"Well, then, tell me. Which one of the soldiers fired?"

"I can't remember which one."

"You can't remember because you are an out-and-out liar,"
DeBerg said harshly.

Hawley tapped his gavel in admonition.

"Now, Corporal Jackson," DeBerg continued, "since you say you
were in the house all that time, tell me this: when Private Peter
Curry showed up, through which door did he enter?"

"The front. Like everybody else."

"Would you like to think about that, Soldier?"

"Nope. He come in the front."

"That is another lie, Soldier. He came in through the rear,"
DeBerg said hotly. "A final question, Corporal Jackson. There was
a Sergeant Dukes who was injured in the melee. Did Sergeant
Dukes sustain the injury upstairs or downstairs?"

"Well, since I was downstairs an' didn't see him," Cpl. Jackson
hedged, "it must'a happened upstairs."

"How sure of that are you?"

"Well, in thinkin' about it, I'm real sure."

"Mr. President," DeBerg said to the senior trial officer. "I have eight statements, all attesting to the fact Sergeant Dukes received his injury downstairs. Even the police will agree to that. Please excuse this perjurer."

Jackson was excused. Three other witnesses came forth with brief testimony that loosely matched the corporal's. As with Jackson, DeBerg, taking the lead, proved they were not all unassailable.

Untroubled, the prosecution called for Sgt. Odell Odums.

The I Company first sergeant's lengthy testimony was to prove critical.

With the president of the court pushing for speed, the prosecutor forged ahead and caused Sergeant Odums to shock the troops by boldly stating that a rebellious attitude had existed in Company K even before getting to Houston. He testified that he knew the company was bent on disruption by the very fact that Poole had stolen some drums and instruments to augment the ones he had already borrowed or stolen for the arrival. It was King Company's intention to be loud and *stir things up*." Even before that, when things were normal, he said, K Company was loud and strutted around the battalion area as though they owned it.

Odums established that the three King Company NCO's, McClellan, Dukes and Poole, were ripe for the Houston rebellion because of the disciplinary actions the men had received. It was something that had never been imposed on the company before. He stated that all three first sergeants, McClellan, Williams and himself, had been ordered not to have their companies sing or march that night when they first arrived at Logan because it would only serve to inflame. McClellan, he said, had willfully violated the order, and the company marched and sang louder than he had ever heard in the past. When asked why his company had not done the same, the I Company First repeated the orders given to him by his C.O., Capt. Whitney. *"Silence was the order of the day,"* he recalled.

Without being asked, he stated that he never did — and never would — have his company sing "that song that McClellan was callin' the Negro national anthem." When asked why not, he stated flatly, "It was *trouble-makin'*." It was, he said, getting stirred up over the term Negro, when the word *nigger* would do.

Boatner, having learned before trial that he had a verbose and excellent witness in the sergeant, pressed harder. Ingratiating himself to the whites, the big, black man with concrete hands fabricated much, and everything he said was to the extreme detriment and ire of McClellan and the prisoners.

Although he sat inscrutable, McClellan, like the troops, was jolted by the I Company first sergeant. He didn't so much mind when he was speaking the truth, which was rare and in itself irredeemably harmful, but the lying and slave-like condescension baffled him.

Odell Odums, whom the aloof McClellan had talked with only once or twice since being in the battalion, seemed like a person who would go to the ends of the earth for blacks. Now on the stand, the former pugilist, who had spoken so vehemently about the status of the blacks at the hand's of the white man's deceit in Verl's saloon that Saturday afternoon back in Houston, turned gutless and showed his true colors by wilting on the stand and speaking in a thin, sing-song voice. Gone were all traces of the deep, boisterous voice and utter contempt for the white man. It was difficult to understand.

Reiterating that his company did not *sound-off* the night they first entered the Logan grounds, he affirmed that en route to the post he did see something afield that could have been Negro effigies and burning crosses that night. They were unavoidable. Overall though, he said, they were not all that disturbing; and, in the proper light, they could have been fun-like. He also said that since being in Houston, neither he nor his troops had been subjected to anything but respectful hospitality. Without even being questioned in that direction, he told of how proud he was to serve under Lt.

Col. Briggs. Under his leadership, the sergeant said, the battalion couldn't have been treated better. And, as he had once told his bent and Uncle Tomming mess sergeant, Sgt. Stanley G. Robertson, as far as making a contribution to the war effort, as a *"professional colored,"* it was his opinion the Army was entirely right in denying blacks front-line duty, "cause the coloreds can best serve the country by cookin' and cleanin', an' bein' in service of the whites."

There was no question in anyone's mind that for the troops Sgt. Odums had been a one-man wrecking crew. According to the looks he received from the prisoners, had he not been on the stand, and had they not been surrounded by guns, Odell Odums would have been killed. A livid Cpl. Tholonius Poole would have led the charge.

DeBerg sat pensively. Several times Jennings shifted uneasily. It was clear she thought Odums was nothing short of a Benedict Arnold. She had difficulty believing one Negro would do that to another.

Later, for flavor and orientation, and like pounding more nails into an already sealed coffin, Boatner led the big I Company first sergeant into all sorts of areas. On many, the defense objected. The court overruled but a few.

Spilling over to the fourth day with most of the questions having already been asked and answered, and, again, over the overruled objections of the defense, the prosecution was now repeating and paraphrasing for unneeded clarity.

"And so, Sergeant Odums," Boatner repeated, "regarding that evening in the tent before you and Sergeant Williams of L Company left, what was it that Corporal Poole said?"

"He kept askin' McClellan if he was gonna go."

"Go where? To do what?"

"Into town, and knock off the police station."

"When you say 'knock off the police station,'" Boatner redundantly asked for the benefit of the court, "what exactly does that mean?"

"It means to attack it."

"As in to conduct an assault on it?"

"Yassir."

"Was there any talk about policemen?"

"Yassir. Plenty."

"With reference to the police, what did Corporal Poole have to say?"

"He didn't like 'em."

"And you know that for certain, don't you, Sergeant?" Boatner asked. "You know that Poole and all the rest of the men had a passionate hatred of the police —"

"You sho' 'nuff is right about that. Poole really hated 'em."

The prosecutor returned briefly to the table to scan something written on a pad. "And for that matter, Sergeant Odums, so did First Sergeant McClellan. He had developed an even greater hatred for the police because, as I understand it, he was particularly enraged because his longtime friend Field Sergeant Dukes had been incarcerated. Is that not correct?"

"McClellan didn't say nothin', but —"

"McClellan didn't say anything — *at the time* — you mean. But you all knew what he was thinking?"

"Objection."

"Overruled, Lieutenant," said the President of the Court. "Continue, Colonel."

"You all knew what First Sergeant had in mind, didn't you, Sergeant Odums."

"We know'd McClellan was gonna do somethin' 'cause he was steamin' inside."

"Why?"

"Cause of the police. 'Cause they had Sergeant Dukes locked up. He was really crazy 'bout that old man. He'd do anythin' for him."

"To include placing his career in jeopardy?"

"His career an' anythin' else he had."

"And the police action that afternoon, it all boiled down to a hatred that McClellan and Poole were determined to do something about, did it not?"

"Sho' did."

"And this passion carried over to the First Platoon tent that evening, meaning that revenge was in the air, isn't that right?"

"Yassir."

"And in order to seek revenge — to carry out that incendiary hatred, McClellan and men were going to march on the city of Houston."

"Come hell or high water."

"And the men weren't summoned or ordered or told to march on Houston by any authorized command, were they?"

"Nosuh."

"Everything that happened, particularly the meeting that took place in K Company's First Platoon tent that evening was in direct response to what had happened earlier that day, wasn't it? And because Dukes had been incarcerated."

"Yassuh."

"By the way, Sergeant, who called the meeting?"

"Only First Sergeant McClellan could get everybody there."

Jennings was on her feet again, but the objection was over-ruled.

But Odums was wrong again. If McClellan had called the meeting, he would not have invited anyone from the other companies.

"And this meeting, Sergeant, for want of a better term, was to map plans for getting even? To quote 'settle the score' for what had happened in Houston earlier that day?"

"S'right, Sir."

"The legalities didn't mean anything, did they?"

"Nosuh. Nobody never said nothin' like that."

"Did you hear anyone say, 'We might have been wronged in town, and some of our jailed boys might be mistreated by an over-zealous police, but let's take this to the C.O.'? Or let's take our case to an executive officer or to the battalion commander'?"

"Nosuh. An' Colonel Briggs was always there to listen to us."

"And the troops knew this, did they not?"

"Yassuh."

"They knew that Lieutenant Colonel Briggs — as one of those rare battalion commanders who was always accessible to the troops — was never one to concern himself about chain of command. He had an open-door policy for the men. Because he believed in his men."

"Sho' did."

"And even if the colonel had not been available — for whatever reason — and since whatever was bothering them was so important, or since it was remotely possible that they could have had legitimate concerns, they could have gone elsewhere, could they not?"

"Y'right, Sir."

"Did you hear anyone say, 'Let's skip chain of command and take our grievances to the *post commander*'?"

"Nosuh."

"And since the concerns were so grave, was it ever suggested to take them all the way up to Division?"

"Oh, nosuh."

"Or maybe, since it would not be a violation of chain of command, did anyone ever say, let's try and find a chaplain? Let's talk to him about what's wrong."

"Nosuh."

"You never heard anyone say, 'Let's stop this nonsense, let's not violate the law; let's not act like beasts; let's act like soldiers and take this thing and lay it square in the lap of someone with authority.' Did you hear *anything* like that?"

"Never heard nothin' like that, Sir. 'Course, me an' Sergeant Williams said, 'Please, y'all, please, don't do it.'"

"You and Sergeant Williams said something? You and Sergeant Williams dissented?"

"Yassuh."

The rail-thin Col. Ballentenkoff of the board leaned forward again. "What exactly did you and Sergeant Williams say, Sergeant?"

"We said we was against it."

"You two NCO's were against marching?"

"Yassuh."

"And all those in the tent heard you say you were against march-ing?"

"Every one of 'em."

"Did you or Sergeant Williams try to discourage any of the men from marching?"

"Oh, Yassuh. But we was at K Company, so we didn't have no voice. Wont nobody gonna listen to us."

"Thank you, Sergeant."

Boatner picked up. "There was not a slightest hint of dissen-sion — or being 'against it' — from McClellan or Poole?"

"Nosuh."

"Nor were there voices of dissent from any of the other mem-bers of Company K, were there?"

"Nosuh."

"Could something have been said and you, perhaps, had stepped out of the tent and weren't in a position to hear it?"

"Couldn'ta. Me an' Sergeant Williams never left the tent 'til we was gone for good. Befo' that, we was sittin' right there in the middle at the foot on one of the cots, listenin' to every word."

"Thank you, Sergeant," Boatner said. Again he'd received more than he asked for. "Now, to repeat, Sergeant; the march on Hous-ton had a target, did it not?"

"Yessir."

"And what was that target?"

"The Houston Police Department."

Boatner allowed the point to soak in, then asked, "They were going to fire on the Houston Police Department?"

"Yessir. An' kill a policeman."

"Oh? They were going to specifically kill a policeman?" the man with the patrician bearing asked, as if struck by newness. The act was strictly for show, because Odums had headed in that same direction before. "Any particular policeman on the Houston Police Department?"

"Any of 'em they could find. But partik'lar that Quackenbush."

"Officer Elmore Quackenbush, a sergeant with the Houston Police Department? And that was made very clear?"

"Yassir. Poole even said the name."

"So there was no doubt in anyone's mind as to what the leaders' intentions were?"

"Not a bit."

"The troops were going to march on San Felipe and conduct an assault on the district's police station."

"Yassir."

"And kill a policeman."

"Yassir."

"And in stating those intentions, did Poole or anyone — *anyone* — say that maybe there should be a change of heart and that maybe — *maybe* — they would take care so as not to cause harm to a peace officer other than Quackenbush?"

"Nosuh."

"They were going to attack anyone and anything that got in their way, weren't they?"

"Yassir."

"They were going to attack, attack, attack, attack, attack and attack! Isn't that so?"

"Yassir. Me an' Williams said they was crazy to do it."

"Did *anyone* — any member — of K Company express a similar sentiment?"

"Nosuh."

"Not a single person?"

"Not that I know of, 'cept Sergeant Willie Powell."

"But he was just a cook."

"Yassuh. An' even he left."

"I'll be getting to that later," the prosecutor said. He had the mess sergeant's favorable statement on hand and knew he would be putting him on the stand.

"Now, Sergeant," Boatner continued, "the company's position was just the opposite of what I just said, wasn't it? In other words, under the leadership of McClellan and Poole the troops *wanted* to march — and they were *going* to march."

"They was gonna march, no matter what. Like I said, they was gonna do it, come hell or high water."

"From the highest to the lowest — their attitudes were 'to hell with what you and Williams think. Damn what this cook thinks. To hell Damn what the Army thinks. Damn what anybody thinks. To hell with being good soldiers; to hell with law and order. Damn the United States. We gonna go to the city of Houston an' do some damage. Serious damage. We gonna draw blood. We wanna kill somebody. We gonna break their laws, an' make our own. We gonna kill the police. An' we don't care who we hurt, kill, or mutilate in the process. An' we care even less about the consequences.' Isn't that right, Sergeant?"

Jennings stood. "I object."

"Overruled."

"Now, again with reference to the police, Sergeant Odums, what did Corporal Poole say to the participants?"

"A lot. All Poole want'd to do was to get out of that tent an' get the police."

"He wanted to kill them. And he was angry when he said it?"

"Yassuh."

"And once again, Sergeant, did Poole ever say or give any indication, as the defense will claim, that they were going to limit their intentions to just freeing the prisoners? And, other than Quackenbush, maybe simply injure other policemen if they got in the way?"

"Nope. He wont talkin' no injurin'. He was talkin' 'bout killin'."

"The men who marched were going to *deliberately* shoot and kill the police."

"Yassuh."

"And he meant any policeman whom they could find, didn't it?"

"Yassuh."

"Now, going back to your earlier testimony, after Poole had finished with his haranguing, what happened?"

"He asked for volunteers to go with him."

"Then what happened?"

"Only about three or four men stood at first, and then Poole got real mad an' started callin' the rest of 'em a bunch'a names —"

"What kind of names? Give me the specifics. What *exactly* did he say?"

"Well, after he called one of 'em a faggot, he said to the rest of 'em, 'You these same ignant blankety-blanks that come runnin' to the Army 'cause somebody told you a nigger could *be* somebody here, that you could prove your manhood here.' An' he said, 'I'll be blankety-blank if I sit here an' let these crackers get away with this crap. I'm sick an' tired of it. Sick an' tired of lettin' the white man walk all over me.' An' he said, 'I'm thinkin' the time to do somethin' about it is right now.' An' then he —"

"Still talking about Corporal Poole?"

"Yassuh."

"Continue."

"An' after that Poole said that they was too scared to fight for what they believed in, but they still wanted to go overseas to fight the Germans, a blankety-blank —"

"Say the words," the President of the Court ordered. This was an area they had not gotten into.

"They bad words, an' we in a church, Suh."

"*Say* the words, Sergeant!"

Odums swallowed, his once dark, powerful voice becoming even more accommodating and servile. "He said they wanted to go overseas an' fight a — a — a — sunovabitch they ain't never seen before an' a — a — a sunovabitch that ain't never done them no harm. An' Sergeant Williams said —"

"Objection," said Jennings.

"Sit down, Lieutenant. And *stay down*," the brigadier said, his temples pulsating.

"Continue, Sergeant."

"Sergeant Williams said the Germans would'a done somethin' if they could get to the coloreds, an' that one time they'd killed somethin' like a hunnert thousand natives in Southwest Africa."

"And what was Corporal Poole of K Company's response?"

"He said that where he was born, somewhere in Mississippi, the white peoples lynched a boy, an' twenny thousand crackers showed up just to have some fun."

"I don't understand the term, Sergeant," Boatner said. "*Crackers?* You mean *cookies?*"

"No, crackers is white peoples."

"*Nice* white people?"

"Oh, no. Low-down white peoples. Ain't nothin' nice about 'em."

"*Crackers*. Is that the same as calling a white person a *nigger?*"

The question caused a burst of loud murmurs in the court.

"I object!" Lt. Jennings was standing. "This is simply going too far, General."

Hawley was on fire. "Shut up, Lieutenant!"

"But, Sir, this is inflammatory. This entire line of questioning is totally uncalled for."

"Might I suggest you not say anything further, Lieutenant."

"Sir, we're not being fair here —"

"The court is giving you fair warning, Lieutenant. One more word and you're through. Do you understand me?"

Wisdom prevailed. "I understand the order of the court."

"Sir!"

"I understand the order of the court. *Sir*."

The stumpy brigadier with the closely cropped hair gave her a stern look, picked up his gavel, and hammered it on the table, ending the session for the day.

Chapter 27

The next day Sgt. Odums was back on the stand, his big broad shoulders appearing even larger under the morning sunlight that filtered through the stained glass windows and infused the stand with a mixture of colors. The I Company first sergeant's demeanor had not changed, and he was still the recipient of hard glares from the prisoners and Jennings. Only once did he look in the direction of the prisoners, and it was at this point when Poole was more than tempted to jump up, grab a rifle from one of the guards, and start shooting. McClellan felt every ounce of what his corporal had in mind and eyed him down.

With the brigadier pushing for closure, Col. Boatner indicated that there were just a few more points he wanted to bring out.

"Sergeant, late yesterday afternoon after I personally became shocked to learn that there was carnal depravity and deviancy in the ranks of Company K by the *"faggot"* term Corporal Poole had used, and before the intrusion by Lieutenant Jennings of the defense, you were testifying that the coloreds normally referred to the whites as crackers — "

"This is disgusting," Jennings whispered aloud to DeBerg, who paid her little attention. "That wasn't his testimony — on either count. And only one person used vulgar terms, and on neither did he say anything about them being normal."

"Sergeant," Boatner continued, "would the term *cracker* apply to a white in uniform, as well?"

"A cracker is a cracker no matter what he's wearin'."

"Even someone in uniform with a position as high as — let's say, Colonel Sarno, the commanding officer of the 24th Infantry Regiment?"

"Even a gener'l," the I Company first sergeant said, sneaking a subservient look at the President of the Court. The reply and act drew a searing look from Hawley. He also cautioned the defense not to stand.

"And, to repeat, Sergeant," the prosecutor continued, "a *cracker* is not at all an endearing term, is it? It is an opprobrious, disgusting and contemptuous term colored people use in voicing their hatred of whites — "

"Yassuh. If you sayin' what I think you sayin'. When the colored folks don't like 'em, that's what they call 'em. An' sometimes when we talkin' by ourselfs, that's what they call 'em."

"And particularly when they want to kill them."

"I object!" Jennings fired.

"Continue, Colonel," the President of the Court said with a hard look to the lieutenant.

"In desiring to kill whites coloreds will use that term, will they not, Sergeant?"

"Yassuh."

"And, as said, its usage, '*crackers*,' would be akin to the word *nigger*."

Once again there were loud murmurs in the court. Brigadier Hawley silenced them by pounding his fist on the table.

"Yassuh," Odums said. "Crackers an' niggers is the same thing.

Only crackers is bad white peoples."

"*Crackers*," Col. Boatner re-emphasized for effect. In the court's silence, he repeated, "The United States Army colored soldiers were going to kill crackers. *Whites*."

"Sir, I must object!" said the lieutenant. "I *have* to. This is base, scurrilous and inflammatory. It is beneath the dignity of this tribunal."

"Sit down and shut up, Lieutenant," Brig. Gen. Hawley ordered. It took a moment, but the lieutenant sat as ordered. After a pause, Hawley nodded for the prosecution to continue.

"Thank you, General," Boatner said. "Now, Sergeant, just one more question along those lines. Are we — the whites — called any other names by the coloreds?"

Jennings could only turn her head away in disgust. Without leaning closer, the chief defender muttered to his aide, "Why are you taking this to heart, Lieutenant? This trial was designed to be an outrage."

Boatner heard the second part. He was singed. "What the coloreds did was an outrage, Major. Deviancy in the ranks is an outrage. To sit in conspiracy and use derisive and race-hating names is an outrage. To kill a defenseless driver and march into town and carry out that incendiary hatred on innocent civilians is an outrage. Killing a poor, little helpless child is an outrage. Killing United States Army officers is an outrage. Murder and lawlessness is an outrage. By the most recent count, nineteen dead and eighteen human beings wounded — *that* is an outrage."

A stern quiet filled the court. The one-star general waited for a protracted period and then asked the sergeant the question Col. Boatner had posed. With the court staring and the prisoners glaring, Odums responded that blacks, in time of heat, often called the whites *rednecks, peckerwoods, and pasty-faced juggies,* words that were often preceded by a profanity. Col. Walt Miller, sitting next to Col. Ballentenkoff on the trial board, leaned forward and asked the sergeant an off-the-record question dealing with the general attitude of the blacks as a whole towards the whites — specifically in the military. Odums said that most of the blacks he knew, except for members of K Company, loved the whites and had a great deal of respect for them. He went on to explain that he could speak more knowledgeably about the subject, at least more than other blacks, because as a former prizefighter before getting into service, he had traveled the country with his white manager, and that had allowed him access to the views of both races. As for his personal beliefs, specifically military, the big first sergeant gushed that for a black to be in uniform was a privilege not likely to pass their way again, and that for the 11 years he had been in the military, nothing had pleased him more than to serve under a white man and to be under the white man's chain of command. He praised the white man's intelligence, his reasoning, his sense of impartiality and his honor. He delivered a few more sugary accolades and concluded by saying that, just as he had learned much from every white who had trained him and every white whom he had had the occasion to box in the ring, in the Army he had learned from every company commander he had served under. He said that the Army was right in essentially not having any colored officers, because the white man was a born leader and he likened his charity and sense of fair play to that of Jesus.

The court was pleased.

What the court didn't know, and certainly was not about to hear, was that this was the same Sgt. Odell Odums who, in his conversation with Sgt. Williams and the disappointed Sgt. Dukes in Verl's saloon on the day of the insurrection, had said in a voice saturated with contempt, *"The white man you done beat in the ring can call you Sir, Champ, or any damn'd thing you want him to call you. He'll do that, while you lookin' at 'im. But the minute you turn your back on him or any one — an' I mean any one — of them suckers, you know what you gonna be? Another nigger. An' if you was champ? Just'a nother nigger that got lucky. An' if you think you done truly beat that sorry sumbitch at any time, you a fool for life. An' I ain't* just talkin' 'bout in no ring. Here, there, everywhere, the white man is the most snakiest sunovabitch the Lord ever put on this earth."

It was the same sergeant, too, who tagged his contempt by saying, "The white woman is just as bad as the white man. He got you thinkin' that pasty-faced thing'a his is the most precious thing that ever walked the earth, an she's just as bad as he is. An' she hates you just as much. An' you better b'leevit. Don't none of 'em like you, me, your daddy, your momma, or your daddy's momma's momma. An' it ain't gonna change. There ain't a white man alive who's taken twenny seconds out'a his life to know a goddam'd thing about you, but when it comes to talkin' about you — or talkin' about what you want, where you from, where you goin', or what you're thinkin', don't you say nothin' — not a damn word, 'cause he ain't gonna hear it. He's gotta do the talkin', 'cause he's knows everythin' about everythin' there is to know. An' above all, he's an expert in niggerology. An' the worst of all'a them sonsabitches is in this goddam'd Army. I hate every one'a them skunks."

The one-star general turned the witness back over to the prosecutor.

"Thank you, General," Boatner said, moving back to the stand and pleased by everything the witness had said. He knew that even if the I Company First had said nothing, his appearance alone worked heavily for the prosecution. The antithesis of McClellan, and as the King Company First was thinking at the time, Odums was everything a lot of whites thought a black leader should be — big, black, pugilistic-looking, and servile; a throwback to the fieldhand/plantation mentality.

"Mr. President — " Lt. Jennings said, depleted.

"From this point on, Lieutenant, I would personally ask that you not say anything, at least for a while. If you have anything to say, I would appreciate it if you would say it through the chief defender, Major DeBerg. Continue, Colonel."

"Now, Sergeant Odums," Boatner said, realizing the lieutenant would not push the court's president. "You're a good colored soldier and a truthful man. Tell me this, after Poole said that twenty thousand *crackers* showed up to enjoy the lynching of this fellow, did he follow up by saying anything equally vituperative and contemptible?"

"Beg y'pardon, Suh?"

"What did Corporal Poole say after he stated twenty thousand 'crackers' enjoyed the lynching of this boy he spoke of?"

"Oh, I forgot," Odums said, still averting his eyes from McClellan and men. "Poole said somethin' 'bout the KKK floggin', burnin', and murderin' somethin' like two thousan' coloreds in Louisiana. An' he said nobody can't count all the coloreds the white man's done lynched in this country."

"And he was very angry when he said that, wasn't he?"

"Oh, Man, he was steamin'. He was mad as a some-buck."

"He couldn't possibly have had anything to say after that."

"Oh, yes, he did."

"He did?"

"He sho' nuff did."

"And — ?"

"He said our war is here — an' it's gonna — "

"Pardon me." The prosecutor faced the spectators in mock alarm.

"He said *what?*"

"He said our war is here."

"Our war is here." The TJA turned back to the stand. "Corporal Poole actually used the term *war?*"

"Yassuh."

"War." Boatner emphasized it for the benefit of the court. He faced the pews and repeated the phrase. "Our war is here. A United States Army *colored* corporal said the words 'our war is here'?"

"Yassuh."

Drama on his side, the prosecutor shook his head as if almost unable to proceed. He wearily motioned with his hands for the sergeant to continue.

"An' he said — "

"He? Still meaning Corporal Poole, an NCO — a noncom — a noncommissioned officer from K Company?"

"Yassuh. He said as long as there's a white man an'a black face on this earth there's gonna be somethin' to war about, 'cause he is always gonna think you're a horse's ass, an' the best you can do is clean up after him. An' he said he didn't come into the Army to be nobody's lackey. An' — "

"One moment. Just one moment. Please, Sergeant. Let's be certain that I heard you correctly. A United States Army corporal talked about *war*. And he followed that up by saying he *'didn't come into the United States Army to be nobody's lackey'?*

"Them ver' words."

"In other words, Sergeant, it was like saying this he enlisted in the Army of the United States to expressly — *solely, only* — to learn the ways of war. And then, upon discharge, this man — Poole — would eventually use that knowledge in civilian life to — to inflict.... My God, my God; this is too horrifying. I shudder to think of the consequences," the prosecutor said dramatically. "Please continue, Sergeant. Please."

"An' then Poole said that when the war over there is over, ain't a damn thing changin'. We win, they lose, an' we'll still be niggers."

"My Lord," Boatner said with more feigned weariness. "Sergeant, I don't see how it is possible, but did Corporal Poole say anything after that?"

"Yassuh."

"You mean after saying all those things, he had *more* to say?"

"Yassuh."

"I'm afraid to ask," said the trial judge advocate with continued histrionics, this time with a contemptuous look to Poole, and then looking at the defense's table. "But we are convened here in search of truth. No matter how odious, repellent, or execrable, the truth must be heard. What else did this — this — *corporal* say, Sergeant Odums?"

"On top of that, he said, all the Germans we didn't kill over there was 'gonna get on the boat an' come over here an' join the rest of these white sonsabitches, an' you'll be a nigger all over again.' He said, 'He's from Europe, we'll still be niggers, and with his no-English speakin' ass, it'll be his country.'"

"This is truly incredible. Absolutely *Incredible*. Such venom. Such filth. Such depravity. What have we wrought here? What kind of people *are* these?"

The prosecutor took a moment, and again wearily sighed. "On the issue of motive, I want to go back for a second. When Corporal Poole said, 'He's always gonna think you're a horse's ass,' who was he talking about?"

"The white man, an' the way y'all thinks of colored folks. 'Course I don't agree with that at all."

"Sergeant, I want to clarify what you've just said," the President of the Court intervened. "Corporal Poole of Company K was referring to the notion that whites — these *crackers* — these *pasty-faced juggies* whom he spoke of, looked upon the coloreds as horses' asses?"

"Yassuh."

"And he was speaking of the military as well?"

"Yassuh."

"To include officers in the military."

"They the only ones we know. We ain't never 'round no regular white troops."

Leaning forward and speaking for the first time was board member, Brig. Gen. Robert W. Wyman. By nature a quiet man, he was small and was sitting to Brig. Gen. Hawley's left. "Sergeant, this is the same Corporal Poole who referred to whites as *crackers, pasty-faced juggies, rednecks, and peckerwoods,* including those in the military, for whom he had a particular loathing?"

"S'right, Suh. If I understan' wha'chu sayin'."

"And to go back just a bit, Sergeant," continued Gen. Wyman, "In Poole's statement — indicating revolt — indicating that he did not 'come into the Army to be nobody's lackey', he was referring to himself? And as if he wasn't going to take it anymore?"

"Yassuh."

"And that would include lawful orders? He wasn't going to obey or be subject to lawful orders anymore. Was that your understanding?"

"S'what it sounded like to me."

"Thank you, Sergeant."

As though a runner's baton had been passed, the prosecutor raced on.

"Sergeant, after Corporal Poole — this *soldier* — this NCO, this colored noncom of Company K who was not going to subject himself to any more lawful orders, in talking about the Germans, Sergeant, after he said 'we win, they lose, and we'll still be niggers' and went on to imply that the coloreds will be niggers all over again because of our government's policy towards European immigration — which he knows absolutely nothing about — what happened?"

"He said to the men, 'Let's go.'"

"And then what happened?"

"Some of the men that was standin', they followed him out of the tent."

"About how many were there?"

"A few."

"A few, meaning how many? Approximate the numbers for the court."

"Three or four."

"So, then, his speech did have some effect?"

"A lot."

"What did the remaining men do?"

"I don't know, 'cause we left right after that."

"The 'we' being — ?"

"Me an' Sergeant Williams."

"Sergeant Williams, the first sergeant of L Company?"

"Yassuh."

"Where did you go?"

"Back to our companies."

"You, as first sergeant of I Company, and Sergeant Williams, first sergeant of L Company, returned to your tents?"

"Yassuh."

"And why did you do that?"

"We didn' want to be no part of nothin' wrong."

The prosecution dramatically repeated it: "*We didn' want to be no part of nothin' wrong.*"

"S'what we said."

"You knew — and every single person who was in that tent on the evening of August 25th knew — without any doubt whatsoever, that if they participated in the march on Houston, they were wrong. Dead wrong. Is that not correct, Sergeant Odell Odums?"

"You right, Suh."

"And when you and Sergeant Williams left, there was nothing to prevent anyone else from leaving with you?"

"Nosuh. We even told everybody they should leave with us."

"Were there any weapons present?"

"Nosuh."

"So no one pointed a gun at anyone, saying that they had to stay in the tent that evening?"

"Nosuh."

"And there were no threats made."

"Nobody threaten' nobody."

Boatner moved in closer. "And you left the tent, and Sergeant Williams left the tent — and perhaps a few men left the tent with you because — *what?*" His ear was close to the man's mouth.

"Like I said, we didn't want to be no part of nothin' that was wrong."

"*We didn't want to be no part of nothin' that was wrong.*" There was nothing else to be said.

Sgt. Odums was thanked and complimented for his testimony. A satisfied Boatner offered him to the defense, knowing well that if they conducted a cross of any measure and tried to destroy the witness's testimony and credibility, they would risk having him repeat the more inflammatory and damning statements. Even if not, the prosecution would bring them back via re-direct.

There was stillness in the court.

DeBerg wanted nothing to do with the big, lying, groveling sergeant from I Company. Neither did Jennings.

Next, Sgt. Williams, L Company's First was called and took the stand. Though briefer, he went through almost the same series of questions as had Odums. He was more intelligent, but he sounded like the I Company sergeant when it came to indicting the troops. With the prisoners deflated and the defense flattened, Col. Boatner was moving around the tense courtroom with ease.

"And, Sergeant Williams," he continued, "some of your men were in on the meeting that took place that evening in the First Platoon tent there in the K Company, were they not?"

"Yessir."

"Did any of your men say anything?" asked Maj. Wally Guggenheim, another member of the board.

"Not while we was there, Sir."

"Before returning to your companies that evening," the major continued, "did you or Sergeant Odums make any statements agreeing with Corporal Poole?"

"Absolutely not, Sir."

The major withdrew. Hawley continued, "You were opposed to marching on Houston, weren't you?"

"Oh, yes, Sir."

"And so was Sergeant Odums?"

"Yes, Sir."

"And you and Sergeant Odums said as much in the tent that evening, didn't you?"

"Yes, Sir."

"You said, 'don't do it.'"

"Yes, Sir."

"And, again, Sergeant Williams, upon the battalion's arrival in Houston, and indeed during your stay, you, Odums and your men had been subjected to the very same levels of treatment as had McClellan, Poole and all the members of K Company?"

"Yes, Sir."

"But you didn't riot? You didn't harangue? You didn't threaten good order?"

"No, Sir."

"You didn't find the need to use vile and gutter-like invectives to describe the whites?"

"No way, Sir."

"You didn't seek to castigate the government of the United States because of any of its policies?"

"No, Sir."

"Particularly any of those that were far beyond your scope of knowledge, such as immigration?"

"No, Sir."

"You didn't seek to violate any of the codes of military conduct?"

"No, Sir."

"You didn't resort to murder and mayhem?"

"We never would'a done nothin' like that, Sir."

"And finally, in these regards, Sergeant, you have nothing against the white man, do you?"

The man who had always secretly wanted to taste a white woman said, "I wouldn't want to live in a world without 'em."

Pleased, the cultured colonel from San Francisco turned and looked over the court, then returned to the table. He took a moment to review a paper that his assistant, Algonquins, placed before him and then returned to the witness. "Now, Sergeant Williams, digressing for a moment, you've testified that Corporal Poole definitely stated that his intentions were to go to the City of Houston, free Sergeant Dukes and the men from confinement, and then they were going to kill the policeman Quackenbush — and any other policemen who were around. Is that correct?"

"Yessir."

"And he made these intentions known to *all* the men who were present in the tent on the evening of August 25, is that not correct?"

"S'correct, Sir."

"Can you tell this court why the other men didn't follow the corporal out?"

"Objection," said Lt. Jennings, knowing she broke her promise to keep silent.

"What are you objecting to, Lieutenant?"

"The sergeant is not a mind reader. For him to answer would call for conjecture. And it distresses me that the trial judge advocate has continued to use this tactic."

"Tell that to the deceased," Hawley said coldly.

Something about his look told her she had gotten away with it for the last time.

Boatner repeated the question. "Why didn't the others follow the corporal out?"

"Poole wasn't the leader," Sgt. Williams replied.

"They would have followed the leader?" Col. Boatner asked.

"Absolutely."

"And the leader of Company K was who, Sergeant?"

"First Sergeant Obie O. McClellan."

Chapter 28

The days came and went in the chapel. There was no contest. Witness after witness crucified the troops and annihilated any hope for the defense. By the end of the third week, even the prisoners had all but thrown in the sponge. On the stand, in eye-blinking succession, the prosecution presented no fewer than 15 witnesses, all testifying that they had seen the troops marching into town. Eight testified that they actually saw the troops firing on the police station and the surrounding area. A distraught Mr. Coglen, father of Marci, the 16-year-old girl who had been killed, told how Poole pointed his rifle at the second floor of the house, delivered reckless and incessant fire, and caused the bullet-riddled body to fall, crushing the skull on the cement below.

It was an exceptionally chilling moment in an already cold court.

Reeking of alcohol, the truck driver P.K. wandered onto the stand after an all-night session of exploring and drinking in a city he had never been to before. He testified that McClellan fired at the cell locks in the police station that night, freeing him and others who were imprisoned inside. The pitted-faced troublemaker dramatically stretched a series of lies by saying that he fought release and never would have left confinement *"if the niggers hadn't forced me out at gunpoint."*

A black, civilian drunk whose cell was not even close to P.K.'s supported his testimony.

The following week, as it turned out, it was the final full week of trial, because an angry Col. Stout still refused to appear out of retirement unless subpoenaed, three policemen took the stand. All gave slanted versions as to what happened, and all pointed to McClellan as the leader who invaded the station.

One policeman testified that the sergeant entered the station with a machine gun.

Quackenbush followed. As expected, he was equally damaging. He started lying from the moment he took the oath. He testified as to how he had been summoned to break up the crap games, and that he and his men, following the law of hot pursuit, followed some of the soldiers into Nell's house of prostitution. Once inside to make the necessary arrests, he said, he was met with a fired-up group that took their venom out on him and his men by throwing and swinging anything they could get their hands on. He told how he was knocked unconscious by several men who jumped him from the rear. As to the shots that were fired, the big policeman said that the soldiers started firing first. They used guns they had obviously secreted from camp. He swore that he and his men fought and fired back in self-defense, finally restoring order.

"An' after the colonel left, we had to march 'em from the whorehouse. They was too many to ride in the paddy wagon," the policeman testified. He conveniently overlooked his statement that he didn't want even the injured blacks to ride because they would smell up his vehicle. "When we got 'em to the station, that's when they really started actin' up. They went wild. We had a rough time lockin' 'em up, but we did."

One of the other trial officers asked, "And as to the allegations they were treated poorly?"

"Bullpucky," replied Quackenbush. "I treated every one of 'em fair and square, like we do with all the prisoners. Fact, 'cause they were soldiers, I think I gave 'em too much slack. 'Course I must say, I never had a worser bunch."

"What exactly did they do?" Boatner asked.

"At which time?"

"Let's say, when they first arrived at the station-house."

"Acted like heathens, that's what they did. Never heard so much cussin', threatenin', an' goin' on in all my years as a policeman."

"And how long has that been, Mr. Quackenbush?"

"Goin' on eighteen years."

"Thank you. Go on."

"Well, from the time they got to the station-house to the time I left, they didn't do nothin' but raise hell an' talk 'bout killin' people. Got so bad that even the civilian niggahs couldn't stand it."

Jennings spoke. "If I were the court, I would consider that editorializing."

"Fortunately, you are not the court. And you won't be *in* the court if you continue to interrupt," Hawley retorted. "Continue, Colonel."

"Now, then, Mr. Quackenbush, at some point you went back to the cell to check on the men before you left, is that correct?"

"Yep. I was try'n to quieten 'em down. But I couldn't stop 'em. An' that lil' one over there, he was the worst one of all. Him an' that other one they say shot hisself."

"Let the record show the policeman was referring to Private Peter Curry. And Sergeant Abraham Dukes, deceased. We might also note for the record that the mutineering Field Sergeant's death was a cowardly act, performed by his own hands," said the prosecutor.

"Noted," responded the brigadier.

For the first time McClellan lost stoicism and winced.

Quackenbush continued. "They tolt me straight to my face that some of their boys was on the way to come an' get 'em out. An' they had nerve enough to tell me that I'd better not be aroun' when they came. They was gonna shoot to kill."

"Shoot to kill?"

"Yessir."

Col. Ballentenkoff of the board leaned forward. "Mr. Quackenbush, it is your understanding that a reinforcing group of colored soldiers was en route to the police station there in San Felipe to free the prisoners, and they were going to '*shoot to kill*' policemen?"

"S'right. An' that there *shoot to kill* is a direct quote from more'n one of the prisoners I had there in my station-house."

The prosecutor turned to the court. "The rest of the colored soldiers of the Third Battalion of the United States Army were coming into the Houston city limits on the evening of August 25 to '*shoot to kill*.'"

"That's what they said," Quackenbush added. "A battalion of their boys was comin' back an' free all the prisoners, and was gonna 'shoot to kill.' I didn' even know what a battalion was."

"But you were told that the remaining colored soldiers of the Third Battalion were en route to the station-house, and the sole purpose of these colored troops coming to the station-house was to free the prisoners and shoot and kill any and all policemen?"

"That's exactly what they told me. They said their boys was comin', an' they said they was gonna be gunnin'."

Boatner allowed the words to sink in, then said, "Is there anything else you'd like to add, Police Officer Quackenbush?" He used the term "police officer" for effect. Though he wasn't in uniform, everyone knew who the Houston policeman was even before he was sworn in. Badge pinned on his lapel, he had created something of a show when he entered court.

"I'm only able to add what I said before. Some of our best men are dead, the station-house is done been shot up. An' the prisoners is gone."

"Thank you, Mr. Quackenbush," said the TJA. "I have no further questions."

"Your witness, Major."

The major didn't move. A clearly agitated Lt. Jennings stood. She had been silent long enough. "Mr. Quackenbush, I've been sitting here listening to you. You never said who, specifically, told you that the remaining troops from the battalion were en route to the police station. I also noticed how conveniently you skimmed over the details of the raid on the house. Would you mind repeating that portion of your testimony before we move on?"

"Lieutenant," the President of the Court intervened, "in view of the fact the testimony was not directly related to the 64th, the 66th, the 92nd or any of the Articles of War having to do with this matter, the court shall disallow the request."

With controlled heat, Jennings said, "First of all, General, I'm requesting a *repeat* of testimony. Secondly, how can the court possibly now say that the witness's testimony is not related to the issue when it was this gentleman's action that precipitated the later action?"

"The court is not entirely sure that is the case," Brig. Gen. Hawley responded. "The court is not sure. And neither are you."

"The court *has* to be sure, Sir. We've already heard the testimony. And even had we not, the court *can* be sure if the defense is allowed the right to properly cross-examine."

"The right to cross is not being abrogated," the brigadier responded, "the procedure to do so incorrectly is. Change your line of questioning."

The female defender suppressed her anger. "Mr. Quackenbush," she asked, "what right did you have to enter the home of Miss Nellie Moore?"

Brig. Gen. Hawley spoke up again. "The police officer has already testified that he pursued the violators under the rule of *hot pursuit*, which is entirely legal. The court is mindful of the fact that the testimony may not have been necessary in its entirety, but a purpose has been served. That said, may I further remind Counsel that it is not the purpose of this assembly to delve into matters relating to the operational policies and or procedures of the Houston Police Department or any other civilian institution. We are concerned here with the violations of *military* law, and I would thank Counsel to restrict her concerns to those issues and those issues alone."

Before the lieutenant could respond, the general intoned, "Court is adjourned for today. We will convene at 0800 hours tomorrow."

As the gavel cleared the court, an exasperated Jennings watched DeBerg silently shuffle away without saying a word to her. Foolishly she had been the last to realize that not even the pretense of a fair trial was to be had in this court. The uncommitted DeBerg knew it, the Army knew it, the Board knew it, the TJA knew it, the spectators knew it, the witnesses knew it, the prisoners knew it, and now, like an idiot, she knew it. It wasn't so much that she hadn't known it, she wasn't that naive. It was more like something she simply didn't want to believe.

She was in a hurry to get away.

Lt. Col. Briggs, who had been quiet throughout trial, sat watching the disappointed woman with the long body for a few minutes and decided to wait a bit longer.

Added to the woman's woes was something about the colonel that she found distasteful. It was pure intuition. Before even gathering her things and leaving the building, she saw him out of the corner of her eye. He had delayed his exit several times before, but she always managed to avoid him by pretending she was leaving with one of the spectators. She couldn't do it this time.

Now that she was ready to leave, so was the colonel, and there was no way to avoid him. She removed her eyeglasses, left the chapel and moved purposefully across the long, barren field. Briggs came out into the cold, stood on the step for a second, picked a fast pace, and caught up with her.

The Third Battalion commander was jovial and upbeat. "Mind

if I walk with you a bit, Lieutenant? That is, if I can keep the pace."

The lieutenant walked on without saying anything.

"And we're headed?"

Her voice was controlled and distant. "*I'm* headed to my quarters, Sir. And it's quite a walk."

"If your billets are where I think they are, it's a hell of a walk. And at this pace I'm not certain you or I will make it."

"A swift walk on a cold day. I find it appropriate, Colonel."

"Not exactly my idea of fun."

"Sorry to disappoint, Sir."

"And sitting back there in that cold court doesn't help matters."

"I'm sorry about that, too," she said without sincerity.

"Ah, but you don't have to be disappointing. May I ask why you are rushing?"

"You're in court every day, Colonel — a procedure I find somewhat strange, to say the least. But you know how much work there is to do."

"There shouldn't be any work to do, Lieutenant. The trial is supposed to be swift and decisive. You don't appear to be serving those ends."

"I'm here to serve the ends of justice, Colonel," the woman said curtly. "By the way, Sir, why are you walking? You're a command officer. You have a staff car at your disposal."

"Actually, I'm walking because I wanted to get a chance to talk with you."

"About the case, I hope."

"I was thinking about making the chat more personal."

"Then you've lost me, Colonel."

"I certainly wouldn't want to do that."

"I do have a question for you, Sir."

"What's that, M'dear?"

"My *dear?*"

"Well, alright. Lovely lady."

"That's just as bad, Sir." Moving on, she said, "Colonel, whom do you think should be blamed for the Houston episode?"

"First, I wouldn't call it an episode. It was a goddamned riot. A rebellion is what it was. An insurrection at its fullest. The Army can't let a thing like that happen without exacting maximum punishment."

"For the truly guilty, I agree. But, Sir, whom do you think should ultimately be blamed?"

"Who do I think should be blamed?"

"Ultimately."

"'Ultimately' or any other way you choose to put it, Lieutenant, the blame rests with that bunch who are on trial. That's why there is a trial. Even at that, they're lucky. There was a time when the coloreds weren't allowed to have a trial in this country, or even sit on juries or testify in a court of law for that matter. These people, and the others to be charged, should consider themselves fortunate. If you don't know that, you're in serious trouble. Now the way I see it, the niggers started — "

She stopped abruptly. "I resent the term, Colonel."

He was glad she'd stopped. He needed a breather. "Alright, maybe it was an unfortunate use of the word. But I say again, the people who should ultimately be blamed are those birds on trial. And maybe Farrell, if you want to get technical."

"The birds aside, Colonel, you don't think you should bear any of the blame?"

"Where'n hell would you come up with something like that?"

"The Inspector General's investigations, which have been renewed back in Houston, and are still being conducted, even as we speak." She started walking again.

Briggs caught up with her. "Now, that's something I had no knowledge of. With the remaining charges already set to be filed, it was my understanding all investigations were closed."

"They were. Until Washington got involved."

"Washington? I hadn't heard anything about that."

"I didn't think you had, Colonel," Jennings said. She glanced at him. "You wouldn't mind my revealing something I've learned about you?"

"No, not at all. I love the idea you've learned things about me. I'd like to learn something about you."

"I was referring to what I learned at a meeting, Colonel."

"What kind of a meeting?"

"An informal one that I attended a few nights ago, Sir. And the kind that's going to lead to a formal hearing after trial. The kind that's going to pinpoint command responsibility. I'm sure one of the highlights, among other things, is going to be why you didn't respond when Captain Farrell told you it looked as if McClellan and the men were marching on the police station. The inspector general's office is most concerned about that."

"I did respond."

"Did you, Sir?"

"Of course, I did."

"But, Sir, wasn't it Colonel Stout who took direct action?"

"Stout didn't do a damned thing. If anything, he made the entire situation worse."

"On that account, Colonel, he probably could defend himself far better than I. But I'm interested in learning how you feel the colonel could have made the situation worse?"

"Quite easily. Had he followed my advice when we first arrived at that God-forsaken place, except for the bellyaching from the niggers — troops, excuse me — everything would've been fine."

"I doubt that, Colonel."

"I was there, Lieutenant."

"I'm fully aware of that, Sir," the lieutenant said. "I'm aware of it, and so is Mr. Emmit Scott."

"Scott? Who the hell is that?"

"Special assistant to the Secretary of War. He's a Negro, by the way."

"Oh, God. Spare me."

"Colonel Briggs, I know this is a rather sensitive subject, but didn't Colonel Stout always speak in favor of the Negroes?"

"Speaking is one thing, *doing* is another."

"I know that, Sir. But wasn't the post commander in favor of having the Third Battalion on post?"

"Maybe that's what caused the problem."

"Perhaps so, Colonel. But it seems logical to conclude that if Colonel Stout was in favor of having the troops at Logan, he certainly wouldn't have been the cause of the problem."

"That's your opinion. The facts say differently."

"Colonel, may I ask you a personal question?"

"Ask."

"Why do you have such loathing for the Negro?"

"How do you know I have loathing for them?"

"You are rather obvious, Sir."

"Well, if I'm that obvious, there's no point in my saying otherwise."

"I suppose I shouldn't expect you to, Colonel."

"And I won't, Lieutenant. I won't be like any number of others you've probably come across in your career, which has been for —?"

"Two years."

"Starting as —?"

"A solicitor in England."

"And ended up in the U.S. Army —?"

"Because of a combination of things, Colonel. But let's just say I have a fondness for this country."

"And assigned to this case because —?"

"I believe in justice."

"And because the case is hopeless, I'd say."

"Maybe so, Colonel. But you still haven't answered the question."

"Don't think I'm avoiding it. In plain English — and it's been said long before I came around — coloreds don't make good soldiers. And it's a proven fact, they aren't good for the country. Even you should know that."

"If they aren't good for the country, Colonel, why were they training so hard to go to Europe to fight for the country?"

"First of all, I'm not convinced they wanted to go overseas to fight."

"Oh?"

"I think a lot of what any colored has to say is just plain ol' b.s. — particularly when it comes to war. Those birds are all talk. And born complainers. They're always crying about this or that. Whining is a way of life with these people. They're worse than another bunch that comes to mind. Not knowing your heritage, I'd better not say who. But I'll tell you this: when the coloreds say they want to go to Europe, I can assure you it's not because they want to fight for Old Glory, or for what this country stands for. Don't make the mistake of believing that. They want to get over there to show off. Coloreds are like that. They always want to show off. They want to be big shots. An' if they've got a few legitimate bucks in their pockets, they're even worse. Most of these people here wouldn't have a cent if it hadn't been for the Army. Clothing and shelter neither. It costs our government over a hundred U. S. dollars to uniform each and every one of these people, and they *still* complain. But mainly, since they can't do it in this country, they want to go overseas and get to — and ultimately impregnate — white women. That's what they want. And we shouldn't forget that. But I'll tell you this: I'd sure hate like hell to see what would happen if one of those birds came back to the docks with one of those European women tucked under his arm. You'd see a real war then. But let's be real about this thing, Lieutenant. Courage and national conviction have never been the colored man's strongest suit."

"And you're sure of that, are you, Colonel?"

"Positive."

"Then tell me why, Sir, five thousand of them fought in your Revolutionary War? And why, at Valley Forge, the Negro deserted less than the whites? And why, at seven dollars a month — six dollars less than the whites, by the way — two hundred thousand of them fought in your Civil War? And why over sixty-eight thousand died?"

"Aaah, I see you know a little about American history. I like that. You're unusual for a foreigner. Next, you'll be telling me these boys on trial are angels. And then you'll probably follow up by saying they weren't in rebellion."

"Thank you for answering the question, Colonel. But, no, I wouldn't be saying that at all."

"And you shouldn't. And couldn't. Don't forget, Lieutenant, these people arrived in Houston in rebellion. K Company marched on post in contempt and promoting division and insurgence. For instance, I had said that silence was the order of the day. I gave specific orders against calling cadence and sounding off. I said the same thing about any and all sideshow antics. And what did they do? Violate every order I gave. And not only was there cadence-calling and beating on drums, washboards and banging on anything else they could get their hands on, these people — again, against orders — were singing their own national anthem. Their own *national anthem!* Not ours. *Theirs!* The nig — the coloreds — have got their own national anthem. Now, how does that piece of idiocy sound to you?"

"Ordinarily I would say that it's obstinate folly. I heard Sergeant Odums refer to the anthem during his testimony. In my view, this is one country; one people. One anthem should be sufficient. Beyond that, I'll reserve comment."

"There's nothing to reserve, Lieutenant. To even think that a group in this country is separatist enough to want their own national anthem has got to be one of the most moronic things I've ever heard of. And to add some scoundrels in the military to that line of thinking makes me want to throw up. What gall. These people are sick. Disgusting. If they want separatism, go to a separate country."

"Colonel, I think it would be wise to remember not all the Negroes in the military were in on the march. Even in the battalion a clear two thirds of the men had nothing to do with — and *wanted* nothing to do with — the march on Houston. They are loyal, law-abiding Americans."

"The count in Houston is nineteen dead and eighteen wounded — or something like that. It seems to me, somebody was in rebellion."

"Which is why we are in court, Colonel, and for what I had hoped would be a search for truth. It is also why I wanted to be on this case so badly," said Jennings. "At present my job is to defend, but there are some deep problems in this country that can't be addressed by continuing to bury our heads in the sand and ignoring the reasons why certain things happen. Now, I am not saying the men on trial are angels — to use your term. They are far from it. Nor am I saying some of them weren't in rebellion."

"You're damned right, you can't say it. Colored people are rebellious as all hell."

"But, Colonel, rebellions are nothing new to this country. I'm not for them — not in the slightest, but the country was conceived in rebellion. And it paved the way for many others. Would you like to discuss one? Name your poison. There's the Dorr, the Shays, the Whiskey, the Turner, the anti-Rent and a dozen others. We can have a field day talking about rebellions in America."

"I can see why DeBerg looks at you as though he's made a mistake. Maybe we ought to get back to the case. I'd like to find out what you really know. Maybe go back to all the problems Stout created."

"Problems Colonel Stout created? That's not the way I heard it, Colonel."

"Well, what way did you hear it?"

"I'm not permitted to go into that."

"Oh, so now you have something to hide. Which one did you get your information from? And who are you going to cover up for ultimately, Stout or that idiot Farrell? Stout's in hiding, so it must be Farrell."

"I can assure you, that is not the case, Colonel. I'm not certain I agree with everything the captain did in Houston — or before Houston, for that matter — but he doesn't need any assistance from me. If you want an opinion based on what I know, I think Captain Farrell should have been much more assertive as a commander. I know he had to do a balancing act, but I think he allowed First Sergeant McClellan far too much latitude in running the company."

"And there are other things about him as well, to say the least. There are some pretty damning statements he's made. There's his attitude about the military, and the list goes on. If you haven't found out about them yet, you'd better start before you place your career in jeopardy by asking certain questions if and when he takes the stand — and I can tell you'd like to do that without Boatner's or DeBerg's consent. But if you do, and if you still have a commission, you'd better stick around, because I'm bringing him up on charges."

"Are you, Sir?"

"You're damned right, I am. And if I had my way, I'd have somebody in Washington haul Stout back into uniform and charge him."

"I don't really think you'd want to do that, Colonel. To either one of them."

"Why not?"

"Because from what I understand, Sir, from the outset Colonel Stout recognized the volatility of the situation. He sought to ease tension by recommending passes —"

"Which started the problem."

"I'm not certain about that either, Colonel. But Colonel Stout did other things favoring good order. And when he heard about the troops marching to Houston, he took quick and decisive action. You, on the other hand —" She stopped. It was an area she shouldn't be going into.

"Me, on the other hand, *what*?"

She declined comment.

"You might as well spill it, Lieutenant. I don't think you know it, but I've been a friend of your boss for more years than he or I would care to remember. If anything's up, he's going to tell me."

"I wouldn't bet on it, Colonel."

"Why not?"

"Sir, if Major DeBerg hasn't told you anything by now, he isn't going to."

"Maybe there's nothing to tell."

"To that, I'd say what I've just said, Colonel: don't bet on it."

Briggs pressed, but the lieutenant wouldn't yield.

"I can understand your curiosity, Colonel. But let me wrap it up by saying this, Sir. It was Colonel Stout's automobiles that were fired upon on the night of August 25th. Not yours. It was Colonel Stout who was on the road hoping to stop the march. Not you."

"Obviously I don't agree with a damned thing you're saying, and neither do the facts. But look, let's call a truce on this thing for the moment. Why don't I take you to the Officers' Club and buy you a drink. Perhaps I can clear this whole thing up. There's been a great deal of speculation and misconception as to what role I played in this entire matter. I don't like what I'm hearing, and I don't relish being out here in the cold, in the middle of nowhere discussing it."

"Thank you, Colonel. But, first, I'm an officer in the United States Army, and you don't *take* me anywhere. Second, I don't drink. And third, I'm not the one you're going to have to explain matters to."

"Touché on the first two. As to the third, you know a lot. You'd be someone good to start with."

"I think it's the ending that you're going to have to be concerned about, Colonel."

"Well, until that time, maybe we could get started on something else."

"I don't think so, Colonel."

"Afraid of men?"

"If I were, Sir, I really don't think it should be your concern," the lieutenant said, picking up the pace.

"Oh, but it is," the Colonel said without relenting. "I've watched you in court. I'd like to watch you elsewhere. Sometimes I listen to that beautiful voice of yours in trial and close my eyes. You can't imagine what I'm thinking."

"Sir, I think you should stop while you're ahead."

Briggs slowed to get a better look at her form. Catching up, he said, "I wonder what you really look like under that coat — with your hair down and out of uniform."

There was no comment.

"Alright, let me try it another way."

"I would suggest you not try anything, Colonel. You've already overstepped the bounds of common decency."

"Ah, but you don't know what I'm going to say," Briggs replied. She chose not to respond. "Okay, perhaps you're intuitive enough to read my mind?"

The lieutenant refused to say anything. The colonel continued to walk with her. They were about midway of the empty training fields when he said, "If you're going to turn me down, at least you ought to say something. I don't think you're going to get a better offer. Or at least you shouldn't. Look at it this way, both of us are getting up there. We both are getting gray around the edges. Me, of course, more than you. All I have are edges. But I think we have a lot we can offer each other — given the right positions."

She picked up the pace and ignored him.

"Slow down, Lieutenant. You're moving as if you're trying to defy the laws of nature. If a man sees something he deems desirable, surely he can't be faulted for trying." He paused and said, "That is, unless her inclinations are of a different persuasion." She stopped cold. She stared him directly in the eyes. "I don't fully understand you, Colonel."

Briggs, though uncomfortable, wouldn't back down. He moved

closer to her. "You're in the military, a man's world. You're a lawyer, a man's occupation. You're making history, Lieutenant. But I wonder how much of a woman you are? — which side of the fence are you really on?"

"None of your goddamned business, Sir," she said in that elegant, clipped voice before stalking off.

The colonel caught up with her again. "If I offended you, I'm sorry. I'm just a soldier from the old school, and there're a lot of things I'm not accustomed to. This modern world is moving too fast for me. So is the Army, for that matter. Sometimes I think I should've taken that bride who was offered to me many years ago. But I just couldn't bring myself to commit. Funny, I was afraid of women, but not afraid of Army. I guess I had it all wrong. Wrong because I've since learned the Army ties you down more than a piece of ass. Of course, if you'd like to help your fellow officer catch up, stop by the Officers' Club with me. Have a drink, fill me in."

"Colonel, present mistake aside, I prefer not being in your company — here, there or anywhere."

"I can *order* you there, Lieutenant."

The colonel knew better. He was trying to be facetious in making the remark. Facetious or not, Jennings was on him. "If you do, Colonel Briggs, the next trial won't be for the other Negro troops. It'll be for you, whether I still have my commission or not."

"You'd bring charges against a colonel?" Briggs asked, chuckling.

"Try me." She was serious. He was not.

"I like your grit. I can see why you left Great Britain. Though, I've got to admit, at first I thought you were one of those trouble-making suffragettes they wanted to kick out of the country. Listen, you just said you prefer not going to the Officers' Club — "

"No. I said I prefer not being in your company."

"Well, you must prefer something. Whatever it is, I'd like to have a hand in it. No pun intended."

She walked on without comment.

The colonel was undaunted. "Other than conducting investigations and defending coloreds, I'll bet you don't do much of anything, do you?"

"On the contrary, Colonel, I do everything."

"Oh? Such as what? And with whom?"

There was no comment.

"I'd bet you'd like it to be with the coloreds. I say that because in court it seems you have such passion for them. I found myself wondering why. And then you know what I asked myself? If given the chance, how far would she really go with one of those birds."

"Colonel Briggs, you're bordering on the despicable again."

"Well, now, that's a matter of opinion," Briggs said. "Then let me ask you this: I know you're a late starter, but how did you get from England to the States, get in the Army, make lieutenant, and end up on a trial like this? I mean, you're making history, and I'd really like to know something about it."

"I got into law and the military by working my butt off."

"I hope you saved a little."

"I did," she said, again hoping to end the salacious advance.

"For my husband."

"Your husband? Now, that is news. I didn't know you were married. I thought you were like me — not that it would make any difference," the colonel said, chuckling again. "How come you're not home taking care of the little man? In the proper way, of course."

She stopped. She'd had enough. "Colonel, let me tell you this, and perhaps it'll end it. When my husband and I — and our children — left England not so very long ago, we found that from the moment we touched shore, there was something wonderful about this country, that it was a country worth fighting for. We found that in its charter for freedom and hope, it could be an even better country. Common sense stepped in and told us that in order for it to *be* that better country, everybody has to pitch in and do their part — as best they can, in any way that they can. There's a war going on. I wanted to contribute. I would have worked just as hard being a nurse, a water-bearer, a runner, or anything else. But I ended up here, and I am damn thankful for it. Now, as I've tried to make clear to you before, whether that fight — that freedom and hope — comes through war, the courts, or through repelling seedy old men intolerant of others and undeserving of command, it is still war, and it still has to be fought. It is obvious victory is not in sight. And, it might not be in sight for a very long time. But we keep on trying, Colonel. One day we'll win."

Chapter 29

It was the end of the third week of trial, and it had been raining for two days. Cold and mud slipped under and through the thin walls of the tents in the stockade, and days later the interior would still be damp.

Sunday evening, after another dull, worrisome day, Jody thought he saw a flicker of renewed life in his friend. It was a mistake. Still, he sat on the cot next to the outstretched Pete, and, as he had done during the week, tried to explain what had transpired in court.

"T'wont a good week, last week, Pete," said the little soldier, whose twelfth year of living had passed a month ago without notice. He was sitting on the cot in his usual state of confusion. "They was talkin' fast an' funny. An' they was usin' a lotta words I didn't understand again. Hope they don't do that next week. Wonder why they do that? I got kinda tired sittin' there. I'm tired of sittin' there, anyhow. An' it's cold in there. Wished they'd light that stove. Bet you'd say the same thing, if you could say somethin'. But I guess that's all they want us to do. Sit there. But, I'm gonna tell you somethin, Pete. I'll sure be glad when this thing is over. Lotta things we gotta do. I s'pose the first thing is, we gotta get you to the hospital. Then maybe I can get to see my momma one more time, and we can get on overseas where we belong."

Jody never took into account the prosecutor's *the mockingbirds must die* statement, and as dreamlike as his thought was, reality said there never could be an overseas for him or Pete — or any of them, for that matter.

As for Pete, even if his mind had shown that flicker of renewed life, it was still over for him. His hands had gotten worse. Earlier they had been medically treated, but it was too little too late. The rags that Jody, Simms and Boland had found and wrapped them in told the story. The guards were made aware of the worsening ailment, and further medical attention had been promised. Weeks passed and still nothing had been done. To help, Jody and Simms tried washing both the hands and the rags periodically. Each time, though, the hands would end up soggy with drying blood and stains of greenish pus. The tissues in and around both hands, hands that had been inspired by the elegant snip of a barber's scissors, were decayed to the point of being gangrenous. Amputation was the only solution.

The crawl toward the inevitable end had slowed just about everybody's movement but Jody's. The men were sluggish coming and going to court. Most of them had given up. Even before that, though, the weekends in the stockade were long and uneventful. Nights were the worst. Home was fading. And it got so that the one or two who used to lie in the cold and wait for the man the next cot over to drift off to sleep so they could comfort themselves with thoughts of women which sometimes led to half-hearted attempts at masturbation had changed. They became like the rest. They simply lay there. No longer were there any up-and-down strokes under the moth-eaten blankets.

Only a few of the men were holding on. Simms was among

them. Normally he would return from court and, in his quiet way, would offer a comforting word or two to Boland, and sometimes to anyone else close by. He would do the same over the weekends, just before stretching out on his cot. Then when the guards lined them up for the last meal of the day, as unappetizing as it was, he would think of something else and hold the positive thought until just before *lights out* was given. "It's going to be alright," he would say softly to Boland. It was probably said to comfort himself as well. Sometimes, even before *lights out*, if there were no tears in his eyes, he would turn his head and extend his slender hand to the cot next to his. Sometimes in return, Boland's fingertips would reach out and touch his. The ray of hope on the beefy soldier's face would carry into the dark.

On this occasion the touch hadn't occurred. *Lights out* had not been given. Boland lay on his cot, deep in thought, his eyes transfixed. Simms was worried about him, particularly since he hadn't moved from his cot since late the day before. Simms was also worried because the prosecutor had introduced the term *deviancy* to the court.

Suddenly Boland's eyes started blinking rapidly.

"What's wrong?"

The eyes continued blinking for awhile, then Boland lifted his big head thoughtfully and shoved a hand under it. "Y'know, this whole weekend, I been thinkin'."

"About what?" Simms asked, thinking it was something intimate between the two of them.

"I been thinkin'.... I been thinkin' most of us is gonna go free," Boland said, as if having figured it all out.

Carter, who occupied the next cot down, was blowing on his harmonica, forlornly searching for the melody of *The Battle Hymn of The Republic*. Knowing that it was the first sergeant's favorite, he had been taking stabs at it since arriving at the stockade. Suddenly he stopped, looked at Simms with a delayed alertness, and asked, "What'd he say?"

Boland lifted himself from the cot, spun into the upright position, and spoke with more voice. "Most of us is gonna go free."

It took a while but another voice asked, "Did somebody say sumthin'?"

"We gonna do *what?*" another delayed but incredulous voice asked.

Boland repeated it simply. "Go free."

"*Go f-f-free?* How you figger that?" Andrews asked from down the line.

"Well, I been thinkin' — "

Caution was swept aside. Crawford mustered excitement. And then just about everybody did. The word *free* generated its own momentum and had most of the men moving in, surrounding the beefy soldier's cot in anticipation.

"*Thinkin' what?*" Rochester urged.

Puerto Rico Hicks was more forceful. "Wha' — wha' — wha'cha sayin', Man?"

"'Member before the trial started?" Boland replied, his eyes thoughtfully searching. "That captain who was innerviewin' us — ?"

"Yeah, yeah, yeah," Crawford said, breathing heavily. "Captain Thurston. Wonder what ever happened to him, anyway?"

Though he had the name wrong, Crawford was asking about Capt. Donald Thoren, the aide who, as DeBerg had suspected, had removed himself because of the hopelessness of the case.

"I don't know what happen'd to him, but I do r'member when he first started talkin' he said it was gonna be up to the Army to prove what they charged us with."

"We know that," Yancy said. "That's why we in court."

"An' that's why they havin' all'a them peoples to testify against us," Crawford commented.

"But, if you think about it, so far ain't nobody done that," Boland said. "The trial is almost over, an' they still ain't sure of who did this or who did that."

"I don't get'cha," said Calvin Yancy.

"I do," said Boot of Company I, with growing enthusiasm. "Even after talkin' to us, that captain wont even sure himself."

"If he wont sure, why'd he leave?"

"We ain't got time to go into that," said Boot. "Go on, Bolly, I hears you. I think you on to somethin'."

"Well, if an eyewitness can't point you out an' ain't nobody can say that they actually saw you do somethin', the Army ain't got no proof. Not if none'a us ain't gotta take the stand."

"Yeah, but that ain't gonna make no difference," Rochester said. "Sgt. Yeager an' all the guards say they gonna convict us, anyway. That's why the major's been so quiet."

"He ain't been doin' nothin'," Puerto Rico said. "Absolutely nothin'."

Yancy joined in. "All he's been doin' is jus' sittin' there."

"Like a bump on a log," Crawford added.

"Yeah, but that woman is sho' 'nuff been fightin'," Boot Talley said.

"That don't mean nothin'," Yancy said.

"Wha'chu mean that don't mean nothin'? Every lil' bit helps."

"A white woman defendin' colored folks?" Yancy asked rhetorically. "They might lynch us even quicker."

"Yeah. An' she might be on the other side, anyway," said Crawford. "Never can tell 'bout them people."

Boot Talley fumed. "As hard as that woman's been fightin'? Why you wanna say somethin' stupid like that?"

"She white ain't she?" retorted Crawford. "My daddy used to say the apple don't fall far from the tree."

Rochester came back with, "Y'all can say all y'all want, but it ain't gonna do no good. Like Yeager an' the guards is been sayin', they gonna convict us an' they don't care who's doin' the talkin'."

"That's what *they* say," argued Boland. "Like the Army, they got it wrong. I mean, like in court, they keep sayin' we was in columns when the officers in the cars was shot. But we wont in no columns."

"What difference do that make?" Carter asked.

"Well, if they don't know if we was layin' down or standin' up in the field — which is the easiest thing to know — they don't know nuttin'," Boland said, holding his ground. "An' anyhow, you don't ambush by bein' in no columns."

Crawford, now anxiously sitting on the corner of Boot's bunk, spoke. "What about all them peoples that's done testified 'bout what we done done at the station-house?"

"But most of 'em didn' actually see who did what," Boland countered. "All they know is we did it together."

Rochester asked, "What about Quackenbush's testimony?"

"He ain't seen nothin'."

Andrews backed the question with, "An' that corporal from I Company? The one who pointed somma us out."

"Jackson."

"Yeah."

"He ain't seen nothin', either. All he knows about was what happen'd in the ho' house. An' that's a separate issue —"

"Same as Quackenbush."

"Right. An' anyhow we can prove both of them was lyin'," Puerto Rico said, joining Boland's optimism.

"An' if we goes free, we ought'a go back to Columbus an' find both of them bastids an' hang 'em."

"Hangin' is too good for 'em."

"Hey, y'all, cut that out," said Carter. "We in 'nuff trouble already."

"I'm gonna be in a whole lot more if I ever find them bastids," Puerto Rico added.

"G'won, finish what you started to say, Bo," urged Crawford. "I wanna hear this."

"Yeah, tell us wha'chu been thinkin'."

"Well, the whole thing is: what the Army is mad about most of all is the ambush."

"An'," Yancy soberly added with a lowered voice, knowing that

Poole could possibly hear him from the other section, "they really mad 'bout Corporal Poole shootin' at that house next to the police station an' killin' that little girl."

"But," Boland continued, "other than that, nonna the whites knows who did the shootin'."

"But they provin' that in the tent we was all in on a mutiny. You know, the conspiracy thing? Sergeant Odums did that. He killed any hope for us."

"Did you hear what that Tom was sayin'?"

"I couldn't b'leevit."

"Lord, he sho' better be glad we can't get to him."

"Sergeant Williams, too."

"Everybody that testified was just as bad."

"A bunch'a Toms," Pedro Grahm reaffirmed. "That's all they was. A bunch'a nappy-headed Uncle Toms."

"They ought'a be shot."

"Lynched."

"Forget them," said Puerto Rico. "Let's talk 'bout the ambush. All'a us wont in on it."

"We know that," Carter said, "but even before the trial started, the officers that was in the cars said all of us did the firin'."

"Yeah, but they didn't *see* any of us doin' it. An' *that's* what we got to hang on to. That's what the Army is gonna hang onto. Like the man said, *What did they see?*"

"How could they see?" Pedro Grahm responded. "We black, it was black out there — an' on top of that, we was in a ditch."

"Even the Uncle Toms don't know nothin' 'bout that," Puerto Rico said, sticking to his theme.

"I dunno, Man. I dunno."

But optimism had grown. Boland, as if on appeal, looked to his silent mate on the next cot for confirmation. "Wha'chu think, Simmy?"

"Yeah, Simmy-boy, lift yourself up an' talk to us," said Carter. "You got all the smarts. Do we got a chance?"

They had, of course, not presented an acceptable argument in any sense. It was sightless, fragmented, inconsistent, filled with omissions and they hadn't taken into account the logic of opportunity, the Articles of War, an unyielding trial board, and the Army's unswerving determination to convict. Still, what some of them said was worthy of at least a modicum of thought.

But not really.

In his quiet way, though, Simms did them one better. He gave it more than a modicum of thought.

Aside from the NCO's, Pfc. Adrian Simms, like most company clerks, had always been regarded as the smartest man in the company. He was light-skinned and curly haired. To them, he *looked* smartest. Added to that, he was the company guidon bearer, and he had one stripe. Without the First, whom they certainly wouldn't have gone to, they truly needed his validation.

The tent fell breathlessly quiet. Even Jody, down the line with Pete, waited to hear what Simms had to say. The rhyming trio — Roosevelt, Menyard and Andrews — who had come midway down the aisle to listen, also waited. Crawford, already sitting and listening attentively, moved in closer, as did the others. Only Jody, Pete and Cpl. Poole, reclining in another section, remained in place.

Menyard of the trio broke the impatient silence. He was edgy. "Whaddya say, Simmsy, do he got a point or not?!"

The gentle-hearted Simms didn't want to answer. But he was glad they were not looking at him as a deviant. But they were grabbing at straws. Straws on their own meant nothing.

Yancy spoke. "C'mon, Simmy, c'mon. Help us out. Tell us somethin'."

"Yeah," said Pedro Grahm, "tell us wha'cha think."

Simms was slow. Very slow. When he finally spoke he was devoid of optimism. "Well, I think Sergeants Odums and Williams —"

"C'mon, Simmsy, forget them!" Andrews said before the words cleared the tall soldier's mouth. "Think pos'tive! Y'gotta think pos'tive!"

"I don't know," Simms surrendered. "I just don't know."

A disappointed voice groaned, "Awww, Mannnn."

"You can do better'n that, Simmsy," Menyard of the trio pleaded. He was growing desperate. "You gotta do better'n that, Simmsy. You got to! We gotta get out'a this mess."

"Don't just sit there. Say sump'um."

"I can't say," said Simms earnestly.

"But if you had to guess — ?" Boland implored.

"Yeah. If you had to guess, what would'ja say?"

"Say somethin'!" Menyard blurted again.

From the horizontal position on his cot, Simms looked up at his mate. For the first time there was real hope in his lover's eyes. There was eager hope in the eyes of the others. They gathered even tighter between the two bunks, sitting and kneeling imploringly. All eyes were on the quiet and slender company clerk and guidon bearer who, until Boland, had often been shunned and derided because of his sexual predilection. Boland had always protected him, and now he couldn't let his mate down. He didn't want to let any of them down.

"If — if — if I had to guess — "

"Yeah? Yeah? — if you had to guess?" Pedro begged as Simms broke off.

"What, Simmsy, *what?*" Andrews and Roosevelt pressed, almost in unison. But now Menyard, the third member of the trio, and the one who had been pushing hardest, didn't say anything. "C'mon, Simmy. Like Nigeral was sayin', you got the smarts," Rochester said. "Tell us wha'cha think."

"Talk to us!" demanded Puerto Rico.

"Please, Simmy-boy. Please," Boot implored. "Please talk to us."

Simms looked at them again. He turned his head and looked down to the far corner of the tent to where Jody was nursing Pete.

The guidon bearer and company clerk, still in the supine position on his cot, turned his head back to the group and began insecurely. "I'd guess —"

"Yeah? Yeah? Yeah?"

"I think —" He dropped it again.

"Aw, c'mon, Simms," Crawford said with a tear in his eye, "say it. Say it. You gotta tell us. *Please*, you just gotta tell us."

"We gots to know, Simmsy. We just gots to know."

"Please — please."

That time it was Boland.

Simms digested quietly, looked at them again, and said ever so slowly, "I'd guess — guess —"

"Yeah?! Yeah?! Yeah?! Yeah?!"

"S-s-some of us are going to go.... free."

He said it without conviction, and he turned his head away even as he said the words. They didn't care. No larger words could have been spoken. The men jumped into each other's arms. Swallowed in infectious hope, they whooped, hollered, hugged and ran up and down the aisle congratulating each other. It was as if the war had been won. Carter grabbed his harmonica and started blowing merrily. The dancing started. The celebration got so loud and festive that the guards raced to the door. The men didn't notice.

"Freeee! We gonna go freeee! *We be's freeeeeeee!!*" Andrews and Roosevelt said, getting set to start a rhyme for the occasion.

Menyard, strangely, was slow in joining the huddle.

Poole, locked in a separate section, had found a nub of a pencil and a crumpled sheet of paper and was sketching a Christmas scene to send to his children. He bolted from his cot and hollered, "What's goin' on out there? What's goin' on?"

"We gonna go free!" Boot Talley said, dancing arm in arm with Puerto Rico. "We gonna go free! *We gonna go freeeee!*"

Poole was beside himself. "How y'know? Who said so? Who tolja?"

The men didn't hear him. They were much too ecstatic. Poole then figured it out for himself. Sickened, he mumbled something, and went back to his cot to lay down.

McClellan, chained at night in the farthest section of the old brick building and cut off from everyone, heard the yelling but remained on his brick bunk. He hadn't heard the dialogue, but his imagination went to work.

All night long the troops carried on, causing the First to spend the first part of his night wondering if false hope was better than no hope at all. He concluded that while hope was often false and, cloaked against truth, made for a greater disappointment, it nonetheless provided temporary relief. And that, in the long run, he thought, was better for the troops.

The First spent the remainder of the night thinking about Dukes and Jody; the old and the new. The ancient and the underage. He thought about how loyal one had been, and how brave the other turned out to be. The old and the new. The old had him thinking about the company's predicament; the new caused him to think about the draft. He hadn't thought about it in a long time. He wondered how many blacks had registered; how many had reported.

One and a half million was the count.

Chapter 30

Sunday night evaporated rapidly. The crack of dawn found the prisoners wide-awake and feeling jubilant. Most hadn't slept at all during the night. Others slept with the rapture of a new born baby. Boland's *"we gonna go free"* pronouncement, which had been reluctantly backed by the respectfully intelligent Simms, rejuvenated itself at every turn. Whereas the heavy, round-shouldered soldier and the shyly bent soldier with the effeminate tendencies had once been ridden, berated and chided for their relationship, they were now the back-slapped favorites of the hour among the troops, and their words did everything but bounce off the canvas walls that morning. Besides praising Boland and Simms, the men were loose with each other, and some, so optimistic as to be planning for the return to duty, took first-time advantage of the basins of water the guards usually left at the tent's entrance. Some of them washed and tried to shave by using lids from tin cans. Later, those who had appetites ate heartily. It was thought that even breakfast, the normal staple of hardtack, molasses, and water, sometimes replaced by oats and sausage, was prepared by better hands. For certain it tasted better.

When it was time to go to court, the men were chatty and friendly to the guards. Even the route getting to Gift Chapel seemed brighter. Inside, they nodded courteously to the bewildered spectators and the few reporters. They were not like they were before, starting with when the guards had led the 63 into the chapel on that very first day, when they moped and sagged, entered with bowed heads, and sat with a seeming indifference that later grew into routine defeat. On this morning, except for McClellan, sternly attentive, and Poole, resistive but not quite as surly as he had appeared before, the men entered court with upright heads and wide grins. Those who had to climb to the second or third tier, instead of plowing and stumbling their way up, moved with exceptional politeness and jauntiness and sat eagerly on the pine benches. Boland and Simms were given first-row-center seats.

Again the court was packed. Everyone felt this would be an unusual day. The prosecution still had a number of witnesses to call, among them Lt. Col. Briggs, the battalion commander, and the questionable Capt. Farrell. Off the record, the court had cautioned both prosecution and defense that Briggs was to be on the stand for only a moment.

Farrell was questionable because it was rumored that at some point he was about to become dangerously vocal. Word had circulated that he was in touch with a newspaper reporter from court and was about to openly challenge Capt. Whitney's testimony and Col. Briggs's account of what had happened in Houston. It made for interesting gossip, but it simply wasn't true. First of all, as President of the Court, Brig. Gen. Hawley wouldn't have allowed it. And Farrell wouldn't have been that naïve. In truth, Farrell had not spoken to anyone — at any time. On the days that he attended court he was silent. His nights were spent alone in his quarters, worrying about his wife and father-in-law's reaction to his involvement in the proceedings. His weekends were spent thinking and reading and writing long letters to family and friends. But without bothering to check what amounted to self-generated scuttlebutt, and without waiting for something to actually appear in print, Briggs had already begun to counter the captain by going to the Officers' Club and dropping loose references about the captain's 201 file, his religion, and his earlier statements on not going to war.

Those smoldering embers aside, the general mood in the court was that the prosecution had, up to this point, done much to substantiate what was believed to be an open-and-shut case — which was the absolute opposite of the prisoners' thoughts. The only thing remaining before the defense made its presentation, court observers felt, was to bring further clarity as to who had been involved with the ambush, that is, those who actually fired on the vehicles, killing the officers. To some, McClellan's earlier statement seemed sufficient. Boatner, the trial judge advocate, felt that the statement was self-serving and not sufficiently indicting. He wanted testimony from a King Company member who had actually marched and had either seen or heard what took place in the ditch that night.

Feeling that he had overlooked something or someone, and secure because of a rereading of a law, a week earlier the prosecutor had sent his investigators poring back over files and records. The investigators were swift and thorough. By midweek they had even checked friends and family members from all over in hopes of finding some tidbit that could give them insight into the one possible member whom they could now legally call to the stand. Preferably, it had to be someone Boatner could intimidate, someone who would go against the defense's wishes, crack, and tell all — and, by so doing, indict all. The prosecutor could freely employ this tactic because, in microscopically rechecking the books, he had the U.S. Constitution on his side.

Sgt. Yeager had already clicked his heels and announced court was in session. DeBerg and Jennings sat quietly.

When all was ready, Brig. Gen. Hawley leaned toward the prosecution table. "Counselor?"

Boatner stood, patricianlike, "Forgoing our other witness for the moment," he said, surprising everyone but the trial board, "if it please the court, the prosecution calls Private Jody Cunningham."

Amiability and brightness along the hardened benches instantly vanished. *"The prosecution calls for who?"*

The prisoners looked at each other. None of them was supposed to be called. Baffled looks went to the prosecutor, and then down to the first row, where the puzzled young soldier was sitting. Because of the commotion created by the prisoners, the spectators were in an equal quandary. They didn't know who Jody Cunningham was, but they followed the lead and eyes of the prisoners. McClellan, centered on the first row, bent over for a quick look, as did the perplexed Poole, who, as ordered by McClellan, had positioned himself far down in the corner of the second row. The First wanted him farther from the guards.

DeBerg held firm, but he actually motioned for Lt. Jennings to stand for the objection. She rose to her feet, though she didn't think it necessary to say much. For the prosecution to call a defendant to testify against himself was such a flagrant violation of the Constitution, nothing much had to be said. Most of the spectators didn't believe it was lawful to call a defendant.

"Mr. President," said the lieutenant, "if it please the court, may I remind you, Private Jody Cunningham is on trial. He is a defendant. He is with the body of the accused. As was the case with First Sergeant McClellan, it is a violation of the Fifth Amendment to the Constitution for the court to allow the accused to testify against himself. To do so strikes at the very foundation of justice in the country. It splinters the principles of equity, and is antithetical to everything our founding fathers stood for."

"This court is still very much mindful that you stood and voiced your objections when the prisoner McClellan *voluntarily* stood to make a *statement*, which, in this court's view, did not amount to testimony, Lieutenant. I will tell you now, as I told you then, you can assume the court knows as much about the Fifth Amendment as you. Apparently you disagree. Now, you state that this court would be in violation of the Fifth Amendment should this young man be allowed to take the stand, having been called by the Government. For the record, I ask you, what does the Constitution say in this regard?"

The brigadier made the statement and asked the question in a manner that indicated he knew where the lieutenant was headed and that he was fully prepared to counter the argument.

"The Amendment is quite clear in that regard, General," Jennings said, her voice calm. "No person shall be compelled — and I quote: 'in any criminal case to be a witness against himself.' I am very much surprised the court isn't at least aware of the wording, if not the intent. The Fifth Amendment has been in effect in this country since 1791."

"How right you are, Lieutenant," said the bulldog general, without consulting books or colleagues, his Kentucky voice resolute. "That particular Amendment has been in effect in *our* country since 1791. It is the cornerstone of justice, and I am glad that you are aware of it. However, I do wish you had read the Amendment in its entirety. Preceding that which you have just quoted, the document states — unequivocally "that no person shall be held to answer for a capital or otherwise infamous crime unless on a presentment or indictment of a Grand Jury except' - '*except*,' Lieutenant, 'in cases arising in the land or naval forces, or in the militia, when in actual service in time of War or public danger."

"Sir, the issue here is not presentment or indictment. We are in court. It is the matter of self-incrimination. The language — and indeed the *intent* — of the Amendment is infinitely clear in that direction. I say again — and my contention is supported by the Manual of Court Martial —"

"Are you referring to the most recent manual — the 1908 manual, Lieutenant?" the general interrupted.

"Indeed I am, Sir," the lieutenant said, now with manual in hand. "And fearful that the prosecution might come up with statements *presumably* made by the defendants, I also ask you to consider that affidavits taken *ex parte* and not as depositions under the 91st Article of War are not admissible as evidence unless expressly consented to by the accused with full knowledge of his rights."

Even the reticent Maj. DeBerg was impressed at that moment. It was something he hadn't known. He even smiled at the revelation.

"I believe that was a finding, Lieutenant," the President of the Court said.

"It matters not, General. It is the law."

"And it is equally lawful to allow the defendant to make a statement," the General said, holding firm. "I quote: *The accused — where he has not testified — may make a verbal or written statement as to the case. The statement should not be sworn to, and if sworn to should not be received as evidence by the court.*"

DeBerg joined in. "Which means, General, Private Jody Cunningham can not be called to the stand."

"On the contrary, Major. The defendant has *not* testified, therefore he can — and *will* — be called upon to make a statement. It will be unsworn. The prosecution will be limited to that extent."

The major relented. The lieutenant did not.

"But, Sir," said Jennings in frustration, "no matter how it is phrased, no matter what restrictions you place on the trial judge advocate, it takes us back to the prime issue, which is this young man's constitutional rights — rights guaranteed by the Fifth Amendment. I quote again: 'No person in any criminal case shall be compelled to testify or be a witness against himself' — which is precisely what this court is asking this young man to do. It simply cannot be done."

"Except,' Lieutenant, 'in cases arising in the land or naval forces, or in the militia, when in actual service in time of War or public danger,'" the brigadier quoted. "That is what is stated in the law. That is the intent of the law. And in this court, that is what will stand. It will stand, Counsel, because the defendant is in the militia and, I need not remind you, the country is at war and the public is in danger."

The defense had been silenced. All they could do was watch.

Nine times out of ten, Jody never even heard his name when it was called. He sat there, his body positioned in support of Pete's, staring at nothing, understanding nothing, his mind wandering. He was with the company, and that was sufficient.

"For the purposes of making a statement, the prosecution calls for Private Jody Cunningham," Boatner said again.

The TJA called the name again, and it finally dawned on the young soldier not yet in his teens that his name had been called. With his eyebrows forehead-high and a question mark sealed on his face, he looked around the roped-off area to see who had called him.

"Private Jody Cunningham will take the stand," the brigadier called again. As Boatner had done, he reiterated the law he had quoted earlier.

Realizing it was he who had been called, a puzzled Jody stood and looked at the man.

"Come forward. The purpose is for making a statement."

Jody was frozen in place.

"Take the stand," the other important voice commanded.

The boy didn't know what to do. He simply stood there.

All eyes were on him, penetrating eyes that now had the youngster's eyes darting from person to person in the court. He turned around, and the eyes went from Pervis Boland to Adrian Simms to Calvin Yancy to Cpl. Poole, up and down the tiers and back again. They didn't go to McClellan, because he had always been afraid to look the first sergeant directly in the eye.

As if appealing to the unable-to-communicate Pete, Jody whispered, "What's it all about, Pete?"

"Soldier, will you take the stand!"

He still couldn't move.

"Private Cunningham, take the witness stand!" the trial judge advocate repeated.

Since they were glaring at him, Jody started to bend under the rope. Boland said in a half whisper, "Don't do it, Jody. You don't have to go over there."

Other voices supported Boland.

For guidance, Jody, still in the bent position under the rope, his high-riding eyebrows lifted even higher, looked up in the direction — but only in the direction — of the first sergeant. It took a while, but after seeing the helplessness of the defense's table, the First looked at the youngster and nodded for him to take the stand.

As the boy bent completely from under the rope and started to inch forward, a barrage from the prisoners drew a blistering attack from the President of the Court. He concluded by saying that if any one of them came even close to another outburst, all 62 would be remanded to the stockade for the duration of trial.

The brigadier then took it upon himself to order the confused young man the rest of the way to the stand. Jody nervously did as ordered.

On the stand, the youngster tried staring at his lap. Boatner wouldn't allow it. He forced eye-to-eye contact and skillfully weaved in and out of a scenario that placed several of the accused in the column that had fired on the vehicles containing the officers. Though not sworn in, Jody was then asked for comment. The young man's confusion got him in trouble again. He made an indicting statement that had Jennings on her feet. After Hawley again set her down, the trial judge advocate, taking every liberty he could find, asked the skittish and stammering young soldier exactly who had fired on the convoy of officers.

What the prosecution didn't know — and was not concerned with — was that Jody had not been with the firing party and that he, along with half the members on trial, had remained deep in the field. Sgt. McClellan, Jody tried to explain, had divided them into two groups. Before that, he didn't know what was going on because he was too busy attending to the needs of Sgt. Dukes and Pete.

Col. Boatner, disregarding the explanations, pushed his attack.

"Young man, I have already explained the crime of perjury —"

"It cannot be perjured testimony because the defendant was not sworn in," Jennings said, this time too frustrated to stand.

She was ignored. Boatner continued. "Soldier, do you realize the trouble you're in already?"

Jody looked over at his fellow prisoners.

"You are to refrain from looking at the prisoners," Boatner cautioned. "You are not to be influenced by anything but the truth. Is that clear?"

Jody nodded affirmatively. He was a child. And he looked every inch a child sitting there.

The President of the Court instructed him. "Nodding your head is not acceptable to the court. You will answer 'yes' or 'no.'"

"Yessir."

"Your Honor, this is an outrage," Jennings said.

Hawley looked at Boatner. "How far do you intend to go in eliciting your statement, Colonel?"

"I'm about through, General," the prosecutor dissembled. "We are only interested in establishing culpability here."

"If it is establishing culpability," a frustrated Jennings said, "it is incriminating. It makes the procedure illegal."

The prosecutor overrode her. "As I intended to say, Sir, the government is trying to get a full and complete statement. The defense is attempting to frustrate those ends. In addition to not heeding the court's admonitions, I feel the lieutenant is conducting herself to the prejudice of good order and military discipline and, as the court has so wisely interpreted for the defense, against the tenets of the Constitution."

"Sir —" Jennings wearily began to the President of the Court.

She was cut off.

"We are conducting a trial here, Lieutenant, not a debate. Continue with the witness, Colonel."

"Now, I'm going to ask you again, Private Jody Cunningham. Were you with — or were you present when the column — or detail — fired at the vehicles?"

"I wont there, Sir."

"You were," Boatner said with a modest flare, "you were there. Everyone in this court knows you were there. I have statements proving you were there."

Jennings voiced her disagreement to DeBerg. He said nothing.

"But I wont there, Sir," the boy protested.

"You are lying," Boatner said angrily. "You were there! You know who fired!"

"Are you trying to impede progress, Lieutenant?"

Jennings couldn't contain herself. She wanted DeBerg to stand, but he wouldn't. She felt like kicking him. Instead, she stood. "I object. And I object most strenuously. The prosecution has no such statements. If he had the needed incriminating evidence, this young man would not be on the stand."

"I am not trying to impede progress, General. I am trying to foster justice. I am trying to get to the truth. I am trying to get —"

"Then don't interrupt!" Hawley said harshly. "Continue, Colonel."

"Thank you, Sir," Boatner said. "Now, Private Cunningham. Were you, or were you not, with the column or detail when the vehicles were fired upon on the night of August 25th, in the Year of Our Lord 1917?"

"I wont with them, Sir."

"You are an unmitigated liar."

"I object!" Jennings was on her feet again.

"Sit down, Lieutenant!"

"I'm asking you again," Boatner insisted. "Were you with the column when the volley of shots were fired?!"

The trial judge advocate had come down so hard on the little soldier that confusion again took over and he surrendered.

"Yessir," Jody said. He quietly lowered his head as if having let his sergeant and the prisoners down.

"Yes, Sir — *what?*"

"Yessir, I was in there."

"In there *where?*"

"The column."

"*What* column?"

"The column that shot up the cars."

But the prosecutor still was not satisfied. "And every man — every single person — in that column fired, didn't he?"

"It-it-it was dark, Sir," Jody said, stumbling. "I-I couldn't tell. I-I don't know w-w-who was in it."

"They all fired, didn't they? Every man in that column fired, didn't they?!"

Jennings stood heatedly. "I object! The prosecution may or may not have the right to put this witness on the stand, but the prosecution does not have the right to wantonly force an incriminating admission and then follow up that illegality by badgering the witness. And he continues to do it, Mr. President."

"It is not badgering, Lieutenant," Hawley said.

"The testimony was forced. It is badgering. Furthermore, it was impossible for the witness to see who was in the column — *if* — there was a column!"

"Will you sit down, Lieutenant!".

"No, I will *not* sit down!"

She shocked the court — and herself. This was the military; she was a lieutenant talking to a brigadier general. She knew she was wrong. With an apologetic air, she would express regret. But she would not back down. "I apologize for the statement, Sir. I truly do. But this blatant miscarriage of justice simply cannot go on. This trial is a charade. In addition to badgering, the prosecution has been argumentative, leading, intimidating, and putting words into every witness's mouth who has appeared before this court. The colonel has violated rules of law and protocol. And he has done so shamelessly and flagrantly. It is a horror I find intolerable, and a condition I would hope the court finds unacceptable."

"You can find it what you wish, Lieutenant. The court is infinitely satisfied with the conduct of the trial judge advocate. If you do not agree, and if you find the court's position intolerable, you have the court's permission to remove yourself."

It was a proposition the female defender hadn't anticipated. The question now was, what was she going to do about it?

Still seething over what she considered the general's blatant misinterpretation of the Fifth Amendment and his outright nescience of the Manual of Court Martial and law as a whole, she gave the matter soul-searching consideration. The court was silent; the prisoners, worried. Everyone was waiting. DeBerg purposely looked in the other direction. His gaze even bypassed McClellan at that point. The bulldog face of the Kentucky-born general who had dropped out of law years ago but had been tapped to handle this trial because of rank and a hard-line reputation had a challenging look to it.

The first-time female defender knew the entire matter had been reduced to an exercise in futility. The court was going to convict, and it was going to mete out the death penalty, no matter what. It was all there, hopeless and unchangeable, and there was nothing she could do about it. She didn't want to throw in the towel, but she felt she had no choice. She was certain of reprimand. It would be vacuous and for show, meaning nothing, but she would get over it. She had to. On the heels of this trial, there would be another one, possibly two. It didn't matter, because long before, she had made up her mind that she was going to be a part of it, and that she would not be shut out of pretrail again. And whether there was one trial or a dozen, as an officer and as someone who really cared, she would take a much more significant role. In any case, whatever her involvement, even if it were that of a law clerk, she knew she would be better prepared.

Still she was in a quandary. She would appeal to her immediate superior.

"What would you advise, Major?"

The chief defender with the compelling presence wouldn't advise anything. Purposefully, he was still looking in the other direction.

Without waiting further, the lieutenant speechlessly gathered the papers that had been spread on the table and packed them into her briefcase. She stood and, preparing to leave, nodded deferentially to the President of the Court. He did not nod back. To Col. Boatner, the trial judge advocate, she said curtly, "I'll see you on the next trial, Colonel. We can only hope that it will not be as big a travesty as this honorable court has made this one."

Part of what she said had been for Brig. Gen. Hawley's benefit. If he or the prosecution had wanted to respond, it wouldn't have had much effect. In an instant, she was marching down the aisle and heading for the doors.

Col. Briggs, sitting in the rear of the chapel, rose and, trying to establish eye contact, held both of the double doors open for her. The lieutenant walked out as if he hadn't been there. The colonel closed the doors and returned to his seat.

Once again, he had been unsuccessful with the woman.

Except for McClellan, Poole and a few others, the black prisoners were feeling the loss, not so much because of the drain on an already weakened defense, but because now they didn't even have a pleasant face to look at.

DeBerg sat silent. After a while, for the first time, he scanned the roped-off area. Except for McClellan, he hardly ever looked at the prisoners, and certainly not with any depth. He didn't know them. Before trial, he hadn't talked to them. The departed Capt. Thoren had done the primary talking for him. Jennings had wanted to do it, but couldn't. The stated reason was that the Army had regulations against allowing females on stockade grounds. The lieutenant had always believed there were other reasons. It had something to do with the age-old fear of black men around white women.

As stoic and as unconnected as he appeared, DeBerg had mixed feelings about the lieutenant's departure. All along he had felt that she was woefully naive. As he had tried to get across to her before trial, in the little that they spoke, the blacks didn't stand a chance, and anything beyond a heartfelt effort would be a waste.

Thinking about the lieutenant, it was true, the major felt something. But he wasn't down on himself. He remembered that at the outset he had been fair enough to tell the her that a few contesting issues could be raised, but in the end, he said, they would all be for naught. Now the feeling centered on whether the woman's departure had been an act of courage or one of female naiveté and impetuosity. It was a thought he would put on hold until later.

The lieutenant's departure did force the old defender to come to grips with just how negligible his involvement had been. Yet, like everything else about him, he was not going to allow himself to worry about it. He quickly dismissed the question of another assistant, because trial was all but over. What did concern the major, strangely, was the attitude of the inscrutable McClellan.

From the outset the first sergeant was an object of riveting interest to the old defender from North Carolina. Day after day he would sit in court looking beyond the stove, observing the sergeant, saying nothing and doing nothing as the case, hopeless as it was, was slipping away.

What had so stirred Maj. DeBerg was that in his personal pretrial investigation, as cursory as it had been, he had gone back through the records to compare the Houston insurrection with what had happened in Brownsville years before. He had discovered the first sergeant's secret. Through an eyewitness, he learned that McClellan had been in service before, under the name of Pulham. It was an astonishing revelation, and to this moment it created an inner problem, because the defender had said nothing about it to anyone. He wondered why. Why was it that he hadn't revealed that extraordinary fact to the court? Why hadn't he told the prosecution? — or Briggs? Why had he never said anything to his own assistant, the departed Capt. Thoren? Or even Jennings? Why had he not confronted the first sergeant with the information? Other questions stymied the defender as well. The main one was: Why would a man who had been dishonorably discharged from the Army risk going to prison by re-enlisting? He would eye the sergeant over and over again with that question in mind. It was the only thing he had fought hard over since taking the case. Still the answer wasn't at hand.

Jody Cunningham was still nervous on the stand. Col. Boatner was still on him. "Now, Soldier, I want you to walk over there to where the prisoners are seated, and I want you to point out every single man who was in that column that fired on the officers' vehicles on the night of August 25th."

The young man's stiffness returned. He couldn't move.

"Let me repeat. I want you to go over there to the roped section in this court and point to every man who was in the column that fired on the vehicles containing the U.S. Army officers on the night of August 25th in the Year of Our Lord 1917."

Once again Jody's eyes scanned the prisoners' section. He was unwilling to move.

Poole, like a lot of the men, was looking at the troubled soldier with strong connections. Jody was not looking at him. He had momentarily buried his fright of the First, and his raised eyebrows and sad eyes were imploring. He didn't look the First directly in the eye, but he was looking in that direction. Understanding his plight, McClellan caught his eye, took his time, and gave the youngster a small, almost imperceptible nod. It also could have been — it was certainly more likely — interpreted as a nod to come and point him out.

It was an emotion-filled moment when the youngster from

Chugwater, Wyoming climbed down from the stand, moved around the stove and slowly back to the roped area under the unmoving stares of the court.

Menyard of the rhyming trio and several others appeared to duck as the young soldier approached.

With tears in his eyes, Jody faced all of them for a long moment. But that's all could do. He couldn't bring himself to point anyone out. The First nodded again. This time it was more readable.

Boatner was on the youngster again. Even before getting to the stand, the tall, fastidious, unyielding man with the thick facial hair had terrified him. Now Jody was shaking and couldn't bring himself to comply even with his first sergeant. The First had sent a definite signal that he wanted to be pointed out. Jody couldn't do it. For the first time ever, he looked the First directly in the eyes. He shook his head "no" to his leader.

He turned and faced the court alone.

From the other side of the court, the prosecutor pushed. "Turn around and point! Point the men out!"

"I can't do that, Sir."

"Why can't you?!"

"Because I was by myself. "

The youngster said it, then slowly turned to go back under the rope.

But Jody was not by himself in court, for just as he lowered his head to be with his comrades, First Sgt. McClellan bent from under the rope and stood with the boy-soldier, who, swallowed in a soiled uniform that had never fit properly without help from safety pins, now looked even smaller.

The others saw what their leader had done. They saw how he stood there — out front, erect, soldierly, manly — appearing as black as charcoal in a room of whites, his eyes front.

The prisoners no longer remained glued to their seats.

Simms was the first to stand. On the upper tier, he was standing ramrod straight, almost as if had the guidon in his hand. Boland looked around, thought about what he had said in the tent last night, and surrendered. He reached forward for a quick touch of his mate's hand. The brief touch was accepted. Boland rose, and he and Simms stood side by side. Down below, Carter stood. On the second row, Poole rose, moved down front, and took it upon himself to gently lift Pete into a standing position. Together they stood.

Jody bent back underneath the rope. He stood next to Poole and Pete.

But only two of the rhyming trio stood, Roosevelt and Andrews. Menyard remained seated. His head lowered, he refused to return the look of his two friends who were standing on the second row. They were hurt. Very hurt.

From another section, another man stood — Puerto Rico Hicks. And then Yancy and Pedro Grahm. Boot Talley of Company I stood. And yet another. Soon, with the first sergeant standing out front, there were 13 black faces spotted on different tiers.

Thirteen men stood tall in the roped-off area in the church.

The Army was satisfied.

"The Government of United States rests," said the prosecutor.

• • •

Breaking the long silence that followed, Hawley, the President of the Court ordered the men to their seats and looked to the defense. "Major DeBerg?"

At the start, he wasn't firm. The arthritic old veteran of the courts was slow in standing and was equally slow in his delivery. He hadn't done the job, and he wasn't expected to be aggressive in his summation.

"This is not — nor has it been — within the bounds of military procedure. It is without precedent," the major summed up. He surprised even himself with the depths he had begun to feel. "Much,

I am saddened to say, has been lost by the earlier statement made by the first sergeant — " The major stopped. He became lost in thought for a moment.

Totally unexpectedly, the answer the old defender had been searching for came by way of something he had said to Briggs in the Officers' Club. He looked over at McClellan, the man to whom he had never spoken, shifted his weight, and said aloud, "I now understand, Sir." It was a simple statement that bespoke volumes.

"You wanted to be a soldier."

The chief defender did not elaborate.

McClellan knew that the major's statement had been directed to him, but he didn't know why. He turned the phrase over in his mind: *You wanted to be a soldier.* He still was not sure. Equally interesting was that the major had addressed him as *Sir.* Even more interesting, he had been somewhat deferential in the manner in which he said it.

The court was incensed by what the major had said, and by his delay. Brig. Gen. Hawley wouldn't comment. He made his feelings clear by tapping the gavel for the summation to continue. DeBerg acted as if he hadn't heard it. Possibly the sound had passed him by. He was deep into what he had said to Col. Briggs in the Officers' Club that night. *"I'm just a tired old North Carolina lawyer who many years ago made the mistake of thinking he could be a soldier."*

P. D. DeBerg never became a soldier.

There sat a black man who did.

The major withdrew the look and started his summation again.

"As I started to say to the court, much has been lost by that earlier statement made by the first soldier — and I do mean *soldier*, First Sergeant Obie O. McClellan. Much has been lost now by the actions of this naive young lad. Much has been lost by the standing of these other boys. It saddens me. I am saddened all the more by the repugnant notion that even before amassing all the evidence for trial, the Army had promised the citizenry back in Houston there would be executions in this case, regardless of the degree of guilt. *Executions regardless of the degree of guilt.* Think about that, Gentlemen. In a democracy, *executions* — regardless of the degree of guilt. What an outrage. What barbarity. Such is the quality of your justice, Mr. Trial Judge Advocate. 'In the interest of the nation,' you may now lead the sheep to slaughter.

"Now, then, without my assistant whom, as with these troops here, I foolishly did not support and whom I should have spoken up for earlier, and a person whom the court has seen fit to demean, berate, and insult, but, that aside, it is not for me to stand at this troubled moment and say that I have worked long and arduously for what I had hoped to be an adequate defense for these boys, for I have not. Nor has my search for fairness taken me well past many a midnight hour, as it should have. It did not. It is not now for me to stand in the sunlight of this court, cloaked in my still-not-totally-accepted Jewish ancestry, and say that — as you — I am without instinctive prejudice. I am not. Bigotry runs deep within me; it is a curse of nature. But, different from you, my innermost thoughts about the coloreds, and the march on Houston itself, would not have been permitted to rise to such an extent that they would have obscured the miscarriage of justice carried out by this court in this, the largest trial in the history of the Republic — and what is certain to be the largest execution in the history of the military. In the foregoing, if the sole purpose of a defender is to defend, I have lost nothing. On the contrary, I have gained. I will be better in the pursuit of justice — somewhere. If permitted by health, I will rise to defend again. I will rise because the Army has no intention of letting these remaining boys — and others of the Twenty-Fourth — go without being under the shadows of the gallows, or the recipients of some extended penalties of imprisonment. The gluttony of full revenge has yet to be served, and you will seek to serve it. Though in truth I am wont to say that it is this nation, the nation's military, and those imbued with the audacity to call themselves commanders of any station who should be on trial, we must move on. We move on because the underlying issue is still before us — ignore it if you will — but it is still before us, and before the nation as a whole. And that is this: Take this recently freed man, infuse him with the false and deadly pride of the military, arm him and promise him the glories of battle, speak to him of justice and equality, and then make him secondary. Compound it at a greater distance by subjecting him to less than he would receive on any plantation, and you shall always have your insurrections, perhaps not of this magnitude, but surely of sufficient strength and numbers as to forever cause heartbreak and discord. In a larger sense, in this view, I am not so much restricting my concern to these, the condemned — pressed by the contempt of a feared people, the outright cruelty of a lying and brutal police, the wrongful and surely shortsighted might of the military, and the outright abandonment of law and its jurisprudence — for the damage has already been done; the verdict, as I mentioned earlier, already in. I had only hoped to speak and dilute the sentences of the innocent; I had hoped to speak, too, for those who are *not* among us today, but who will someday be before a tribunal of some sort. But, here, now, on this day, before this body — in this hallowed place of God — I had hoped to speak. I had hoped to speak for those among us who are wallowing in ignorance and condemned by color. I had hoped to speak for those too disciplined to resist and too frightened to fall out when First Sergeant McClellan gave that awful, but understandable, order before marching: *if anybody falls out, shoot them.* For the different breed, the obviously guilty, those spurred by hatred and poisoned by position, there was not — nor shall there ever be — a defense *ever*, only the hope that society does not, and more importantly the military, will not cause or produce any more of them. For the innocent, those who did not have — and those who will not have — the choice of obeying or disobeying, following or not following, I had hoped to speak for them.

"May God have mercy on their souls."

Chapter 31

By tradition the fourth Thursday of November was observed to commemorate the feast held at Plymouth in 1621. For some it was marked by going to church and giving thanks to God for harvest and health. Those desirous of using Gift Chapel on this Thanksgiving could not do so. The chapel was still bedecked with all the trappings of a court, and on November 26th, nearly four weeks from the beginning of trial, Brig. Gen. Hawley's conflicting procedure had it that the findings and sentencing for the insurrectionists were to occur at 0800. No one was late.

Outside, it was gray. Inside, it was cold.

The sentences were to be final. In time of war it was not necessary for an authority higher than the department commander to review case or sentencing.

Brig. Gen. Hawley was on firm ground.

"May I remind you when sentences are announced, there will be no audible comments or demonstrations whatsoever. There will be absolute silence in the court."

Those were the words of the president that morning. He said them to an expectant court packed with spectators, officials and reporters.

Capt. Farrell was seated near the stove on the same front row he had sometimes occupied during trial. Lt. Col. Briggs had changed positions. He was behind the captain, and almost at the prosecution's side. Throughout trial, going or coming, Briggs made it a point to avoid the captain and looked toward the nape of his neck now only because it was unavoidable.

The feelings among the prisoners were mixed. None of them had slept during the night, yet the expected somberness and taut-ness were absent in court. Unlike before, with the bursts created by Boland's optimism, none had the feeling they would escape pun-ishment. A few missed Lt. Jennings. Still grabbing at straws, some felt that since they had been tried in a chapel it would still prove to be a good omen. Others believed that since the case against them was never proved with the required exactitude — at least in their view — the Army would come down on the side of leniency. Most thought they would be dishonorably discharged and that the Army would let it go at that.

A few of the 63, remembering bits of the prosecution's damning opening statement, had resigned themselves to the idea that they would receive prison sentences ranging up to 10 or 15 years. Twenty years would have been stretching it. Where any of the ideas along those lines came from is not known. The day before, on Thanksgiv-ing Day, when First Sgt. McClellan was asked by some of the men what he thought, he wouldn't comment directly. As he had done throughout trial, he maintained a reserved silence, saying only that whatever the Army meted out, they were to accept — and accept bravely. It was to be the same as if they had been on the front lines in Europe.

The First said it knowing full well that some of them were go-ing to die.

As the defense had said, the Army promised the people in Houston there would be executions in the case *"regardless of the degree of guilt."* What's more, the trial judge advocate had made it clear in his opening statement that some of them would die.

The only question in the First's mind was how many.

Long ago his premonition had said 13.

As Brig. Gen. Hawley leaned over to engage Brig. Gen. Wyman and two of his colleagues on a last-minute matter, Sgt. Yeager of the guard detail went over and handed McClellan a note he had received the previous evening. The contents of the note had an obviating effect. It removed the sergeant's look of impenetrability and replaced it with one of sadness. He fingered the note for a while, then bent over and looked down the line at Jody. He started to say something to the youngster, but decided against it. Resignedly he folded the note and placed it in his pocket. He was still holding onto the letter he had carried with him throughout trial. As the trial officers continued conferring with each other, every now and then he would read a line or two from the letter, then he would turn his head around to look at the rest of the men. They were quiet looks, brief and unreadable. They were not like the looks he was receiving from the major. DeBerg's looks to him were not unreadable and he knew why. The First, early on, could tell that the old defender had found out about his past. But it was not a worry, as it was too late for the Army to do anything about it now. Dismissing the thought, he noticed that the usual morning sunlight was no longer slipping through the stained glass windows.

Down from McClellan, Jody, in all his youthful innocence, was still with Pete, and Cpl. Poole, unusually relaxed, was seated prominently in the center on the first row of benches. Lost up top now, having been unseated from front row center, Simms sat next to Boland.

As the minutes ticked on and the wait for the trial board's findings grew longer, Boland's fear was coming on strong. His brutish hands were sweaty and itchy, and he was fidgeting. Simms was holding one of the hands, and he was attempting to hold it low and out of view of the first sergeant and the court.

The trio of Roosevelt, Menyard and Andrews were no longer seated together. Menyard had moved to the end of the middle section. Boot, Puerto Rico, Rochester and Yancy were seated close to each other on the second tier, and, while not totally composed, they did display a detached interest. Almost like Boland, Carter and Crawford were showing signs of becoming wrecks.

Withdrawing from the last-minute consultation with the other trial officers, and with a final word with an apparently dissenting Gen. Sudhenhow, the brigadier from Kentucky sat erect. He cleared his throat and looked sternly over the room before starting to read. To the prisoners he said in a taut voice, "When your name is called, you will stand."

The statement caused prisoners and spectators alike to tense.

The guards moved into position.

The brigadier read aloud.

"Master Sergeant McClellan, Obie O."

The first sergeant put on his glasses and stood. As he waited for the general's next words, he thought of a saying he had read when he had access to his books. *"Such is your luck, such you are called to see."* In his mind, he dedicated them to his men.

The general continued:

"Cpl. Poole, Theolonius
"Pfc. Carter, Nigeral O.
"Pfc. Simms, Adrian
"Pvt. Andrews, Gilbreet
"Pvt. Boland, Pervis
"Pvt. Cunningham, Jody
"Pvt. Grahm, Pedro, of Company I
"Pvt. Hicks, Puerto Rico
"Pvt. Rochester, Junius

"Pvt. Roosevelt, Bubba

"Pvt. Talley, Boot, of Company I.

"Pvt. Yancy, Calvin

The standing men were looked at closely. There were 13 of them. They were the 13 who had voluntarily stood earlier.

This time they had been called alphabetically by rank.

The President of the Court continued without solemnity or emotion. "The court finds you: Of specification One, and of Charge One, Guilty. Of Specification Two, and of Charge Two, Guilty. Of Specification Three, and of Charge Three, Guilty. The court, upon secret written ballot, two thirds of the members present concurring, sentences you, the accused, to be hanged by the neck until dead, dead, dead."

Involuntary gasps accompanied murmurs from the spectators, all uttered as if there could have been no holding back.

In the roped-off area, there were sounds, too. They were low. Carter, Crawford and a few others were sobbing. Boland's knees took a leave of absence. He would have gone completely down had it not been for Simms and the strong arms of Bubba Roosevelt.

Poole was standing with a kind of controlled defiance. Occasionally he would send an arm out to help Jody stabilize Pete. They were standing next to him. First Sgt. McClellan stood alone, his face impassive. Not so the faces of the men whose names had not been called. They were squirming with a certain relief covering their faces. Many thought sentencing was over.

They were wrong.

The President of the Court speared the silence and called 46 more names. Reluctantly the men stood. To them he said, "The court finds you: Of Specification One, and of Charge One, Guilty. Of Specification Two, and of Charge Two, Guilty. Of Specification Three, and of Charge Three, Not Guilty."

The brigadier added, "The court, upon secret written ballot, two thirds of the members present concurring, sentences you to be dishonorably discharged from the service of the United States Army, to forfeit all allowances due and to become due, and to be confined at hard labor at such place as the reviewing authority may direct for the term of your natural life."

The brigadier's voice snapped on. Three more men were now standing. "The court upon secret written ballot, two thirds of the members present concurring, sentences you to be dishonorably discharged from the service of the United States Army, to forfeit all allowances due and to become due, and to be confined at hard labor as such place as the reviewing authority may direct, for two and one half years."

To one lone person the court intoned, "To be confined at hard labor at such place as the reviewing authority may direct for a period of two years."

There were no acquittals.

In time of peace the President of the United States would have to approve executions. Not so now. The brigadier general ended the pronouncements by saying, "In time of war, the Forty-sixth Article of War authorizes department commanders to carry into execution sentences of death without reference to a higher authority. This court is now adjourned."

The brigadier general pounded his gavel.

Trial was over.

Caught off guard for a moment, Sgt. Yeager bounced back and immediately called *attention* to the already standing court. The man from Kentucky with the closely cropped hair, shortened frame, bulldog face, and small silver star on each epaulet of his tight-fitting tunic slid his chair back, stood, and scanned the court. He led the 13-member trial board away from the tables, down the aisle, and through the double doors. They moved with snap. After the board was fully out, the spectators started leaving. They cleared the chapel slowly and quietly.

Young Lt. Davies waited until the court was nearly empty, then directed Sgt. Yeager and the guards — now numbering 21 — to move the prisoners back to the stockade. They left through the rear door.

The 13 sentenced to die would later be separated and shipped to another camp.

After the prisoners were gone, a few of the spectators remained in court and did nothing but stare. No one mentioned it aloud, but by morning the modest A-frame building, dwarfed and aloof amid spacious grounds, would again be a chapel. The pulpit would be restored, the bibles would be back in place, the hymnals would be out, the religious icons would be up, and in two more days the pews would be occupied by military church-goers.

A spent Capt. Farrell was anchored to his seat. He couldn't move even to retrieve his overcoat. He hadn't looked at the prisoners as they left, but he thought about them. He decided that whether the Army would approve or not, he'd be with those sentenced to die at the end. As to his future with the military, he couldn't say. He'd give it more thought later.

Disturbed because Col. Briggs had moved down to a seat in front of him, Farrell finally summoned enough energy to move. He got his coat, nodded to the defender, and left the building.

The colonel, seemingly untouched by Farrell or anything that had happened in court, buttoned his coat and moved to DeBerg's table.

"Well, Pee," he said, attempting to glad-hand the defender, "at least you tried. Commitment to anything has never been one of your stronger suits, but you did make up your mind to come down on one side or the other — *finally*. And the speech? A little holy. But nice."

DeBerg said nothing. Inside he was angry. Briggs watched him as he packed more papers into his briefcase and repeated, "I said I loved your speech. You almost had me believing it. But I noticed you got carried away at one point. How did you phrase it? — those imbued with the audacity to call themselves commanders of any station who should be on trial.' Dangerous thinking, Sir. Very dangerous. I'm sure somebody is going to call you on it, but what exactly did you mean by that?'

"You figure it out."

"Then let me get to something that really touched me. It was that bit about your 'still-not-totally-accepted' Jewish ancestry. That almost had me in tears."

DeBerg was ready to leave. "Heinrich," he said, "your mother couldn't bring you to tears."

The Third Battalion commander chuckled and left without further comment.

Col. Boatner of the prosecution finished inserting folders and papers into his briefcase and looked thoughtfully over at the defense counsel. DeBerg, knowing that the prosecutor would soon be stopping by to talk, slowed his movements.

Boatner approached. "Charges have already been filed against the next group, Major. They're going to need a good defender. Can I expect to see you in that role?"

"Hell, no," DeBerg responded.

"Oh?"

"Not unless you're coming to my home in High Point, North Carolina."

"That sounds like retirement talk."

"It doesn't *sound* like retirement talk. It *is* retirement talk."

"But in your speech — well done, I thought — you said you would 'rise to defend again, because the Army has no intention of letting the remaining boys go.' I think I'm quoting you correctly."

"You are. I would love to've done that, Paul. But now that the passion of the moment has receded, disappointment, hardened arteries, inflammation of the joints, common sense, and practically everything else you can think of, tell me to get the hell out. And I also think in my speech I said I will stand *somewhere*. That doesn't mean it has to be here. Maybe I'll take a look at the coloreds in trouble in civilian life before I pass on. There's sure to be plenty of them. Attitudes in the country aren't about to change."

"But it seems to me you're going back on your promise."

"So what? The Army went back on theirs."

"I don't see it that way," Boatner said.

"You wouldn't. You engineered it."

"I did my job."

"Your job was to seek justice. Not wholesale executions. This is the *United States*, for God's sakes. This is the cradle of justice, the *home of equity*."

"There's no point in discussing our differing views, Major," Boatner said. "You're not going to change and neither am I. And, I'm proud to say, neither will the Army in its pursuit of law and order."

"Law is the very last thing you should be talking about, Colonel."

"Actually it should be first. And let me remind you, Major, at least there was a trial. Let me ask you, since the next trial is going to be about the same as this one was, if you're not going to be around who would you recommend we get to defend? And don't say that damned woman, even though I expect she'll be fighting to be on it. That is, if she's still in the Army and still has a commission after I file a report on her. I'm sure Hawley is going to do the same. We're not going to let her get away with that nonsense she's pulled."

"Then I recommend you don't get anyone — for the next trial, or the one after that."

"No one?"

"To do nothing," the major said, shuffling over to remove his coat from the coat rack. "Which would be just about one step beneath what I've done."

"Well, you were getting there."

"I wasn't getting anywhere. I wasn't worth a damn, and you know it," DeBerg said. "Common sense told me a long time ago that anything I might do wouldn't make a damned bit of difference anyway."

"Not true."

"Hogwash. Like you, Paul, the Army doesn't want a defender for coloreds. The Army wants people like me, people who are too old and too self-absorbed. Vague and indifferent people; people who wait much too long and far too late before they know what in the hell is going on. People like me, Colonel; people who should have jumped off or should have been thrown off the merry-go-round long ago. All we do is watch the ponies. At least McClellan took the coloreds for a ride. They didn't get anyplace, but at least they went for the ride. I suppose that's the main reason I became so fascinated with him. He was committed. That's something neither you, I, nor the country are accustomed to, Paul, a committed Negro, willing to lay down life and limb for a belief."

"And murder and revolt in the process."

"I am a long way, a *very* long way, from suggesting that McClellan was in the right. He was wrong. *Dead* wrong. He knows that. He said so. He stood in this court and *said* so. He was as wrong and as shortsighted as the military. As for the others, there is the question of following orders. It is a dilemma that will be around for as long as there is a military, for as long as there are leaders and followers. Either you or one of your witnesses said it best: 'blind, puppy-dog allegiance.' *Following orders.* That's what the troops were guilty of. That's all. That's what McClellan was guilty of instilling — blind, puppy-dog allegiance. But then again, if he was guilty, the Army has to be guilty. Ask yourself, what did the Army instill in him? McClellan became a man committed — *the military way.* He was so committed that this was his second time around in the military. Did you know that, Paul? No. No, you didn't. Why didn't I tell you when I found out? What kind of a trial would it have been with that hanging over his head? McClellan — or Pulham, as he was once known — was probably born seeking commitment. There's nothing wrong with that. But pride, race and the Army turned his commitment into a combustible dogma. Perhaps if he hadn't been the product of the military, the man and that prideful commitment to race could have taken on another form. And, if allowed — *if we had listened* — maybe from a man like that we all could have learned something."

"It's a damned good thing you're retiring."

Coat buttoned, the major tucked his briefcase under his arm and moved away a few steps. He turned back to the colonel, "Trial for the next bunch should be in about a month or so?"

"Something like that. But rest assured, Major, there will be a trial. And it will be speedy. Speedier than this one."

"I certainly hope so, Colonel. This was the largest murder trial ever held in the United States, and it was an embarrassment. It was charade, mockery at its highest. But let's not fret, Paul. It did have its benefits. It was held in a chapel — and that proves to the world that the Army of the United States is bigger than God Himself. But then it took almost four weeks to do it. *Four* whole weeks, Paul. My Lord! If word ever gets out that it took the U.S. Army that long to try sixty-three coloreds in a church — *sixty-three* coloreds in a church at the same time, mind you — why, it might set off another revolution! But I think I have a solution for you. For the next batch, why even have a trial? We know what the outcome will be. Why not just have some photographers show up for the lynching? Take pictures of it. Lots of them. Plaster 'em all over the country. Make it front-page news. But be consistent, Paul. Don't call them soldiers. Call them what they are. Do that, and then caption your photographs with something like *Crows*... No. No. A man of your brilliance and sensitivities can do better than that. What was that fancy term you used to describe them? *Mimus polyglottus?* Nice. I was impressed. Now, how would you label your photographs to get the point across? Let's see now. How about something like 'Goodbye, Mimus polyglottos'? *Farewell to the mockingbirds.* That's it. And between you and I, there's a little bonus hidden there. Mockingbirds will even attack people.

"*Farewell to the mockingbirds,*" the old defender said, leaving. "I like that. It says it all. But whatever your caption, Paul, treat it like you've treated justice. Do that, and I'll guarantee you it'll achieve the desired effect. It'll sure as hell teach the other niggers to stay at home."

Chapter 32

December came, and with it some changes. For all intents and purposes, King Company was no more. The decision as to how long it would remain on inactive status hadn't been made. The men of King Company, and there were only a few who weren't in the stockade awaiting the second trial, were transferred to Companies I and L. Columbus was still the home of the Third Battalion, but it had undergone change. No longer could one hear loud cadence-calling or spirited marching. Everything was subdued.

Col. Briggs was no longer in New Mexico. He had been reassigned to the Eighth Illinois. Although it was denied because of the nation's emergency, he had, upon arriving at the sprawling post, immediately applied for retirement. The Eigth Illinois (Colored) was scheduled to go overseas.

The stockade at Fort Bliss, El Paso, Texas became the new home of the prisoners. It was a secure, colorless place, and the 13 men who had been sentenced to die had a section all their own. They were rarely seen or heard by those already imprisoned there, or by the remaining 50 from King Company who were still waiting to be shipped to a federal penitentiary in Kansas.

For the short period all of them were expected to be at Fort Bliss, there wasn't much activity. McClellan, confined to another section, but with access to the 12, had told them that they were to relax as much as possible, think pride until the end, and keep their spirits up. He told them that they had every right to be afraid but that they shouldn't appear weak before the guards, nor should they feel weak in any way. Weakness, he said, was cowardly, and they had done nothing cowardly. In the end, he promised, they would find a way to triumph over tragedy.

It was not that the young men had lost faith in their leader. They hadn't, and they wouldn't. But with death staring them in the face without appeal, it was hard to imagine how triumph could overcome tragedy. And so the First's words held for a while, but, in the main, the condemned slipped back into a disheartened state. They were not helped by the news that the French had just executed a woman — Mata Hari — for spying. She hadn't killed anyone. They had. If the French could execute a white woman for doing less than they had done, one of the men opined, then it was certain all was lost here. The speaker got no argument.

Gloom settled heavier.

In the mornings the men woke up in cold tents, tried to eat the beef and beans that had been prepared for them, and milled around. Noon didn't bring about much change. In the evenings, those who had developed appetites ate, then went back to their cots to toss, turn and wrestle with sleeplessness.

Most times, late in the evenings, and sometimes during the day, Carter, still wanting to please his First before the end by finding *The Battle Hymn of The Republic*, would pull out his harmonica and idly float something close to the melody up and down the dimly lit aisle. Occasionally the men welcomed the searching. Often they did not. It wasn't because the playing intruded upon conversations. The men didn't talk much. They rarely huddled in groups and talked among themselves. They never talked about hometowns, families, friends, places they had been, or places they wished they had seen. They didn't talk about the war, training, marching or the great reputation King Company once had. And, as if they had never been there, Houston never came up. Nothing interested them. The harmonica intruded upon nothing.

To some it could have seemed that the First had backed off too much. He hadn't. He didn't expect the men to be buoyant, but he had instructed Poole to keep an eye on them, and he managed to give them an occasional talk. The talks, while short, effectively kept the men out of the depths of depression. To help, he also had Poole resurrect the morning and afternoon calisthenics. Exercise was good for the mind.

In backing off, McClellan held two thoughts in mind that he was sure would be of benefit. Ironically, one was to go over the execution in great detail. He felt that talking about the end would release pent-up emotions. His other idea concerned the letter from Sgt. Newton he had promised Sgt. Dukes he would read.

In the chapel, when staring at the stained glass windows, McClellan often thought about his old friend. The connection was religious. It was interesting because before being tried in the chapel neither he nor Field Sgt. Dukes had ever been on the inside of a church. They had never opened a bible, didn't know one hymn, nor had they ever been on their knees in prayer. Like Dukes, McClellan did have an unshakable belief in the Man Upstairs. He felt that He would understand their lack of traditional participation and would welcome them home when the time came. It was this philosophy that enabled him to get over Dukes's death. He knew early on that he would be seeing the old sergeant again, and he thought it would be soon. He remembered thinking he was going to see him in death the night they marched back to Camp Logan after the uprising. He glossed over it, but he thought he was going to be shot once he was inside the gate.

Obie McClellan didn't know if he feared death. Other than his mother and father who passed when he was a child, and except for Sgt. Dukes and Toho Fujiyama, the troubled young Japanese who had taken his life back in Columbus, and, of course, excusing Houston, the First actually hadn't seen much death. He was ready for it, but he didn't know if he actually feared it.

It was not necessarily a new thought for the first sergeant. Often while training the troops, particularly when the company had been handed down the used machine guns a few years back, he thought of the ease of killing in war, which, as a matter of course, led to thoughts of how easy it was to *be* killed in war. For a long time, he thought there was a certain nobility attached to both. But here, facing the end, all dignity and honor had been stripped away. That nakedness was bound to be surrounded by fear. He didn't want to be fatalistic, but truth held that if you live, you must die. The only trouble was that here, death would come because of a court edict. Unlike in war, or as it had been when wonderful Sgt. Dukes met his death and at that moment or two when he had lost rationale in the fields, he was directly responsible for having the ignoble arms of death enfold a group of young men who truly belonged elsewhere.

The Army didn't know these young men. He did. And all along he had felt that not knowing them had been the Army's and the country's loss. There was something wonderful about each and every one of them, and for the nation not to have seen them at their best was as big a tragedy as anything. This the First did not like to think about.

Remarkably since being there at El Paso, there had been no outward bursts from the men, and none of the faces were bloated with tears and fear. Death did not command the eyes. But fear had to be a factor. As the scaffold hour grew closer, fear was going to be an even larger factor. It was inescapable. It could not be eliminated, but it could be dealt with. The most effective way, thought the First, was to establish preoccupation, to have something else to take precedence over the chilling thoughts of the end.

Even if it had to be masked or coated or buffered by the now artificial call of a higher duty, something had to be done beyond exercising in the yard and giving the occasional talk.

As he had done before, the First permitted his mind to momentarily leave the confines of the stockade and drift all the way back to his days just before he left college, back in Tuskegee. Rarely did he think of the all-black Alabama institution, but he was trying to remember what it was like when he was in his mid-20's, which, except for Poole, who was 38, was the average age of his men. If he had had to face death in his 20's, what would have braced him? What could have been said or done to ease the mind of young Oliver B. Pulham? There would be no answer, because young Oliver B. Pulham was of a different mindset. His mind had already been seized by the military.

This time the First did not remain thinking of his two years in college for long. In going back to the early years, though, he thought of another New Englander. In such a reflective moment, the brief and long-ago romance with Flora Pound should have come to mind, but it didn't. It was not that he had completely dismissed her. He hadn't. She was tucked somewhere deep in the heart, and he always prided himself on knowing that if they had ever married he would have been faithful and true to her until the end.

But, ironically, McClellan thought of Harriet Beecher Stowe. Moreover, he thought of what President Abraham Lincoln had reportedly said upon meeting the widely acclaimed author: "So, you're the little woman who made this great war."

Many agreed that *Uncle Tom's Cabin* had had a great deal to do with bringing the issue of slavery to the nation's conscience. And now, 55 years later, McClellan and his men were going to die because the nation's conscience was still an issue. What irony, he thought.

According to some of the men, still livid over the testimony given by Sgts. Odums and Williams, they were going to die because of two Uncle Toms.

That was an even bigger irony.

Harriet Beecher Stowe notwithstanding, the First found nothing else in his past that would serve the moment. He came back. He thought about what had started it all. What did it mean? How did he get there? Before marching, Col. Briggs had used the term "anarchist." The prosecution had also used the term. As contrary as it might have appeared to the whites, neither he nor his men were anarchists.

McClellan could never see himself as anarchist. A true anarchist, he believed, had been Nat Turner. He was a long way from agreeing with the man and, from what he had read, he really didn't like him. He admired Harriet Tubman because of her life-on-the-line, unflagging courage in conducting the underground railroad for escaping slaves. Excusing Fredrick Douglas, the First's all-time favorite was almost a contemporary, Tuskegee's Dr. George Washington Carver. Southern industry would be saved because of the brilliance of this quiet and dignified man who was born a slave. But Turner entered into the sergeant's thinking because far back in history he had suffered a similar fate, and, as an exercise he began to toss the revolutionist's last words over in his mind. He recalled that they had been written in prison while Turner was awaiting execution.

It led the First to wonder how much of a similarity there was.

Turner was a quixotic slave leader and preacher who sought to take over Jerusalem, Virginia, in 1831. He and his band had killed 57 whites and caused 55 blacks to be executed and another 200 to be lynched. Turner, before his execution, wrote, *"I saw white spirits and blacks spirits engaged in battle and the sun was darkened — the thunder rolled in the heavens, and blood flowed in streams. And I heard a voice saying 'Such is your luck, such you are called to see.'"*

There was a similarity.

Blood flowed in Houston. To combat the fear, the first sergeant had already thought about rehearsing his men for the thunder of the heavens.

Nothing could be done to eradicate what they had done in Houston, and to some of the on-looking whites who would be at the site, staring silently up at the gallows, even the act of hanging was not good enough. And thunder or not, no one needed to be reminded that these people had been led by this strange man, this man who was neither fleshy nor muscular and whose receding hairline of kinky gray made him appear too old for the rigors of first sergeant, yet who was the insurrectionist leader that had masterminded chaos and anarchy.

With his black skin and broad negretic features this man, they were sure to say, was the epitome of wrong, the incarnation of evil itself. He had been blessed with a mind and an ability to read, grasp, interpret and lead. He could have led in the American way, but he chose not to. He decided he would become the very symbol of everything not good in America. He was the symbol of every-thing that was to *become* not good in America. And the defense attorney had, for once, been right in saying that he hoped the Army would not see his kind again. And even if the others had not been sentenced to die, he should have been — he and that black, arro-gant corporal up there with him. It should be just as the President of the Court had said: hanged by the neck until dead, dead, dead. Three times, said the brigadier general. Three times the man should die. The sentence was justified because this man was the architect of rebellion. The defense in his closing said he hoped to stand for all those who will someday be before a tribunal of some sort. Well, the on-lookers were sure to think, not if there are no more McClellans.

Chapter 33

As the unknown date of execution grew closer, the troops who had received prison terms were in a kind of distant suspension over the 13 who were scheduled to die and whom they had soldiered with, some for two or three years or longer. Only a few words were spoken. Undoubtedly some of them would like to have said more. Perhaps they had intended to say more to their condemned comrades, but now they were unable to do so. A week earlier the 50 who had received the prison sentences were shipped to Kansas in the middle of the night. They were ordered to be quiet. There were no good-byes.

Having put the Battle Hymn of the Republic on hold for a short while, two days before the end Carter was on his cot, playing *Near The Cross.*

There was something about the old gospel hymn that sounded prophetic, even though the lyric was more baptismal and thematic than anything else. The song reminded Carter of something he had thought of earlier when they were informed that their end would come "sooner than expected." He thought about it again. He stopped playing and said to no one in particular, "I wonder if we ever gonna get to see a chaplain."

If Carter was heard, no one responded.

Crawford had saved his lid from a sardine can and was quietly trying to dry-shave. Puerto Rico gave him a pained look and asked him if he knew something the rest of them didn't know.

"Just wanna look my best," came the answer.

Junius Rochester lifted his head to a cot down the line. "Pedro, you and Boot done finally made it to King Company."

"Yea, Man," Pedro Grahm said with surprising gladness. "An' feelin' good about it. You glad, Boot?"

"Yep," said Boot Talley. He was munching on a strip of beef jerky he had saved from a previous meal.

Yancy noticed that Boland had gotten up from the cot and walked to the tent's entrance, leaving Simms sitting alone. He was stopped by a bayoneted guard. Resignedly, he returned to the middle of the tent and simply stared into space.

"What was you lookin' at, Boland?"

"I was just tryin' to exercise my legs. An' I want'd to see if I could see the sarge out there." He sat and shoved two hands under a chin that held an all-too-heavy head. "An' I was thinkin' maybe somebody would be comin' with the mail." Then he mused to himself, "I'd sure like to hear from her just one more time."

Simms, on the next cot over, heard it. He knew who Boland was talking about. Colette. It was the girl he was going to marry. Simms had always wondered what she looked like. Pretty, he thought. Colette. She certainly had a pretty name. In a way, Simms thought it was too bad she would never get to see her soldier again. He wondered if she'd miss the adorable bear as much as he would.

Responding to Boland, Roosevelt and Andrews, the two remaining members of the rhyming trio, tried to get a rhyme going but were unable to think of anything new. They went back to an old standby.

"Mail — . Mail — . Mail — .
You can't read an' yo' momma can't write —
If it wont for the Army,
You pickin' cotton all nite."

It didn't sound the same. It was lacking in timing and efferves-
cence. They missed the traitor Menyard. Not sentenced to die, he
was among those who received life at hard labor. The sentence did
nothing to ease the hurt of the two. They spent their time quietly
wondering why he had not stood with them in court.

As crude as it was, the offering by Roosevelt and Andrews did
highlight another pitiful fact. Despite McClellan's attempts at teaching during the trouble-free days in Columbus, most of the men still
couldn't read or write. If Simms or Carter or John Chin or a few
others didn't write for them, or if they didn't manage to go home on
pass, which was not at all frequent because of distance and lack of
funds, they were virtually without communication. Analphabetism
took its toll both ways. Any number of family and friends back
home couldn't read or write either, and it often happened that when
a young man left home, he left home and communicating with home
for the duration of his military stay. Sometimes the simple act of
not knowing their own home addresses contributed to the problem.

Digesting Andrews and Roosevelt's half-hearted effort, Jody, as
innocent as ever, thought about his plight, and his mother's. He
didn't know his home address. Certainly he was not alone, but he
was heard to say, "My momma don't know where I'm at. I'd sure
like to wish her a Merry Christmas in a couple of weeks."

It would have been interesting if First Sgt. McClellan had heard
him. Earlier that morning the First went into the tent and called
his young soldier aside to have a talk with him. Besides praising
him, he wanted to talk to him about his mother, but he cut the

conversation short.

A number of men were surprised at what Jody said. They had forgotten it was that time of year. To some, it didn't make any difference. Before the Army, they never had anyone with whom to share the holiday.

• • •

All along the First was mentally mapping additional plans for the end. Now it was quickened. He didn't know the date, but he knew it would be soon.

He was right.

December 10th came with a suddenness, sudden because it seemed to have come from out of nowhere, and sudden because it came with the news late that morning that Maj. Gen. Hilliard Laird, the department commander, had approved the findings of the court. Within minutes, the first sergeant of Company K was informed that he and his men were to be executed at sunrise.

It was ever so abrupt. A jolt, really. But then again, it wasn't. The First accepted the news without a display of emotion. Escorted by a guard, he went at once to the tent where the men were. He broke the news matter-of-factly to the last of his company, and made certain that his voice was devoid of stress or strain. He was direct and thorough as he told the men not to be ashamed, and if necessary, to find comfort in each other. He spoke of character and honor and said he was proud of the way they had conducted themselves throughout the entire ordeal. Saying nothing more, he moved Poole aside and spoke briefly with him. After that he went outside and spent the rest of the day alone, away in the farthest corner of the stockade. At noon his guard came over and asked him if wanted to eat. The First declined the offer. He had already eaten his last meal on earth.

Later, a quieted Poole gave the men a talk, and following McClellan's orders, at 1400 he ordered them into a rehearsal. They did so with remarkable restraint and obedience. It was a strange sight watching twelve men moving back and forth, practicing until late afternoon the steps to hang from the gallows.

That evening, they tried to eat what would be their last meal.

Only three were able to do so.

Poole, Jody, Pete and Simms were the only ones who slept at all that night.

Chapter 34

Very early on that next morning a frost crawled over Texas and a peculiar chill hovered over the stockade. Away from the tents, away in the farthest corner of the stockade yard, McClellan could be seen under the big lights. He had been up for hours. With his arms draped behind him and his fingers curled around the watch Sgt. Dukes had given him, he was gazing out into the nothingness.

Daylight was still hours away. The quiet man was moving slowly and thoughtfully in the strange cold. Trailing him now was a guard, but the first sergeant was a man alone, wandering in the frost, slow and easy, no hat, shirt opened, unshaved and, like his men, needing a bath.

When the moment came, the stockade's big, thick gate creaked open and Capt. Farrell entered. Trailing him were Lt. Davies and a sergeant of the guards who had replaced Sgt. Yeager. Close on their heels were four more guards who augmented the six guards already there.

As the new guards stopped in front of the big tent, two of them were laboring with a trunk which resembled a footlocker. As they allowed it to drop in front of the tent, it gave off a loud and distinct clank. Even though he knew what was in the trunk, Capt. Farrell gave a small, chilled reaction at the sound. He slowly continued to where he saw the first sergeant, his back turned, in the far corner. Farrell had left the lieutenant behind. He knew the young officer was going to poke his head into the tent and say to the men inside, "It's time." It would be that simple.

McClellan, lost in thought, was still looking in the opposite direction when the captain approached. They hadn't seen each other since the trial. They hadn't talked since Houston.

The First turned and saw the captain approaching under the stockade lights. He gave him a small, almost surprised look and saluted. It wasn't a snappy salute. It was one of pleasantry. Farrell smiled. When he was close enough, he responded by extending his hand for a handshake.

"It's good to see you, Sergeant."

McClellan put the watch away and shook the captain's hand. "It's good to see you, Sir." His voice was low, barely above a whisper.

The captain was surprised at the sergeant's obliging demeanor. He had expected at least a touch of bitterness and rancor to accompany the unexpected unkemptness of the once proud, neat man.

The First knew that the captain didn't know what to do or say after the greeting, so he helped him. "How is the war effort?"

"We're winning."

"I'm surprised," McClellan said, calling on a humor he never used.

"The Negro units are helping," Capt. Farrell added, pleased by the thought.

"Negroes in Europe," McClellan said reflectively. "That's what I call real good news."

"I can give you a little more of the same," the captain said. "Because of Houston, Colonel Briggs is in a world of trouble. He's been trying to retire."

"Will they let him?"

"No. His papers were held up. Because of the war I doubt if he could have gotten out, anyway. Then he was supposed to be on his way to Europe with the 8ᵗʰ Illinois, but those orders were rescinded."

"The 8ᵗʰ Illinois is a Negro unit."

"I know."

"He really must be an angry man now."

"He'll be facing charges soon."

"Maybe now you won't have to give me my orders of demotion."

The captain laughed. "You don't mind if I take a little more time to think about that, do you?"

"Take your time, Captain. Take your time."

"I wish I had all the time in the world."

"Considering the circumstances, I wish you did, too."

Farrell smiled. So did McClellan.

After a moment the First asked, "You think the colonel will be out there?"

"Oh, I'm sure he'll find a way. He'll be there if he has to walk from Illinois."

"I've always found the colonel interesting."

"Why?"

"His manner. The way he strutted around with nothing ever touching him. I'd always wondered if he was a peacock or an ostrich, whether he thought he was above it all or whether he was content to have his head buried in the sand."

"If I were asked, I'd say he was more like the former. And you?"

"The latter."

"I'll tell you something I'd noticed," Farrell said. "I don't think I've ever heard the colonel refer to the men as soldiers. He'd use the word 'troops' when he had to, but never 'soldier.' In fact, I don't believe I ever heard him say 'men.'"

Silence came. McClellan reflected aloud. "December 1917. In the world's first great war. Negroes on the battlefield."

"They're attached to the French Divisions."

"I wonder how they are doing?"

"From what I hear, excellent."

"That's wonderful. Magnificent."

"Have you always wanted to be a soldier, Sergeant?"

The first sergeant broke his trend of thought. "Strange you should ask, Captain. I was just thinking about that a few minutes ago. But no. Being a soldier was not exactly a burning thing in my youth, growing up in Rhode Island. But I did manage to find out the Army offered a spirit of adventure and a sort of isolation or refuge, if you will, from a country that seemed to've had nothing better to do than to constantly remind you of your second-class citizenship."

"And that doesn't happen in the Army?"

"Well, yes. Yes, it does. The military is only an extension of the country. But here, at least, there is purpose."

"And war."

In rethinking his feelings about not always wanting to be a soldier, the First wanted to amend his answer. He had always loved the military. He didn't go back to rectify the reply, because he felt that it would lead to a deeper conversation and he would then have to explain the change of name and all that went with it, even though it was possible Maj. DeBerg had already revealed the secret.

The First came up with another thought. "Captain," he said, toeing in the cold, hard dirt, "I've always felt you never really wanted to go overseas. I never got the feeling that it was because of us, even though I know there are a lot of officers who wouldn't feel comfortable being with Negroes on the front lines."

"I know. Colonel Briggs is one of them."

"He has a lot of company," the First said. He shifted back to the question that had troubled him from the very first time he heard his C.O. speak. This time he was more direct. "Captain, are you a pacifist, Sir?"

At first the captain was hesitant, but then, as if he no longer had to hide anything admitted, "Let's put it this way. I was raised a Quaker, I'm now proud to say. I believe they were among the original pacifists."

"They can't be all bad," smiled the First. "During slavery they sided with the abolitionists."

"I didn't know that."

McClellan smiled and shook his head in irony. "But this is something. This is really something. A pacifist in charge of troops who, after all is said and done, are going to hang because they wanted to go to war. What a world."

"I detest war," the captain said, finally revealing the truth. "And, no, my mind was made up at the time. I would not have gone."

"Maybe they'd better bring a rope for you."

"I'm white."

Both men laughed. They had to. It was getting too somber, so McClellan said, "I think all sane men fear war. It's only a strange sense of bluster and bravado that causes us to say differently. But your secret is safe, Captain."

"I'd like to thank you for me and my family, but it's no longer a secret. Colonel Briggs knew about it, and, therefore, so did a lot of others. My hearing is next week."

"What are you going to do?"

"I don't know."

"Even a pacifist should know that for some people there is equality in war."

"I don't know if I agree with that or not."

"That's because you have nothing to prove," the First said conversationally. "You are not, to quote the trial judge advocate, a beast or cowardly rot from the jungle. You are not primitive and vulgar. You are not a scab masquerading as a soldier, nor a mimic of one. You are not the morally corrupt, or the intellectually inferior."

"The trial judge advocate was wrong in saying those things."

"The prosecution merely said what others believe. Whites are oblivious, and will always assume we are less. It is up to us to know we're more."

"It's rotten that things have to be that way."

"They don't *have* to be that way," the First said easily. "We've all got a lot to learn. For instance, I wonder if most blacks know just how difficult a lot of whites have it."

"How difficult the *whites* have it?"

"Yes. Think about it. There are about a billion African descendants covering the face of the earth. It's got to be hell trying to hate a billion people."

Farrell offered no comment. He looked up at the moths and the other winter-defying insects fluttering around the big arc light, and back down at the sergeant. "I've got a question: are you satisfied with what you've done?"

Answering was not easy. "I regret what I had to do. I regret, very deeply, the loss of life, the harm inflicted upon others. I regret the sacrifice these young men have made — and all the others who will be in prison for the rest of their lives. It is hurtful to know that they will not grow to make a contribution. I don't like the fact they will not become leaders — fathers. Leadership and responsible fathers are sadly lacking in this race of ours. I'm afraid we will always suffer from that. And to that end, we can look elsewhere, but the fault will always be ours — and ours alone. And in this case — mine."

"And Houston?"

"As far as Houston is concerned, something had to be done."

"Do you think there will be more Houstons?"

"Always. Perhaps not to this extreme. Maybe even worse, I don't know — but something will always have to be done. The struggle for racial equality, the fight for manhood and dignity in this country is not a momentary thing. It'll be around for as long as there is an America."

Again, the captain didn't quite know what to say. McClellan relieved him of the discomfiture by asking if he knew anything about the rest of the men.

"I've been back to Houston and saw the rest of the men who've been charged, they're doing fine, under the circumstances. The few others have already been transferred. I also had the chance to visit the penitentiary at Ft. Leavenworth, Kansas."

"How did you manage to do that?"

"Through the inspector general's office, with the help of Major DeBerg. Lieutenant Jennings helped a lot," the captain said. "Major DeBerg — he retired, by the way — but before leaving he said the word is, the results of the next trial won't be quite as bad as this."

"I should hope not," the First said soberly. "It really isn't deserved. For thirteen men — when there should've been only one — two, including Poole. But for thirteen men to be sentenced to death in a chapel in Texas doesn't do much for the image of God — or the military, for that matter."

"As a Quaker," the captain said, then corrected himself, "as a former Quaker, an Inner Light Quaker, really, I thought to hold the real trial in a chapel was really going overboard. But I'm told the reason why they held it there was because it was the largest facility around."

"I'll mention that to God as I'm passing through."

"Do you think God will want to hear from you after you've led the march on Houston? Where innocent people were killed?"

"I take no pride in that, Captain. None at all."

"But as to what I was asking, whether or not God will want to hear from you?"

"It was a good question, Captain," McClellan said, provoked to a deeper seriousness. "A very good question. I don't know if I can answer that now."

While the captain was wondering what else to say, Lt. Davies came over with two of the guards.

"It's time," the lieutenant said. He was respectful. McClellan broke his thoughts. "And we're due to hang at sunrise?"

"0517. At a clearing in the woods."

"Lieutenant, a week ago I made a request for the company guidon —"

"The request was denied by the departmental commander. No flags, banners or insignias."

"I'm sorry to hear that," the First said. He again toed at the hard ground beneath a foot that had been quiet. "Back in Columbus when I had access to my books and pamphlets, I became interested in a couple of young organizations. One was called the National Association for the Advancement of Colored People, and the other, I believe, was The National Urban League. Have you ever heard of them, Lieutenant?"

"No, Sergeant," the lieutenant answered, knowing full well the sergeant knew better.

"Have you, Captain?"

"No, I haven't," Capt. Farrell said, feeling as uncomfortable as the lieutenant.

McClellan continued. "I imagine the Army has tried to keep this thing somewhat of a secret, but I managed to get word that they and one or two other Negro organizations have found out about it and have requested attendance —"

"Disallowed," the lieutenant said before the question was completed.

"The colored newspapers?"

"Disallowed."

"No Negro witnesses?"

"That is correct. No Negroes or coloreds."

McClellan gave him a wry look. "Is there a difference?"

"I couldn't tell you," replied the young officer. "The Army just wants to make sure all bases are covered."

"I get the feeling the Army would like for us to be dead before we die. But we'll hang on."

They were off.

At the tent, the guards had ordered the men out into the frost and were already connecting the chilled leg irons that had been removed from the trunk. When McClellan arrived, two of the guards moved to do the same to him. The First waved them off. With the lieutenant's agreement, the guards backed off.

McClellan stepped forward to address the men. First he took another look at the chains and leg irons, and by the impuissant stream of light that slithered from the tent he searched their faces and tried to brush away humiliation.

Farrell and Davies stood to the side.

"Gentlemen," began the sergeant, his voice low and instructional, his manner urbane, "however wrong I was in leading you to this point, and whatever the Army's, and the country's yet greater wrong, I must ask that you keep in mind you are not so much going to your deaths as you are refuting certain beliefs about us as a people, and that no matter what the adversity, our heads will remain unbowed. As soldiers, we will soldier to the very end. Nothing should ever deter us from that, not the military, not the people who will always be against us, not even the sometimes troubling voice of our own black, hot-headed bourgeoisie. Do you read me, Corporal Poole?"

"Very loud and very clear, Sergeant."

"Now, before leaving New Mexico, Gentlemen, I spoke to you about the insurrection in Brownsville back in 1906 and how, by order of President Theodore Roosevelt, an entire battalion of our boys were dishonorably discharged from service without trial. I said, too, that there was talk of never letting any of us wear the uniform of a United States soldier ever again. But that did not happen, and, as you can tell, even by the presence of brave young Jody here, our people are now being drafted. We are restricted, we have not been accorded the simple dignity of man, the nation is still more than suspicious of our courage, but we are still here. It is not an overstatement to say that there will always be those who will wish — and will try — to get rid of us in any fashion they can. It is not overstating the case, either, to say that there will always be those who, seeing only the worst in us, will discourage progress. But we will not be stopped. We will always be here, forever ready to prove our worth and allegiance to a growing nation. It is not to say that as a people we are without fault. Like the country itself, like the whites themselves, we have fault, and we have it in a most shameful and debilitating degree. There is fault in our ignorance of the world around us, and of our own history; fault in our ever-declining moral values; fault in our penchant for the shallow and self-defeating; fault in those of us who use our race for detestable and self-serving ends, and fault in our blind acceptance of it — as well as allowing charlatans to be cloaked as leaders. There is fault in our continued satisfaction with less than our God-given rights, fault and ignorance in our failure to unite and fully value ourselves, and to walk with dignity and inspire our young and pay tribute to our old, we, as a people, are not without fault. But, again, we are still here; and, again, we will be here. In the military we are not that many now, but in the days and years to come, our ranks will grow. There will be a true coming of the troops — a coming of all the troops — even from the best of us, our women. In one way or another, the American white woman has served the services since 1775, winning, even, the Congressional Medal of Honor. They will one day be called upon to do even more. Ours will serve, too — officially — as nurses, and as canteen workers, and maybe one day even as flyers in this new aero-plane I've read so much about. Led by the Alpha Kappa Alphas and the Delta Sigma Thetas, and other colored sororities and organizations, the black woman will serve in areas you and I have never dreamed of. She will not always be undervalued and ignored. As the African proverb says, 'touch a rock, start an erosion; touch the black woman and start an ava-lanche.' The black woman's day is coming. Along with that accep-tance and change there will be many others. The complexion of

America will change. Our borders will be lowered, and ships the world over will one day flood the nation's ports, but it is a sad truth that it is our people who must be vigilant, as our stock will not rise in the eyes of many. Few from abroad will hold us in high regard, and in the main we will continue to stand alone. It will be so, too, that the colored man, weakened at home and not knowing his place in the world, will be sacrificed on the field of battle proportionately more than any other race, for the nation will come to learn that this war, and all the wars to come, cannot — and will not — be restricted to honor and glory alone, for when all is said and done, war is nothing but death in the marketplace. No matter how noble the aim or how just the cause, war is death in the marketplace, and neither prophet nor poet, soldier nor scholar can change that. War, Gentlemen, is death in the marketplace."

The man with the lowered voice paused, dug into his shirt pocket, and extracted the letter he had carried with him since leading his men to what would be buried in history as the Houston Insurrection.

Continuing, he said, "It does not serve me well, as, in the interest of soldering, I have lived a lie. But I should now tell you that under different names, good Sergeant Dukes, myself, and a Sergeant James Newton, a once brilliant field sergeant now reduced to serving as an orderly for the white troops in France, were all once members of that battalion I spoke of in the 25th Infantry Regiment. It is ironic, but on the day of our march on Houston, I received a letter from the former field sergeant, a letter which I suppose made an indirect contribution to our being here now. I would like to share a portion of it with you, as I had promised Field Sergeant Dukes.

"My friend, and a friend, I might add, whom I've known since way back in college — where we both became followers of the late, great Frederick Douglass there in Tuskegee, Alabama, begins by saying that he and some other orderlies, and stevedores, ditch and grave diggers, some having been doctors, and teachers, and lawyers in civilian life, and other colored professionals who had volunteered for the cause, were very excited because they had finally made their way overseas. They arrived in France on the United States battleship Virginia. They were, of course, segregated aboard ship, but before getting even close to shore the ship's executive officer had them removed on the grounds that an Act of Congress once barred coloreds from serving in the United States Navy, and as a result no coloreds had ever sailed to a foreign country aboard a United States naval vessel. My friend, and all the other coloreds in the service of their country, were accordingly removed to a tugboat. Over there to dig trenches and tunnels, they were called sappers and mudlarks.

"My old friend from Tuskegee Institute goes on to say that even though they were odd-looking to the French, odd enough for some of the French to want to feel their skin, and almost as with the Sudanese and Senegalese of Africa, they wanted to turn them around to look at their rear ends to see where and how their tails grew. It is all the more strange because France has had colored troops ever since it has had colonies. But the American coloreds were nonetheless welcomed. Immediately thereafter, a United States Army Divisional Order Number 40 was issued, proclaiming the following — and is herewith quoted:

'It is important for French officers to have an idea of the position occupied by the colored race in the United States. The coloreds are a menace of degeneracy. They are designed to play inconspicuous roles of laborers. The black man as a citizen of the United States is regarded as inferior. He is noted for his lack of civic discretion and professional conscience. Among other things, he is given to the loathsome vice of criminally assaulting women. The French, therefore, are called upon not to treat the coloreds *with familiarity and indulgence. To do so would be an affront to national policy. French officers are advised to prevent the rise of intimacy between them — that is to say, they are not to eat, seek, talk, or even shake hands with the coloreds. And while it is all right to commend the good service qualities of the coloreds, French officers are asked not to commend them too highly in the presence of any and all whites.*"

The first sergeant returned the letter to his shirt pocket. "Divisional Order Number 40 was from the headquarters of the commanding general of the American Expeditionary Forces, General John J. 'Black Jack' Pershing.

"Gentlemen, the general represents the best that a great country has to offer. But despite all things said by man — here and elsewhere — we, the coloreds, are a great people. Much to learn, and a long way to go, but we are a great people. God would not allow us to endure as much if we were not.

"As colored soldiers, you and I must endure a bit more. The time has come for us to carry out the sentences of the court. This morning we must die. The prosecution said it is in the national interest. You and I know better. You and I know, too, that there is nothing unique in the act of dying, though not welcomed, death is but our Father's final earthly signature. Having the privilege of choice, at the clearing in the woods our government has prepared for us, we will go to our deaths representing the greatness of our race, the dignity we hold as men, the distinction of our soldiering, and knowing well our only aim was to serve the country honorably."

Chapter 35

First Sgt./Master Sgt. Obie O. McClellan and Lt. Davies spoke of the clearing in the woods. It was not a clearing in the truest sense. The site was on a military reservation, about eight miles northeast of Camp Travis, and long before the men arrived, a bonfire was cutting through the stilled and darkened trees, kicking at the chill of a departing night. In addition to the bonfire, there were a number of U.S. Army trucks whose headlights were used to illuminate the work area.

Col. Boatner, the TJA, in his opening statement back on November 1st had said that the gallows were ready. He was wrong. It was said for effect. On this December morning, soldiers from the post had been cutting trees and working on the construction of the gallows since the previous morning, and even though the time for execution was drawing closer, they hammered and sawed and nailed without hurry. Dawn would have caught them had they not cut short the work, leaving one or two insignificant chores undone. Still the area with the big gallows with two levers and two lines of traps that ran six in front and seven in the rear loomed surrealistic — ethereal, even. But the size of the gallows and the smell of the fresh new timber mixed with the still-burning wood and grounded itself into a ruthless reality. It was affecting.

A group of officers and a few official-looking civilians had arrived earlier. Some were at the location even before the workers were part way through. They were affected. But they did not leave.

Standing amid the curious were two members of the trial board. Also present were three officers with Capt. Algonquins, representing the trial judge advocate's office. Neither the President of the Court nor the prosecutor cared to attend.

Getting to the site presented something of a problem to a few because military officials wanted to maintain as much secrecy as possible, yet they were faced with the dilemma of getting the word out. The Army wanted particularly to assure the Houston populace that, as promised on the day after the insurrection, executions would be carried out. Electing to exercise caution, the Army chose to withhold official word of time and place of executions. Because reporters had been in court, the newspapers knew of the event, but they were cautioned to be discreet.

The execution site was set deep in the woods and was accessed by a road especially cut for the occasion. For the prisoners, the road seemed bumpy and inhospitable and was made all the more jarring by the two creaking carts that carried them. They were sandwiched between two Army staff cars containing Capt. Farrell, Lt. Davies, and five other officers. The truck that trailed the carts contained the sergeant of the guards along with his detail. Their guns were aimed directly at the shackled prisoners. Harmonica out, Carter was now back to searching for the last touches of *The Battle Hymn Of The Republic.* The melody was just about perfect now.

A glum Boland was sitting with Simms, holding nervously tight on his slender hands. Boland had developed the shakes, and he was clearly agitated with Carter's selection. Finally he snapped,

"Why don'cha play somethin' happy?!"

"Compared to where we goin', this *is* happy," Carter said. He went back to playing.

When the convoy cleared a few downed trees and came to a stop, the guards quickly hopped from the truck and, as if prearranged, formed a corridor from the carts to the gallows. Capt. Farrell brushed his way through a cluster of onlookers and landed at a position just forward of the scaffold steps. If he had moved eight more feet to his right, he could have touched the first step.

Poole, who of late had adopted a low profile, seemed to have sparked at the situation. He was first off his cart and was feeling talkative. Catching up with McClellan, who had been first climbing down from his cart, the corporal looked up at the gallows, hesitated and said, "That's a high some-bit, ain't it?"

The shackled First, continued chain-walking without looking up. He had seen it before. Many times. "We can handle it," he said, thinking of the last premonition.

Poole, moved closer. "Sarge, you know what made me mad?"

"I was wondering why you'd been so quiet."

"We didn't get that peckerwood Quackenbush. I been mad about that since we left Houston. It really burns me up. An' them Toms, Odums and Williams, I could just — Man, I can just see my fingers around their necks. I don't want to shoot 'em. I want to strangle 'em. Nice an' slow."

"Odums and Williams did what they thought they had to do. There's no point in being angry about it. They didn't know it, but they could have gotten on the stand and Tommed and lied in our favor until the cows came home, the results would have been the same. We were going to hang, no matter what. The saving grace is, we don't have to leave this earth being bitter. And if this race of ours is ever going to enjoy higher ground, the very first thing we have to do is get rid of anger. Particularly black-on-black anger."

"I'll say a good *Amen* to that." Poole took a few more short steps. Then the First's statement fully settled. "Get rid of black-on-black anger. If that ever happens, wow! What a race we could be. Is that why you don't hate me for what I did back in Houston?"

"How can I hate you? I believe in you."

"Good God, Sarge, I learn somethin' new from you every day."

"And, Poole, as far as wishing we had gotten the policeman Quackenbush, he was never really the objective."

"He wont?"

"The real objective was to free the prisoners, not kill a policeman."

"We still should'a got that peckerwood."

"Let me ask you something, Corporal. If we had gone overseas and killed the Kaiser, would it have stopped the war?"

"Hell, no."

"There are about a hundred thousand Klansmen in this country. They are not very bright people. If we were to break away from here right now and go and kill one of them, would that make the other Klansmen any smarter?"

"Wha'cha sayin' is, one monkey don't stop no show."

"Not when it comes to race. Never has. Never will."

Observing the guards as they chain-walked a bit more, Poole nudged the sergeant. "Y'kno, Sarge. I figured it out. Look. See? Notice how low them guards is carryin' them Springfields? We can overtake all of'em. We can get them rifles, break away from here, go to Mexico, an' get lost forever. The Mexicans'll help us out."

"Poole," the First said, "we have only minutes left. I'm going to make a soldier out of you if it kills me."

"Well, guess we better stay put. 'Cause we sure don't want you to die too soon," Poole said, chuckling. They clanked on for a bit, then he said, "Y'kno, Sarge, the one thing I always wanted to be in life? An' it's really gonna s'prise you."

"What?"

"An artist. That's somethin' I always want'd to be. If I was an artist, I could'a just painted my troubles away. Wonder if my wife ever knew that?"

The first sergeant was surprised. He didn't know the rabble-rousing corporal could ever have been interested in being something as sensitive as an artist.

"Maybe in your next life, Poole. Maybe in your next. Maybe somebody will give you a brush instead of a gun, then you can paint all your troubles away," the First said. "By the way, did you write to your wife to tell her that you won't be returning?"

"Nope," said the corporal. "She knew I wasn't comin' back when I left."

The men had automatically formed a line, and Capt. Farrell was up front, shaking each man's hand firmly and saying a word or two as they filed past him before heading up the stairs.

When Jody assisted the foggy-minded Pete into his view the captain's eyes were just returning from observing the odd sight of Boland holding on to Simms's hand as they moved away. He attached the right significance to it, but it was another slice of life he knew nothing about. He wondered if McClellan did.

"How's he doing, Jody?" the captain asked, directing his attention to Pete.

"He's gonna live," Jody said.

The captain didn't know how to respond to the youngster. He fished for a moment and asked, "And how are you doing?"

"I'm doin' fine, Sir."

"I'm glad you are. I'm really glad you are," the captain said earnestly. "Tell me, Jody, do you think you've been a good soldier?"

He smiled proudly. "Yessir. Pete thinks so. An' First Sergeant McClellan told me b'fore I was. After the trial, he come in the tent with a guard just to tell me that. He spoke to me all by myself. An' he talked to me a long time."

"I wish I had done the same. You are a good soldier, Jody. You're a damned good soldier. And you taught me something about courage. I think you've taught us all."

"Ooooh, thank you, Sir. Thank you so much."

The company commander gave him the firmest of hand shakes, saluted him, and said goodbye.

"Bye, Sir," Jody said. "Oh, an' Sir; in a few weeks, when it comes, have a nice Christmas."

The captain hesitated for a second. "I suppose I'm like a lot of the men in that regard, Jody. I'd almost forgotten, it's only two weeks away."

"Well, you have a good one, anyway."

The nice little underage soldier with the peach-fuzz face gave the captain another smile, took his friend under arm, and moved up the 13 steps to the gallows.

Poole was next in line. Before speaking to the captain, he turned back to McClellan, last in line, and said, "I apologize, Sarge."

The captain overheard it. "What are you apologizing for, Poole? Houston?"

"I wouldn't apologize for Houston if my life depended on it," Poole said. "If you was me, would you apologize?"

"I wouldn't be you, Poole, if my life depended on it."

Poole laughed. "You got me with that one, Cap. Not bad for a white man."

"Cut it, Poole," McClellan said, still standing in back of him.

"Okay, Sarge. Just one more thing, Cap. What's next for you? I spent most of my time in court thinkin' about that."

"I'm glad to know my future kept you company. But what's next for me will not be what you think."

"I hope not. But that ain't tellin' me nothin'."

"I'm going to find — and command — another King Company. This company can never be replaced, but I'm going to find another one. And I'm going to try like hell to make it half as good as this one was."

"Is."

"Alright. Is."

"Thank you. Now, just let me say this: I'm happy to know you ain't scared of coloreds no mo'," Poole said, playing with the words.

"An' it's even better knowin' you ain't a fish out of water no mo'."

"I may have been a fish out of water, Corporal. But I was never afraid. Just cautious."

Poole laughed. He thrust his chained hands out for a dubiously accepted handshake. He capped it by saying something else that irritated the sergeant. "An' say goodbye to the colonel. Sorry we didn't get him."

"Careful, Poole," Farrell said. "You're still in the Army."

Poole laughed again. He moved away laughing.

With McClellan the captain couldn't find the words. He settled on a long, exhausted exhale. He finally said, "God, it's such a waste."

"Not to be respected is an even bigger waste," McClellan replied.

"That's true. And most unfortunate. I wish we had gotten to know each other better. We should have talked to each other. We were both wrong in not doing that. Communicating is so vitally important. People *have* to start doing that. We *must* start talking to each other. There is no reason on earth for not doing it."

"The sooner, the better."

The captain fished for something else to say. "Realizing what you stood for, and what the coloreds are going through, I would have appreciated knowing your views on fighting for, as they say, 'the liberation of the oppressed in Europe.'"

"As a soldier, I wouldn't have commented. As a man, I'd have to say that with one out of every three Americans being either foreign-born or the child of a foreign-born, America *is* Europe."

"No difference?"

"Not when it comes to human beings."

"The world is in trouble then, isn't it?"

"That's why there's a war going on."

"You mean the war over there or the war here?"

"Back when we were talking a little earlier, Captain, I didn't think you really knew there was one here."

"I didn't know it before. I know it now. The question is, can the war be won?"

"Not if good people stand idle."

The captain smiled hopefully.

McClellan smiled appreciatively.

"Captain," McClellan said finally, "in thinking over what you asked me about whether God wanted to hear from me after leading the march, I think so. I think He's going to ask 'why Houston?' I will explain it the very best I can, and then I'm going to ask Him, in His kindness, goodness, and infinite wisdom, 'why America?'"

The captain was unable to respond. He didn't have to.

McClellan extended his hands. The captain sent his hands clasping around the chains and said goodbye. The sergeant moved off.

Midway of the scaffold steps, the first sergeant stopped, turned, and looked down at the captain. He gave a good man the *thumbs up* sign.

The good man responded quietly. "Stand tall."

The captain had never said that before.

Hurrying up the remaining stairs, the first sergeant said loudly, "Spirits up; triumph over tragedy. In the interest of the nation, where are we Corporal? Where are the '*mockingbirds?*'"

"In the interest of the nation, the *mockingbirds* are one pace to the right and two paces to the rear of the traps, Sergeant!"

"Perfect," said the First.

The 13 individual strands of rope swung down and to the left of the double-line formation. Second and third in line on the second row, Simms and Boland were next to each other. Boland was obviously the more frightened of the two, but for the first time Simms was showing traces of uneasiness. It didn't stop him, though. He was still looking at his partner with eyes of enduring support. He always knew the feeling he had for the beefy soldier would last until the end. And no longer now did he have to think about Colette, the girl his mate was going to marry.

"Togetherness," Simms said to the First when he stepped in front of them. McClellan smiled and moved on, intending to stop in front of each man with a word of comfort.

He looked back and noticed that Simms had sent his chained hands over for Boland's. He had never been open in the first sergeant's presence.

The deliberateness was acknowledged, but McClellan didn't say anything.

Simms wanted to know. He *had* to know. It was something he had always wanted to know. Hesitantly he asked, "Did you approve, Sarge?"

Recalling that the prosecutor had said there was deviancy in the ranks of Company K, the question did more than stop the forcefully moralistic sergeant who had never voiced an opinion on the sobering and far-reaching subject. Knowing of the union, and fond of both, he was troubled, and he had been troubled by it for quite some time. Now he was forced to comment.

The First took his time and moved back, stopping midway between the two men. He was not certain of the rightness, or even that the thought — let alone the act — could ever be condoned. Man was born to be with woman. Woman was born to be with man. Without that natural order, there could not be procreation, no future generations, no need for biological orderliness, nor anything of the sort. But there was a chink in nature's code. There must have been reasons why. These two who had bonded together in far-reaching contradiction had not been the first to do so, nor would they be the last. And on earth things did not simply happen. There were reasons. There were reasons, and somewhere there were answers. But they were not to be found here. Not on this earth. In a matter of minutes all such answers would come. In a matter of minutes he — *they* — would be at the summit, the zenith. There, the culmination of all reason and knowledge would be at hand, apt and full, vast and indisputable. But again, not here. Here, it was beyond him. Everything was, really. Here, he was only man; only human — military. The only thing he knew for certain was that the man-with-man issue would be around for as long as there was a military, for as long as there was man.

To the gazelle-like soldier who used to carry the guidon with polish and ramrod rigidity when he marched and was the very symbol of a proud company, and who was now seeking approval of a different nature, the first sergeant answered in the only way he knew how. With compassion in his voice, he said, "Approval will have to come from a source higher than me. We will be seeing Him in a very few minutes. Here, I can only do as I've always done, try for understanding."

Simms was satisfied.

Junius Rochester was next.

"You're looking good," McClellan said to him.

He smiled ruefully. "I wish'd I felt good."

"You'll be fine," the First said, returning the smile.

Still with an easy, comforting smile, the master sergeant stopped in front of Carter. To him, he said, "Nigeral, you did some mighty fine work for the company. You never failed to make us look good."

The first drummer and harmonica player replied, "My pleasure. Wish we could do it again."

"You never know," McClellan said. "You never know." Before he stepped to his left, Carter had one more comment.

"I finally learned your favorite song, Sarge. The Battle Hymn of the Republic."

"I heard you over in the tent working on it. That woman and the gentleman wrote a fine piece. I heard how you've mastered it coming here. You never gave up. That's what we're all about. That's what being colored is all about. Never giving up. Do you know the words?"

"Some of 'em."

"My favorites are *He died to make men happy, let us die to make men free.*"

"Do you think that's us?"

"I certainly would like it to be."

Carter got the message. He felt better.

Boot Talley was next in line. He was from I Company. "How do you like being in King Company, Son?"

"I'd do it again if I could."

McClellan thanked him and moved on. Henry Crawford was next. The 24-year-old soldier from Beaumont, Texas, was shaking uncontrollably. He'd been sobbing for a long time. The first sergeant, though his hands were still chained in front, gently took the young soldier's chained hands into his. "You have family?"

"Yessir. A mother."

"And your father?"

"I never knew him."

"Does your mother know anything about Negro history?"

"Yessir. She learned how to read. She did it all on her own."

"I guess she's like so many of our women, having to do everything on her own. But at least she's learned, and that's good. Very good. One day she'll get the truth about what we did, and why we did it. She'll understand. She might not agree, but she'll understand. And she'll be proud of how you faced the end."

"How will she know?"

"She is a mother," the First said calmly. "She'll know."

The young soldier was greatly relieved. "Thank you, Sergeant," he said.

Bubba Roosevelt and his rhyming twin, Gilbeert Andrews, were next.

The first sergeant said to them, "I hope you don't hold a grudge because you're missing a part of your team. In our race there will always be those who will desert us in our hour of want. They will elect to go their separate way without commitment to self, race or conscience. Will they ever be satisfied? I don't know. Menyard did what he thought he had to do. He was not unique. I've known others like him."

When he said that, McClellan was also thinking of how damning and indicting the turncoats Odums and Williams had been in court. What made it worse was that they were leaders. But, as he told Poole, the idea was not to leave this earth bitter.

Continuing with the two, he said, "Whether those who take that separate path are right or wrong, in the long run, it really is not for us to say. We can only try for understanding. What is nice about our race, what is wonderful about our people as a whole is that there will always be people of courage among us. People of fortitude; people of conviction and sacrifice. In our race, too, there will always be people like you, people who entertain, people who make us laugh, who push worry away, and say, if only for a little while, 'come on in, Fun. Make yourself at home.' You did that for us. Thank you."

"And thank you, Sergeant."

The First had started in the rear. Now on the front row, and careful of his footing, he was moving left to right.

Puerto Rico Hicks was next. He asked the sergeant, "Is it gonna hurt?"

"Only for a fraction of a second," said the First. "There'll be a flood of light, then darkness will come. You'll lose the senses. Shortly after, you will be awakened by some of your people — from perhaps, as far back as your forefathers and your foremothers — then, through an everlasting and unworldly brightness, God will appear. He will touch you, and all things will become clean and clear. You will never know pain or prejudice again."

It was ever so comforting to the young soldier, not born in this country. "Thank you, Sergeant. I never thought about that before," he said. "But, Sarge, God — what I mean is, where I come from, we wasn't much for church, y'know. Do y'think — ?"

"God didn't build churches. Man did. God created hearts. And from what I know, He did a pretty good job with yours."

The young soldier was ready to go. Right then and there, he was ready. And so were the two standing next to him. They had no questions. The First simply gave them a smile of confidence and stepped away.

Pvt. Jody Cunningham, standing proudly next to the mindless Pete, was next.

"It was brief but pleasant, Son," the First said to the boy-soldier.

"I'm glad I was here, Sarge."

"We were fortunate to have you," the first sergeant said. He paused and thought about the contents of the note Sgt. Yeager had given him in court. He still had the note in his pocket. "Jody, first of all, I hope you will forgive me if I didn't tell you all that I should have when I spoke privately with you in the tent the other day. I believed it was in your best interest. Will you forgive me?"

"Yessir," said Jody. He had not the slightest idea what the First was referring to, but his eyebrows were lifted to an all-time high. They were up there with good reason. The *first sergeant* was asking *him* for forgiveness. Not a bad way to die. Not bad at all.

"Next, I would like to say that of all the soldiers in the company, you, I think, deserve to live. You've shown courage far beyond your years. In combat, you would have been just as brave. Valiant. You are a trooper if there ever was one. In court you almost had me in tears. As I told you in the tent, I am very, very proud of you. I can never thank you enough. And I'm truly sorry you're here. It isn't deserved."

"Thank you, Sir. But I d'serve to be wherever the company is."

The First leaned in to embrace him. He smiled and moved down to where Calvin Yancy was positioned. He gave him words of encouragement and was about to put on his noose when Jody called down.

The boy had recalled something Pete said when they first met. "Sarge," he asked, "is we still king of the hill?"

"No," the First said easily. "We're on our way home to see the true King."

Jody couldn't keep the feeling to himself. "Pete, did'ja hear? Did'ja hear, Pete?"

For the first time since that late afternoon of August 25th, Pvt. Peter P. Curry spoke. He was difficult to understand, but he spoke all the same.

"We never did send your momma that bed."

Now, for the first time, the youngster with the arched eyebrows wanted to cry. But he wouldn't do it. He was a King Company Soldier.

If he had known, Jody could have had something else to cry about. Besides praising him when he went into the tent and called him aside that morning, there was something more personal the First wanted to say. He wanted to relay the contents of Yeager's note, but he just couldn't do it. Even at this moment he wasn't sure he had done the right thing.

The simple truth was that the first sergeant didn't have the heart to tell his youngest soldier that his mother was dead. The hard Wyoming winter had finally claimed her.

"Alright," said the First, standing tall at the end of the line. "Let's do justice to the occasion. Give the first command, Poole." Poole prepared himself.

The statement "let's do justice to the occasion" was bad enough, but the by-standing whites were totally stymied by the follow up. They had no clue as to what the hurrying first sergeant meant by the words *give the first command*. They automatically assumed that the eight armed guards and the two standing by the levers would come with hoods or blindfolds and then put the nooses over the heads of the men, or, perhaps, the sequence would be reversed. But when the man in charge, still wearing his spectacles, said *give the first command*, everyone, everyone, that is, but Farrell and the troops was mystified. Their mystification turned into suspicion. Was this a kind of code, they wondered, meaning was it time to try to escape? Anything was possible. They were, after all, still being led by a man who had deserted sanity and, for four terrifying hours, allowed a fiendish monster to reign. When it was over, 19 men and a child lay dead or dying. They died because the troops, like sheep, blindly followed this archetype of arrogance, this pretense of a soldier who, with 62 others, sat unreadable in a chapel that served as a court; this man who, in God's House, on that first day of a trial that lasted from November 1 to November 27, stood and said, *I trained my men for war and I led them to a war,* and then had the gall to imply in that same speech — in God's House, no less — that the attitude of the country was wrong in its treatment of the coloreds and the colored soldier.

It was 0501.

With the dawn still held at bay and a winter's mist seeping through the trees and across the gallows, everyone was ready for something. A strained and eerie mood prevailed.

The two guards carrying the hoods were waved off.

Capt. Farrell understood it. He knew that, under McClellan, there would be no hiding, no ducking. And the former Quaker from St. Agatha, Maine, knew that this was not to be a maudlin event, that the departure would be one of swelling and monumental pride. That was one of the reasons he lipped the phrase *stand tall.*

The captain knew they would.

"Nooses!" called the erect Poole.

All hands were chained in front, yet the command had the men roping their own necks with the thickly knotted nooses.

The corporal was manning the second row at the farthest end. For observation and command, the first sergeant was positioned at the opposite end. His was the last noose on the first row.

The double-line formation was precisely one step to the right and two paces to the rear of the traps that would spring when the two levers eventually were pulled by the guards.

Now McClellan was no longer the reserved leader. Now there was a growing intensity about him. He was uncharacteristically edgy.

Paraphrasing Nat Turner, the man he didn't admire but whose anarchism he understood, the First said, "Alright, this is our lot. This we are called to do!" He shouted down the line. "Give us, *the* mockinbirds, a command, Poole!"

Poole was all business. "Two paces, forward — huhh!"

The two chain-burdened steps were taken. It placed the men exactly one pace to the right of the traps.

The move was ragged.

For the First, it was dismaying. The men hadn't done it with nearly the precision and militarism expected by the first sergeant. He ripped his noose off over his head and charged up the line in front of the traps. "No, no, no!" he fired. "What'n the hell are you doing?! This is not the best you can do! This is not soldiering! This is not *standing tall!* Where is your pride? Your dignity? Your honor? Where is the distinction of your soldiering? Where is courage and conviction? We shouldn't want to go around the corner looking like this, let alone to our deaths. Gentlemen, you are soldiers in the Army of the United States. You are expected to die as soldiers in the Army of the United States. Your people expect you to die as soldiers in the Army of the United States. Bring them back, Poole! Bring them back! And let's soldier, people. Let's sol-dier. Do I hear you?!"

"Yes, Sergeant," answered a few.

"Louder!" demanded the First.

"Yes, Sergeant!"

"I can't hear you!!"

"Yes, Sergeant!!"

"Poole!!"

The corporal quickly commanded, "Detail! Two paces to the rear — !"

"No, Poole! No!" yelled the First. "We take no *backward* movement! That's the whole point! It is forward or nothing!!"

"Yes, Sergeant!" Poole responded. "Dee-tail! About face! Two paces forward, huhhg!"

Quickly and impressively done, they were turned again and were ready to start over.

McClellan, itching for perfection, stayed in the center, making sure that all was going to go right. Now when he gave commands, Poole, as had Dukes, repeated them.

"Two paces, forward — !" called the First.

"Two paces, forward!" Poole echoed.

"....Huhhhgg!" McClellan said.

The move was good. It was not perfection.

"If you could have soldiered in war, you can soldier here! Do it again! Bring them back, Poole!"

Poole was swift with the appropriate commands. "Detail, tenn-hutt! Abooout face! Two paces forrwarrddd, huttt! Abooout face! Ready, Sergeant!!"

They had returned to the starting point with speed and precision, but according to the First, something was missing. He made them try it again — and yet again, but the results were the same. The troops just didn't have it in them. It was useless to rehearse the move again. "Alright," said the disappointed man, "let's just get it over with."

Looking disconsolately at the line, he chain-sauntered to the end and put his noose back on, tensing the onlookers and sending the lever-pullers hopping into place.

"Okay, let's just do it," the First said, his voice drained of energy.

"One step to the left. Hughhh!" Poole called.

The move placed the men directly in line with the traps.

McClellan was just about to give the last command when into the area came Lt. Col. Briggs. Most didn't notice him, but Capt. Farrell did. They didn't acknowledge each other's presence. The colonel did acknowledge someone else, however. It was Lt. Jennings. She had arrived a little earlier and was standing quietly in back of the crowd. Of the 47 spectators on the periphery, she was the only woman. She had been driven to the site by the former post commander of Logan, Col. Stout. Comfortably retired and out of uniform, he was hardly noticed. Col. Briggs sent them both a baleful look and directed his attention to the scaffold.

McClellan's disappointment hadn't receded. "Alright, the least we can do is to keep it together."

"*Together!*"

McClellan spun around and looked down the line in astonishment. The surprising word had come from the men, and it was loud and strong. Poole had been behind it.

As if he couldn't believe what he had heard, the First bellowed, "What'd you say?"

"*Together!*" the company responded.

Spark rekindled, the First yanked the noose from around his neck and over his head and flew up and down the line in excitement. "Yes! *Yes!!* That's what we want! That's the way we go!" He stood in the center. "What're we gonna do?"

"Soldier!"

"How're we gonna soldier?"

"Together!"

"Say it with thunder, say it like you mean it!"

"*Together!*"

"Because you are — ?"

"*KING COMPANY!!*"

"Well, all right, King! In place! Mark time!"

"Mark time!" Poole said.

"Hugghh!"

The First began to call cadence. As the chain-burdened feet marched magnificently in place, he called for Poole to pick up the count.

"Alright!" hollered the First. "Are we gonna stir it up and sound off?!"

"Loud and strong!"

"With Poole giving the count, the First called, "King Company! Making the best of a bad situation! Stomach in, chest out! Your heads held high! The last of it! Let 'em hear you, King Company! Let 'em *hear* you! Sing a song! Sing it like you mean it!"

"Stony the road we trod...!!"

"Stony the road we trod
Bitter the chast'ning Rod
Felt in the days when hope
had died;

Yet, with a steady beat —
Have not our weary feet
Come to the place where
our fathers sighed?"

Out of the gloomy past;
Til now we stand at last..."

The only person not absorbed was Lt. Col. Briggs. He went over to Farrell, looked back at the scaffold, and scowled. "What the hell are those sonsabitches doing, Engineer?"

"Soldering, Sir," the captain said proudly. "Those 'sonsabitches' are soldiering."

"And still singing that damned song."

"You ought to learn the words, Colonel," the captain said, moving away so that he could concentrate. "If not the words, certainly the meaning."

McClellan, back in position, put his noose back on. The troops' singing continued to boom, the clanking chains had become more precise than ever.

Everywhere, emotions were drained; the spectators were spellbound. Even those who had hidden behind face-covering hands and peeped through barely spread fingers no longer did so.

"Spirits high! Triumph over tragedy, Gentlemen," McClellan hollered.

Then, over the chains, the singing, the pride, and the tears, the

First, his voice almost gone, called out, "Let's go home, Black Lightning! Let's go *home*. Poole! Call it! Call it, Poole, call it! *HURRY UP AND CALL IT!*"

Poole called it. The line moved forward in crackling unity.

— After the thunder and amid the stony silence of a cold and distant December morning, the swaying bodies turned some, then stopped.

The mockingbirds had gone home.

Epilogue

The bodies of the 13 men of 24th United States Infantry (Colored) were buried in unmarked graves. By midmorning the scaffold had been disassembled and sent to Fort Sam Houston.

The Army of the United States needed the lumber for the trial to follow.

Another trial was held in the chapel at Fort Sam Houston. Six more men were scheduled to die. Bowing to waves of protests, however, President Woodrow Wilson finally commuted their sentences to life in prison.

Between the two trials, 103 men were convicted and received various terms of imprisonment, 66 of which were for life in the United States Penitentiary at Ft. Leavenworth, Kansas.

Eight of the soldiers escaped punishment for the march on Houston. They disappeared that night of August 23, 1917 — the actual date of the march.

They were never heard from again.

In September 1950 — almost 34 years after the uprising in Houston, the 24th U.S. Infantry Regiment was assigned to Korea.

Two months after the start of the Korean War, the troops — still led by white officers — were charged with desertion, cowardice and unworthiness, and were deemed incapable of carrying out missions against the enemy.

Thirteen months later, the 24th U.S. Infantry Regiment was disbanded.